PERFECT KILL

Helen Fields studied law at the University of East Anglia, then went on to the Inns of Court School of Law in London. After completing her pupillage, she joined chambers in Middle Temple where she practised criminal and family law for thirteen years. After her second child was born, Helen left the Bar. Together with her husband David, she runs a film production company, acting as script writer and producer. The DI Callanach series is set in Scotland, where Helen feels most at one with the world. Helen and her husband now live in Los Angeles with their three children.

Helen loves Twitter but finds it completely addictive. She can be found at @Helen_Fields.

By the same author

Perfect Remains
Perfect Prey
Perfect Death
Perfect Silence
Perfect Crime

Perfect Kill

HELEN FIELDS

avon.

Published by AVON
A division of HarperCollins*Publishers* Ltd
1 London Bridge Street
London SE1 9GF

www.harpercollins.co.uk

A Paperback Original 2020

First published in Great Britain by HarperCollins*Publishers* 2020

A catalogue copy of this book is
available from the British Library.

ISBN: 978-0-00-827524-2

Typeset in Bembo Std by Palimpsest Book Production Limited,
Falkirk, Stirlingshire

Printed and bound in the UK by
CPI Group (UK) Ltd, Croydon CR0 4YY

MIX
Paper from
responsible sources
FSC™
www.fsc.org   FSC™ C007454

Acknowledgements

Getting a book from concept to shelf is not unlike agreeing to host Christmas Day for your family, extended family, friends and neighbours (bear with me here). It's all fine for the first half of the year, then as the months pass, you realise the magnitude of what you agreed to do. It's still exciting and you have a warm glowy feeling when you think how nicely it'll turn out, but still, the burden's on you and it feels terrifying. Except that it's not really all on you. Because along the way, different people will turn up to make all the tiny pieces come together.

So as the dreaded but much anticipated day draws nearer, and you begin shopping for ingredients and researching recipes (or in the actual book writing world, that's plain old writing, editing and polishing), the design team gets moving. They make everything look wonderful and shiny, with clever graphics, eye-catching roundels and raised print. So now – as if by magic – the tree is up, lights are twinkling, and there's a holly, ivy and mistletoe wreath adorning the front door.

But you haven't invited anyone! Not a problem. You have a publicist, a marketing team and a sales squad to get in touch with all the right people, to persuade them that your Christmas will be better than any before, and that your house will be the place to be come December 25th. They'll make sure people turn up on time, dressed in their ridiculous jumpers, ready to make merry.

So things are still looking a bit messy and not quite ready for visitors . . . no problem. Editors will save the day. They'll spot the dust left on the mantelpiece, the odd sock hidden behind the sofa, the unplumped cushions, and they'll make it all perfect. There won't be a bauble or a candlestick (or a typo or a comma) out of place. Gosh, it's all starting to look great.

But then the guests begin to turn up, and everyone's still running around like crazy, you've forgotten to make the gravy, one group of people had no idea that they were supposed to bring mince pies, and communication has stopped. Luckily your commissioning editor is there to liaise with everyone. To cast a wise overseeing eye across the proceedings. To tell you when you're about to overcook the turkey, or remind you to add more brandy to the sauce. She'll get everyone around the table, take control, and suddenly it will all fall into place.

And where are you? You're still in the kitchen, stirring something, feeling pleased but exhausted. That's when your agent will walk in quietly and slide a large glass of white/red/port/tea – whatever you need (she'll just know what that is) and tell you it's all going to be okay, just when you need to hear it most.

As you're finishing dinner, and you think it can't get any better (the pudding was divine and there's still plenty of silliness left to enjoy) the audio team turns up singing metaphorical carols at your door, and it's perfect. Even the stuff you never knew about or thought about. It just works.

The analogy is flawed, I know, but the point is valid. Getting a book into readers' hands is a monumental team effort. The best writing in the world is just a series of words put together until the work is done to make it a book. And for the record, my agent does a lot more than just hand me a soothing glass of something when necessary, but my goodness is she always there when I need her!

This isn't a jolly Christmas book (far from it) but I still have a team to thank for making it as good as it can be. Any failures are mine alone from this point forward. So with no more ado, my unending gratitude to Avon's publicity superstar – Sabah Khan. Also Ellie Pilcher, Dom Rigby, Beth Wickington, the brilliant Oli Malcolm, Anna Derkacz, Hannah O'Brien, Kelly Webster and Catriona Beamish, not to mention the fabulous designers, Claire Ward, Ellie Game and Holly Macdonald. To my editor – my guiding light – Helen Huthwaite, there isn't enough gratitude. To my agent Caroline Hardman, without whom not a single word I've written would have been read by anyone other than my friends, you are both the most patient and grounded person I've ever met. Never change. And to all at Hardman & Swainson Literary Agency working so very hard – Joanna Swainson, Thérèse Coen and Nicole Etherington. You all made this book, and those stories that came before it, and I never forget it, not for a second.

But imaginary Christmas lunch wouldn't be the same without bizarre relatives and too-drunk friends, so I'm also inviting Andrea Gibson and Ruth Chambers without whom I would have fallen apart years ago. To Neil Broadfoot, fellow author, fellow giggler, fellow twitterer, because I couldn't have a virtual party without you. To the kids who tolerate their mother being distracted, unavailable and often weird when writing – Gabriel, Solomon, Evangeline – please don't get any older/taller/more grown up while I'm not looking. It's unfair. And lastly to a few new American friends who learned to put up with incessant book talk as they got to know me, and who've helped me transition to a new continent. Heidi & Rob Jessup, Jodi & Chris Queen, Marie Lewis & Matthew

Sparks – thanks for reading/listening/supporting/musing and for the food & drink.

I hope you enjoy *Perfect Kill* – it took a whole lot of people to get it to you.

HF xx

For David

Who always told me that I could and I would
Who catches me when I stumble
(literally and metaphorically)
And who never stops laughing at me

Chapter One

At precisely the same time Bart was coming round from a chemically induced sleep, his mother was waking from a herbal insomnia remedy and wondering why the house was so quiet. It wasn't a Sunday. On Sundays, Bart neither had college nor work, and occasionally he slept in. Not all that often, but sometimes. Maggie rolled onto her side and rubbed bleary eyes, trying to focus on the small travel clock perched on her bedside table – 9 a.m. She'd overslept. Not that she had anywhere to be in a hurry, but mornings – it was a Wednesday, she realised – were marked with the clanging of crockery, the pouring of cereal, and the sound of the dishwasher being loaded before Bart exited the house. He was a good boy. The sort of boy her friends were rather jealous of. She was conscious of the fact, once in a while moaning about him a little to make it clear that he wasn't perfect, although secretly she knew he was. She might tell her neighbour that he played his music too loud, or pretend to her weekly library social group that he was forgetful about tidying his room. But Bart was neither loud nor untidy. In fact, he was independent, considerate and helpful. An exception among other twenty-year-old men. (Boys, Maggie thought.

Twenty was no age at all. Certainly not mature enough to comprehend all the cruelties the world had to offer.) But then Bart had grown up quickly after his father had been killed serving in Afghanistan. Not in battle. That would have been devastating, of course. The truth had garnered more pity and less admiration from the community. Her husband had choked in the mess hall one night when a fellow officer had cracked a particularly hilarious joke. The steak he'd been chewing was sucked up into his airways where it had stubbornly lodged and refused to move in spite of no end of back-smacking, then a desperate attempt at the Heimlich manoeuvre which had broken ribs but not allowed any oxygen to his lungs. How did you explain that to a fourteen-year-old boy? That his father, who'd been a military man since before Bart was born, had been dispatched not by bomb or bullet, but by a mouthful of protein.

Perhaps Bart was ill, Maggie thought. Or maybe she'd taken too many sleeping tablets and not heard him leave the house. That had happened before. Distracted after a long shift at the call centre, she'd returned home and taken a SleepSaver, eaten dinner, then swallowed another pill without thinking. Such were the perils of tiredness. Living on a military widow's pension and her wages was too tight for comfort, even with Bart earning a few extra pounds waiting tables on a Saturday.

'Bart, you all right, love?' she called, pulling her tatty pink dressing gown over bare shoulders. Bart had bought her a new one for Christmas. It was exquisite. Cream, and so soft it was like one of the really posh cuddly toys you seemed always to find in bookshops, for some inexplicable reason. It was hanging on the back of her bedroom door, and she stroked it every time she entered or exited. But it was too nice to wear. She'd only spill coffee down it, or splash it with the remnants of the previous night's pasta sauce. The thought of spoiling something so luxurious and thoughtful was enough to keep her in her threadbare robe, at least for another six months or so. She'd start wearing it before Christmas came around, she told herself.

Bart hadn't replied by the time she'd reached his bedroom door, knocking politely, always mindful that her boy needed his privacy. He'd never brought a girl back for the night, not that Maggie would have minded if they'd been discreet, but Bart conducted his relationships elsewhere. He obviously had girlfriends. He was a good-looking lad, and that wasn't just the blur of seeing him through mummy-goggles. At six foot he was big enough to stand out but not so tall that he attracted silly comments on the street. His father had been six foot four and once threatened to deck a man who had somehow imagined that no one had ever asked her husband what the weather was like up there. Maggie's husband – God rest his soul – had been a decent man, but not blessed with looks, all sharp features and eyes closer together than suited the average face. She was the exact opposite. Broad, flat face, wide eyes (wide hips too, and getting wider by the year, she reminded herself). Perhaps their differences had endowed Bart with the sort of symmetrical, well-balanced face that wasn't exactly attention-grabbing, but with which no one could find a single fault. Great skin, even teeth, good bone structure, and a fair brain. He was in his final year of a business studies college course that he was hoping would offer a career in London. Plenty of work in Edinburgh, Maggie always told him. Or Glasgow, if he wanted to leave home. Anywhere in Scotland. But London was his dream. Always had been. Even that was too distant for her liking, but she knew that letting go was all part of the painful parenting experience.

In the absence of a reply to her knocking, Maggie opened the door slowly, calling his name softly as she put a foot inside. The curtains were open and the bed was made. Nothing surprising there, his lectures started at 9 a.m. every day. He'd have left an hour ago to make sure he was in good time. Bart wasn't the sort of student who ever turned up late. But he hadn't woken her up. His normal routine was to wake, shower, have breakfast, clear up the kitchen, and to take her a cup of tea before leaving the house. She in turn would rise later, do the washing, shop and leave something tasty in the slow cooker before going off for her shift, which started at lunchtime and went on until 8 p.m. Telesales was thankless but they hadn't missed a mortgage payment yet.

It wasn't the lack of a cup of tea that bothered Maggie. Her son was entitled to forget doing that for her. She counted her blessings on a daily basis for him, with or without his little kindnesses. What she couldn't understand was why his mobile was still sitting on his bed, charging, exactly where he'd left it the night before when he'd dashed out to grab an extra shift at the restaurant. Another waiter had called in sick. Bart had been offered the hours, and the thought of boosting his savings account was too tempting to refuse. The pay wasn't great but the tips were, and he always attracted enough customer good-will to make a night's work worthwhile. His phone had been running on empty so he'd left it on his bed charging ready for the next morning. Maggie had watched him plug it in as she'd delivered a pile of freshly ironed clothes for him to put away. Those, too, were sitting patiently on the bed for his return.

She squashed the stupid maternal panic that made the stable bedroom floor feel suddenly like quicksand. So her boy hadn't come home. Perhaps he'd met up with friends and gone for a drink, or had a better offer from a pretty girl. Only normally he'd have called her, however late. Let her know to put the chain on the door. Tell her not to worry. Bart was thoughtful like that. His father had taught him well. Maggie took the stairs carefully, and checked the answerphone on the landline. No message. She didn't have a mobile. It was just one more bill that she didn't need. Plastering an optimistic smile on her face, she popped her head through the door of the lounge, all ready to have a good laugh in case he'd had a few too many and slept on the couch. She was fooling no one with the false jollity, least of all herself. Bart wasn't an excessive drinker. He'd never reached a point where the couch looked like a better option than his own bed. Before she could stop it, her mind began conjuring the ghosts of accidents. Somewhere in there, a misadventure with a steak loomed large. Like father like son. Wouldn't that be the ultimate irony? Both of them gone, cause of death unchewed meat.

'Stop it, you silly woman,' she scolded herself, wandering into the kitchen to make her own cup of breakfast tea. 'Your boy'll be back any minute.'

But the truth that Maggie had felt, in that secret, vile part of the brain no parent ever wanted to hear pipe up, was that her boy wouldn't be back in a minute. Not by any stretch of the imagination. Because by then, Bartholomew Campbell was already two hundred miles away.

It was the stench that woke him. Something acrid with a heavy undertone of sulphur had filled his sinuses and was threatening to make him gag.

'Mum?' His first thought was that she must be ill. That she'd gone down with food poisoning or a virus overnight and been too embarrassed or too thoughtful to have disturbed him. Only he couldn't remember getting home. And now that he registered the pain in his body, Bart realised he wasn't in his bed. Or any bed at all.

He sat bolt upright, head swimming, before collapsing back down to the floor. Everything was dark. Not the dark of Scottish nights away from the city camping by a loch. Not even the dark of the private rooms at the back of the night club he occasionally attended with his friends. True dark. Not one star.

No bloom of pollution. No crack or spill from beneath a door or the edge of a blind.

'Hello?' Bart shouted, braving movement again, sitting up more slowly. That was when he felt a tugging on his leg.

He froze. Something had hold of his left ankle. He breathed hard, twice, three times, tried to get to grips with his fear, then he lost it.

'Get off me!' he yelled, wrenching his foot upwards, trying to scrabble away. He hit a wall with his head shortly before his foot locked solid and his hip popped from its socket. The scream he let out was loud enough to wake the entire terrace where he lived. He rolled right, instinct kicking in, and the displaced hip shifted again back into the socket, easing the dreadful pain and allowing him to lean forward to take hold of whatever had his foot.

He didn't want to extend his hand. There was something about reaching his fingers out into the black void that seemed to be inviting a bite. Like slipping your hand into a murky river in the sort of place where, when animals attacked, the general reaction to the news was: *What the hell did the idiot tourist expect?* What Bart found was both less and more terrifying. His ankle was bound by a leather strap. There was no bogeyman occupying the darkness with him. Not one that had hold of his leg, anyway. The strap was thick and sturdy, with a chunky metal link sewn through it. At the end of that, he realised miserably, was a chain. What was at the end of the chain, Bart wasn't sure he was ready to discover yet. So he did what all cautious people would do in a foul pitch-black room, finding themselves inexplicably chained up. He began calling out for help.

His cries went in an arc. He called for help. Stopped, listened. Called out again, this time louder. Stopped, listened. Bart could feel the rumbling below the floor more readily than he could hear the engine, but an engine it unmistakably was. He put his hand down flat. The surface was rough but not cold. Neither wood nor metal. More like the sort of industrial liner that was used to insulate modern houses. He'd seen it being carried in huge sheets into Edinburgh's ever growing new housing estates. Perhaps he was in a factory then, in a room high above the machinery. That made sense. The low-level growl of metal and the lack of sharp sounds from the outside world. He pressed himself closer to the wall and began yelling afresh.

'Hello! Anyone! Can anyone hear me? Help. I need help.' His cries got louder, his voice higher. He banged on the wall first then the floor between phrases, punctuating his cries for assistance. His cries became screams. Bart had never heard himself scream before. It was terrifying. Then he was hammering on the wall and stamping on the floor at the same time as he screamed. Just make noise, he thought. Someone would hear him. Someone would come.

But what if it was the wrong someone?

No, he told himself. Not that. Those thoughts were what would stop him being rescued. If all he had was a short window of time before whoever had chained him up was due to come back, he had to make all the noise he could right now. He took some steadying breaths. Think. The chain on his ankle allowed him limited movement. He walked along the wall as far as he could, tapping as he went, feeling for the edge of a doorway or handle, listening for a place where there might be an exit. Nothing. Then he walked the other way along the wall. Tapping all the time.

A crash at his feet made him leap backwards. He tripped and fell, scrabbling away. The darkness made everything nearer and louder. He'd never considered what a threat the lack of light was before. Everything was alien. His sense of distance and direction had completely gone. As the noise faded, he reached out tentatively, groping the floor for whatever it was he'd hit. His fingers found the bucket a couple of feet away on its side, still rolling gently to and fro. He grabbed the handle and pulled it closer, exploring its edges, neither brave nor stupid enough to put his hand all the way inside. The smell coming from in there was its own unique warning. Human waste was remarkably distinctive. Neither cat, cow, dog nor pig excrement came close to replicating its odour. Bart contemplated what it meant. The bucket's edge was rough with what could only be rust. Its outside was dry and there was no liquid slopping anywhere. Not recently used then. Yet it was there for a reason.

'It's here for me,' he whispered, not liking the rawness in his throat from all the yelling. He'd lost track of the time he'd spent calling out to apparently absent listeners. He'd be lucky if he could speak at all within the hour.

Setting the bucket down, he took stock. There were two options left. Sit down, huddle, wait it out. Someone had delivered him there, yet he had no idea how that had happened. His new girlfriend, if he could even call her that so early on, had met him in the restaurant as he'd finished his shift, and he'd been about to go back to her place for a while. After that was a steady blank in his memory, but his situation couldn't be accidental. His captors would be back. If he chose not to simply wait, he could assess the situation, explore his surroundings, try to figure out the state of play. That was a phrase he remembered his father using on his infrequent trips home from active duty. He summoned whatever genetic courage might inhabit his DNA. What he learned was that bravery was a myth.

In the end, fear was a more generous motivator. If Bart waited, things could only get worse. He could think of no earthly reason why anyone would want him. Perhaps it was a case of mistaken identity by some chancer who thought he was from a wealthy family able to pay a ransom. Maybe it was some sort of bizarre terrorist event. And they were the better options. More likely – much more likely – it was some sick fuck who wanted to rape then kill him. He wasn't sitting on the floor and waiting for that.

Forcing himself to get to his feet, Bart checked his pockets. His wallet was gone, not that he'd imagined it might still be there. The only item still on him was the photo of his father that he carried everywhere, his dad in full uniform, carrying his baby son in his arms. On the back his father had written the immortal words, 'Bart, I may not always be by your side, but I will always come back to you. Love Dad xxx.' He clutched the photo for a moment then shoved it securely into his pocket again. Whatever else he'd lost, he couldn't bear the thought of losing that too. He felt for the wall, arms stretched out so that only his fingertips were touching it, and tried to measure the space. Four walls, rectangular, maybe twelve foot by twenty. Then he followed the length of chain and found that it was attached to a central metal loop in the floor and secured with a hefty padlock. No discernible door. Five other objects turned up as he searched the floor on his hands and knees. A coarse blanket that reeked of damp and sweat. He bundled it up and kept it close to his chest, as much as a comforter as for warmth. A woman's shoe, its high heel snapped and hanging half off, lay on its side in a corner. A large container of water that smelled fresh enough. A box of food – packets of crisps, biscuits, and chocolate, he decided from the smell – all junk, nothing fresh, but it would keep him alive for a couple of weeks. The thought that he was supposed to stay alive quelled his immediate panic. The cell was part of his journey, not his final destination. He had time to take stock and prepare for whatever lay ahead. Finally, standing, he bumped into something dangling from the wall, also chained, that squeaked back and forth when he knocked it. Reaching out, he identified its hexagonal shape, felt the chill of glass around its sides, then his fingers found the dial. He turned the metal cog.

Light, enough to barely illuminate a one-metre radius, spilled from the lamp. Bart let out a soft coo. Amazing how such a simple thing could suddenly mean more than all the money in the world, given an appropriate degree of terror. The colours it shed were dappled. A sickly yellow nearer the top from the old bulb, graduating into a dull pink in the middle, then brown at the bottom. Bart stepped closer, letting his eyes adjust. It wasn't that the glass panes were coloured, he realised. Nor that a special effect had been used on the bulb.

The outside of the glass had been spattered red. He reached out his fingers hesitantly, wanting to know, not wanting to know. The lantern's panes were bloodied with delicate streaks, settling at the bottom. Different layers. Subtly varied shades. A mixture of very old, crackled blood, like a glaze on an antique vase, then newer congealed blood. A single blob came away on his finger. Congealed but not yet fully hardened.

Bart sank to the floor in the small circle of light, an actor mid-stage in a spotlight with no audience to appreciate the beautiful tragedy being played out. Then he pulled the blanket around himself, and wondered how long both the lamplight – and he – would last.

Chapter Two

Elenuta ran.

Three flights down the staircase, she headed for the exit onto the street, hoping no other door opened as she passed it. Each of those other apartments was as dangerous to her as the one she had just escaped. Dressed only in a tattered halter-neck top and Lycra miniskirt, no underwear, no shoes, she raced downwards, jumping the last three steps, praying her ankles wouldn't sprain. She needed to be able to run. Looking upwards, she checked the situation. No one was following. Yet. It would only be sixty seconds or so before they realised she was missing, though.

Forcing herself not to barge through the outer door and have it slam, she moved carefully, slipping out into the night air. Dumbryden Gardens was still unfamiliar after the month she'd lived there. Inevitable, given that she hadn't been allowed out of the flat. Planks over the inside of the windows meant she couldn't even assess the terrain from above. She'd wondered why the police hadn't become suspicious. Windows covered from the inside were never indicators of lawful activity. One of the women who'd been held in the flats the longest had explained.

'Looks perfectly normal from outside. Kids' curtains, flowery curtains, princesses, bullshit rainbows and hearts. They put the planks on with the curtains still up.' A week later, the woman had disappeared, never to return. None of the other girls knew a thing about it. There were hypotheses and horrified speculation, but nothing solid save for one scrap of information that had got Elenuta where she was now. Perhaps a client had got too rough and killed her, was the most popular opinion. Then there was the option that she'd contracted a disease that would render her useless for sex trafficking purposes. Finlay did his best to keep his girls clean – not for their sakes, but so that his punters kept coming back for more. No one was going to do that with their dick resembling a root vegetable and leaking pus. Perhaps she'd escaped, one of the other women had whispered. There was a rumour about a key being sewn into the hem of one of her skirts. That was why Elenuta had requested that any spare clothes in the house be given to her. She'd pleaded that hers were no longer fit to be worn, and that hadn't required much acting. Finlay had given her grief about it. As one of the newest members of what Finlay laughingly called his 'team', Elenuta was popular with the clients and made more money than anyone else. The clothes landed at her feet one day during her allotted shower time. The key had been shoved roughly into the picked-open hem of a pair of shorts. After that, the problem had been finding a moment when no one was guarding the outer door. That hurdle had suddenly and bizarrely been overcome when a man had walked in carrying a bulging newspaper package smelling of hot chocolate and shouting, 'Deep fried Mars Bars, you fat fuckers!' Without a second thought, Elenuta had grabbed the key and gone for it.

Now she had no plan. All she could do was follow her instincts. Turning left, she raced through an alleyway between the block she'd left and another that sat at a right angle to it.

Put some distance in place first, then consider what to do, she told herself. Several of the street lights were broken. Sometimes during the day she heard the sounds of rocks being thrown, the odd cheer when there was a hit. The darkness provided both shelter and a disadvantage. Her pursuers knew the area well. A line of terraced houses was on one side, the rear of another block of flats on the other. She couldn't see a main road, which was what she'd been hoping for. Flagging down a car would be her fastest way out of the area, and it wasn't as if there was any definable risk of being raped. Not after twelve different men had been allowed into her room already that day. There were rewards and penalties depending on your behaviour. If you wanted to eat, you did what you were told without complaint. If you didn't want to be beaten raw, you did what you were told. If you didn't want to be injected with heroin against your will, you did what any man asked you to, without moaning and without tears. Unless they wanted to see you cry. Several of them did.

She wasn't sure exactly what time it was, but it had to be after 2 a.m. That was when the stream of customers began to tail off. Few lights shone from the windows of the houses. Pausing to get her breath – it had been several weeks since she'd walked more than a few paces in one go – Elenuta considered her options: stand in the middle of the housing estate and scream like a banshee to attract maximum attention and scare off her pursuers, or run from door to door hoping some kind person would open up, immediately believe what she told them, and protect her until the police arrived.

A slammed door, cursing, then a shout from behind her helped make her mind up. She needed to buy more time. If they saw her, they'd be on her in a matter of seconds. The front doors weren't worth the risk. Dipping low, she headed for the rear of the properties, knowing the problem would be dogs in the back gardens, but discounting the danger. She'd been throttled, beaten, drugged and assaulted more ways than she'd known were possible since being kidnapped in her native Romania. Getting into a fight with a bullmastiff looked like a clean exit from her perspective. If they barked, they were going to give away her location. That was a risk she had no choice but to take.

Her whole body ached. The adrenaline of escape wouldn't last much longer. Tiredness was setting in, partly through sheer terror, partly because her food had been rationed to weaken her. It was working. She took the first fence easily enough, scratching the inside of her leg on the chicken wire. Didn't matter. Just one more injury to add to the multitude of others.

The next garden had a higher wooden construction. She looked longingly at the back door, wondering if she could risk giving up running and starting to wake people. The problem was that back doors didn't have doorbells. She would have to knock and call out if she was going to rouse people at that time. She steeled herself. Better to be cautious and make sure she was safe before revealing her presence. It seemed wiser to get at least four houses in before starting to hammer on a door. Climbing first onto a wheelbarrow, then a barbecue, she took the high fence, making it over the top then losing her hold and falling to the ground, a tool of some sort smashing into her ribs. Still she didn't cry out. The worst of the noise was soaked up by the mud and wet grass she landed in but there was nevertheless a dull thud as she hit the earth. She'd learned the hard way recently how to stay silent and endure pain. It turned out to be a useful lesson now. Light-headed and suddenly overwhelmed with nausea, she stayed where she was before daring to move.

A light came on in the upstairs window, attracting her attention, and undoubtedly also alerting her pursuers to her whereabouts. This was it then. Just two houses in, and that would have to do. She was hoping a woman would live there, maybe fifty years old, mature enough to know desperation when she saw it, and compassionate enough to want to help. It shouldn't be a family with young children. They wouldn't want to invite her in and wait for the police to attend. No one in their right mind would want someone as battered and unclean as her in the same house as their babies. Rolling onto her stomach and pushing herself up, she knew she looked awful. There weren't any mirrors in the flat, mainly because it would be too easy to break them and create a weapon. It had the benefit of stopping the women from realising how dreadful they looked, but imagination worked just as well.

Elenuta began banging the back door with both hands, with her fists curled one around the other, kicking it at the same time. The owner was already awake. She just had to get them downstairs.

'Please,' she shouted. 'Help me. Need help. Call police. I am kidnapped.' Her English was good but not perfect. Enough to make herself understood which was all she needed.

An upstairs window slid open at the house next door. 'Would ye shut yer fuckin' hole, wench?'

'Help me . . .' she screeched. The window slammed shut.

'She's in the gardens,' a man shouted. 'Chunky, get over there and shut her up.'

They were coming. Last chance.

'Which house?' another man yelled in response.

'Second one in, I reckon . . .'

Not going back. I'm not going back.

'Somebody help, please?' she screeched into the sky. 'Call police! Police! Help!'

Bending down, she grabbed a large stone frog from the path, turning her head aside to avoid the shrapnel, and lobbed it

15

through the glass pane in the back door. It shattered instantly, and lights were suddenly blazing in the kitchen. A man's hand, then his leg, appeared over the wooden fence.

The door opened. 'Get in here!' a man hissed, grabbing her by the arm and yanking her into the kitchen, shutting the door behind her just as heavy boots thumped down into the dirt.

'Please, you must call police,' Elenuta said. 'They will take me.'

'Don't you worry yerself,' the man said. 'I know all about it. Finlay, is this what you were looking for?'

Finlay Wilson appeared in the kitchen doorway. Five foot four, skin and bones, with tiny wide-set eyes that made him appear more reptilian than human.

'Aye, that's ma skank,' he grinned. More teeth were missing than not, and those that remained were a shade of yellow usually reserved only for dog vomit. 'Good man, Gene. We'll be out of your way now.'

Elenuta looked from Finlay to the man she'd assumed was about to save her, to the huge figure – presumably the man called Chunky – who was outside the back door ensuring she couldn't escape into the garden. There was going to be no escape, no police rescue, no return to her home and family. Served her right for falling for such an old trick. The promise of a better job, flattery, more money. Just a job interview to go through. Then there was the back of a truck, a gag over her mouth, ropes around her wrists and feet. Days of travelling like that, lumped in with a few other women, in a wooden box in the centre of a cattle transport. It didn't matter how much noise they tried to make. They never had a hope of being heard. From there, they'd been transferred into a lined cargo container and lifted onto a ship. Insufficient water had left them all dehydrated. At some point she'd lost hope that they would survive. When they'd reached land, she'd begun to wish they hadn't. She'd given it her best shot. There wouldn't be another chance to escape. That left only one option.

Throwing herself forward, she grabbed a knife from the block next to the sink, diving into the opposite corner of the room and holding it to her own throat.

'I rather die,' she said, her hand shaking fiercely enough that the blade was already leaving a ragged trail over her skin.

'Would you now?' Finlay asked, stepping forward, a smile playing at the corner of his lips. 'That's as may be. But what'll your wee friend back at the flat do without you? There's a special event on soon, see, and I've had my eye on you for it. Problem is, if you act like a little bitch right now and mess up my plans, there'll be a vacancy.' He got up close into Elenuta's face. 'What's that kid's name? Anika, that's it. I was touched by how you looked after her on her birthday last week. Sweet sixteen. That's a bit younger than the girls I normally race, but if you fuck with me, I'll make an exception.'

Elenuta lowered the knife. She didn't need any time to think about it. Finlay had proved multiple times in the last month that he never joked about anything. Whatever race he was talking about, Anika wouldn't survive it. It was a miracle she'd survived the trip across Europe to start with and she'd grown more withdrawn with every man they sent into her bedroom.

Not your problem, a wormy voice whispered in her ear. End it now. Better like this. Only that wasn't her. Anika reminded her of her little sister. It could as easily have been her trapped like a tiny bird in the disgusting cage on the fourth floor of flats, all of which seemed to be controlled by Finlay and his men.

'Sensible girl,' Finlay whispered, taking the knife from her compliant hand and getting a grip on her upper arm, ready to march her out.

'Fin . . . man . . . do I no' get a free suck-off at least, seeing as I told you she was in my garden? After she broke my window too,' Gene whined.

'You've got your right hand. That'll have to do. This girl and I have business to sort out.'

Finlay dragged her towards the front door.

'Am I supposed to pay for the broken window? You fuckin' wanker. Is that all the thanks I get? I should call the bloody polis on you, see how you like that. Treating everyone round here like shite, thinkin' yer the big man.'

Elenuta caught the single nod Finlay issued to the man who'd been guarding the back door and who was now standing with his hand through the glass she'd so recently smashed.

'Well, I'm no' scared of you. You've got some paying back to do. Did you really think we'd all stay quiet about what you've got going on up the road?' Gene continued, oblivious.

There was a single gunshot, more whoosh than bang. The louder noise was the splatter of blood and bone fragments hitting the wall.

Staring at the mess, Elenuta came to terms with what she'd already known, even if her stubborn brain had kept on trying to see a light at the end of the tunnel. She'd left one shoe inside the container on that ship. One of her best shoes, that she'd thought she was wearing to the job interview that would change her life and her family's fortunes. With it, she'd left behind both hope and her faith in human nature. In every way that mattered, she was already dead. Finlay dragged her across the broken glass and through the back door into the garden. She didn't even feel the shard that pierced her heel.

Chapter Three

Malcolm Reilly would have been staring at the ceiling of the mortuary if his eyes were still in their sockets. Detective Inspector Luc Callanach found it harder to stare at the young man's face than the bodies he'd seen before. There was something so macabre, so alien, about a face without its eyes. And that wasn't all that was missing.

'Eyes, heart, liver, lungs, pancreas . . .' the French pathologist listed, 'gall bladder, kidneys and testicles.'

'But the penis is still there?' Jean-Paul asked. As the Interpol agent heading up the investigation in conjunction with French police, Jean-Paul was in charge.

That was fine with Callanach. He was only in France as Scottish liaison officer to Interpol temporarily, or so he'd been told on arrival three months earlier. After nearly two years in Scotland, he was still more accustomed to hearing English than French, and his head was performing a bizarre unnecessary translation between the two. He'd spent the previous twelve weeks trying to trace human traffickers who were allegedly moving women from Eastern Europe to the west, and from Spain and Portugal up as far as Denmark and

Scotland. Now the body of a Scottish national had been found in the housing projects at Flandres, north-east of Paris' city centre, and it had made sense for Callanach to attend. Local police had reported a corpse. The truth was that only a shell remained.

'See for yourself,' the pathologist told them, peeling down the sheet. The body was one long open wound, cut from sternum to groin, with a cross cut below the ribcage.

'You didn't make any of these cuts?' Callanach clarified.

'I didn't need to. Whoever opened him up didn't make any effort to sew him back up. This was how he was found. The incisions were made with a scalpel, though, and with some care. The cuts were deep enough to allow entry but no organs would have been damaged. I'd imagine the organs themselves were removed cleanly. There's little additional trauma, technically speaking. Whoever did this knew their way around the inside of a human body.'

'You think we're looking for a doctor?' Jean-Paul asked.

'I wouldn't insult my profession by calling whatever maniac killed this boy a doctor, but someone with medical knowledge, certainly.'

'So all the organs were removed in a single operation then?' Jean-Paul clarified.

'I would say so.'

'What else can you tell us about his death?' Callanach asked, taking photos he wished he wouldn't have to print out and stare at on a police station wall several hours a day. What most people didn't understand about a crime scene wall was that the photos weren't simply there for evidential purposes. Those visuals also ensured that you would work every single minute just so you could take them down again.

'His stomach was half-full when he died, and he would have been an average weight. His external skin was clean. Save for the removal of his eyes – also surgical in nature – there are no scratches or contusions on his face, nor the rest of his body, save for some old bruising on his knuckles. Chafing on one of his ankles suggests that a restraint was used at some point but that it was padded. It's hard to talk about cause of death without the major organs to examine, but there's insufficient other trauma for me to conclude that this young man died from anything other than the result of this surgery.'

'Given the attempt to dispose of the body, I guess we can discount any legitimate form of organ transplant surgery,' Jean-Paul commented.

'I'd say that was a fair assumption,' the pathologist agreed. 'There's no brain trauma, and no signs of long-term illness, but I'm severely limited in reaching conclusions. Superficially, he seems to have been healthy.'

'Someone looked after him,' Callanach said. 'They wanted him in good shape.'

'It must be organ harvesting,' Jean-Paul intervened. 'Except for the testicles, obviously.'

'No, even those can be transplanted actually,' the pathologist said. 'It's rare, but feasible.'

'Interpol helped close down an international operation like this two years ago. Most of those involved are now imprisoned, but there were inevitably a few who escaped, mainly on the administrative side. We'll review the case. It might give us somewhere to start.' Jean-Paul started texting something on his phone as Callanach stepped up to take a closer look inside the body cavity.

'How long do organs last outside the body before they absolutely have to be transplanted into the new host?' Callanach asked.

'Depends on the organ,' the pathologist said. 'Typically a maximum of thirty hours for a kidney, up to twelve for the

21

liver or pancreas, no more than six hours for lungs. Recent developments with storage boxes have meant that we can now keep a heart functioning outside the body for up to twelve hours but you're talking about having access to the very best technology.'

'Not a problem if someone's willing to pay,' Jean-Paul said.

'But the chance of having all the recipients ready at the same time – at best within a day and a half of one another. That seems . . .' Callanach stared grimly into the half-empty abdominal cavity, 'well, difficult, given that we're talking about an off-the-grid transplant.'

'You don't understand how professionally these operations are set up,' Jean-Paul told him. 'They run fully staffed clinics that look completely above board. Take the donor, have patients ready. It's last chance for most of them. They're too far down the waiting list to have a realistic shot at getting a donor through normal channels, or they don't fit the right model because of lifestyle or genetics. Those people, if they have the money, will try literally anything. The more desperate the patient, the fewer questions they ask. Most have some idea there's criminality involved, but if it's that or death, then the thought of prison isn't so daunting.'

'If it's that well-financed and professional they should have been able to find a better method of disposing of the body than dumping this boy on the street,' Callanach said.

'Not on the street. In a building site. Perhaps they were planning for him to be concreted in, then got disturbed.' Jean-Paul stripped off his gloves as he stepped away from the body. 'These people get other people to do the dirty work. Hired thugs. They were probably paid to dispose of the body securely but got lazy or thought they were being observed and just ditched him the first chance they had.'

'That doesn't explain what a twenty year old from Scotland

is doing here. It would have been quicker and less risky to have abducted someone locally,' Callanach said.

'Maybe he was a good match for one particular donor and they decided to harvest everything else that was usable to justify bringing him over,' the pathologist suggested. 'You should have your Scottish colleagues gather all his medical and personal information. Anything that might have made him a target.'

'Of course,' Callanach agreed, knowing that meant having to contact DCI Ava Turner. Wanting to and wishing he didn't have to at the same time. He and Ava had been dancing around the edges of a relationship for a couple of years. Just when it had finally seemed about to start, he'd screwed up and Ava had lost faith in him. Since then they'd barely spoken. Now, a phone call was inevitable. An international abduction and a death under these circumstances meant she would want to visit the victim's family personally.

'You coming?' Jean-Paul asked from the doorway.

Callanach hadn't even noticed him moving across the room. 'Sure,' he said, taking one last look at Malcolm Reilly's incomplete face and catching an odour on the waft of air-conditioning. 'Can you smell that?' he asked the pathologist.

The two of them bent over the body, breathing deeply. The top notes were all gassy – sulphur and rot – with the metallic twang of old blood, but then came something earthier, nutty with a hint of spice.

'All I'm getting above the normal odours is latex, and we don't use that in our gloves,' the pathologist said. 'I agree, there's something unusual.'

Callanach started to sniff around Malcolm's face, moving around to the crown of his hair, putting his nose as close to the hair as he dared without risking contamination. 'It's strongest here,' he said.

The pathologist took his place and breathed in deeply. 'I'm

not sure what that is. I'll swab the hairs again to see if we can trace any chemicals.'

'Can you keep the body sealed in an air-tight container so we don't lose the smell and we'll arrange for an aromachologist to come in and see what they pick up?' Callanach asked.

'No problem. That was a good call. I'm very careful about using my sense of smell during postmortems but I missed that one. Can you have the expert here within the next twenty-four hours? The scent will begin to fade if we leave it longer than that.'

Callanach looked to Jean-Paul for confirmation. Interpol wasn't his to make demands of any more. Everything he needed had to be assessed and confirmed by someone else. Jean-Paul nodded, then looked at his watch.

'We should go,' Jean-Paul said.

Callanach said goodbye to the pathologist and followed Jean-Paul to the car, trailing a few paces behind the man who had once been his closest friend, in and out of work, who had travelled with him, got drunk and partied with him, and who had unintentionally set him up on a date with a woman who later falsely accused him of rape. His reputation in tatters and his career at Interpol crushed – notwithstanding the fact that the case had never gone to trial – Callanach had left France and made a new start in his father's home country, Scotland. Jean-Paul had disappeared from his life when Callanach had needed him most, ensuring the stain of potential guilt hadn't rubbed off on him by association. Since he'd left France, they'd spoken only once about a case, managing polite professionalism but nothing more, the gulf between them unbridged.

'Still top of your game then, Luc,' Jean-Paul muttered as he climbed into the driver's seat of his old Maserati – handed down from his father, as Callanach recalled. Jean-Paul had always found it an excellent way to attract women's attention. A certain type of woman, anyway. It wasn't a judgement. In his twenties, Callanach had regarded almost every part of his life as disposable. Women had shifted in and out of his life like a tide. These days the opposite was true. Every decision he made was measured and careful, and he was an expert on consequences.

'Just luck,' Callanach replied, pulling a Gauloises cigarette from the pouch in his pocket and dragging on it, unlit, tasting bonfires and sunsets, and a thousand different red wines. He didn't bother lighting it. Smoking, like so many other pleasures, was one he had to forego these days. His move from France to Scotland had prompted a number of changes. Giving up smoking was the most public one. Away from work, he drank less wine and spent more time at the gym. But the real change since the rape allegation was post-traumatic impotence. That one was proving much harder to come to terms with.

'It was never luck with you,' Jean-Paul said, pulling away roughly from the kerb. 'You were always in the right place at the right time. You always overheard exactly the phrase we needed for all the pieces to fall into place. I often wondered if moving to Scotland had changed you. Apparently not.'

Callanach stared at his former friend's face as he drove. His chin had slackened and there was grey showing prematurely in his muddy blond hair. Jean-Paul had aged considerably since they'd last seen one another, his mid-thirties proving unkind.

'Let's not do this,' Callanach said.

'Do what?' Jean-Paul laughed. 'Be honest with each other? Be real? You've barely said a word to me since you came back to Interpol. Are we supposed to act like we don't know one another – all polite bullshit and small talk? Screw that.'

'What is it you're angry about, Jean-Paul?' Callanach asked, winding down the window and letting the weak sun warm his arm.

Jean-Paul laughed, but his face was all bitter after-taste. 'You think I'm angry? Jesus, Luc, are you ever going to forgive me for what happened? Astrid Borde is dead. You watched her die. I know you went through some bad shit, but the woman who accused you of rape is gone. It's time to move on.'

'I have,' Callanach said quietly.

'Like fuck you have. You know what? I messed up. I didn't know what to do when Astrid accused you, but I've said sorry. Do you think I haven't spent the last couple of years regretting what happened?'

'Jean-Paul, Astrid Borde played me, and you, even my mother. She was smart, devious, and the evidence she set me up with was overwhelming. Was I angry that you seemed to dump me? Damned right I was, for a long time too. But hindsight's no bad thing. If a woman you'd been out on a date with turned up with bruises, scratches, internal injuries for fuck's sake, and you'd lied about what had happened on your date, I'd have done exactly what you did. It's important to believe victims, even when the accused is a friend. You did the right thing. I'm not angry with you. I'm just sick of thinking about it – of it being a part of my life. That's why I left Lyon and Interpol, only now I've been sent back. It wasn't my choice. I'm not trying to punish you. This just isn't where I want to be.'

'So you just what . . . rose above it all?' Slamming a foot on the brake pedal, Jean-Paul pulled the car roughly in towards the pavement. 'You've decided to forgive me? I guess you expect me to thank you for that. God, you're unbelievable. Do you ever fuck up? It took about ten minutes after you were back at Interpol to have every woman in the place fawning over you. Did you know they've found photos of you on the internet from when you were modelling? And the false rape allegation has just made you even more of a hero. All you went through, and you've come back stronger than ever, and now twice as magnanimous. Do you need to sleep or are you actually superhuman?'

Callanach knew what women thought of him. His looks were as much a curse as a blessing. Dark hair that curled as soon as it grew more than a couple of centimetres, olive skin that tanned with the slightest hint of sunshine, and a smile that could persuade women to do almost anything he wanted. Not that he wanted anything from women any more.

'What's going on with you? You were never like this, Jean-Paul. As for the way I'm being treated within Interpol, I haven't noticed anyone paying me any attention. A lot of the faces have changed from a couple of years ago. I just want to be left alone to get on with my job. I didn't ask to be partnered with you on this.'

'No, you didn't. I asked to head up the investigation when I realised you were being assigned to it as Scottish liaison officer. I thought that maybe we could reconnect, put the past behind us. I don't know what I was expecting, Luc. Anger maybe, some bitterness. I was hoping I could help you through the transition to living in France again . . .'

'I'm not living in France again,' Callanach said. 'I'm visiting.'

'You're not visiting. It's as if you're not here at all. I knew you better than anyone, but I don't know the man you've turned into. It's like you're a ghost. You don't talk to anyone. You sit silently in meetings. You work, go to the gym and disappear off to wherever you're staying. If you want to punish all your old friends then go ahead, but did you ever stop to think that we suffered too?'

'How *you* suffered? Is that a joke?'

'Yeah, that's right. It was hilarious being the best friend of the guy awaiting trial on a rape charge. No one knew what to say to me. Half the squad stopped talking to me altogether. Astrid told everyone that I'd introduced you to her, and made it sound as if I set the whole situation up. And you just disappeared. You wouldn't take any calls, you refused visitors . . .'

'You were a potential witness. My lawyer told me not to see you under any circumstances.'

'Luc, I was your best friend. You didn't rape that woman any more than I did, and I knew it. You just never gave me a chance to say those words to you,' Jean-Paul shouted.

'You're right. I'm sorry. I should have been more thoughtful when I was facing the prospect of spending fifteen years behind bars, then living with the label of sex offender and doing casual labour because my career had been stolen from me. It was a lot to deal with,' Callanach replied quietly.

'Even now you can't see it from anyone's perspective but your own, can you?'

Callanach stared at him, arms folded, one side of his mouth twisted up, half smile, half grimace. 'Well, now you've said everything you wanted to. I've heard your side of the story. And I'm not superhuman, I'm just doing my job. As for women paying me attention, I think you're a lot more interested in that than I am. Maybe you need to figure out why that is. You always did hate the way women reacted to me. At least you're finally being honest about it. But I'm here to work, and that's all. I want to find Malcolm Reilly's killer, close down this human trafficking case and go home. No drama, no conflict, no amateur psychotherapy, and – in the unlikely event that anyone does ask if I'm single and available – the answer is no. I'm committed elsewhere. Now, I'm pretty sure we were headed towards a crime scene, so let's go.'

Chapter Four

Detective Chief Inspector Ava Turner's first thought of the morning was that sex was simpler at the anticipatory stage than in the ramifications phase. Staring at the shoulders of the man asleep next to her, her second was to wonder how he ever found shirts to fit. He awoke, stretched, sighed heavily and ran one hand through his long hair before rolling over to greet her with a wide smile.

'Tell me it isn't time to get up yet,' he said. 'I need at least another twelve hours with you before I'm prepared to let you out of bed.'

'That's nice,' she said, sitting up and wrapping his discarded shirt around herself until she located something more appropriate. 'But I have to get to the station and I'm no good with early morning company, so if you could . . .'

'Get out?' DI Pax Graham asked. 'Ava, we both knew this was going to be complicated when we came back here last night, so let's go easy on one another. I've got no intention of making this difficult for you at work. I'm not the enemy. Far from it. All I want is to make this happen between us, on whatever terms you can deal with.' He reached out and took her fingers in his hand, stroking her palm gently with his thumb.

Fuck, Ava thought. Fuck, fuck, fuck, and one more for good luck. She was such an idiot. Sleeping with an officer under her command was stupid enough, but choosing one who seemed to genuinely care for her was a recipe for disaster. And that was before she pulled back the psychological curtain to take a look at her motivation.

'This was a mistake,' Ava said, voice soft, face as neutral as she could make it. 'My mistake, not yours. I'm really sorry. It was a combination of having some downtime and too much beer – not that I needed to be drunk to sleep with you. I've been out of a relationship a long time, and I suppose I got lonely.'

That wasn't the truth and she knew it, but the lie was easier.

'You know, you're allowed to be lonely.' He sat up, showing off the sort of chest an MMA fighter would be proud of, and leaned over to kiss her bare shoulder. 'Being a detective chief inspector doesn't mean your feelings have to get shoved into some lesser status. Also, if I leave now I won't be able to impress you with my bacon sandwiches.'

'Could I maybe take a raincheck on the bacon?' Ava asked. 'Not that it doesn't sound good . . .' Her mobile ringtone burst through the excuse session. She grabbed it and stood, pulling the shirt fully closed, hating her self-consciousness in the cold light of day. Opening a drawer with her free hand she rummaged for underwear and socks as she answered. 'Turner.'

'Ma'am,' Detective Sergeant Tripp said. 'We've got a dead body, single gunshot wound to the head. Deceased is a Caucasian male believed to be in his sixties.'

'Where?' Ava asked, perching on the edge of her bed to pull on knickers, as she motioned at Graham to keep quiet.

'Dumbryden Gardens, Wester Hailes. The crime scene

examiner's already there. The deputy pathologist's on his way, as Dr Lambert is away on a lecture tour this month. Uniforms have sealed off the roads locally. Can you come, only I've tried DI Graham, but it's his day off and he's not answering his phone?'

Ava walked around the bed, picked up Graham's jeans, reached in the pocket for his mobile and tossed it onto the bed next to him.

'Try his mobile again. He was probably sleeping. It's only . . .' She checked the bedside clock. 'God, I overslept, how is it eight thirty? I'll be with you in half an hour. Ask DI Graham to meet me there and keep the scene secure. It's not the easiest of patches on a good day.' She ended the call. 'Your phone was off. Tripp's about to call you. We need to go in separate cars.'

'Can you drop me back to mine on the way?' Graham asked, standing up and giving Ava the benefit of all six foot four of him stark naked. She looked away, wondering what would be a good alternative career for when she got fired from the Major Investigation Team.

Graham's mobile rang. Ava's followed suit. She walked into the bathroom to avoid anyone overhearing their voices on their respective calls.

'No, it's fine. I've got no plans so I'll be there,' Graham was saying as she pushed the door half shut.

'This is Turner.'

'Ava, it's Luc.'

She opened her mouth to talk, catching sight of herself in the bathroom mirror, socks in one hand, mobile in the other, hair wild, mascara smudged beneath her eyes, skinnier than she'd been for years. It wasn't a flattering look. She didn't recommend a diet based solely on stress and insomnia.

'Can you hear me?' Callanach asked.

'Yes . . . yes I can. Sorry, you caught me at a busy moment.' A sheen of sweat suddenly glimmered on her forehead.

'Shall I call back later? This can wait an hour or so. Where are you?'

Ava coughed, and forced some authority into her voice. 'At home but I'm just on my way to an incident. Go ahead. Tripp's covering it so I've got two minutes.'

'You're at home? I thought I heard Pax Graham's voice before . . .' Callanach sounded distant, foreign. But then he was – both things – Ava thought.

'He stopped to pick me up en route to the scene,' Ava thought on her feet, feeling sick, hating the ridiculous sense that she'd been caught cheating, ridiculous given that she was single even if things with Luc hadn't been properly resolved. 'It's a shooting so all hands on deck. MIT went out for drinks last night and I left my car at the station. Is there an update on the trafficking case from your end?' she asked, moving the conversation onto safer ground, wishing for the tenth time in as many minutes that she'd stuck to beer and not chased it with shots, and that she'd equally stuck to dull celibacy instead of trying to distract herself from the memory of the near miss with Luc by filling her bed with a convenient warm body. She'd broken her self-imposed rules pretty impressively. Drinking with her team was supposed to be limited to one quick glass, then head for the exit.

'No, this relates to a Police Scotland missing persons case, Edinburgh area. Young man by the name of Malcolm Reilly. His DNA was put on the Interpol database two months ago. A body was found and we've only just had official confirmation that the DNA is a match. It's a definite homicide. I'm sending an encrypted email with the details.'

'Okay, I'll have DS Lively take a look at it.'

'It'll have to be you, Ava. It's a bad one. Interpol has been asked to assist local French officers. It appears to be an organ harvesting case. The victim's been pretty much emptied out anatomically speaking.'

Ava sat down on the edge of the bath and ran a hand over her eyes.

'You need me to go and interview the family,' she said softly.

'I'm afraid so. I'll send you all the details. We'll need Malcolm's medical records, and we're chasing known suspects from our end. When we have any potential names we'll cross-check to see if anyone was in the UK at the time the victim was abducted.'

'Okay, I'll send uniformed officers in advance to break the news and offer support, then I'll get on it later this morning. Give me an hour to check out the shooting then I'll head directly into the station and take a look.'

'Sorry to land this on you. Sounds like you're busy enough already,' Callanach said.

'Until a few minutes ago we were almost having a quiet period.' She paused. 'How're you doing?'

'Fine.'

'Good. That's good. Well, I'll call if I have any questions once I'm up to speed.'

'Jean-Paul would like a conference call, tomorrow morning preferably. Is nine a.m. okay with you?'

The bathroom door opened. 'Hey, Ava, we'd better . . . shit, sorry.' Pax Graham exited quietly. Ava cursed inside her head.

'DI Graham's calling you Ava now?'

'You've been calling me Ava since we met, Luc.'

'When we met, you and I were the same rank.'

Ava tried to formulate a response, and failed. 'We should probably talk some time, about things.'

Things, Ava thought. As if the dead bodies, trafficked women, and the ocean between them weren't enough. Talking about things meant acknowledging the fact that for two years they'd pretended to be just friends when there had always been something more than that beneath the surface. Then at the moment it had been about to become something tangible, everything had gone horribly wrong.

She hadn't sent Callanach away exactly, but the request for a Scottish liaison officer to work with Interpol had been good timing. Ava asked herself, for perhaps the millionth time, if in different circumstances she'd still have chosen Callanach to go. She knew better than anyone how hard it was for him to go back to France after everything he'd been through. For a while she'd persuaded herself that forcing him to return was in his best interests. That everyone had to face their demons at some point. Of course, Callanach facing his had meant that she'd been able to delay facing hers. Successful relationships had eluded her all her adult life. There had been a brief engagement a while ago, to another police officer who had turned out to be less than charming. There were the odd random flings over the years but nothing that had lasted beyond the magic make-or-break six-month mark. Then there was Callanach, and in spite of waiting for the right moment and making sure it was real, somehow it had all ended in pain, regret and devastation for them both. Not all of it was his fault, either. Ava had taken a long hard look into the face of potential hurt/failure/let down, and chosen to sever whatever affection lay between them. Irrevocably. The man she'd woken up with this morning was simply her way of decorating her very own poisoned chalice with an extra cherry. Well done her.

'Ava?' Callanach prompted.

'Yeah, sorry, I was checking my diary. Sounds like we're both going to be too busy to do any talking in the near future. Let's leave it until we're in the same country.'

'Of course,' his voice was abrupt. 'I should let you go. Don't worry about the conference call. We'll exchange details by email. Tell Pax I said hi.'

He was gone. Ava closed her eyes while her hands stopped shaking.

She had to get a grip. Malcolm Reilly's family needed her. Whichever poor soul was lying in a pool of his own blood and brains over at Dumbryden Gardens needed her. Her personal screw-ups were just going to have to take second place. Like always.

Chapter Five

Ava stared through the hole in the glass pane at the crumpled body on the floor. The bullet entry wound was clear, as was the fact that the victim had been standing right next to a wall that had caught every fragment of bone, blood and grey matter expelled under bullet force from the exit wound.

'Did the bullet go through the glass?' Ava called inside to the technician who was busy collecting fragments from various kitchen surfaces.

'Unlikely. We suspect something much larger and more blunt given the size of the hole in the pane.'

Ava opened the back door of the terraced house cautiously, careful to sidestep any glass on the floor. Only there wasn't any.

'Have you already swept up the glass for forensic testing?' she checked.

'No, nothing's been moved from the scene yet. We need everything in place to track the likely journey through the property.'

'Do we have an estimate for time of death?' Ava asked, checking her watch.

'Six to seven hours ago.'

'Thanks,' Ava murmured as she made her way further inside,

mindful that it had to be scene examiners first and police officers second, to avoid contamination. Stealing a glance at the victim – scrawny, neck covered in what looked like jailhouse tattoos – she left the kitchen and went into the lounge. Hand-rolled cigarette ends overflowed from every conceivable container, and a few had missed judging by the blackened holes in both the furniture and carpet. Takeaway cartons were strewn liberally about. A yellowing sofa that had obviously been chewed by a dog at some stage sat sadly at one end of the room, collapsing in the centre. It looked embarrassed to be there, Ava thought. Rightly so. The whole place stank. An old vest had been used to soak up some sort of spillage on a cardboard box that was doubling as a coffee table, and the curtains were makeshift scraps of material, hung with gaffer tape.

Ava took the stairs, aware of the carpet sticking to her shoe coverings, glad of the gloves she was wearing that protected her hands from contamination as much as protected the scene from her. Straight ahead was a bathroom she didn't even dare enter. The stench coming from it was nauseating. The first boxroom bedroom was jam-packed with bits of broken furniture and old suitcases. Beyond that lay the other bedroom, housing an equal number of cigarette butts as the lounge, and a bed with sheets that might never have been changed. No curtains at all upstairs, and no clothes in the open wardrobe. What clothes there were had ended up scattered across the floor in varying piles of slightly worn to absolutely filthy. Next to the bed was a pile of red-inked bills. Ava picked one up and opened it. Apparently Mr Gene Oldman hadn't been meeting his electricity payments. She looked around. It was a tip. Every surface in the entire house was dusty or sticky. Except one.

Ava took the stairs back down two at a time.

'Everyone stay still,' she ordered. 'Wherever you are. The kitchen floor's clean.'

'Ma'am?' Tripp queried, staring at her from the hallway.

'Every other surface in this entire house is a bacteria brothel. There's a dead man lying in the corner of the kitchen with his brains marking the walls – no effort to clean that up – and yet the kitchen floor is absolutely spotless. Somebody cleaned it, so whatever was on there was more important to the killer than the body itself.'

'I need a complete window blackout and luminal spray asap,' one of the scene examiners shouted. 'If the surface was bleached and the victim's been dead seven hours already, whatever was on the floor will be fading fast.'

Ava stood back and let them work. Every window was lined with blackout blinds and every door shut until no light could enter, then four officers waited to spray a section of floor each.

The entire floor began to glow immediately.

'That's the bleach,' an officer explained. 'You were right. It's been recently cleaned, but it was fast and areas have been missed. There,' he pointed in the direction of the back door, down in the corner near the skirting board. 'And there. Photos immediately please.' A faint blue glow came from two lines of grouting, and a semicircle roughly two inches across could be seen clearly near the back wall, furthest from the door.

'Why does it glow blue?' Ava asked.

'The chemicals react with the iron in the blood's haemo-globin. We're on borrowed time though. It's fading. That's why we have the cameras ready to record areas of the floor where we need to pay special attention afterwards.'

Ava trod carefully in the dark, moving towards the semicircle that was the boldest of all the glowing sections of floor.

'It's the edge of a footprint,' she said. 'Just the back of the heel. Can we get an accurate foot size from this, do you think?' she asked the lead scene examiner.

'I'd say there's enough definition there for that, and now we know where the blood is, we might be able to ascertain more with further testing. The fact that we're seeing this much glow probably means the bleach wasn't very strong.'

'Any hope of getting DNA?'

'Depends if we can find a sample unaffected by the bleach.'

'All right,' Ava said. 'The victim's name is probably Gene Oldman, the property owner. Could you double-check against other fingerprints and DNA in the property? I didn't see any photo ID lying around.'

She made her way outside. In other areas of the city the presence of so many police officers would have triggered the build-up of an automatic crowd. Onlookers would be waiting for a body to be brought out on a stretcher. Speculation as to what nightmarish events had occurred would be circulating. But this was the heart of Wester Hailes. When the police arrived, doors were slammed and curtains were closed. No one stood out on the street. A loathing of authority overrode natural curiosity.

'DI Graham,' she said. He was in the throes of organising a nervous-looking bunch of uniformed officers. Conducting door-to-doors in that region of the city was about as much fun as a colonoscopy.

'Ma'am,' he said, face straight, no sign of what had happened the night before. He was professional and discreet, which made Ava feel worse rather than better about what she'd done.

'I'd like to knock on the immediate neighbours' doors myself to get a feel for what's happening, but would you do the talking?' Ava asked. Years of working undercover meant Graham had developed an easy tone which had the hardiest of potential witnesses opening up to him. In spite of her long, curly hair and unthreatening physique, her English accent courtesy of an expensive education insisted on by her parents rendered her something of an affront to some people, particularly in an area as deprived as Wester Hailes.

They knocked on the first door and waited. Not so much as one curtain twitched, yet there was a clear sense that the property was occupied. Ava motioned to a uniformed officer to check round the back. It took no more than two minutes before a young couple were being escorted around from their back garden.

'They were just headed through their back gate, ma'am,' the officer explained.

DI Graham took over. 'Well, thanks for coming to chat. Won't keep you long. You've probably noticed activity in your neighbour's house.' No response. 'Were either of you in last night?'

'We went to bed early,' the man said, glancing sideways at the woman.

'Did you? It's really helpful that you were in your property. We have reason to believe there might have been a gunshot. Did you hear anything?'

'Slept right through. Didn't hear nothin',' the man declared.

'Is your bedroom at the front or the back of the house?' Graham asked.

'The back,' the man said. 'So what?'

'So that would have been above and right next door to the room where we think the gun was fired, likely around three a.m. Are you sure you didn't wake up at all?'

They both shook their heads.

'A window was broken, too. I'm guessing there'd have been quite a disturbance. Did you know your neighbour well?'

'Not really,' the man said.

'So you knew him a bit then,' Graham said. Ava had to give him credit. He was a thousand times more patient than her. 'What was he like?'

'He was a creep,' the woman said. The man gave her a sharp look that Ava didn't like.

'How so?' Graham asked.

She shrugged, suddenly finding the pavement of huge interest. Her partner took over. 'You know what some blokes are like. Can't keep their eyes off a woman's tits when they're talking to her. That's why we never chatted to him much. Now we didn't hear anything and we didn't see anything, so are we free to go?'

Graham looked at Ava, who nodded. 'Give your details to the uniformed officer behind you, then you can go. And if either of you should suddenly remember anything, get in touch, okay? We know not to use your names.'

'Don't know what the fuck you're talking about,' the man said, putting an arm around the woman and pulling her away.

It wasn't a surprise. There were areas of the city where it was understood you just didn't speak to the polis. Not if you didn't want your windows smashed first and your face shortly thereafter. Life was tough. Just buying food and staying out of prison was hard enough for some people. You got a reputation as a rat and you'd be looking for somewhere new to live before you even smelled the petrol being poured through your letter box.

'Let's try the other side,' Ava said.

The door opened before they'd knocked and a stout elderly lady stood, hands on hips, ready to do business.

'Are you here about my disability scooter?' she shouted.

'I'm DI Graham and we were wondering if you know your neighbour, Gene Oldman?'

'I reported it missing two months ago. Left it outside my front door. Do you know how many polis came to see me about that?'

'I can certainly check up on what's happening with that case when I get back to the station. Could I take your name?'

'If you haven't got my scooter, you can get off my doorstep. I've got nothing else to say to you.' A bunch of kids who'd assembled behind Ava's back began giggling. She left Graham to deal with the woman who clearly had a prepared script that she was going to stick to no matter what, and turned to the kids.

'Live round here, do you?' she asked the group. There were four of them. Three boys and one girl who was trying to make herself look tougher than the company she was keeping – shoulders back, chin stuck out. Necessary, Ava guessed, so she didn't get ditched. Gender equality wasn't a priority on Edinburgh's backstreets.

'Fuckin' pig,' the girl said. The boys laughed.

'What do you lot know about the man who lives in there?' She motioned towards Gene Oldman's house.

'My mam says he never washed his clothes, not ever,' the smallest boy said.

'Would you shut your gob? You know we're not supposed to talk to 'em,' the girl warned him.

'Is he dead? He's gotta be. My dad said the polis never bother with us here unless someone's dead,' the boy continued.

The girl dug him in the ribs.

'So none of you are supposed to talk to me, then,' Ava said. 'If I was going to ask who's in charge round here, who would that be?'

'Dunno what you mean,' the girl said.

'Yes, you do. The person your mums and dads warn you to steer clear of. Everyone either goes quiet when they walk round the corner, or talks to them like they're the headteacher. Who does that sound like?'

'Are you stupid?' the girl asked.

Ava looked at her. She wasn't being cheeky. There was genuine curiosity on her face.

42

'You think I should be too scared to ask?' Ava directed at her gently.

'Fuckin' right you should,' the girl replied.

'Are you scared of him?' Ava continued.

'You kids, get out of here!' The woman DI Graham had been questioning stormed down her front path, waving her arms at them. 'Go on, get home, right now.'

In the second Ava turned away to tell her to leave them alone, the kids were gone, sprinting along the pathway between the terrace of houses and a tenement block.

'I'll look into that problem with your scooter,' Graham told her as he approached Ava.

'Don't bother,' the woman said. 'I just remembered, I sold it last month.' She waddled back inside, slamming her front door.

'Nothing?' Ava asked him.

'I learned a few new words,' Graham said. 'Which is impressive given how much time I've spent undercover with drug dealers and gangs. What next?'

'I'm going in to the station,' Ava said.

'I'll follow you in.'

'No, don't worry. It's your rest day. We won't get much further until the postmortem's been done and we've got the forensics report. We sure as hell aren't going to get anything useful from local witnesses.'

'I'd like to come in and help,' Graham said. 'And you could use some breakfast.'

She began walking towards her car. He fell into step beside her.

'Listen, Pax, last night was . . . a one-off. It can't happen again. It makes things too complicated at work.'

'I hear you,' Graham said. 'But you should know that I've never given up on anything I really wanted in my life.'

'I'm not an achievable goal. Also, I'm not worth the effort.

43

I don't do healthy relationships. I guess I'm asking you to forget what happened between us. Would you try to do that?'

He dug his hands deep into his pockets, head to one side, his long hair moving in the breeze, jaw flexing.

'You're not particularly forgettable, I'm afraid,' he said eventually, smiling before turning slowly and walking away.

Ava searched for an expletive that would adequately give voice to her frustration and failed to find one.

Chapter Six

A building site just off Rue Curial, at the side of a hotel whose star rating Callanach estimated to be in the negatives, was where Malcolm Reilly's body had been dumped, and it was about as far from the image of romantic, starlit Paris as it was possible to get. No building work had taken place there for several weeks while the builders settled disputes over safety regulations, so Malcolm had lain face down, between a cement mixer and a cherry picker, until some unfortunate labourer, who couldn't possibly have been paid enough to have discovered a hollowed-out body, had turned up on a routine safety-hazard walk-around one day, only to have the site immediately closed down again as a crime scene.

Callanach looked around. There was some regeneration happening in the area, but he guessed that was only because land in that district was so cheap. Low-cost modern flats rose above lock-ups that harboured decades-old secrets. Cracks in walls were papered over with plaster, and alleyways led into dark places that no sensible person would enter. This was not the Paris of tourist fantasies. It was a world riddled with debt and a multitude of illegal ways to pay it off. This was a space where a body could rot and no one would notice, or care if they did.

A tarpaulin shielded the patch where Malcolm's body had lain. Beneath it, a brown stain marked the concrete and brick rubble.

'Was he naked when he was found?' Callanach asked Jean-Paul.

'Wrapped in a plastic sheet. We're assuming he was left here at night to avoid witnesses. He was there for several days before the corpse was found. Did you speak to your boss about getting his medical records?'

'It's in hand. So how did they get access to the building site?'

'They forced open two sections of wooden panelling and walked in. Dragged the body across the site – there was a build-up of rubble around the plastic sheet – left him, then put the panel back in place. We know from the construction company that building work was behind schedule though. It's possible they'd planned to dump him in a foundation pit ready to be cemented over, but their timing was off.'

'Fingerprints on the sheet?'

'None. All the DNA belongs to the victim. The only unusual chemical identified was lanolin, and that was in quantities found only by swabbing the sheet. Not large patches or smears. Nothing visible to the naked eye.'

'Lanolin's from sheep's wool, right?' Callanach asked.

'Yes. We're compiling a list of possible sources – farms, animal movement vehicles, textile factories.'

Callanach looked upwards, checking which buildings had aspects that overlooked the building site. 'And all these properties have been canvassed to check if they saw anything suspicious?'

'As much as we could. We'd have needed twenty different interpreters to get round every apartment. You know what it's like here. The police are the enemy.'

'These people don't want dead bodies in their back yard any more than anyone else,' Callanach said.

A brick whistled past Callanach's head and smashed at his feet. He leapt away and dived towards a cherry picker for cover as another hit Jean-Paul on the knee. Clutching his leg, Jean-Paul limped towards a half-built wall, crouching down with his back to the brickwork as a broken metal pipe smashed into an abandoned paint can.

The projectiles were flying at them from behind the main entry gates, and the aim was accurate enough that whoever was throwing had a decent view of them.

'Get their attention,' Callanach shouted to Jean-Paul.

'Just stay where you are. I'm calling for police backup.' Jean-Paul waved him back into the sheltered area.

'Don't do that. As soon as they hear sirens, they'll scatter. Just divert their attention for a minute,' Callanach said, ducking low and running towards the far end of the site where pallets had been stacked precariously high near the boundary.

Jean-Paul took a few steps away from the wall, shielding his head with one arm as he bent to pick up the broken pipe, then swung it high in the air and back over the fence from the direction it had come.

There was a cry, followed by a furious yell. As Callanach allowed himself a glance over his shoulder, multiple projectiles appeared over the top of the fence. He hoisted himself up on the nearest pile of pallets hoping they'd been stacked carefully, disliking the wobble as he rose higher. Jean-Paul yelled. Callanach turned to check he was unharmed. His foot slipped, the pallets groaning beneath his weight, and he grabbed at the stack to his side. Splinters slid diagonally into his right palm.

'Fuck,' he muttered, seeing Jean-Paul using a stray sheet of corrugated iron as an anti-assault umbrella. He smiled in spite of the pain in his hand and his concern for Jean-Paul. It was such a throwback to years gone by. He and Jean-Paul had travelled the world assisting police forces from other countries to track drug cartels, arms dealers and money launderers, and situations like these had been the days they'd looked forward to. Just enough physical jeopardy to get their pulses racing with the unshakeable belief that a few hours later they'd be sitting in some bar, empty beer bottles spread like trophies, and another credit on their Interpol files. Simpler times.

He hauled himself upwards, the splinters folding beneath his skin as he closed his fist, knowing he was facing a lengthy session with a needle and antiseptic later that night. The top of the fence was too thin to do anything except angle his foot onto its side to give him the boost he needed to jump. He took a literal leap of faith, hoping there wasn't too much smashed glass or jagged metal on the other side. Landing well initially, he stumbled over a half-buried paving stone, falling sideways to avoid planting his splintered hand in the dirt. He opened his eyes to stare into the empty barrel of a syringe, the needle encrusted with blackened blood and pointing in the direction he needed to be going.

Getting to his feet carefully – avoiding the needle that he could see and what he presumed were several others better hidden – Callanach rounded the edge of the fence and sprinted for the far corner. There he paused, putting his mobile in camera mode and exposing it beyond the edge of the fence, filming as he assessed the situation.

Between eight and twelve young men packed into a tight group were picking up whatever they could find at their feet and lobbing it over the wooden security fence. Two others were standing with eyes pressed up to the gaps in the vertical planks, yelling instructions to the others. Middle Eastern in appearance and speaking rapidly in a language Callanach couldn't understand, they looked more like bored teenagers than a serious threat, except for one who was keeping his distance, watching the others, making the odd comment. Callanach focused his camera as tightly as he could on the faces, hoping the sound recording wasn't too muffled, as he decided what to do. These were local boys, that much was clear. It was a fair bet they realised he and Jean-Paul were police officers.

Calling for backup was the only way to ensure controlling the youths until each could be spoken to individually, but it was hard to achieve a completely silent police approach anywhere in Paris with tail-to-tail traffic. He wondered how much longer Jean-Paul could remain unhurt with so many projectiles raining down.

A gunshot stopped his strategising. The boy who'd been keeping out of the fray had apparently grown tired of the situation, aiming directly at the wooden fence and sending shrapnel flying at his mates. They leapt away shouting as the man-boy walked forward, gun out in front, towards the hole he'd created. Callanach knew that Jean-Paul would be calling the situation in and searching for better cover. More of a problem now would be stopping the inevitable move of the gang towards the entrance Jean-Paul and he had used, thereby preventing a safe exit. He and Jean-Paul were both unarmed. Interpol agents rarely took guns out during investigations unless there was a known or specific threat. Today was supposed to be about information gathering, not engaging in an anti-police showdown. Worse than that was the prospect that a stray shot might hit an innocent passerby. There was only one thing left to do.

'Police!' Callanach shouted. 'Put down your weapons. Hands up and get on your knees.'

The shot came in his direction before he saw the young man move, glancing the corner of the fence and pinging away at an angle. Callanach ducked. Feet were pounding concrete but the high rise of flats in a square around them created an echo

49

chamber. There was no way of knowing if the gang was running towards him or away. Callanach bolted for a nearby doorway.

There were shouts from just beyond his line of vision, frantic fury mixed with questions and instructions. Callanach forced his body back further into the recess. Footsteps indicated an approach in his direction, and he readied himself to fight.

Sirens sounded in the distance just as he was about to throw himself out of his hiding place. There was an instantaneous hush – everyone listening, trying to assess the direction from which the emergency services were coming. Then the scatter began. People running in all directions, calling to one another, their panicked voices revealing their immaturity. Less aggression, more uncertainty.

Callanach stuck his head out and watched them go. They ran at extraordinary speed, jumping railings, disappearing across the road, one leaping from a garbage can to grab a second-floor railing and haul himself up onto the exterior corridor of flats. Only one voice remained, calling, listening in silence, calling again.

'Huznia.' A pause. 'Huznia!'

Callanach looked around. The caller was nowhere to be seen and his voice was fading. The sirens were getting closer, closing in from both ends of the road.

'Huznia!' The shout was more insistent.

A scraping noise came from behind a pile of bin bags. Callanach crept over to take a look as Jean-Paul appeared from the far end of the building site sporting a large graze across his cheek. He gave a thumbs-up. Callanach responded with a nod and a finger over his lips to keep him quiet.

Covering the final distance to the bin bags quickly, Callanach found a young girl crouched, tears in her eyes, looking absolutely terrified. He smiled at her gently, hands slightly raised in the international signal that no harm was intended. She looked less than convinced.

He spoke in French to her, quietly, slowly and clearly. 'Everything's all right. Do you speak French?'

There was a brief pause then, 'Yes,' with a sob.

'Are you Huznia?'

She looked surprised, then relieved – nodding – young enough to believe that anyone who knew her name must be friend rather than foe. Callanach wished life was really so black and white.

He smiled gently. 'My name is Luc. Don't be scared. Who are you waiting for?'

'My brother,' she said, looking away to the side. Her French was good considering her age – he guessed she was five or six years old – but then desperation was often the most compelling teacher of foreign languages.

'Who's your brother?' Callanach asked.

'Azzat,' she said quietly. 'Do you know him?'

'I think he's looking for you. Are you hungry, Huznia?' Callanach asked, lowering himself to one knee to get closer to her.

She frowned. Good girl, Callanach thought. At least she'd been taught to be wary of strangers.

A pair of boots appeared in his peripheral vision, scruffy, a hole in front of the big toe of one. Callanach took his time turning round to assess their owner. The boy was in his mid-teens, but his eyes were older. He was ready to fight, ready to run, ready to do whatever he had to. His clothes were in the same state as his boots, ragged and ill-fitting. Stolen or hand-me-downs. His face and hands were bruised, and darkened with the sort of dirt you couldn't really shift without soap. He and his sister were obviously living rough.

'Leave her alone,' the boy said. His French was fluent, not just the words but the accent, impressive for a second language.

'I'm not going to hurt your sister,' Callanach told him. 'I'm not here for you, but I have some questions about the body that was left at the building site. Do you know about that?'

'Huznia, come to me,' he said.

Callanach took a few notes from his pocket and held them where the little girl could see them.

'Your sister's hungry,' Callanach said. 'And she needs new clothes. I just want some information.'

'We don't need your money,' Azzat said. 'We're fine. Now get out of the way and let my sister get by.'

'I'm not going to stop her from getting to you. You have nothing to fear from me. We're just talking.'

A police car roared into view. Azzat pushed forward, grabbed his sister by the arm and began pulling her out from between bin bags.

'But I am hungry!' she whined.

'I'll get you food,' Azzat said.

Callanach stepped aside to let them get past him. 'Where are you from originally?' he asked.

'Afghanistan,' Huznia said. 'Do you have food in your pockets?'

Callanach passed her a twenty-euro note, keeping another in his hand but on show. Other police officers were approaching cautiously.

'Do you live near here?' The two children stared at one another. 'All right. You don't have to tell me. Take my card, though. Keep it. I need to find out who brought the body that was found in this building site. Call me if you know anything. Maybe I can help you.'

'You'll take my sister away from me!'

'Will he?' Huznia cried.

'No, I won't. And I won't let anyone else either. I can see how much you love each other.' Callanach held a hand up to the approaching officers, keeping them at bay some twenty metres away. 'Take this money, buy some food and make sure you have somewhere safe to stay. If you get in trouble, call me.'

Azzat snatched away the cash and the card, shoving them in his pocket as he and his sister began to run.

'Huznia, don't let him throw my card away,' Callanach shouted after them.

The girl looked back, gave a half wave, then they were gone down an alley that was no more than a crack between buildings.

Callanach supposed he should have called family services and had them taken to a children's shelter. There was obviously no adult caring for them. They were skinny and unkempt. But there was every chance they'd be separated. It was difficult housing a young girl with a teenage boy. The psychological damage done by separating dependent siblings was enormous. They would get lost inside a system that did its best, but which too often left children sitting in the dirt at the bottom of life's slide. The truth was that maybe they were happier living rough, but together.

'Why didn't you bring him in?' Jean-Paul demanded from behind him. Callanach turned round. His colleague was holding a gauze pad to a bleeding wound on his head, and looking shaken.

'He wouldn't have told us anything,' Callanach replied.

'He might have, if he'd thought the alternative was having his sister taken away,' Jean-Paul said, tossing the gauze into a skip and setting his free hands on his hips.

'I wasn't prepared to do that.'

'Yeah, well lucky for you, you're not the person who's going to have to explain to Malcolm Reilly's parents how he died. Did you go soft in Scotland?'

'Maybe I just grew up a bit,' Callanach said quietly, wondering where Ava was at that moment, part of him wishing he could have been with her to give the news to Malcolm Reilly's family, and the other part equally glad he wasn't.

Chapter Seven

Bart woke up feeling sick, rolling dramatically to his left and smashing his face against the wall. Metal screeched and the world shifted around him, tilting forwards then back, until he lurched for the ring in the centre of the floor and held tight. The feeling of movement wasn't new. His world had been unstable since he'd first awoken, but this was something different. Almost – although he told himself it was the lack of fresh water and decent food making him delusional – like flying.

The box he was trapped in shifted again, and this time there was a different noise. Whistling, a gust, then a spinning turn. He gripped his stomach, wishing it would stop. It was a desperate thing to have become resigned to dying alone in what amounted to little more than a cell. The air stank from the bucket he'd had no choice but to fill, avoiding the overflow where it had tipped twice during the journey. Despite turning off the electric lamp for increasingly lengthy periods whenever his sanity could stand it, the battery was fading now. Alone in the dark, cold and starving, at least fear had deserted him too. There was nothing with him in the dark that could hurt him more than his own imagination, and he had conquered that. For the briefest of periods he had managed to meditate, sitting upright, blanket wrapped around his stiff body, breathing in a rhythm with his heartbeat, imagining sitting on a beach at sunset, listening to the waves. Just the waves. Letting nothing else in. It was a neat trick when you learned to do it well. Having an ex-girlfriend who'd been training to become a yoga instructor had helped. The effects just didn't last very long.

His ribcage protested as a huge crash beneath his prone body reverberated through him. Bart realised the sensation of flying hadn't been a product of his nutritionally starved mind. Whatever container he was in had been moving through the air. No more, though. All movement, the sense of rocking, had ceased. New noises invaded his space, muffled and distant, but there were definitely voices blended in with the mechanical din beyond his walls.

Bart stood up, listened, strode towards a wall and took a deep breath. Hammering on the wall he began to shout. He bolstered the noise of his fists with one foot. When that was bloody and raw, he used a knee instead. Nothing. No response. Letting his fists rest – by now his hands resembled a cage fighter's – he took the strain with his forehead. Unfamiliar with the art of giving a Glaswegian kiss, Bart didn't let himself be deterred. He headbutted the wall as if his life depended on it, mainly because by then he'd realised that it did. He would die inside that box if something didn't happen soon. Slamming his forehead into the wall three, four, five times, he went reeling backwards, losing his balance and ending up back on the floor. On his knees, he went for the wall again. The electric lantern finally gave up the ghost. In the perfect dark he hammered, shouting, yelling, screaming, until his voice was nothing more than a whisper. Then an engine started up and everything started moving again. Bart lay down and let defeat shrivel him into submission.

★ ★ ★

It was impossible to know how long the journey had taken. Bart had either slept or passed out. His head was thumping and there was blood crusted on his forehead and down his cheeks. The memory was vague, but at some point his body had assumed control of his brain and apparently tried to break through the walls. He was paying for it now. Bart tried to stand and failed.

From the far end of his prison box came the squeal of metal then something else, and for a moment he couldn't identify the change. The quality of the blackness changed. Not dramatically. No one switched on a light, but there was a new duskiness to the dark, shifting from black to the deepest of greys. Particles of light were invading his atmosphere. He'd assumed the space was completely sealed. Not so. Crawling on hands and knees, he made for the wall closest to the noise.

'Open it up,' a man shouted. Someone answered with an accent Bart recognised as French even if he couldn't speak the language.

He stared at the walls, as if by concentrating hard enough he would be able to see the faces that lay beyond. Were these his rescuers? His assailants? Raising one bruised and shaking hand, he paused before knocking. He had no idea how long he'd been trapped inside – days, he assumed – but already his prison felt safer than the unknown beyond. In the outside world he'd been kidnapped and removed from everything and everyone he loved. He had no idea why or by whom. He'd never expected to fall victim to such evil. Now it was all he could think about. Every face he saw would be a mask, every word a lie. He would never be able to trust anyone again.

A scraping-crunching came from one upper corner of the cell before Bart found his courage. He backed away. The first clear light pierced the gloom to reveal a scene that had him cringing with embarrassment in spite of the horrors he'd endured. A blast of fresh air only served to intensify the stench of human waste that Bart had become used to, but now he could see it. The bucket he'd been using had overflowed with the journey and the floor was awash. He held his filthy hands in front of his face. Now he could smell himself, too, and felt a desperate urge to vomit as the end of his prison was crow-barred away to the sound of ripping wood. Beyond the opening it was too bright for his eyes to focus.

'Help me,' he whispered.

'Pick him up,' a man said. Heavy boots crossed the wooden cell. Two men took an arm each in gloved hands, dragging him out into the daylight.

Bart breathed deeply, his eyes closed, feeling weak sunlight on his face and doing his best to muster some strength in his legs. His eyes were taking their time adjusting to the brightness. After a few steps, the men lowered him to the ground and he sank gratefully to his knees. An open bottle was thrust into his hands. He sniffed it, registered nothing but cold water, and swallowed the bottle in one go. A car park appeared in blurred patches. A few vans, gravel, brown grass around the edges, no buildings in sight – nothing that gave him any indication where he was. Behind him, on the back of a massive lorry, was a cargo container. He blinked, made an effort to keep down the water, and rubbed his sleeve over his eyes. Inside the container was a thick-walled wooden cell, the end wall prised off. A second bottle of water was handed to him.

'Slowly,' a man said. 'Then eat.' A loaf of bread in a tatty brown paper bag was thrown down to him. The tone and the treatment were all the confirmation needed of his status. His vision was clear now, as was his sense of smell. He stank. Not like he imagined a human who'd been incarcerated would, but like an animal. All filth and sweat, the sort of smell found in farms and abattoirs. The men around him seemed not to notice.

They weren't surprised by the state of him. Which meant they'd done it before.

He grabbed the bread, which looked like a gourmet offering compared to the box of stale snacks that had been left in the container for him. Even so, he'd consumed it all early in the journey and been left desperate for more. Once you realised what true hunger was, seizing food no matter what position you were in was more instinct than choice. As he ate, men wandered into his former home with buckets. The sound of sloshing water hit the floor and streams of filth ran out. Another brought several heavy-duty plastic cartons from the back of a van, with boxes of what must have been food supplies, similar to those he'd found.

'I can't go back in there,' he told the man closest to him through a mouthful of bread. 'Can't do it.'

The man ignored him, and barked orders to others, tapping on his watch. Faster movement followed, guns were drawn and men approached the backs of two vans.

'Head down,' Bart was ordered. When his reaction time wasn't fast enough, he was assisted with a slap to the back of his scalp.

He kept his head angled down, but his eyes up. The van doors opened slowly. The men reached in, pulling out the occupants of the vehicles. One by one, women appeared, hands tied, moving slowly, blinking at the sudden change in environment. Their faces were dirty and their clothes shabby, but they weren't in the same dreadful state as Bart. Not yet, but then they were ushered towards the container. One woman began to cry, and it spread through them like a virus, the women either side succumbing to tears, another going straight into a wailing sound as if she had only been waiting for a prompt. Bart kept count. Four women from one van, five more from another. He hoped for their sakes that they were given several more buckets for the journey.

One woman fell to her knees, then let herself go to the floor face first, sobbing, begging in the universal language of terror and desperation. A guard gave her an order. She didn't move. That earned her a kick. She reached out for the man's ankle, grabbing it, pulling herself towards his feet. He leaned down, snatching a bunch of her already matted hair, wrenching her face upwards to look into his eyes. He spat, waved the gun in her face. She sobbed some more.

Bart wanted to say something. In the dim recesses of his mind he imagined a braver man, a stronger male specimen who had not been so broken by his ordeal, springing up, wrestling a gun from one of the men, shooting off a couple of bullets to show he meant business, before taking command of the situation and freeing them all. What he did was let his face fall to the dirt. What he didn't see couldn't hurt him. Instead, he heard all he needed. In spite of the constant mechanical noise of the previous days – he wasn't quite sure of the time period – his ears were as alert as ever. He heard another kick, that soft whoosh of air as foot contacted stomach. More crying. Laughter. Another man's footfall, heavy, slow, deliberate. Then the unmistakable sound of a zip being lowered. Liquid hitting skin in a constant stream. The woman let out a howl that was end-game hopelessness. The reduction to nothing more than disposable goods was complete. As Bart opened his eyes, the woman was crawling away through the dirt, following the others into the black hole that he'd just escaped. The men picked up the wooden end wall of the cell, took nails from their pockets, gathered hammers, and began to seal it up. The hammering from the outside was matched blow for blow by the sound of fists hitting the inside of the wood. Bart had time to wonder if the men had bothered to replace the batteries inside the lamp. As pathetic as it was, that tiny spark had been everything to him in the endless dark.

He looked past the man standing over him.

'I need to pee,' he said. 'Where do I go?' The bottles of water had run through him like fresh rain off dried mud.

The man pointed at the ground where Bart sat. He was going nowhere. If he needed to piss, it was right there or not at all. He did what he needed, watching as the enormous container door was swung shut. A wooden cell within a metal prison. Enough noise externally that no one would ever be heard within. He wished vaguely that he hadn't bothered ripping his vocal chords to shreds for nothing. With one hand taking care of business, he used the other to dip into the rear pocket of his jeans, clutching his most treasured possession, loath to sacrifice it, but who knew where he might end up next? If this was his only chance to leave a note, a record of his passing, then he had no choice. He waited until all eyes were elsewhere, then dropped the photo of his father behind him in the dirt as he zipped up his jeans.

Ten minutes later and the container was gone, driven away on the back of a lorry by three of the men. Two others climbed into the unmarked white vans from which the women had disembarked, leaving one final van and a car. The women were obviously being trafficked, presumably for sexual exploitation or into slavery. What he had no understanding about whatsoever was why he was there. He figured he would find out soon enough, and the answer wasn't going to be one he wanted to hear. So he just didn't ask. He wondered what the men thought of him, on his knees between a puddle of his own urine and a stream of someone else's, not even asking for his freedom. Not begging, not trying to run. Just doing nothing. His life had gone from hopes and dreams to a nightmare in such a short timeframe that his head was spinning with it. Just survive for the next five minutes, he thought. After that, I'll worry about another five. If I make it to tonight, I'll worry about the morning. The bread sat in a hard lump in his stomach. He would comply. There was no point annoying his captors. He would watch and learn. Information, he heard his father say inside his head. You can't run if you don't know where you're running to. You can't fight if you don't know your enemy's strengths. And you can't do anything at all dehydrated and starving. Eat and drink whatever they offer, Bart told himself. Sleep when it's safe. Don't hope. Plan.

'Car,' one of the men said. 'Now.'

Bart stood up and stretched.

'More water?' he asked.

The men looked at one another, until someone shrugged and reached into the van, throwing another bottle in Bart's direction.

'Piss in my car and I'll cut your dick off,' he was warned. 'Turn round.'

He was marched to the boot of the car and told to climb in. The floor was covered in old blankets that smelled of dog. He was given a moment to take another drink before his hands were tied behind his back.

'I hear you bang or shout, I pull over and fucking gut you. Get in.'

Bart did as he was told. The container lorry had headed north, as far as he could tell from the position of the sun and the fact that the day was still warm with some hours of sunlight to go. The car was pointed in the other direction. It was a straightforward exchange then. Made sense. Why pay for a container if it only held goods to trade in one direction? Two or three of the men had spoken French to each other. His journey, while it had seemed endless, could only have been a couple of days. France seemed like the logical point for them to have docked in that timescale. The women had spoken a language he hadn't recognised though. A couple of them had been very dark-skinned, but the majority looked more Eastern European. Either they'd been kidnapped or they'd thought they had found a passport to a new and better life. That was almost crueller. Paying their captors for the prospect of safe passage and finding the opposite, their families left to wonder what had happened to them and why they'd never contacted them again.

It made Bart think of his own mother. She, at least, would have called the police by now. People would be looking for him, retracing his last known steps. His friends would be plaguing social media with requests for shares and information. Somewhere, someone had to have seen something that could lead to him. The woman he'd dated twice, if meeting for coffee could be considered a date, had offered him a lift home from the restaurant. Her name had been Kitty, or maybe she'd said it was a nickname. They hadn't progressed to surnames. That was as much as he could recall. There was no CCTV in the main restaurant dining room, but there was a camera on one of the doors to capture images of any diners who decided that paying for their meal was not a good option. Would Kitty have thought of that? Perhaps she'd worn a wig, or changed her face with makeup. Even he couldn't quite reconstruct her in his mind.

His poor mother. She would be frantic. That was a good thing in the circumstances. She wouldn't rest until he was found. The car started up, and he jammed his feet to keep from rolling around and hurting himself. Steady, he told himself. Don't get injured. He tried to focus on the distance as they travelled. He tried to figure out the left and right turns, and to create a map in his mind. But it was warm, the car rocked gently, and the stinking blankets were a soft enough bed. And he was exhausted. When Bart woke up, the first thing he saw was chain-link fence.

Chapter Eight

Indrani Desai was waiting in Jean-Paul's office – currently also Callanach's desk space – at 7.30 a.m., wearing a traditional sari and spaghetti-strap gold sandals. Jean-Paul took the seat nearest her, offering drinks that she refused and his hand that she also opted not to shake. Callanach watched Jean-Paul look at her admiringly. His old colleague had never had much of a poker face when it came to women.

'Forgive me if it seems rude, but I try not to transfer any oils onto my own skin. Sometimes a residue of a scent can throw me off when I'm working,' she explained.

'You've been to see Malcolm Reilly's body?' Callanach asked.

'I have,' she nodded. 'Not a normal part of my job. Aromachologists design scents for shops and supermarkets. Sometimes I work with athletes putting together aromatherapy packages for them. That was the first time I've worked on a dead body and even though I only saw the head uncovered it was . . . awful.'

'I'm sorry,' Jean-Paul said. 'It's the worst part of what we do. I know it was an unusual request for you to smell his hair. Were you able to pick anything up?'

'I was,' Indrani confirmed. 'He was in a sealed bag, so when the plastic was first opened I caught a strong whiff. It dissipated in minutes though. I'm afraid it wouldn't pass a scientific test if you were looking for me to give evidence in court.'

'At the moment we just need whatever leads we can get,' Callanach said. 'What was your conclusion?'

'Myrrh. Burned near to his head. The smell was smoky and slightly impure, but myrrh itself has a very specific liquorice note to it. Earthy and rich, but with a contrasting lemon scent. Some people say they smell latex, too. It's quite unique. I'm surprised you picked it up given all the chemical odours in the mortuary,' she told Callanach.

'Sorry, how did you know it was me?' he asked.

'The pathologist described you to me. He said you were the one with the symmetrical face.'

'Yes, well, Detective Inspector Callanach gets a lot of that,' Jean-Paul snapped. 'Could you tell us where someone might get hold of myrrh and what it might have been used for?'

He gave Callanach a look that was a throwback to days Callanach was happier not remembering, when they'd spent weekends and holidays partying together, and women had been their constant companions. Indrani Desai was far from the first woman Jean-Paul had been attracted to who had seemed more interested in Callanach. In their younger days it had been a source of simple ribbing. Now it seemed Jean-Paul didn't find it quite so amusing. Callanach himself wasn't the slightest bit interested. He was only there for Malcolm Reilly.

'It can be anything from just making a place smell good, to a belief that myrrh is an antioxidant. It's from a tree sap. There are all sorts of claims made about its medical properties, including a treatment for arthritis, neuropathic pain, for asthma and indigestion. It's generally regarded as being purifying and cleansing; certainly it has antiseptic properties. It can also be used for embalming. Historically, it's been used for centuries as part of rituals. You know the Bible reference, obviously, but most cultures have used myrrh at some point. Today you find it in candles or essential oils.'

'Thank you, Miss Desai,' Jean-Paul said. 'I'm guessing it's easy to get hold of then?'

'It is. Can I help with anything else?' she asked, standing up.

'Just this. The other chemical found in relation to the body was lanolin. Would that ever be used in connection with myrrh that you're aware of?' Callanach asked.

She paused, twisting a bracelet around her wrist a few times, and frowning slightly.

'The only thing I can think of is that it might have been added to create an ointment, maybe for dry skin, or as a way of applying the myrrh, but you have to remember that myrrh's medical properties are still doubted by many. There's not much western acceptance of its uses. It's more often found in Chinese herbal medicine.'

'Thank you,' Callanach said. 'We appreciate your help. I'm so sorry you had to be involved in these circumstances.'

'I'm sorry for the boy,' Indrani said quietly. 'The look on his face. I assumed emotions would leave your face after death. Even with his eyelids shut, I could read the terror, as if his muscles had frozen. It's etched into him. I consider myself an advocate of peace, yet for the first time I can see why people call for the death penalty in such cases. Why should the monsters who perpetrate such evil continue to have a place on this earth?'

Jean-Paul showed the aromachologist out of the building.

Callanach stood in front of the board in their room, covered in photos of Malcolm Reilly's body and the building site where it was found. He wrote a series of notes around the images. 'Organ harvesting?' 'Lanolin – uses, sources?' Then 'Myrrh – healing, antiseptic, embalming'. The last option made no sense to him at all. Why consider embalming Malcolm Reilly's body after his organs had been taken from him so unceremoniously, then dumping him at the building site? His body had been used. That was the tragic reality. There was no emotion involved. No crime of passion, or momentary loss of temper. Whoever had taken his life had calculated the value of killing a human being for their own ends, whatever those might have been. He checked his watch. Hopefully Ava would be at her desk soon for him to share what he knew. Not that she'd be in the mood for chatting. Interviewing grieving parents about their dead child was about as depressing as policing got.

Chapter Nine

Ava knocked on the Reillys' door. Eight a.m. was too early really, but if years of policing had taught her anything it was that grief guaranteed both exhaustion and insomnia in equal measures. The Reillys would have cried, ranted and been consumed with every negative emotion in the dictionary until they'd finally fallen asleep, then awoken only to lie in the cold, early dark knowing that every day would start like that in their foreseeable future. Yesterday, she'd let specially trained police officers break the news of the death and remain with the family for as long as their presence was welcomed. They would continue to offer support in terms of answering day-to-day questions. Now she had to try and figure out why Malcolm Reilly had been chosen as a victim, and how he'd been identified as a target. Nine times out of ten that meant causing offence. She took a deep breath.

The door opened quietly, and a large woman stood, hands on hips, woollen cardigan stretched over a flowery blouse. Her face looked as if it had been attacked by gravity, jowls hanging, bags stretching for the floor beneath her eyes.

'You'll be DCI Turner. We were told to expect you. I'm

Malcolm's grandmother. If you'll take a seat, I'll fetch my daughter and son-in-law. They're upstairs. It wasn't a good night.'

'I understand,' Ava said. 'Thank you for letting me in.' She sat quietly in a living room that had become a tomb to a missing young man. They'd been expecting him back, of course. Most young men in their twenties who disappeared suddenly also reappeared. The same was less true of missing young women, but males weren't as likely to be kidnapped, raped, murdered. Not so today.

'Good morning,' a man said, walking slowly forwards and offering Ava his hand. It was shaking as Ava grasped it. He looked broken, tall but bent at the shoulders, his hair greasy and unkempt, his shirt untucked at one side. Grief was the enemy of both the physical body and the mind.

He was followed by a sweet-looking woman, dressed in pale grey – trousers, shirt, jumper, even her socks. She looks like a ghost, Ava thought, literally as if the life had bled from her. The woman tried to smile, but the wobble it brought was too much.

'Mrs Reilly,' Ava took over. Sometimes it was easier to speak than wait to be spoken to. 'Forgive me for asking to speak with you at such a terrible time, but I need to know as much as I can about Malcolm and his disappearance. Interpol is working with the French police, and we have a liaison officer out there making sure nothing is missed. I'm in charge of the case at this end. Could we sit?'

Malcolm Reilly's mother nodded slowly and turned on unwilling feet to head for a sofa. Ava pulled out a notebook, noticing the photos of Malcolm in ski gear against endless bright white backdrops.

'I appreciate your talking to me. I know the shock of Malcolm's death is still new. Telling you both how sorry I am for your loss won't help you, but perhaps finding the person or people who hurt him will offer something more valuable. I want to know as much as you can tell me about your son, particularly about his final day. You'll have given that information to the police before when you reported him missing, but sometimes additional questions occur to me when I'm listening to people talk, and now that we know it's a murder investigation I may have different queries. All I can ask is that you bear with me, all right?'

Malcolm's parents made eye contact with one another, giving their consent only by not objecting. Ava understood perfectly. Words were hard enough to come by when you lost someone you loved through illness or accident. When they'd been cut open and their organs stolen from their body, what could you possibly find to say that did justice to the explosion of horror and grief your life had suddenly been reduced to?

'He went to the gym,' Mr Reilly said. His voice was hoarse. Ava had images of the night he and his wife had spent sobbing in one another's arms as he continued to speak. 'He went most days, unless he had an injury or needed to rest.'

'That was the twenty-four-hour gym at West Side Plaza Shopping Centre?' Ava clarified.

'Yes,' Mr Reilly said. 'He was part of a ski team and they were expected to train regularly. Helps to avoid injuries.'

'Looks like he loved it,' Ava offered, turning her face to the sea of photos.

'He wanted to be in the Olympics. That was his dream,' Mrs Reilly said, her face awash with tears. That was the thing about memories. One day they were just ordinary recollections, with more to be made, expectations keeping them in perspective and ready to be replaced. Once death came, those memories were newly precious, gold to be mined and polished at every opportunity, in the knowledge that the total sum of your riches had already been amassed, and that every ounce, every fleck had to be cherished forever.

Ava paused, letting the Reillys recover, then continued.

'What time did he go to the gym?' she asked.

'About five thirty p.m. He came home from work, had a bite to eat, then changed and went. He was usually out until about eight, but that night he didn't come home. We didn't start worrying until ten, then we tried his mobile but he didn't answer. We tried again half an hour later but by then his phone was switched off. His younger brother went out looking for him. Malcolm's car was still in the gym car park but the receptionist said she'd seen him leave a couple of hours earlier.'

Ava already had a statement from the gym's receptionist in her file. There was CCTV footage, good quality and in colour for once, that showed Malcolm Reilly looking fit and healthy after exercising, exiting the building at 8.38 p.m. precisely. The receptionist's estimate had been half an hour out, but no surprise there. It was a busy place with plenty of people coming and going after work. Malcolm had turned left out of the main doors, bag slung over his shoulder. By then he'd changed out of his gym gear into jeans, a T-shirt and a green jacket – there was footage of him on the running machine earlier for comparison – his hair still wet from the shower, then he'd gone to the coffee shop cum bar. That was at about 8 p.m. No CCTV in there but a few regulars and staff had noticed him going in.

'Did he tell you he was going to go to the coffee shop afterwards?' Ava asked.

'No.' Mr Reilly shook his head. 'But he was well known at the gym. He's been a member there for more than two years. He often met friends and went for a drink or bite to eat afterwards.'

'Anyone in particular he hung out with regularly?'

'Why did they take his insides?' Mrs Reilly blurted, suddenly standing up, fists clenched and pressed into her stomach. Her husband turned his gaze to the floor. 'Even his eyes, for God's sake!'

'That's what we're trying to find out,' Ava replied gently. 'I think that if we can figure out the motive for doing that, we'll be able to catch Malcolm's murderer.'

'So are we supposed to bury only half of him, and do what . . . add the rest when you find the missing pieces?' Mrs Reilly went on.

'I'm afraid we need to keep Malcolm's body at the mortuary until the matter is resolved. We can transfer him back to the UK if you'd feel more comfortable having him in Edinburgh. We're not going to rest until we get answers for you.'

'He'd met someone,' Mr Reilly announced, at little more than a whisper.

His wife whipped her head round, the fastest Ava had seen her move since arriving.

'What are you talking about?' Mrs Reilly asked.

Her husband rubbed a hand across his forehead.

'He asked me not to tell you. I don't know much about it myself. Just that he'd met a woman he rather liked a few times, but that he wasn't sure it was going anywhere.'

'Why not?' Ava asked.

'Why was I not to be told?' Malcolm's mother followed up.

'I gather she was married, or engaged, or something. Malc was vague about it. He wouldn't tell me her name. I got the impression she'd asked him not to talk about her.'

'Why exactly?' Ava pressed.

'He said something about how she wouldn't like him talking about her. I overheard him on the phone one day. Malcolm had sounded excited, younger than normal. He was quite reserved usually, so I asked who it was. I think he wanted to tell me more but was torn.'

'You should have told me anyway,' Mrs Reilly said. It was an accusation.

'Malcolm knew you'd disapprove. He didn't want to upset you. Neither did I.'

'And what if she had something to do with all of this? If I'd known, if you'd told me . . .'

'How could some woman he liked have taken him to France? His passport's still in his drawer. And why would she do that? It makes no sense. That's why I didn't say anything before. It's ridiculous,' he declared, banging his fist against his leg.

Ava gave them both a moment to calm down.

'Which phone did you hear Malcolm talking to this woman on, and when?' she asked.

'His mobile. It was never found after he disappeared. As for when, that would have been about ten weeks ago. It was a Sunday afternoon,' Mr Reilly said.

'So two weeks before he disappeared, then. I'll check his mobile call logs with his telecom provider. I don't suppose you know where he met this woman?'

'I don't, but he was keen on her, and he obviously thought she felt the same or I don't think he'd have mentioned her to me at all. It couldn't have been her, could it?' He stared into Ava's eyes, looking for more than information. Wanting affirmation, reassurance, perhaps forgiveness.

'We have to cover all angles when we investigate. I'll do my best to locate this woman. Until then, it's best not to torture yourselves with hypotheticals. I'll leave you to it. If you think of anything else, please do get in touch.'

'How could you keep that from me?' Mrs Reilly hissed at her husband. 'He was my son, I had a right to know.'

'It was nothing, please, Anne, don't upset yourself . . .'

'Don't upset myself?' she raged, looking around the room before choosing the nearest object to seize. It was a vase. Her

72

husband looked on in silence as it smashed in the fireplace. 'My boy was gutted like a fish, and you're asking me not to upset myself? What is it that you want me to do? Sit in bed quietly and cry into a hankie? What if this woman's husband found out about them and decided to get rid of Malcolm? Did you think of that?'

'No . . . no, I'm sure Malcolm wouldn't have let it get that far.'

'Mrs Reilly,' Ava said. 'I understand—'

'No you don't,' Malcolm Reilly's mother screamed. On the final word she aimed an open palm at Ava's face, slapping hard enough for Ava's neck to crack as her head whirled round. 'Oh my God. I'm sorry. Oh my God,' she gasped, falling to her knees.

Ava took to the floor beside her, taking Malcolm's mother's hands in her own, gently stroking the hand that had slapped her.

'You're right,' Ava said. 'I don't understand. It's okay. The worst thing is, I know that I never want to have to understand, not fully. I never want to be feeling what you're feeling now. That's why I do this job. I want to make sure that as few people as possible have to go through what you're experiencing. All I can promise is that I'll do my best, and that I'll make everyone else do their best, and I won't stop until I can give you answers.'

Mrs Reilly drew herself into a ball, rocking back and forth, eventually letting her husband kneel next to her and wrap her in his arms. Ava suspected they would be there, on that cold wooden floor, for an awfully long time. She let herself out.

An hour later Ava was at home changing out of her uniform. In spite of the Major Investigation Team's non-uniform policy, she had always felt more comfortable treating visits to the recently bereaved with the utmost formality. That mark of respect was the least she could offer. The rest of the day was going to be briefings and normal graft, though, and her jeans were beckoning. She was almost ready to leave for the station when her doorbell rang. Ava sighed. Her cheek was still raw from the monumental slap dealt by a grieving mother. The blow had been well delivered, and while Ava didn't resent it at all, it had left fingermarks that would be like carrying a physical part of Malcolm Reilly with her for the rest of the day. Fitting perhaps, given that so much of him was actually missing. She wandered towards the door, feeling less than charitable towards whoever was out there, ringing her doorbell so persistently.

'Hey you,' a voice said, as Ava began to open the door. 'I was hoping you might be here.'

'Natasha,' Ava said, stepping back to let her best friend in, grinning at the unexpected visit. They didn't see each other often enough, and exchanging texts hardly did justice to the number of years they'd had each other's backs. It couldn't be helped. Natasha was Head of Philosophy at Edinburgh University, not to mention chairing numerous panels and writing articles. The two of them almost never managed to make their free evenings coincide. 'You just caught me,' she checked her watch, 'but I've got time to put the kettle on. God, it's good to see you.'

Natasha turned, shrugging off her coat slowly and putting it carefully on a hook before following Ava into the kitchen.

'You mean you've actually got milk in your fridge that's in date?' Natasha smiled.

'You're so rude. I'm pretty sure I have.' She opened her fridge door and peered at the label on a milk carton. 'Aha, see, still good until tomorrow. Now you'll have to apologise!'

'Apologise my arse,' Natasha said, sitting down. 'Ava, I need to talk to you.'

'Yes, please, anything. I've had a bloody awful morning so far. Seriously, probing grieving parents for details of their child's life at the worst possible moment. You know it's going to be bad, but nothing prepares you for the sense of devastation.' She stretched her arms waiting for the kettle to boil. 'Want some toast?'

'No, thanks. I'm not hungry. Sit down with me.'

'No time.' Ava grabbed a hairband from her pocket and tied her long, curly brown hair up high on her head. 'I've got two different teams working up cases, one here and one in France. Thank God Luc was already there or I'd have lost two officers to liaison posts.'

'Ava,' Natasha said firmly. 'I have cancer.'

Ava looked at her, frowned as she half smiled, shook her head. 'What are you talking about?'

'I found a lump in my left breast a month ago. The doctor was great, referred me straight to the hospital. The consultant's been amazing. They operated two weeks ago, removed a sample and did a biopsy. I got the results yesterday afternoon.'

Ava closed her eyes, waited, opened them again, gritted her teeth.

'A month?' she said eventually. 'You've been going through this for a fucking month and you're at my door for the first time today?' Her voice was at yelling pitch. 'How the fuck could you ever think that was okay?' She turned, tried to pick up the kettle but slopped boiling water across the tops of the mugs and her hand.

'Ava, stop, please,' Natasha said, standing and walking round the table towards her.

'No,' Ava said. 'If you're here, it's because it's bad news, and I can't hear it, Tasha. God help me, I know it's you going through this, not me, but I can't have anything happen to you. I don't want to hear it. I can't stand it.'

Natasha wrapped her arms around Ava's shoulders, holding her tight.

'I couldn't have this conversation before I knew for sure what it was. You'd have made the same choice. It was less painful not to think too hard about it. I knew you'd want to come to every appointment with me, ask every question, cross-examine the doctors, but I just wanted to let it all happen without a fight.'

'How bad?' Ava whispered into her friend's hair.

'Bad, but not hopeless. I won't give you all the medical terms. I've driven myself mad looking it all up already. It's stage two. I'll need another operation, chemo, maybe radiation therapy, then they'll review again and see how I'm doing.' She stepped back, wiping tears from Ava's face with her thumbs.

'Oh holy shit. I'm so sorry I shouted at you. I'm such an idiot. You came here because you needed me, and I . . .'

'Actually, I came here for you to yell at me and get it out of your system. You're nothing if not predictable,' she grinned.

'Go to hell,' Ava said, more tears falling. 'Tasha, I have to ask.'

'It's all right,' Natasha said. 'Roughly speaking, there's a fifty per cent survival rate for the type of cancer I have at this stage. It's nowhere else in my body yet which is the good news. Apparently my aunt had it too, so there's a family history to take into account, although I found out about that, as ever, when it was too late for a heads-up.'

'So you've told your parents then?' Natasha nodded. 'How were they with you?'

'Well, they managed not to ask if it was something I'd caught because I'm a lesbian, so I guess that was progress.' She laughed, and Ava's kitchen rang with the hollowness of it. 'They were shocked, I think, but told me they're sure I'll be fine. Not what I wanted to hear, oddly. I mean, I want people to be reassuring, but it's so bland when it happens like that.

Almost dismissive, like they can't cope with the reality so it's an easy line to trot out.'

Ava sighed.

'Still want that tea?' she asked.

'Damn right I do. I can't drink booze at the moment, so tea's about my only decent option.' Ava busied herself with the mugs and teabags. 'Anyway, I'm here to ask you to just stand by me, I suppose. At the moment, I'm not quite sure what's ahead. I have another appointment at the hospital tomorrow to agree a treatment plan. I know you're busy with your caseload but . . .'

'I'll be there,' Ava said. 'Whatever you need. Just message me about the time. I'll drive you.'

'You don't have to go that far,' Natasha smiled, taking the offered mug and sitting back down at the kitchen table with it.

'Oh, that's just because you're a liability on the road already. I honestly can't let the general public be put at risk if you're even more distracted than usual.' Ava sat opposite her.

'Fuck you,' Natasha grinned.

'I love you,' Ava retorted. 'And I'm so ashamed about how I reacted. I wasn't angry at you.'

'I know that.' Natasha reached across and took Ava's hand in hers. 'Do you remember when we were fourteen and that little gobshite Barry Beckwith told everyone he'd put his hand up my skirt? I came to you crying. Everyone was gossiping about it, and I thought my life was basically over.'

'I screamed at you because you hadn't punched him in the face as soon as you found out. Did you have to remind me?' Ava laughed.

'The next day, Barry turned up at whatever awful party we were at, with a black eye and a cut lip, telling everyone he'd been mugged for his backpack. I knew it was you, even though you never admitted it.'

'I hated seeing you hurt like that.' Ava smiled gingerly. 'I still do. At least I could just go and punch Barry Beckwith. What the hell am I supposed to do with this?'

'Hold my hand, make me laugh, give me space when I ask for it. What actually did happen with Barry then?'

'I called at his house, flirted with him, told him I wanted to do the same as he'd done with you. He invited me up to his bedroom, and as soon as he closed his door I smacked him in the face. He tried to grab me to stop me from leaving, so I headbutted him, only he was quite a few inches taller than me, so I only contacted his lip. I knew he'd never have the balls to admit he'd been beaten up by a girl, so I wasn't worried. He had tears in his eyes as I left, which I figured was almost good enough payment for what he'd done to you.'

'I'm so glad we've always been friends. Mainly because as an enemy you're terrifying.'

'Whatever happens, I'll be at your side,' Ava said softly, the laughter gone. 'You can't leave me, Natasha. I won't let you.'

'Not even you can control this one,' she replied. 'But I appreciate the fact that you're going to try, more than you could possibly know.'

Chapter Ten

Elenuta held a bag of ice against Anika's cheek and waited for the girl to stop crying. Most of the men, and a few women, who visited Finlay's establishment were there for something much less honest than plain old sex. They wanted to violate. Knowing that it was non-consensual was part of what they were buying. Getting away with throwing a few punches, the odd hand around the throat, sticking rough fingers wherever they liked, that was all included in the price too. Paying good money for a chance to express their hatred and rage in physical terms with no comeback was a given. The last bastard had gone too far with Anika though. She had fingermarks on both thighs where her legs had been held open, multiple grazes across her throat where rings had tugged at her delicate skin, and a lump coming up on her face that would take two weeks to reduce.

One of Finlay's men came in, stared around the room at the four women crowded in there, syringe in hand.

'This'll make you feel better,' he said gruffly.

'She doesn't need that,' Elenuta said. 'I look after her.'

'Boss's orders, don't mess,' the goon muttered.

Anika stared glassily at the syringe, then gave a weak nod, holding out her arm.

Elenuta took her hand, tried to pull her away.

'Don't,' she whispered. 'Anika, let me help you.'

'You'll get the same treatment if you don't keep your nose out,' Elenuta was told. The man shoved her away from Anika.

She watched as the needle pierced the girl's skin, plunging its oblivion into her nervous system. Anika's sobs turned into a groan, then a sigh. Silence.

'Why?' Elenuta asked the man, as he withdrew the needle and checked Anika's pupils.

'Finlay's fed up with her crying. She won't last. Too fragile for his liking. He's decided to race her next month. Believe me, a little bit of smack's not going to hurt her.'

Elenuta stared at him. Most of the guards refused to enter into conversations with the women. This one couldn't seem to care less. She wondered if she was being set up for a punishment, then decided it didn't matter anyway. Being scared of every consequence was exhausting.

'What's your name?' Elenuta asked.

'Digger,' he said. 'You should go and eat.'

The rest of the women had already filed out of the room into the small kitchen they were allowed to use, with supervision. There was one dull knife for them to cut up food, and it had to be handed straight back to whoever was in charge once it had been used.

'Not hungry,' Elenuta said. 'What race?'

Digger looked over his shoulder and Elenuta knew he was checking to make sure Finlay hadn't sneaked in. He had a habit of doing that, could be almost silent as he approached. Finlay enjoyed keeping everyone on their toes. Two or three times a day he appeared to check up on them, going from flat to flat, making sure the women were busy on their backs and that none of the men who worked for him were getting lazy or dipping into the takings. Elenuta checked the clock every time he turned up. There was no pattern to it, and that was how he liked it, she realised. She and Finlay had spent what he'd called some quality time together after her failed escape attempt. Her ribs wouldn't heal properly for weeks. He'd spared her face as that was what made him money, but other aspects of his punishment had been sufficiently brutal that she'd simply curled up in a corner and not dared move or speak until he'd left the flat.

'You're better off never finding out,' he replied as Anika began to tip over. Elenuta caught her, and Digger grabbed a cushion off the tatty sofa to slide under her head as she hit the floor.

'Will Anika come back from race?' Elenuta asked quietly.

Digger stood up.

'I doubt it,' he said. 'That's enough questions. You'll get me in a right load of shit.'

'Will I have to race?' Elenuta asked.

'You won't if you keep the clients happy and don't pull any more stunts like running away. The polis have been all over Gene's place since. Finlay's pissed. You got off lightly but I wouldn't push your luck.'

'How many women in race?' Elenuta continued. Digger wanted to talk, she could tell. He was one of the less brutal supervisors. She'd never seen him hit any of the women, or take advantage of the free sex that was on offer. Her assessment was that he liked a quiet life. Not so quiet that he wasn't prepared to shoot heroin in the arm of anyone making a fuss, but that was what Finlay had ordered. If any of the women were trouble, it was procedure to shut them up and leave their warm body on a bed for whatever use could be made of them.

'Four,' Digger said quietly, checking his watch. 'Help me get her back onto a bed. She's not going to wake up any time soon and Finlay won't like seeing her lying there when the clients come in to choose one of you.'

'They race each other?' she persisted, taking hold of Anika beneath the arms.

'For fuck's sake, would you quit it woman?' He picked up Anika's legs and began walking backwards into the narrow hallway, down which the bedrooms were situated.

An arm slithered around Elenuta's waist, crushing the air from her, leaving her lurching forward, trying to hold onto Anika's head before it smashed to the floor.

'Do you really want to know?' Finlay mock-whispered into her ear. She could feel the wetness of his lips against her.

'I told her to quit it, boss,' Digger said, looking miserable.

'I heard you, mate. This one doesn't learn, does she? How are those ribs? Still sore, I'm guessing?' He slid his arm up from her waist to her ribcage, tightening his grip. Tears sprang to Elenuta's eyes as she fought for breath. 'But education's a good thing. Maybe I should show you what the race is all about. It's guaranteed to make you behave yourself. You can manage this other wee cunny on your own, can't you Digger.' It was a decision, not a question. 'And you, you pretty bitch, can come with me. Digger, fetch my laptop from the kitchen before dealing with the whore.'

He took Elenuta by the hair, pulling her backwards up the corridor, feet tumbling over one another, hauling her suddenly sideways when they reached an unoccupied bedroom. Throwing her onto the bed, Finlay climbed on next to her, winding an arm beneath her neck to pull her in close. Digger delivered the laptop, and Finlay tapped a series of icons until a video came up, the first image frozen in place.

'Watch this,' Finlay grinned, holding Elenuta's head in place with one hand, as he took a knife from his pocket and lay tossing it in the air and catching it.

Four girls came into view from a small doorway, each wearing ragged underwear, no shoes on their feet. They looked back as the door shut, grabbing each other's hands, stepping forward inch by inch. Elenuta could hear them whispering in at least three different languages mixed with some broken English. It was clear they had no idea where they were or what to expect. Nothing good, though.

A light came on to one side and a bank of chairs could be seen on a large glass-partitioned balcony. One hundred men, if not more, were seated in rows and looking eagerly down at the women. They began banging on the chairs, the floor, whatever was at hand, slowly at first, the beat increasing steadily, a cacophony of masculinity.

Finally, a man stepped forward, looking smarter than usual. He'd made an effort, Elenuta realised. The thought chilled her. This was Finlay dressed to impress, enjoying a crowning moment. The four women stood, frozen, huddled together.

'Good evening, you bunch of cocksuckers!' Finlay shouted to a gleeful response from his audience. 'Welcome to the third race. Most of you know what to expect by now, so I'll keep this short and you lot keep your hands out of your pants while I'm talking!' He pointed vaguely into the crowd but at no one in particular and Elenuta understood that he'd practised and polished this little speech, self-proclaimed king for a couple of hours.

'Do you want to see your champions?' There was a further hammering of approval, but apparently not quite loud enough for Finlay's liking. 'Well, do you, you bastards?' A much louder roar that time. 'All right then.' He threw back his arms, a circus ringmaster drawing the audience in, revving them up.

Another door opened and three men walked out, each wearing only shorts and trainers. Elenuta's first thought was how ridiculous they looked, like those fake wrestlers whose every blow and fall was carefully choreographed. One was covered in tattoos – literally covered – from ankle to neck.

'No names here,' Finlay said, with a nod of acknowledgement towards the camera. 'But these gentlemen have paid a high price for this honour – higher than the rest of you wankers bid, anyway.' (Another crowd belly-laugh for that.) 'So give it up for them.'

Finlay walked forward, raising each man's right arm one after the other, tattoo's first, then a skinnier man with a scar down the length of his torso, and finally a shorter male with an enormous girth and loose flesh folds dripping from his upper body. The men accepted their applause with chest-beating, raised fists and celebratory middle fingers pointed in the direction of the admiring crowd.

'Now to meet your skanks. Let's hope for their sakes that they haven't got too out of shape, spending all that time on their backs!' Real-life Finlay lying on the bed gave a snort of laughter at his own comic genius for that one. 'Bitch number one!' He grabbed the nearest woman to him and pulled her closer to the audience. 'Great titties or what? Bet you can't wait to see those bouncing up and down when she runs.' He thrust her towards the nearby wall. 'Bitch number two!' The crowd was lapping it up, their appreciation rising to fever pitch. 'Best blow jobs for fifty miles. You'd best hope she's a fast runner then!'

The woman he took by the arm gave him a look that could have burned green wood. Elenuta saw her own loathing reflected in her eyes, and knew she shouldn't look at Finlay while she watched the remainder of the video. What he saw in them would get her killed in a heartbeat.

'Bitch number three!' This girl – definitely more girl than woman – he grabbed around the waist and lifted into the air. 'Grown men have fainted at the tightness of her pussy – we bring you nothing but the best here!' He dropped the girl, who sank to her knees on the floor, hair hanging limply over her face. 'And last but by no means least, the winner from the last race, bitch number four. Can she repeat the brilliance of her last run or did she only have one victory in her?' Finlay circled the last woman, who was looking twitchy, jerking her knees up one after the other, her eyes huge, haunted, like some terrified Olympian on speed.

'Rules – like there fucking are any – the bitches get a sixty-second head start on the hunt. They can run, hide, fight, disable one another, team up, whatever they like. Champions – same applies to you – all you have to do is move like fuck.'

Elenuta felt vomit rising in her throat at the word *hunt*. The women were starting to edge away from Finlay, three of them together, the previous winner – as if that term could ever apply – keeping her distance from the group.

'There are screens above your head that will capture any action you can't see from where you're sitting. Don't worry, we won't let you miss a thing.'

Elenuta couldn't see the screens the audience had access to, but she didn't need them. It was all here, ready for Finlay to gloat over. She wanted to refuse to watch, but even if Finlay would let her get away with that – and he wouldn't – knowledge was a currency, and at the moment she was flat out broke. She needed to know what possible dangers lay ahead.

'Turn up the lights!' Finlay shouted and, like a Broadway show, the camera rose into the air – Elenuta assumed it was a drone – and lights flickered on in what was apparently a vast warehouse, fitted out with a maze of partitions. Here and there, metal staircases, more like ladders, rose above the temporary six-foot walls and facilitated access to a different part of the building, but using those ladders would make the women more visible. There were what appeared to be cupboards, large bins, piles of sheets, all providing the false promise of a place to hide. Elenuta estimated the warehouse interior was maybe twenty thousand square feet. It was hard to tell with the sketchy light and movement of the drone. It was vast, by any reckoning. The drone dipped closer to the floor and lengths of barbed wire came into focus, which would force the runners to either jump, dip below it or turn back. Dappled light on the ceiling caught her eye.

'What's this?' she asked without thinking, giving Finlay a chance to enjoy her interest.

He pointed at the warehouse floor although there was nothing to see from the drone's viewpoint.

'Smashed glass. Five different patches of it. There have to be some handicaps, after all.'

'But they have no shoes,' Elenuta said. 'It's not fair.'

'Not fair? I paid good money for those whores. I need a return on that investment, and that means putting on a proper show. Do you have any idea how much it costs me to house and feed you lot?'

Elenuta stared at him, the space between her eyebrows a knot of wrinkles as she waited for him to laugh. He didn't. He meant every word of it, the resentment at the bills incurred feeding them stale bread and out-of-date chicken nuggets. The heating was turned off overnight and only put back on during client hours so they didn't get complaints. The sheets were the only items washed regularly. The women handwashed their personal items in the sink overnight. Elenuta wondered how far gone Finlay was if he had genuinely persuaded himself that he was somehow being taken advantage of by the women he held captive and sold every day.

'Here we go,' Finlay told Elenuta, his face alight with excitement. 'Now don't you fucking look away. I don't want you missing any of the good bits!'

'One final word of warning to you all,' on-screen Finlay wagged his finger. 'First man to lay hands on any woman gets her to himself. Once a man has her, no other man can touch her. Three men, four women. The last woman standing gets a good meal, a hot bath and a comfy bed with none of you cunts in it tonight. That's it!'

He raised his left hand in the air. 'Countdown! Five.' The last race's winner looked deep into the maze, head down, knees bent. The other women looked terrified, hands still wrapped together.

'Four.' The audience was on its feet to a man, and the noise coming from that side of the warehouse was deafening. Elenuta couldn't hear Finlay count down after that, but she watched his lips move.

'Three, two, one!'

The previous winner was gone. She flew into the maze, taking an outside lane, glancing back over her shoulder only once as the other three women looked on, dazed and bemused.

'Run, you fucking whores,' Finlay shouted. 'If you don't want to die where you're standing, then friggin' run!'

As one, like the herd of zebra that's spotted the lion, they bolted, moving chaotically, tripping over their own feet and each other's. Elenuta wanted to shout instructions to them, as if she were watching in real time, but it was way too late for that. The camera focused on a clock on the wall, the countdown already at thirty-seven seconds and falling as Finlay's champions jumped up and down, ready for the off. Tattoo had his teeth bared. The big man was sweating profusely, sparkling in the half-light. Elenuta prayed that a heart attack might strike him down in his revolting excitement before he could set off. The scarred man, though, was something else. Something bestial, his face twisted with a hatred so terrifying that Elenuta could hardly bear to watch. She pitied anyone who crossed his path. He was a man without limits. She'd met such men before and been grateful to have survived the encounters.

The image suddenly split into four quarters, presumably a reflection of what the audience in the warehouse had seen. The footage was from drones, four separate cameras. This was no small operation. Finlay had to have had four men, one set to follow each woman, to provide constant footage. Two of the women had stuck together, and the others had gone off alone. The countdown was at ten seconds, and the men were poised and ready to sprint.

'Those drones are the bloody best you can get. Cost me a fuckin' packet,' Finlay lectured.

'Uh huh,' Elenuta murmured.

Her hands were gripping the bedcovers, as if to tether herself away from the screen. The previous winner was at the far side of the maze now, pausing, hands on knees and panting, looking behind her, then ahead, to decide tactics. Not getting yourself cornered was the obvious priority, and she wasn't. She had three directions to run in. The next decision was whether to hide, or keep running. The problem with that was exhaustion. Sooner or later the after-effect of the adrenaline would be to drain the women's energy, rather than to provide a boost, and then there would be nothing left to fight with if – when – the moment came.

Elenuta looked at the other screen sections. The youngest woman was trying and failing to open an old metal cupboard, tugging uselessly at the doors which had obviously been deliberately locked and put there to distract the runners.

Horns blasted, echoing hard around the bare walls. The men, like hounds released, began to run. The audience made noises that might have come from behind the bars in a zoo. The scene was nothing short of gladiatorial, if the surroundings were less than Romanesque. The young woman who'd been attempting to open the cupboard had finally given up on that plan and was trying to cover herself with a pile of old sheets that had been dumped on the floor. However slight she was, there was no disguising the person-shaped mound in the middle of the rags.

'Get up,' Elenuta hissed through the screen at the girl. 'Get up now.'

'She can't hear you, love,' Finlay laughed. 'Entertaining, isn't it?'

'Animal,' Elenuta said.

Finlay leaned forward, poking out his tongue to lick her face from eye to chin, leaving a trail of saliva for her to wipe away.

'The big bloke's surprisingly light on his feet. Watch him go here,' Finlay pointed, as the largest of the three men took a corner at speed and caught sight of a woman ahead of him. 'Oh, the tension,' he mocked. 'I should charge ten times what I do for this. People would take out loans if they had to.'

Elenuta chose to look at Finlay rather than the chase underway on the screen.

'How much for ticket?' she asked.

'Ah, see, now you're showing your true colours.' He tapped the side of her head with his forefinger. 'I knew there was a smart wee brain in there. One hundred and fifty for a seat in the audience. One thousand to participate. You can stop looking at me like I'm something you trod in, you snotty bitch. I'm a fuckin' businessman, that's what I am.'

A thousand pounds, Elenuta thought, to be able to chase and capture a woman to rape, beat and abuse on camera, in front of an audience. In the end though, not so different than what happened to all of them every day. Just less of a spectacle.

Three of the screen sections disappeared as one enlarged to follow the progress of the big man more closely. The drone was overhead both him and one of the women, face to face, each panting, him grinning, her glancing backwards at the stretch of broken glass on the floor behind her that was perhaps four metres long. Too long to jump but there was no way she was going to be able to climb the partition. The only other option was to fight the man, and hope she could deal enough of a blow to give her time to escape the way she'd come.

He motioned to her with his fingers, palms up. *Come on then*, was the message. *Just you try it*. The woman whipped round, dipping down as she went, grabbing a piece of broken glass in her left hand. She was no fool. He had several stone on her, and even though they were the same height, fighting him off was going to be tough unarmed. With the glass though, she stood a chance.

He took a step back, taking his time, before pulling a pair of leather gloves from his pocket. It wouldn't stop the glass entirely, Elenuta thought, but it gave him more protection. Certainly he wasn't about to back down now. He'd paid a thousand pounds and he wanted it repaid in flesh.

The woman stepped forward, keeping just out of grabbing distance, but presenting the man with an opportunity to try. He lunged for her and she leapt backwards and to one side, pulling the man's arm and propelling him towards the glass-covered section of floor then letting him go. He fell under his own momentum, helped by his front-loaded gravity. Only letting himself crash to his knees first saved him from being peppered with broken glass from head to toe. Still, he howled in pain. The woman was already gone, leaping back down the corridor in which she'd been caught, glass fragment held out front. The man got up slowly, his knees and lower legs bloodied, staggering slightly before righting himself fully. Wrenching a shard of glass from one leg, he shouted into the empty area. Elenuta's nails were her own shards of glass in her palms. If the man caught up with that same woman again, he would make her pay over and over, once for the pain and again for the humiliation. He hurled the slice of glass at the drone hovering about his head, and spun round to follow her. Slowly this time, though. He wouldn't be sprinting again for a while. Elenuta allowed herself a smile.

The screen returned to its four-way view, and the tattooed man could be seen walking carelessly through the maze, calling out. Of course there wasn't any rush. The sprint at the start had been in the spirit of the race, but the reality was that in a closed circuit the men could take as much time as they needed. Sooner or later they'd stumble across a woman, and then it was only a matter of time until they got what they wanted.

Tattoo walked down a long stretch, suddenly stopped, cocked his head to one side, turned and retraced his steps. There, on the ground at his feet was a pile of old rags, unmistakably shaking. Tattoo located the drone that was recording his progress and grinned widely into the lens. Like some Victorian theatre villain he tiptoed forward, still looking up at the camera with a finger dramatically over his lips, making the most of the moment and the crowd's adulation.

He reached out a hand, held it over the top of the pile, then grabbed the linen and whipped it up. On the floor, huddled, was the youngest of the women, trying to squirm away. He took hold of her by the throat, taking a knee at her side as the camera closed in to capture her facial expression. It was sheer terror. Elenuta thought she'd seen fear before, God knew she'd felt enough of it herself, but this was something deeper, more primeval.

'Please,' the girl mouthed at the man. 'Don't.'

He laughed, roared with it, so much larger and stronger than her that he didn't even bother using his other hand as he picked her up and slammed her into the wall. The back of her skull smashed into a large bolt sticking out of the brickwork, and her eyes floated upwards for a moment. Fighting her way back into consciousness, she clawed at his fingers, slapped uselessly at the pressure on her throat. Her chest hitched as she tried to draw breath, her eyes beginning to bulge. Blood trickled through her hair and down the sides of the neck from the head injury.

'He'll kill her,' Elenuta muttered.

'Well, duh, what did you think they were paying for?'

Elenuta's hands flew over her mouth. The girl was beginning to change colour. The tracks of burst blood vessels were appearing in her eyes and her head was flopping left and right out of control. Her legs were buckling and flapping.

'No,' Elenuta sobbed.

'That's just the first. The other two are much more inventive. Wait and see.'

Elenuta wrenched herself from Finlay's grip, losing a fistful of hair as she threw herself across the room.

His laptop continued to produce a hateful audio, gurgling, choking, wailing, accompanied by the roar of the crowd in the industrial colosseum, each of them desperate to watch that final, gruesome moment of death. It didn't take long.

'Do you not want to know who won?' Finlay asked, climbing off the bed himself and walking to stand in front of Elenuta.

She shook her head.

'Right then. If you can't take it, maybe you should stop asking fucking questions. Have I made my point?'

Elenuta nodded.

'Good. Now that's put me right in the mood for a fuck. On the bed and get your knickers off. I haven't got long.'

Chapter Eleven

Detective Sergeant Max Tripp sat in Ava's office wondering why his boss looked like death but knowing better than to ask.

'How long has this boy been missing now?' Ava asked, scribbling notes on a pad.

'Five days. Bart went to his usual place of work at a restaurant. It's a part-time job as he's a student. Was due home that night. Didn't show. He left his mobile in his bedroom so there's no way of tracking him.'

'Could he have just bailed? Stressed with the college course and the job, dropped off the map?' Ava was going through the motions and she knew it. Tripp was an experienced officer who always covered all the bases.

'His mum's a widow, and they're very close. Great relationship both by the mother's account and by all the family, friends and neighbours we've spoken to. He's got a bright future, finds the college work easy. No indicators for an unexplained disappearance, and he hasn't touched his bank account since he went missing. Plus, his boss at work said the night he went missing, Bart had booked in several extra shifts for the following week, and had said he was happy to wait for his wages until the next night.'

'So if he was about to run, he'd have taken the cash at the very least.' Ava put her pen down.

'That's about it. No regular girlfriend but he was good-looking and a popular lad. He'd never failed to go home unless it was planned in advance, apparently he worried too much about his mum being alone for that.'

'Last known person he was in contact with?'

'One of the other waiters said goodnight to him as he left the restaurant. Bart was planning on cycling home. His bike was found the next day still secured to a fence post. No sign of his belongings. Reporting was fast – his mother called the police the morning she discovered him missing. It's fair to say she's devastated. She has no doubt whatsoever that something terrible has happened.'

'The Malcolm Reilly scenario,' Ava said.

'Exactly. The problem is that with no evidence about how Malcolm disappeared, who was involved, no forensics and no witnesses, linking the two cases relies entirely on the type of victim and the fact that both disappeared in an unexplained manner.'

'Similarities as far as you see them?' she asked.

'Age of the victims – within two years of each other. Obviously they both live in Edinburgh, both schooled here, both have jobs in the city. Both fit, healthy, and well liked. Close family ties. No money problems, known enemies or associates that might cause concern.'

'Drugs?' Ava interjected.

'Malcolm Reilly's tox screen from France came back with mixed results. They did hair testing which is pretty thorough, and which shows absolutely no drug use as that would have lodged in the hair root. There has to be some allowance for the fact that other organs were missing so liver and kidneys couldn't be checked. Brain shows no alcohol had been consumed in the hours prior to death. The stomach had a concentration of oral morphine though, which didn't show in the hair test, so it hadn't reached the hair root. It looks as though a very large dose was given which would have put Malcolm into an almost comatose state.'

'Allowing his killer to do whatever he or she liked,' Ava said.

'Without him registering much pain,' Tripp added.

'What about Bart? Any indication that he had either a drug or alcohol problem?'

'Didn't like wasting his hard-earned money on alcohol, although he had the occasional drink. Drugs were something he said he abhorred, although he wouldn't be the first kid to have one opinion then do something different.'

'Only you clearly don't think that's the case?' Ava commented, studying Tripp's face.

'I don't. He lost his father in a tragic accident, and seems to have worried about his mother constantly. I don't think drugs is a risk he'd have taken.'

'Okay, but let's not discount it entirely. When you care for someone as deeply as he obviously cared about his mother, the simple stress of worrying can make it difficult to cope.' She frowned, picked up her pen again and underlined a couple of sentences as she rubbed her eyes. 'But I agree we have to investigate the theory that the two disappearances might be linked. If nothing else, it could be the break we need in the Reilly case. You can have DC Monroe. Try to recreate the end of that last evening in the restaurant, see if it doesn't jog some memories. Go through the bookings list, get in touch with anyone who was in there that night. Liaise with DI Callanach if you need to about the Reilly case, and see if there's any link between the two men that we're unaware of.'

'Yes ma'am.' Tripp stood up. 'So, will DI Callanach be back after the Reilly case wraps up, do you think?'

Ava didn't look up. 'There's still a trafficking investigation ongoing. He's only assigned as Scottish liaison officer to Interpol on the Reilly case because he was already out there. Honestly, I can't say when he'll be back.'

Tripp shifted his weight from one foot to another until he found the right words to say.

'The squad misses him, ma'am.'

'I should hope so,' Ava responded. 'If one of our officers weren't missed it would be a pretty sad indictment of MIT. As I said, talk to Callanach directly for information. I'm sure he'll also be able to update you as to how the trafficking operation is progressing.'

'Right,' Tripp said gently. 'Oh, and DI Graham asked me to let him know when you were free. Shall I tell him he can come up and speak with you now?'

Ava sighed. 'Um, actually, I have a couple of calls to make that won't wait. Could you message the detective inspector and ask him to email me instead? That way I can deal with it while I clear some other matters off my to-do list.'

'I will, ma'am,' Tripp nodded.

'And tell DI Graham that I want him and DS Lively on the Gene Oldman murder full time. There should be a lead by now. Oldman must have had any number of unsavoury contacts for us to bring in for questioning.'

Tripp left quietly. He knew a dismissal tone when he heard it; not that DCI Turner pulled authority very often, but she obviously wasn't in the mood for small talk. He messaged DI Graham from his mobile as he wandered down the stairs, to find most of the squad gathered in the incident room. A breeze of silence wafted across as he entered.

'You seen the DCI yet?' Lively shouted, breaking the quiet.

'I have,' Tripp replied. He was an unwilling public speaker, but people obviously wanted to know what the structure of the next week was to be. 'I'm going to be following up on the Bart Campbell disappearance with DC Monroe. The chief agrees there's a possible link to Malcolm Reilly which needs looking into. She wants you and DI Graham to keep moving on the Gene Oldman murder.'

'Aye, I bet she wants me dealing with that one, keeping me where I belong, out with the good folk of Wester Hailes,' Lively sniped.

Tripp wandered over to speak with Janet Monroe, as Detective Inspector Graham entered the room.

'Right, there's a lot to do. Sergeant Lively, any news on the footprint we found on the floor in Gene Oldman's kitchen?' Graham began.

'Sure. Given that it was only a partial print the shoe size is estimated to be a five, so we're working on the basis that whoever left the print is either an adolescent, or if it's an adult it's likely to be a female. The foot width is slim, although that may be due to not putting the full foot on the floor because of the injury. DNA profile is definitely not a match for Oldman's.'

'Anything from any of Oldman's family members yet that might help?' Graham asked.

'He's got a sister whose exact words were, "Why the fuck are ye bothering me with this shite? Sodding git got what he deserved."'

'Does she have an alibi for the time of death?'

'Depends if you call long-term residence in Her Majesty's Prison Cornton Vale an alibi or not. I'd say Cornton probably has a better community spirit than Wester Hailes,' Lively sniggered.

'Sir!' PC Biddlecombe arrived in the doorway, panting.

'Yes, constable?'

'Farmer from a pig farm out at Roslin just called in.' She

stood, breathless, staring into the packed incident room as if it were an exam hall and she'd forgotten to study.

'And that would be of interest to us because . . .' Lively prompted.

'Oh my God, right, he found pieces of skulls this morning when he was mucking out a pen. He's certain they weren't there a week ago. Should I . . . um . . .'

'Give Sergeant Lively the details,' Graham instructed. 'And get a crime scene investigation team out there straight away.'

Biddlecombe spun round to exit as quickly as possible, succeeding only in smacking her left shoulder into the doorframe. There was a ripple of laughter that Graham quelled with a look.

'You want me to go out there and take a look in person?' Lively asked.

'Yes, but keep it brief, liaise with the forensic team, then get back on with the Oldman case. The leads are getting staler every day, and these skull fragments may not be human, or they might be from ancient bodies the pigs have just scratched up from the ground. I don't want to get distracted by it until we have some hard facts.'

'Take some gloves, Sarge,' a young officer shouted gleefully from the back of the room. 'That pig shit isn't gonna search itself.'

'Is that right, DC Swift? I'll be needing some assistance then. Grab your coat, lad, you've pulled.'

There was a groan followed by the sound of back-slapping.

'I'm supposed to be helping DS Tripp establish who was in the restaurant the night Bart Campbell disappeared, sir,' John Swift moaned.

'I can spare you, constable,' Tripp confirmed. 'And I'll notify DCI Turner about the skulls.'

Lively threw a hi-vis jacket in Swift's direction, and the two of them headed for the door.

Chapter Twelve

Fleury-Mérogis Prison, the largest prison in Europe, sat in 180 hectares of a southern suburb of Paris, a reminder to all who saw her what good came of criminal enterprises. Sadly, it was a lesson that hadn't been learned by its 4,100 occupants. A central polygon-shaped building off-shot five three-armed wings, each home to four floors of inmates: men, women and juveniles. Wire on the roofs discouraged daring attempts at escape by helicopter, necessary given the connections some of the inmates had. Over the years, Callanach and Jean-Paul had delivered plenty of new 'guests' to Fleury-Mérogis, many of whom were still in residence, some never destined to freely see the light of day.

They showed their Interpol credentials and emptied their pockets into lockers. Built fairly recently in the 1960s, the prison atmosphere was nonetheless tense with an oppressive sense of history, perhaps because time moved so slowly within its walls. They didn't talk as they were escorted to the interview rooms, each of them caught up in their own memories of previous criminal endeavours whose perpetrators had been incarcerated there. A terrorist cell whose movements they'd watched until minutes before an attack. A copycat killer who'd perfected his skills to such a pinnacle that he'd far outshone the man he'd admired. Others whose lives were just pathetic, and who'd turned to crime in boredom and frustration. Fleury-Mérogis was a miniature city, with all its class divides, volatile micro-economies, victors and victims, every conceivable language whispered and screamed in its hallways and darker places. Callanach hated it.

Giorgia Moretti-Russo had been fifty-three years of age when Jean-Paul led the case that resulted in her multiple life sentences. Callanach had spent his night reading the files. Seven counts of murder, all for organ harvesting purposes, and those were just the bodies that had been found. It was pretty clear that Russo hadn't started with those victims, though, and Interpol's internal memos theorised that thirty to forty was a more accurate estimate. A former surgeon in Italy, she had all the skills necessary for the practical side of the business, while her French husband had taken care of the administration. He'd been killed resisting arrest. Her only comment on the subject, reportedly, was how wasteful such a death was, when her spouse's organs could have netted her in the region of half a million dollars.

Jean-Paul and Callanach waited for her, arms crossed, the chill air in the interview room only half the reason they felt so cold. Moretti-Russo had never expressed a single regret for what she'd done, abducting men and women to specific racial and age specifications, killing to order and making herself rich beyond most people's wildest dreams. With better self-control, she could have taken the money and run away to a non-extradition South American country, and lived the rest of her life under the warm sun in luxury. But she'd wanted more.

The woman who appeared in the doorway accompanied by a prison guard was an exception among Fleury-Mérogis lifers.

Incarceration seemed to suit her. Now in her early sixties, she was slim but not skinny, her skin looked as if she'd never missed a day of moisturising, and she walked straight-backed with a confidence that made Callanach feel as if he were the inmate and she the visitor. But then she had nothing to lose, and they did.

'Gentlemen,' she cooed, extending her hand regally, bent slightly at the wrist, as if they should kiss it. Jean-Paul stood up and opted for shaking it instead. Callanach kept his seat, arms folded. Russo wanted them to acknowledge her as if she were a fellow professional, living life beyond the walls she'd made for herself, and he wasn't going to play her game.

She sat down opposite them at the small table, crossing her long legs demurely at the ankles, and tossing her dark, bobbed hair to one side. Callanach saw she must have been an extra-ordinary beauty in her youth, obviously intelligent, used to getting her own way. She smiled at him with perfect teeth, marred only by a black space at the back. Callanach couldn't help himself; intrigued, he tipped his head further to the right to better view the aberration.

'Curious?' she said breathily, leaning towards him. 'Let me open my mouth for you.'

She did so slowly, running her pink tongue across her lower lip, drawing the moment out. Callanach didn't stop her. This was part of her game, and he'd learned with narcissists that it was easier and more fruitful to let them play a while. Turning her head to the side, she slid a finger into her mouth then pulled her cheek away to give him a better view. She'd lost a tooth, presumably while in prison or there was no doubt she'd have had a dentist fit a crown.

'You want to know how it happened, so let me spare you the embarrassment of such obvious interest. A woman who'd been here some time, in for kidnapping I think, although I was too bored to bother with the details, decided she didn't like the way I held my head. She rather stupidly thought that trying to carve her initial into my face in the showers might be a good way of bringing me down to her level. Sadly for her, the shiv she'd secreted in her rectum was slippery from the soap she'd used to get it out. My hands, expecting her as I was, were dry, so the shiv ended up in her temple rather than my cheek. During the altercation she landed a punch that fractured my jaw, and my tooth was the casualty, but it was a small price to pay for the overall victory. She's in a special unit now, and every meal is provided to her by a plastic teaspoon, while she listens to piped music from her wheelchair. Since then my life here has been . . . remarkably peaceful.'

'Mrs Moretti-Russo, we're here to talk to you about a case,' Jean-Paul began. 'I gather you were informed of that when we asked to speak with you. Did you have a chance to consult with your lawyer about the meeting?'

'Call me Giorgia, please,' she said.

'That's not really appropriate, so if you don't mind we'll—'

She cut across the attempt to maintain formality.

'You'll call me Giorgia and I'll call you by your first names, or we don't speak at all. My house, my rules. There's a very attractive young woman in my cell waiting to massage my feet, so don't think I don't have anywhere else to be.'

'Of course,' Jean-Paul didn't miss a beat. Callanach wanted to leave. Giorgia Moretti-Russo was serpentine and calculating. 'I'm Jean-Paul and this is Luc. We're grateful you agreed to see us. Do you mind if we use a voice recorder?'

'Of course not. There'll have to be a deal, after all. I certainly want you to feel as if you're getting value for money.' As Jean-Paul set up his voice recorder, she made a point of turning to look Callanach full in the eyes, with a quick up-and-down sweep for good measure.

'Are you allowed to speak or just here for security purposes?'

'I speak as and when I feel the need,' Callanach replied.

'You don't like me.' She tipped her head to one side.

'Did you expect me to?' he asked, knowing she was drawing him in and wanting to resist, but unwilling to let her dominate the conversation.

'I expect an Interpol agent to keep an open mind and judge based on his own perceptions, rather than having an emotional reaction to a file of papers that tells only half a tale.'

Callanach found a spot on the wall to stare at. She wanted him to look her in the eyes, and he wasn't going to give her the satisfaction. It was her eyes, in fact, that had led the police to her. With one light hazel pupil and the other dark brown, she was too recognisable for her own good, but too vain to have worn coloured lenses as a disguise. She was scouting for victims when she'd approached a plainclothes police officer, and that had been the end.

'Let's get started, shall we?' Jean-Paul interrupted.

'You'll have spoken to the governor already, of course, and agreed terms with him.' She smoothed an eyebrow as she waited for Jean-Paul to open with an offer.

Instead, he opened an envelope and began spreading photos of Malcolm Reilly on the table, starting with three photos as he'd been in life: one in his ski gear, one taken at the gym, and another that had been downloaded from a social media post – Malcolm on holiday, shirtless, tanned, on a beach. That stopped her in her tracks. She reached out her fingers slowly, manicured nails stroking the images.

'No body fat,' she purred. 'Muscly without bulk. He was what . . . five foot nine?'

Jean-Paul checked his notes.

'Five ten,' he confirmed.

'So you believe his organs were harvested, but you have no leads. How much of him was taken?'

'Most of the major organs,' Jean-Paul said, taking out the photos of Malcolm's body as it was discovered, followed by the postmortem photographs.

Giorgia picked them up one by one, taking her time, sliding a slim pair of glasses from her pocket and putting them on, her movements self-conscious for the first time. She hated wearing them, Callanach realised. It made her acknowledge ageing. And the glasses dulled the impact that her extraordinary eyes made, of course. The second she'd finished her examination, she slid the glasses back off, returning them to her pocket rather than leaving them on the table where she would have had to see the space they occupied.

Callanach and Jean-Paul both knew better than to prompt. They sat silently waiting for her to open up. She was enjoying the involvement and the attention. That much was clear from her demeanour. She leaned forward on the table, frowning then closing her eyes, imagining the scenario that had eventually delivered Malcolm Reilly into the hands of the pathologist, no doubt.

'Do you have the postmortem report with you?' she asked. 'I need more details on the incisions and the treatment of the blood vessels. The photos are good but they're not the whole story.'

Jean-Paul passed it over.

They sat in silence again as she read. Callanach had read the documents so many times they were pretty much ingrained in his memory. The oral morphine wasn't difficult to get hold of. It was prescribed regularly to patients with conditions causing extreme pain, particularly those receiving end of life care at home.

'Pen,' she ordered. Jean-Paul handed her a pencil in compliance with the governor's orders. Pens were too easily broken, sharpened and turned into lethal weapons.

Glasses back on, Giorgia began underlining and dashing off notes in margins, drawing circles around certain words. Callanach watched as she worked. This was a different woman, utterly focused and unaware of herself. She was less dislikeable like that, he decided, her vanity replaced with an instinctual return to the professionalism that had marked her early days as a surgeon. This time when she was done, the glasses remained in place. She tapped her fingernails on the desk. It was strategy time. She was obviously intrigued and engrossed, but that wouldn't prevent negotiations.

'Best offer, in one go. Don't mess me around. And before you ask if I can help you or not, yes I can. Your pathologist is good but he's not a surgeon so the insights are, being polite, lacking.'

'A cell to yourself. No more sharing. An additional sixty minutes per day out of your cell in recreational areas. Your choice of jobs inside the prison. One extra visit per month,' Jean-Paul announced.

It wasn't a bad deal, but she was holding the cards and they all knew it. They'd expected her to ask for more, of course, but Jean-Paul hadn't held anything back. There was no point. Anything less than the offer he'd made wouldn't yield results. It was up to her to decide whether she wanted the little extras that the deal would give her. To a life prisoner, an extra hour a day out of her cell added up to an awful lot over the years.

'That's all?' she directed at Callanach, playing games again. He nodded. 'I'll need a week to think about it. Come back again in seven days. If I need more thinking time than that I'll have the governor let you know.'

'Don't bother with that,' Callanach said, stretching his legs out in front of him and keeping his shoulders loose. 'You don't want us to play games, and we don't want you to. You know there's a time issue, we know that life inside a prison – even with your skills at manipulating people – is dull. You may not find it scary any more, you may have become accustomed to the crappy food, and perhaps there's a certain hierarchy that you've topped, but you're bored. An extra hour a day out of your cell, better access to all the people and information you need to maintain your status, is worth a lot.'

Giorgia pushed her glasses to the top of her head. That, Callanach realised, was what she did when she thought no one was watching her.

'It is, Luc,' she purred, 'but there are other things I'd rather have.'

'Name them. Just out of interest. Our hands are tied as far as negotiating goes,' Callanach said.

'Much of my authority in here comes from my former job. I'm a good doctor. Whatever else I did wrong, no one could ever say my expertise was lacking. I want access to the latest medical journals to stay up to date. The library here says they're too expensive to stock and won't make the expenditure for me alone.'

'Noted,' Jean-Paul said. 'I can ask about that.'

'And I'd like a stethoscope and an otoscope. It's designed for checking ears, but works just as well for other parts of the body. Neither instrument costs much.'

'What for?' Jean-Paul asked.

'What do you think?' she snapped. Giorgia took a deep breath and smiled. 'Apologies, I'm not used to being questioned. I run an informal clinic in here. It keeps my mind occupied but there are limits – severe limits – to what I can do with no medical kit.'

'There are doctors here, and for serious cases inmates are referred to the hospital. I don't see the point,' Jean-Paul said.

'Of course you don't. You're not used to waiting a month to see a doctor while your throat's getting sorer, or your urinary tract infection gets so bad you can't piss without screaming. You're not used to having prison guards ask you for favours just so you can be referred to the medical centre. You don't understand how it feels to be laughed at and told it's too bad when you're in pain. I offer a fast way to get medical advice. I even save the doctors here valuable time. I know when symptoms are serious and I can pass that information on to the guards who are the most easily persuadable. Twice I've diagnosed signs of serious illness that the prison doctors had decided were malingering or hyperbole. One of those women got the treatment she needed, and the other at least got proper pain relief and a hospice bed to pass in peace. Not all monsters are useless. It's just a different set of rules.'

'And what do you get in return?' Callanach asked. 'I'm guessing your enterprise isn't entirely altruistic.'

'Cigarettes. I don't smoke of course, but they're bank notes in here. Some women pay me in drugs which I can then prescribe to others who need them for whatever their condition is. Favours, information, beauty treatments, the expertise of others. You'd be surprised how sophisticated this economic system is. The really big earner is the criminal lawyer convicted of tax fraud. Her cell's never empty, as you can imagine.'

'It'll be difficult,' Jean-Paul said. 'Medical implements have metal parts. The governor will be concerned about safety, and even more worried about his liability in allowing you to practise quasi-medicine with no licence. There'll be an issue about getting sued.'

'I'll sign an agreement to say I'm only allowed to perform research with the kit, not to diagnose or treat fellow prisoners. I'll even keep a copy of it hanging on my cell wall for everyone to see. That'll stop the lawsuits. Do you think I haven't discussed this with my friend the lawyer already?'

She'd come in fully prepared, Callanach thought. No doubt she'd been planning exactly this conversation from the second she was notified that Interpol had requested an interview.

'As for the danger posed by a stethoscope and an otoscope, I'd accept having them handed to me at certain times for a specified period, and handing them back to a guard for safe keeping. Say two hours a day, Monday to Friday. That way it'll be obvious if I can't return them or if parts of them have been removed. Not that I'd allow that to happen. I do have some pride, you know.'

'I'll ask,' Jean-Paul said. 'I can do that right now. But the deal's off the table if you try to delay.'

'Did you just grow some balls, Jean-Paul?' she asked. 'I don't recommend speaking to me like that again, though. That might work with the drug importers and paedophile rings you normally deal with, but not with me.'

Callanach guessed she was right. Her IQ was well beyond normal limits, even for a surgeon, and her sense of entitlement carried with it a stubbornness that was their most likely stumbling block.

'Give me a moment,' Jean-Paul said. He knocked on the door for a guard to open up and went outside into the corridor. There, a phone call with the waiting governor was all that was required for authorisation to do the deal or not. It would be a yes, Callanach knew. Interpol didn't have carte blanche, but it still held enough sway to get what it wanted.

Giorgia waited until the door was locked again.

'There's some tension between the two of you,' she observed. Callanach didn't answer. 'Does he compare himself to you, do you think? He won't turn his body towards you fully when you speak. He won't allow himself to nod, or show any normal signs of enthusiasm even when you're working effectively. It's as if he's trying to cut himself off from you.'

'You didn't give evidence at your trial, and yet you'd easily have been a match for the prosecutor. Why did you opt for silence?' Callanach asked. She would immediately recognise the question for what it was – a change of subject – but he wasn't going to discuss Jean-Paul with her.

'Perhaps I wanted to end up in here,' she said. 'You see things as black and white, which is what hampers most police investigations. There's an unwillingness to accept the humanity or the complexity of the perpetrators of crime. Most law enforcement personnel lack imagination. They're so caught up in right and wrong, justice, laws, that they fail to explore the evidence in ways that might be truly disturbing, as in this case. The organs are gone, therefore it must be harvesting. Simple, clean.'

'Isn't it?' he asked.

'Of sorts. Then again, not really. It's your face, isn't it? He hates that women can't stop staring at you. Being with you is a constant drain on him. It must be like being the less attractive twin. He's diminished by you.'

'He's a little old for that,' Callanach said.

'We'll see, shall we?'

Jean-Paul re-entered the room.

'All right,' he said. 'Your requests have been guaranteed. They're being reduced to writing, and will be signed by the governor before we leave. Provided you supply us with valuable information.'

'Fine,' she said. 'I'll need your colleague to take off his shirt.' She turned her head and gave Callanach the tiniest wink at an angle hidden from Jean-Paul.

'No,' Callanach said.

Giorgia grinned.

'Purely for anatomical purposes. I need a specimen to show

you how I'd have made the incisions. This is the easiest way without an anatomical dummy here.'

Jean-Paul gritted his teeth.

'Shirt off,' he growled.

'I'm not part of the deal,' Callanach said quietly.

'Apparently you are,' Jean-Paul muttered.

Callanach had a choice. Continuing the argument would undermine Jean-Paul's authority in the room. Giving Giorgia what she wanted was a backward step in the negotiations, and gave her another reason to draw out the process she was already enjoying too much. He opted for the path of least resistance, gratuitous as it was, undoing his buttons, dropping his shirt on the chair and standing up.

'I need a pen. Not a pencil. I'll be drawing on your colleague.' Giorgia grinned at Jean-Paul who sighed but took a pen from the inside pocket of his jacket and handed it over.

Callanach took a moment to consider how much of a threat the pen was. Shoved into his eye or his neck it could kill him, yet Jean-Paul had handed it over without argument.

'You can relax,' Giorgia told him. 'You're too pretty to kill.'

'Not a consideration you gave some of your other victims,' Callanach said, as she turned him so his chest was facing the single light in the centre of the room.

'Ah, but then there was money involved. Now it would just be gratuitous killing. That's something I could never be accused of.' She ran her fingers down his chest, pressing on the breastbone, feeling the curve of his ribcage and back up to where she left her fingers over his heart. 'You have a very slow heartbeat,' she said. 'You must keep fit. Watch that, though. You'll have problems with low blood pressure if you're not careful.'

'Can we start?' Jean-Paul asked.

Giorgia raised one arrogant eyebrow at Callanach, making it clear she'd won their earlier argument. Callanach looked away.

'All right,' she said, sliding her glasses back on, and looking across the table to where the photos of Malcolm Reilly's opened chest and abdominal cavity lay. 'Let's begin.'

She positioned the pen at the top of Callanach's chest and drew a single downward stroke from the top of his breastbone to the top of his pubic bone.

'This was the first incision. Single cut all the way. Then the second cut was made across the abdominal cavity. If the abdominal cut was made first, there would have been some snagging as the vertical incision hit the wound, and there's none reported. There is, however, a tiny additional nick at the crosspoint of the right-hand section of the abdominal incision.'

She drew one line across the right side of Callanach's abdomen, left a space to show where the snag was, then completed the right-hand section.

'You're assuming that these organs were all harvested at once. Obviously if the donor is deceased you take all the useable organs as quickly as possible. Multiple surgeons on a team, everyone conscious of the ticking clock, putting whatever you can into storage for transportation. It's done under pressure and because there are no options. Also, it's a relatively simple, clean process because without the heart pumping you have less to concern yourself with in terms of blood loss, the cavities filling up, no need to tie off the arteries and so on.

'My experience was different. I performed organ transplant operations on patients who were still alive – kidneys, liver sections, and once a single testicle – and I can tell you that the less damage you do while you operate, the healthier the organs will be when they're transplanted into the new host. For this reason, it only makes sense to perform the operation initially to remove any organs that can be removed without a threat of loss of life. It also allows you to deal with those organs and repair the damage one organ at a time. There's a reason for that.

Black markets operate differently to regulated medical practices. There's an upfront fee – a sort of booking cost – a second payment when the organ is delivered and transplanted, and a final payment is due if the organ has not been rejected after twenty-eight days. Perfectly good commercial practice, and it means the surgeon works harder to do everything possible not to allow the organ to become overly starved of blood or damaged by trauma during the operation. Did your tox screen show anything like propofol, pentobarbital or thiopental in his system?'

'Only liquid morphine in his stomach.'

'Which would have killed his pain, but it's not a proper anaesthetic. It's almost impossible to control anaesthesia through oral drugs. If he'd come round, the surgical team would have been in trouble. So they were intent on taking everything in one go. If they were going to take organs over a longer period they'd have used one of the drugs I mentioned to keep him in a medically induced coma.'

'How would you have harvested the organs?' Callanach asked.

'Well, I'd have kept the stress away from the heart as long as possible, and minimised surgical entry until the very end. I'd have started with the testicles, then I'd have gone into the abdomen.' She drew a short line across Callanach's stomach. 'Liver first as it's so large and I'd have wanted it out of the way, followed by pancreas and gall bladder. For a kidney, I prefer to make an incision in the side, just below the ribcage. It's a cleaner removal system.

'Now, by the time you get to the lungs, the lack of medical knowledge becomes more stark. A thoracotomy, to remove a lung, is properly performed by way of a horizontal incision across the chest, positioned more towards the arm on the left side where the lung is positioned against the heart.' She made a mark several inches long below Callanach's left pectoral muscle. 'Which tells me that they took the heart first as they went in through the central chest incision. Obviously by this stage your young man was dead anyway. Eyes last. Mess around with the brain like that at the outset and the patient goes into shock and the organs would start to degrade too fast, particularly without proper anaesthesia.'

'So it could be organ harvesting,' Jean-Paul said. 'Badly done by an inexperienced surgeon, or someone with some medical knowledge attempting to rip customers off, not concerned about whether or not the organs were rejected by the new host. If they didn't have a contract with a final payment, that would make them less likely to be careful, right?'

'It's possible,' Giorgia agreed. She patted Callanach on the chest as if he were a pet. Jean-Paul rolled his eyes. 'You can sit down now, darling. What you two don't understand is the market. You don't put an ad in the local paper, you know. I located my hosts – my clients – through their doctors. Real doctors, with licences and good reputations, who were more than willing to drop my name into the conversation for clients who were out of time and hope.'

'You never gave up their names to the prosecution,' Jean-Paul noted.

'And I destroyed every contact I had with every one of them, digital or on paper. Why did those men and women deserve to be ruined just because I'd been caught? They were doing their best for their patients, exactly what the brief is when you go into medicine.'

'You killed people,' Callanach reminded her. 'For money.'

'For every person I killed, my work enabled an average of six other people to live. So if, for example, I killed ten people, I saved sixty. I should have been given a reward not imprisoned.'

Callanach stared at her.

'You were only convicted of seven,' Jean-Paul reminded her.

'How sweet,' she replied.

Callanach knew she believed it on some level. Not that she didn't appreciate what she'd done wrong, but her self-justification was genuine.

'We were talking about the doctors in your . . . referral scheme,' Jean-Paul reminded her.

'Ah yes, well, we contacted them, discreetly of course, and let them know that we might have organs available. There was a convoluted system for them to contact us in return, in case any of them notified the police, but they all had one thing in common. Wealthy clients with failing organs who'd been on waiting lists long enough to have lost hope. The organ donation system doesn't work effectively, in spite of recent attempts to impose a scheme where people are assumed to be in until they opt out. People are dying needlessly, on a daily basis. We were oversubscribed at times. For a couple of organs we actually held auctions. That was my downfall, before you feel the need to point it out to me.'

'The doctor who lost the auction was the one who contacted the police and gave evidence against you?' Callanach asked.

'Indeed,' she said. 'But what I was trying to explain is that we had carefully established systems. In our arrogance we assumed them foolproof, but they were good. We made contact with the right doctors. They checked me out. They gave very specific information regarding donor types, blood types, age groups. There was no amateur element to what we did. We ran a private hospital to all intents and purposes. My husband hired premises under a false company name, then we'd kit out the operating theatres and recovery rooms with the best equipment, engage experienced staff, and I performed both ends of the transplant. We paid cash everywhere we went. No one asks questions when you're paying a little extra and they don't have to wait for money to transfer. We were good at what we did, because we knew what we were doing.'

'The relevance?' Jean-Paul asked.

'The relevance, obviously, is that whoever is performing the surgery in this case, while they have some medical knowledge – the incision is correct in depth, so the organs could have been successfully removed – is no expert. No professional anaesthesia. Incisions that do not maximise operability. Any doctor they contacted would check them out immediately and tell their patient not to go anywhere near an organ offered by such a provider. Taking such a risk would only hasten death, not prolong it.'

Jean-Paul wrote lengthy notes on a pad while Giorgia perused her own markings on the copy of the postmortem report.

'What else?' Callanach asked, noting the smile playing at the corners of her mouth.

'Some basics. I'd really need to examine the body myself to be clinically certain, but it looks unlikely that whoever operated left sufficient lengths of blood vessels attached to make for an easy transplant at the recipient end. But they chose their donor well. Someone did research. He was healthy, a non-smoker, no obvious alcohol use, no sign of disease, fit, no body fat. I couldn't have chosen better myself.'

'So he'd have made a good donor? But you're saying harvesting wasn't what this was about.' Jean-Paul threw his pen on the desk.

'I'm telling you he's good marketing material. You choose the donor to make the sale as easy as possible, the same as any other product you're trying to sell.'

'The question is what they were selling precisely, if not organs for transplant,' Callanach said, doing up the last button of his shirt.

The governor appeared at the door with a sheet of paper in his hand, looking as relaxed as if he were about to join them for coffee.

'Dr Moretti-Russo,' he greeted her with respect. 'I'm so glad you've been able to assist our friends from Interpol. That was good of you. If you're finished, you can check this agreement and we'll both sign it.'

'I don't know,' she smiled and ran a hand through her hair. 'Do you think I'm finished?' she asked Luc and Jean-Paul.

'I think we're done here.' Jean-Paul stood up, gathering the photos and report from the table.

'What is it?' Callanach asked her.

'Do you have faith in me?' Giorgia replied.

'I accept your expertise.'

'Cold fish,' she smiled. 'Offer me something else. You won't regret it.'

'I'm afraid this is the best we can do,' the governor interjected. 'We literally haven't the staff or resources to make any further concessions.'

'Shame. You've heard my expert opinion. No one thought to ask me about my gut instinct.'

'That could be anything,' Jean-Paul said. 'We're after hard leads, not fairy tales.'

'But the fairy tale is what's going to help you,' Giorgia said. 'Last chance.' She turned her back on Jean-Paul and the governor, standing directly in front of Callanach instead.

'Your choice. Have a crown fitted to replace the missing tooth or have your eyes lasered so you can lose the glasses. I'll secure funding,' he directed at the governor.

'What the fuck?' Jean-Paul sighed.

'Shut up,' Giorgia told him. 'Tell me which one I'm going to choose and why, then we have a deal.'

Callanach didn't hesitate.

'You'll choose the eyes. The tooth you carry like a badge of honour. It's a war wound that secures your position in here. Repair it and you'll lose credibility because it'll look like it was bothering you. The problem with your vision is that you hate it because you feel it diminishes you. Visible ageing reduces your prowess, both to others and for you internally.'

'More psychoanalysis than I was expecting – or wanted – but fine. Add it to the agreement.'

Callanach picked up a pen and took hold of the contract, scribbling an additional note at the bottom and adding his own signature to it, before both Giorgia and the governor added their own. Jean-Paul held out his hand for Giorgia to return the pen. She did so slowly with a faint smile.

'Your turn,' Callanach told Giorgia, as Jean-Paul secured the pen in his pocket.

'All right,' she said, taking both his hands in her own and staring up at him like a teenage girl waiting for her first kiss. Callanach tolerated the touch of the hands that had killed in cold blood, and waited. 'What's the one thing you need more than anything else in life, that's personal to you? Something that has become so important to you, it's close to an obsession.'

'There isn't anything,' he said blankly.

'Yes there is. Everyone has something. For me it's liberty. I think about it constantly, even when I'm not conscious of it. An hour later, I'll realise I was reliving a walk on some beach, step by step. For the governor, it's time with his daughters. When you're in his office, he barely looks at you. He stares at the photo of him with them, loses track mid-conversation, sometimes calls people by their names by mistake.'

'Do I?' the governor asked softly.

'Think about it. It's important,' Giorgia told Callanach.

He hesitated, threw a half glance in Jean-Paul's direction before he could stop himself.

'Being believed,' he said.

Giorgia took in a sharp breath.

'I wish I could ask why, but your colleague has decided I'm

wasting time, so here you go. People will do anything, sacrifice anything, to get the one thing that means the most to them. It makes them vulnerable. More than anything else, it makes them stupid. Why did your victim's hair smell of myrrh?'

'We don't know that yet,' he said.

She nodded her head.

'Historically it's been used for embalming,' Jean-Paul offered.

'Was your victim embalmed?' she replied.

'Um, no, but . . .' Jean-Paul said quietly.

'Then it wasn't being used for its embalming qualities. The myrrh is what you need to figure out. There's more than one type of doctor in the world, Luc. Some of us use tried and tested medicine. Others operate with smoke and mirrors, myrrh and myth.' She dropped his hands, although her touch remained icy on his palms. 'I'm ready to go back to my cell now,' she told the governor. He gave her a slight dip of his head and knocked once on the door for the guard to open up.

Chapter Thirteen

Ava had taken the opportunity to leave the station, arriving at the farm in Roslin at the same moment Detective Constable John Swift exited Lively's car, misplaced his footing in the mud, and fell flat on his face in a combination of wet earth and animal excrement. She winced, decided against offering him a hand up given the state he was in and the likelihood that she too might end up on the ground, and waited for her sergeant to deliver the inevitable stinging verbal assault. The farmer saved Lively the trouble.

'Is he some sort of clown you bring along to lighten the atmosphere when human bodies are discovered?' the farmer asked. Ava didn't engage. 'This way then. Wee Bobo there can follow the footprints when he's got himself upright. The other lot are already getting set up.' He pointed to the scene examiners' vehicle parked next to a distant barn.

Lively walked at Ava's side.

'I like him already,' Lively motioned at the farmer who was striding off across the field.

'Maybe you were separated at birth,' Ava muttered.

They arrived at the pig enclosures to be handed clean suits

by the forensics team. Ava and Lively slipped theirs on easily as DC Swift struggled to pull one over his muddy clothes.

'Not to judge, ma'am, but how did the inappropriately named Constable Swift find his way into MIT? Did he get lost on the way to the bogs and just forget to leave again?'

'Give him time, Sergeant. He might be a diamond in the rough.'

'Oh aye, he'll be the genius who solves this entire case just as soon as he's learned how to walk. What're you doing here, anyway, if you don't mind my asking? Bit premature, isn't it?'

'Human bones in pig pens? There's only ever one explanation for that.' She climbed a fence and trod carefully, keeping to the hard mats the examining team had put through the mud to minimise disruption to the scene.

'We don't even know if the bones are human yet. I'm not sure the farmer is qualified to be making that assessment, unless he's angling for a job at the mortuary.'

'Farmers may not see many human bones but they see plenty from animals. Makes sense to me that these stood out.'

'A tenner says you've overthought it and we're wasting our time.' Lively held out his hand for Ava to shake.

'I'd happily just pay you a tenner to scrub your nails more thoroughly,' Ava smiled. 'Put your gloves on, and help DC Swift into his suit. I'm not sure he ever learned how to do zips.'

'Definitely human,' a forensics officer said, walking up and holding out a section of skull for them to view.

'Damn it,' Ava said. 'How long's it been here?'

'Not sure exactly but at least two, possibly three, bodies were dumped here. Come with me.'

They trod along the plastic matting to the edge of one pig pen where yellow flags poked their waving heads from the muck.

'This skull section was found here. You can see there's another section of skull still in situ. We want to excise the surrounding mud to see if there's human tissue which would help us get a more precise time on the bodies' arrival.'

'How do you know the bones aren't all from the same individual?' Swift piped up from behind them.

'Well,' the scene examiner said slowly. 'As you can see, the skull section in my hand has the right eye socket still intact. Compare it with the skull section sticking out of the ground, and you'll note that one has both eye sockets still intact, so unless our victim had three eyes . . .'

'Moving on,' Ava said quietly, talking over Lively who was swearing under his breath and shaking his head. 'You said you think there might be a third body?'

'Next pen over,' she pointed. 'We can't go in there yet as we want to preserve the scene first, both to understand the pigs' movements and to protect whatever trace evidence there might be in the mud. We're about to cover it with a tent before the rain starts again. The bone was spotted from beyond the fence at the other side. There's no skull, but we've seen what we believe to be part of a clavicle. It's small and thin, more likely to belong to a female or a child, but that's preliminary. And there's something else. Follow me back out. There's a better view from the far side of the pens.'

They retraced their steps, Ava grabbing Lively's hand as he reached out to slap Swift round the back of the head, before traipsing in increasingly deep mud to stand at a fence where a variety of farmyard machinery had been dumped in front of another pig pen.

'Stand up on the lowest fence rung,' the forensics officer instructed them.

'Carefully,' Lively instructed Swift.

The better view showed several more yellow flags over a wide area, just under a wooden fence where a considerable disturbance had been made in the mud, creating a large dip.

'When we arrived, the farmer had moved the pigs out of the pen we were just in, but what drew our attention was the behaviour of the pigs in the pen you can see from here. There were several of them gathered around the dip in the mud, pushing their snouts up against the fence, clearly fighting each other to get to whatever was this side. We investigated and found the bone next to what appears to be a section of trachea up to the larynx. It's fairly distinctive.'

'You think they pushed it under the fence while they were consuming the remainder of the body?' Ava asked.

'That's the theory. In the other pen, the boards go right down into the earth. Here, because there's the machinery area to keep the pigs in, the fence has a gap at the bottom. No doubt at all that they'd already have consumed that trachea if they'd had the opportunity.'

'Can smell food a metre down, my girls,' the farmer declared from behind them.

'Any idea how long it would have taken them to consume a whole human?' Ava asked him.

'Am I no' a suspect then?' the farmer asked her.

'You'll have to make a statement, of course, and we'll need the names of everyone who works here or has access to the area, any suspicious vehicles or people on your land, but I doubt you'd have called us in if this was your handiwork.'

'Bloody right. And there's been no one suspicious I've seen, or they'd have ended up on the pointy end of my shotgun,' the farmer told them. 'There were three sows in each pen. An average body would be gone in less than half a day. A full day if it was a really big man.'

'Tested that, have you?' Lively asked.

'If I didn't know what quantity of food my pigs consumed daily after twenty years' farming, I wouldn't be much good at my job now, would I?'

'Do they eat anything then?' Swift asked.

'The sections of skull are left over because that's the hardest part for the pigs to bite through, just because of the shape. Left long enough, even the skulls would have gone, with the pigs working on the edge of the skull until it cracked and fell apart. We're sifting the mud in each pen now for teeth. Those don't break down in the pigs' stomachs so they'll give us a good baseline for when the bodies were dumped. If they've already expelled the teeth, the bodies would have been consumed more than thirty-six hours ago, which is the average adult sow's metabolic rate. Given the full day it takes to consume a human, you could roughly time the bodies to have been brought here about two and a half days ago. And yes,' she directed at Swift, 'pigs are the ultimate body disposal system. Human DNA is no longer recognisable after it's been through a pig's stomach. We're lucky we got the trachea, or the chance of getting any positive identification would have been virtually nil. They eat the soft bits first,' the scene examiner added.

'So all the future pig shit needs to be checked to see when they pass the teeth?' Lively asked.

'That's your problem,' the farmer announced.

'Each pig is in a separate indoor pen. We'll check each one on a daily basis until we're confident that all the teeth have been gathered. We don't want them outside until we give you the all-clear, so the teeth won't be affected by any uncontrollable elements,' the examiner explained.

'Well, guess I won't need to feed them for a day or so,' the farmer said, nodding as he left them to it.

'You'd think he didn't care at all,' Swift commented as the farmer disappeared around the side of the barn.

'He raises, feeds, then kills animals for a living,' Lively said. 'Circle of life and all that. I'm guessing he's not a sentimentalist.'

'You were definitely separated at birth,' Ava said. 'What'll happen to the bone fragments now?'

'They'll be delivered to a forensic anthropologist. I'll email you the details. You can talk to them directly for their findings. The trachea will go to the deputy pathologist for inspection. Samples will be taken and we'll keep our fingers crossed for a DNA match.'

'Constable, go after the farmer and take his statement, please,' Ava said. Swift looked happy to be leaving the conversation as the scene examination officer excused herself to rejoin her team. 'The bodies are piling up. Something's not right.'

Lively nodded. 'Malcolm Reilly in France. Three unidentified here. It's a lot, but it's not unknown. These three might have been dead for a year or more.'

'We've also got Gene Oldman in Wester Hailes,' Ava reminded him.

'Gene Oldman pissed the wrong person off, and I suspect the queue to do that might have gone round the block. Whoever shot him in his own kitchen and didn't even bother covering his body isn't the same person who went to these lengths to get rid of evidence. The sudden influx of bodies is a coincidence. These things don't space themselves out considerately over the year.'

Ava turned away from the pig pens, looking across the hills at the view. It was breath-taking. Roslin had become a tourist hub for Rosslyn Chapel, but that wasn't all the area had to offer. There wasn't another building in sight from where she stood.

'Not that many pig farms around here,' she noted. 'Most Scottish pig farming happens further north. Nice secluded farm too. Not overlooked. Pig pens and the barns are a good distance from the farmhouse. Clever.'

'Bugger to get the bodies here though,' Lively noted.

'Not if they cut them up first, which would have made consumption easier. There's enough information about it on the internet that it wouldn't take a criminal mastermind to figure it out.'

'Messy though, and risky. How could they be sure the farmer wouldn't have disturbed them, or found the bodies before they could be eaten?'

'If it were me, I'd have been watching the farmer first,' Ava said. 'Check what time the lights go off in the farmhouse at night. Move the bodies in immediately it gets dark. Give the pigs maximum overnight consumption time. If they were armed, they might not have been too bothered about the farmer's shotgun. There must have been more than one person getting three bodies into the pens. I'd have kept one man back to keep an eye on the farmer's door, make sure he didn't get suspicious from the noise of the pigs, then had maybe two others, three even, dumping the bodies out here. Gets dark early at the moment. They'd have had in the region of twelve hours' dark or dusk to get it done. Chop up the bodies into small enough chunks and streamline the process. That's what I'd have done.'

'Should I be worried about you?' Lively asked.

'Too much time on my hands,' Ava said as she turned to head back into the city. She couldn't be late. Natasha was waiting for her at the hospital.

Chapter Fourteen

Elenuta sat quietly on the kitchen floor, eating her lunch. It was Pot Noodles again, cheap and easy to store, and they seemed never to degrade no matter how out of date they were, which was safer than the questionable meat Finlay occasionally turned up with. Last time four of the women in the flat had been sick for days after eating what they'd been told was pork. The smell of it had put Elenuta off, and her refusal to eat it had meant all other meal options had been taken off the table for the day. It had been a lucky call. Most days she was so hungry she took whatever she could get.

The process of eating was part muscle memory, part fakery right now. As hard as she'd tried to ignore Finlay's laptop after he'd done what he wanted to her then fallen asleep, she'd sneaked back over to it. She'd noticed the email icon at the bottom of the screen while she'd been watching with Finlay earlier. She'd checked over her shoulder but Finlay was still dribbling in his sleep. Clicking twice on the tiny envelope symbol, she'd tried to recall any email address she knew. Her parents, her best friend, even businesses she'd connected with in the past.

'Enter Password', the screen had demanded.

Elenuta's heart had sank. She'd tried the internet search symbol, imagining finding any website with a chat function where she could ask for help. Same result. Only the video gallery and a few stupid games were accessible. Absolutely fucking typical. Access to a laptop and all she could do with it was watch more of the same horrors she was living through. Still, someone had to bear witness. With the volume switched off so as not to wake the sleeping monster, she'd watched the remainder of the race, and for every conscious minute since, she'd wished she hadn't.

The girl had died, as Elenuta had known she would, her back to the wall, pinned by the tattooed man who'd roared his self-approval, banging his chest as he'd let her fall to the floor, stomping around like some triumphant hero. Then the drone camera had swapped over to highlight the race's former winner. Reality TV in its most extreme form of evolution, she thought. The woman heard a noise in the corridor behind her, whipping her head round, freezing, eyelids stretched as high as they would rise. Then she was off again, sprinting forwards, racing away from her pursuer, looking much fitter than anyone living in Finlay's care had a right to. She rounded a corner, one hand pushed out against the far wall for balance, looking lithe and strong.

That was when she ran full force into the race's largest champion, knees still bleeding from his earlier encounter. She was a head taller than him, and obviously fitter, but she was no match for his bulk or his rage. Her own forward momentum worked against her, as he grabbed one of her arms and her body twisted, falling sideways to the floor, her head hitting the concrete with a crack that Elenuta could imagine in surround sound even if the volume was off. The woman tried to get back up but staggered, flat on her face as the big man climbed on top of her, already pulling off his shorts. Elenuta looked away, steeled herself, watched again. After everything she'd been through – the violence, imprisonment and daily sexual assaults – the terrible, sickening truth was that seeing another woman raped had become just a day in the life. Hours of hearing the women in rooms either side of her crying, screaming, calling out, had desensitised her. She simply had to wait for the scene to end. When he'd finished using her, he grabbed his previously discarded trousers and stuffed them into her mouth, pinching her nose. She fought hard, thrashed for more minutes than Elenuta realised it took a person to die from suffocation, and eventually lost consciousness. Still he didn't move, just continued to lie on top of her. Perhaps, Elenuta thought, he realised how he would look to everyone watching through drone vision, his now placid penis flopping pathetically as he retrieved his trousers and put them back on. Or maybe he was prolonging the moment, his one great triumph over the female gender, revenge for every real or perceived slight, every rejection, sating not only his sexual desires but bringing every hate-filled thought bursting into glorious technicolour. Whoever was directing the action finally grew bored. The scene shifted again.

The screen now split fifty-fifty, and two women could be seen. The one who had previously armed herself with the glass was taking stock, standing still, listening – no doubt – to the silence following the previous winner's death. With each scream, Elenuta realised, there would come a guilt-feast of relief and delight that another woman had been caught, and that you were still alive to fight or run. Another woman, just like you, who you might have shared a room or a flat with, who might have tried to distract an angry guard or client to spare you from another fist. That woman's death had just increased your own chance of survival. Good luck sleeping with that in your head.

The other woman still standing was huddled in a corner. Elenuta didn't like her chances. The adrenaline that had got her moving at the start of the race was obviously used up. The man with the scar down his stomach came into view. He stood still a moment as he spied the woman, gave a brief shake of his head as if to say how sad it was that the game had come to such a pathetic end. She put her hands up in the air, slightly in front of her, her lips moving rapidly, cheeks shining with tears. There would be no fight, Elenuta knew. Plenty of begging, but not enough resistance to make a difference. The scarred man stepped forwards slowly, taking his time, the smile on his face that of an uncle Elenuta had as a child who brought her sweets, played games and slid his hand up her skirt whenever her parents weren't looking. When she threatened to tell, he threatened to move on to her younger sister. That smile was everything – a mask, a casual indifference, a confidence, a promise of worse to come. Elenuta put a hand over her mouth to keep from waking Finlay up.

As the scarred man reached the woman, he held out a hand to her. A suitor in a twisted universe. The woman looked horrified, then worse – hopeful – and reached out her own shaking hand, laying her slim fingers on his palm. And that was that.

He pulled her forward into his arms, kissing her cheek softly, then turned her round, her back to his chest, pulling her clothing away. She didn't fight him. Her head was flopped against his neck, her bare chest fluttering with insubstantial breaths, eyes blinking madly.

The scarred man dipped a hand into his pocket, bringing out a silver blade that flashed in the overhead lighting, teasing its presence. She closed her eyes. Elenuta forced hers to stay open. The man held the blade aloft, making a play of it in the air before the drone that was edging closer to get the audience its best view of the final action. The woman was limp in the man's arms, hands at her sides, feet rooted to the concrete.

The man lowered the knife, sliding one hand beneath the woman's left breast, lifting it to expose its pale underside, positioning the knife parallel to the underside. The woman's mouth fell open, what was about to happen written as clearly on her face as if she had typed the actual words. The knife held no quick death for her. What if one breast was not enough for him? What if he didn't stop at two, but decided other body parts were fair game? The dread shone in her eyes. The drone buzzed a little nearer and the scarred man stared at it. He lifted the knife away, pointing the blade into the lens.

'Shall I do it?' he roared, his mouth so large and clear Elenuta could read his lips. It took no imagination at all to hear the crowd's response.

The next movement was a blur. The woman grabbed, finding her strength when she needed it most, taking hold of the man's wrist. She stepped – or perhaps fell – forwards. Turning the knife, she directed it at the side of her neck, letting her body weight fall into it. The crimson stream was evidence of her good aim. The man held her for ten seconds, then her dead weight got the better of him. His triumphant roar became a cry of frustration. As she hit the ground, he kicked, once, twice, three times, but by then her head was lolling, the slowly spreading patch on the ground a river of her relief. Kneeling across her, the man took back his knife, and the blood flowed faster. He stabbed out his impotent fury in her already dead body.

Elenuta smiled and cried as he vented. In the second screen, Finlay had found the last woman standing, still clutching her makeshift glass weapon, and was holding up her arm to proclaim her victorious. Her face was pale. She shook as he touched her, tried to pull away.

'Couldn't resist watching the finale, eh?'

Elenuta cried out, falling backwards onto the floor, hands out in front, both a plea and a defence against whatever was coming.

'Sorry,' she cried. 'Will not touch laptop again.'

Finlay stopped the video and slammed down the lid.

'You're fucking right you won't, bitch. You're not going to be pressing any buttons at all with no hands. I've got a nice sharp knife waiting for you in the kitchen. It'll slice right through your wrists, no problem at all. The only bits of you I need to leave intact are your mouth and your pussy.'

The flat doorbell rang.

'Please, so sorry,' Elenuta sobbed. 'So sorry.'

There was a pause before the bell rang again, this time for longer.

'Answer the fucking door, motherfuckers!' Finlay yelled before looking back down at Elenuta. 'Tell you what, we'll play a game. If whoever's at the door is a good client who pays properly and leaves a tip, you'll keep your hands. If it's some nosy bastard neighbour or those balls-aching Jehovahs, you won't be hitting any targets smaller than an elephant's arsehole for the rest of your natural.' He stood up and pulled Elenuta up next to him, slapping her backside hard enough to leave fingermarks. 'And the next time I fuck you, you'll look me in the eyes and say thank you like a good girl. Got it?'

She nodded.

'Say it then,' he whispered, his mouth millimetres from hers.

'Thank you,' she gasped. 'Thank you.'

Finlay smiled and went to see who was at the door.

Chapter Fifteen

Ava's mobile rang.

'It's Luc,' she told Natasha. 'I'll call him back later.'

'Nonsense, take it. We've nothing else to do but wait for a bloody big needle to be stuck in me.' Ava's thumb hovered over the reject call button. 'Does he know?'

Ava shook her head.

'I've been meaning to tell him, but with him being in Paris . . .'

Natasha leaned over and took the phone from Ava's hand, answering the call on speaker phone.

'Luc, it's Tasha,' she said. 'Ava's too important to answer her own phone these days so I'm doing it for her.'

'Natasha,' his voice was warm. 'She's not making you cook for her too, is she?'

'I keep trying. I'm not sure she eats at all these days. I have a horrible feeling she's gone back to student-style cuisine. How's Paris? I want to hear all about it.'

'You should visit me here,' he said. 'Maybe not until I've made some progress on this case, though. What are you two doing? I can't remember the last time Ava was away from her desk before five p.m.'

'We're at the hospital, actually,' Natasha said. 'Ava's keeping me company.' A doctor walked in, raising a hand in greeting as he flicked through a file.

'Nothing serious, I hope,' he said.

'Ava can fill you in. I've got to go. Mustn't keep the doctor waiting. I'll pass you to Ava. Sit in a street cafe and drink a pastis for me, okay?'

She passed the mobile over and Ava switched off speaker, standing up and making for the door.

'I won't be long,' she told Natasha. 'Luc, it's me. I'm in the corridor but I can't be long. What's up?'

'Is Natasha all right?' he asked.

'Haven't got the time,' she snapped, harder than she'd meant to. 'Any progress on Malcolm Reilly?'

'Of sorts. We're ruling out a professional organ harvesting set-up, at least in the traditional sense. We saw a sort of expert in the field who gave us some insights.'

'A sort of expert? Doesn't sound very scientific. Is that the best Interpol can do?'

'Well, she's a surgeon who specialised in transplant medicine, until she started an off-the-record venture with her husband. After that I suppose you'd more accurately call her a serial killer. She knows her stuff though, not just the medical stuff, but the black market.'

'Okay,' Ava said, pulling change out of her pocket and wandering down the corridor to a nearby drinks machine. 'So did she give you any leads?' She ploughed a few coins into the slot.

'More advice than leads. We're focusing on potential end users for the organs. There'll have been marketing, maybe even an auction. Malcolm Reilly's hair smelled of myrrh. There's a possibility it was a sort of ritual killing. Our expert's last sugges- tion was that there are different types of doctors out there so . . .'

'Witch doctors?' Ava pulled her coffee from the machine and blew on it. 'I hadn't realised there was much of that happening in Paris. Are you sure you're not going off on a tangent?'

'At this stage we're just pleased to have a tangent. We think Malcolm Reilly was chosen specifically for his fitness and physique. It looks like he was profiled, which is something you'll need to check out at your end. It wasn't a random choice.'

'He disappeared after a trip to the gym. His father thinks Malcolm met a woman there he was interested in,' Ava explained.

'That sounds like the priority follow-up. We're heading into some of the less mainstream communities to see if anyone's heard of organs being offered for sale.'

'We may have another problem. A missing male, similar type, no contact for several days now, just disappeared after work. Fit, healthy, non-smoker, no drug use. Out of character not to go home. Couple of years younger than Malcolm. We've been treating it as a possible link so far . . .'

'Raise the priority,' Callanach said. 'And send me the missing person's file. Have you put out a ports notice?'

'Already done,' Ava said. 'I should go.'

'Hey,' he said softly. 'I know your voice better than that. Tell me what's going on.' She sighed. 'Is it bad?'

'It's breast cancer,' she said, choking on the final word and spilling coffee on the floor.

Callanach was quiet for a long time. Ava waited for him to formulate a next question.

'How bad?'

'Stage two. They're operating again this afternoon. They took the lump out already but after some tests they want to take more tissue. The doctors are doing their best to save the breast, but . . .' She took a deep breath and tried to steady her voice. 'You know how it goes. One day at a time. Natasha's being Natasha, and I think that's worse. I sort of wish she'd break down because I'd know how to deal with that. I'm a shitty friend, right?'

'You're more like her sister than her friend, and she wouldn't want anyone else with her except you,' Callanach said. 'I wish I was there.'

'Me too,' Ava said quietly. 'I need to go back in while they prep her for surgery. Call my mobile if you need me. I'll be here a few more hours but I'll go when I know she's round from the anaesthetic. She'll be kept in for at least another day.'

'I'm so sorry. She befriended me for no other reason than I was new to Edinburgh and working with you, and she never once made me feel like I was anything other than a lifelong mate. I can't believe I'm not there for her,' he said. 'Hug her from me and send my love, okay?'

Ava sniffed then cleared her throat. 'I will.'

She ended the call, wiped her eyes, threw the remains of the coffee into a bin, and went back in to hold her best friend's hand, hoping she would never have to let go.

Chapter Sixteen

Bart Campbell stared at the ceiling. He was in a small room with a comfortable enough single bed. The lights turned off and on from the outside, and he could hear other voices in the corridor occasionally, although his view through the ten-by-ten-inch toughened glass pane in the door was limited. It hadn't been a cell originally. A long mark on the wall indicated that a desk had stood there for some time. Boarding had been fitted over the exterior of a window, which suggested they were trying to stop him from getting out rather than preventing others from getting in. It was quiet outside. Few traffic noises, no passing pedestrians. No music or industrial sounds. A meal was delivered three times a day. Breakfast was yoghurt and fruit. Lunch was salad or soup. Dinner was lean protein and vegetables. All low-fat and healthy, with minimal carbs. He was going to lose weight fast, but he could survive on it. He'd eaten all of it and it had tasted fine. He had long since stopped worrying about poison.

The people who delivered his meals appeared only briefly, wearing white balaclavas and never spoke. The white balaclavas had freaked him out initially. They were supposed to be dark-coloured, surely. When had anyone in a movie ever turned up in a white balaclava? Where did you even get them? They didn't look homemade.

When the van he'd been transported in had arrived at . . . wherever he was . . . he'd been blindfolded and walked into the building. The space where they'd parked had been vast, every footstep echoing. With one man on each arm, hands tied behind his back, he'd been guided forward until the breeze on his face had subsided and a door had slammed behind him. There was the click-thump of a lock being secured, then another voice, this time a woman, issuing orders in French. She'd sounded older than him, perhaps his mother's age, and insistent. He'd been moved on again, deeper into the building. The floor had clacked as he'd walked. He'd heard other voices, some whispering as he'd passed them, then he'd turned into another corridor – more locks, more pausing – and a sharp chemical odour had hit him. Not like a hospital exactly, definitely under-tones of bleach, but a curious concoction of the acidic and the sulphuric. The stale waft of air that hadn't been freshened by open windows. Finally, in his own room, a new mattress smell as if the plastic cover had only just been removed. That was when he'd heard the crying for the first time. A woman. Young, but not a child. Weeping more than crying, he'd realised when he listened hard. As if she was too tired to cry hard any longer.

Then a white balaclava had entered and told him to take off his clothes. He'd done as he was told. There were enough locked doors between Bart and the exit to make fighting and running for it a ridiculous choice. He was told to stand at the back of the room, draw himself up to his full height – being kidnapped makes you slouchy, he'd thought – and photographed. Same thing, but the back view, then to each side. Finally with his arms in the air, and instructed to flex his muscles. After that, they'd put away the camera and taken out a tape measure and set of scales. Every conceivable measurement was recorded, from skull to feet. He'd lost weight – no surprise there. Finally, three bottles of water were delivered to his bedside table and he was told to drink them before sleeping, as the white balaclava murmured something about him being dehydrated. He was given escorted access to a bathroom with a shower, where soap, a toothbrush and toothpaste were provided – who the hell needed their captive to brush their teeth, he had wondered as he'd scrubbed the grime of his journey away – and tried to persuade himself that at some point he would understand what was happening to him. At last he'd been returned to his room, left alone, the corridor dark.

'Bart!' A girl's voice hissed across the few metres of void between them. 'Hey, you awake?'

He stopped the memories short and walked to his door. If he stood at the far right-hand edge of the small window, he could just make out her door, and the swing of her blonde hair in the far edge of her own window. Just. Glimpsing more of her had proved impossible. If either of them moved so that their face was on view, they couldn't see far enough down the corridor themselves to make contact. Seeing that hair, those long – if blurred – swinging strands, was the closest he'd come to feeling sane since waking up on the container ship.

'I'm here,' he stage-whispered back. The guards didn't stand in their corridor at night. Their conversations had so far not been discovered. He had no idea what the penalty might be if they were overheard, but the risk seemed worth it. He had called to her as soon as the guard had left him alone that first night. She'd been slow to respond, terrified of the repercussions. Bart had spent the next thirty minutes standing at his window, sipping water, talking to her, trying to draw her out, telling her about himself and what had happened to him. If nothing else, if the girl survived and he did not, he figured that she might one day be able to tell his mother what had happened to him.

But she had spoken, eventually. Not that what she'd said to him was in any way reassuring, other than to have someone sitting beside you on your metaphorical boat trip to hell. 'Skye, you okay?'

There was a sob and a cough. Skye Kelso was terrified. Bart knew how that felt, only she'd been there longer than him, and her previous fellow abductee was gone with no explanation. He had tried, without success, to get Skye to talk about it.

'I have a cat,' Skye said. 'I didn't tell you that, did I?'

'No,' Bart whispered. 'What's its name?'

'Squash,' she said. He could hear the smile in her voice. That was good.

'What colour?' he asked.

'Tabby, obviously.' That time she actually laughed. It was the first time she'd done so since they'd begun speaking, perhaps the first time in weeks – she'd lost track of how long it had been since she was taken – and he felt as if he'd scored the winning try at Murrayfield against the All Blacks. Rugby, he thought to himself. I used to love rugby. Used to. How had the tense changed so fast?

'What about you? Any pets?' she followed up.

'No. I had goldfish for a while when I was six. They all ended up swimming with the fishes – can you say that about actual fish or does it not work?'

She rewarded him with another laugh.

'You're funny,' she said so softly he had to jam his ear against the glass to hear.

'Tell me what you look like,' he said. 'I want to be able to imagine your face.'

'Okay, I'm five seven and a size ten, so average figure, I guess. Blonde hair down to my shoulder blades. I've been thinking about getting it cut though.'

'Don't,' Bart said quickly. 'Not ever.' Seeing her hair was the only good memory he had now.

'I have blue eyes, which makes me sound more glamorous than I am. In reality they're a sort of muddy blue-grey. And my eyelashes are too thin so I have to wear tons of mascara otherwise I sort of fade into a pale mess in photographs.'

'I don't believe you,' he said, and that time he could hear the smile in his own voice. It sounded foreign.

'It's true. And one of my ears is slightly larger than the other. My brother always teased me about it. He called me Lopsy for years when we were little.'

'What's his name?' Bart asked.

'Nick. He's kind. I mean, he's a pain in the ass, right? But he used to hug me when I cried and if he was here now he'd beat the shit out of these bastards.' Skye laughed and sobbed in one go, sucking and spluttering air, thumping her forehead against the glass. They were both silent immediately, waiting for someone to come and investigate. No one did.

'Skye,' Bart said gently. 'Would you talk to me about Malcolm?'

A pause.

'What's the point?'

'I guess, because I want to figure out what we're doing here, what they might have in store for us. Don't you want to know?'

'No,' she said, her voice hard. 'It's nothing good. There's not going to be any happy ending. Figuring it out won't do any good. It'll just mean contemplating the worst before it even happens to us.'

'Are you telling me you're not doing that already?'

'I just want to forget it while we talk.' Her breath hitched.

Bart understood. He felt the same. Having a conversation was real and normal. Hearing about someone else's life – even someone locked in a room in the same corridor where you suspected your life might end quite soon – was better than being realistic about your own mortality. But he needed the reality check and that had to start with information.

'Let's make a deal,' Bart said. 'One question about all . . .' he motioned around him pointlessly '. . . all this.' He didn't want to put a name to it. If he did that, she would never open up about Malcolm. The only reason he even knew the other man's name was because Skye had called him Malcolm by mistake in their first conversation, and then gone on, briefly, haltingly, to explain why. The details had ended there. 'And then one of us tells the other something personal. From home.'

Skye sighed heavily. The sound – and the emotion – were like a curtain coming down. He started on a positive.

'I was in a play at the Fringe festival last year,' he told her. 'Not exactly a starring role. I was the back end of a hippo. It was a mock-up of a pantomime, and they thought a hippo would be funnier than the traditional cow.' A belly-laugh. That was great. Bart found himself grinning more than the audience had at the jokes in the show. 'So Malcolm – what can you tell me about him? Where he came from, how old he was?'

'He was twenty-two. He was from Glasgow originally but his parents moved to Edinburgh when he was twelve. He talked about skiing a lot. I think he was on some sort of team. He was here when I arrived.'

'Did you ever see him?'

'When he was being walked to the shower and back each morning. Then there was a day when a load of people went into his room, all dressed in medical scrubs and masks. They had a load of medical equipment and a video camera with them. Two days later they walked him out of his room. He smiled and waved as he walked past my window, but I think he knew . . .'

'What?' Bart asked.

'That he was never coming back.' Her voice broke on the last word, and Bart gave her time to recover from the memory.

'What did he look like, physically?'

'He was normal, you know, fit and healthy like you'd expect from a skier. He was a bit battered, but then he'd done the journey.' The journey. Skye had talked for a minute or so about ending up in the box then made it clear she never wanted to discuss it again. 'What's your favourite bar in Edinburgh? Mine's The Newsroom on Leith Street. They do this amazing burger with chilli con carne.'

She sounded a long way away.

'Is that the bar that has all the jars with lights in the front window?' he asked.

'It is. My friends took me there for my last birthday. My only regret is that I had too many cocktails and can't remember the last hour, but the next day my face was actually aching from laughing so much.'

'I like Dishoom,' Bart said.

'Amazing Indian food,' Skye joined in.

'I'm more a restaurant person than a bar person, not that I have the money for it very often.'

'You'd hate where I work then,' Skye said. 'It's a bar in a hotel on George Street. Most of the time it's fine but on a Friday and Saturday night it gets a bit out of hand. That and hen parties.'

'Really? I work in a restaurant. Skye, how much do you remember about when you were taken?'

'Do I have to?' she asked, her voice younger, reluctant. Bart wished he could put his arms around her.

'Could you try?'

'Fine,' she said. 'I was working. It was a really late shift because the bar doesn't close until the last guest goes to bed, and some film crew had been celebrating in there. They went through every type of vodka we had until two in the morning, then I closed up. The next thing I remember is waking up. I don't want to talk about that again.'

'That's okay, we don't have to. At the bar, before you left, did anyone buy you a drink? Either someone you knew, or a stranger?'

'No, we're not allowed to drink at work. We can take tips but not be bought anything. The management doesn't like the way that looks, even if it's just soft drinks. I always have a bottle of water around and sip it while I'm working. You get really dehydrated during an eight-hour shift, you know?'

'Is that something you did all the time?'

'Uh huh.'

'So anyone who'd come into the bar more than once might have seen where you put the water bottle back down?'

'I suppose,' she said.

'Was it accessible – the bottle – if you'd been busy serving people, or clearing tables? Could anyone have reached it?'

There was a long silence.

'Yes,' she said. 'Even from across the bar. I wasn't that careful. Shit. Oh shit. I work in a bar. I know what people do. Fuck it, this is all my own fault.'

'Skye, no. It's not. You could never have anticipated this. Not in a million years.'

She was crying.

'A woman I'd just started seeing bought me a drink after my shift and invited me back to her place. She left before me, said she was going to bring her car round. It's all fairly dim in my mind. I remember putting my jacket on, and I must have left on my own two feet or someone would have stopped me . . . then nothing.' Skye was quiet. 'What about Malcolm? Did he remember anything?'

'He was at the gym. That's all he told me. He'd seen plenty of people he knew there so he figured the police would be able to trace his movements. He was freaked out about losing his mobile as he wanted to have his signal traced.'

'You know, it's possible that Malcolm isn't dead. Maybe they were just moving him somewhere else.' Bart did his best to sound convincing and failed.

'For what purpose?' Skye replied.

'Maybe they just decided to let him go,' Bart offered.

'Or maybe not,' she replied. 'I'm tired. I'm going to try to sleep now.'

The inch-wide image of blonde hair disappeared from his view.

'Skye,' he called after her. The blonde mass filled the crack of window again. 'When we get back to Edinburgh I'm taking you to The Newsroom. We'll eat whatever we want and drink cocktails, and I'll make you laugh just like your friends did. That's a promise. First thing we'll do when we get home.'

'Sure,' she said. 'Right. Only I'm not even sure anyone's looking for me. I'd just split up with my boyfriend who was a total jerk, if I'm honest. I'd had a fall-out with my parents over him. I'd threatened to go off the grid and just travel for a year to teach them all a lesson. I'd even started looking up destinations on my laptop. If anyone checks it, the last thing they'll find is me researching flights. The worst thing is, the night I left, I had my passport in my bag. I was thinking about going into one of those high street flight centres and picking a cheap holiday to anywhere.' There was the sound of a fist hitting the wall. 'I'm screwed. We're screwed. We both know it.'

Bart thought about it.

'Your brother will know,' he said. 'Nick will know you'd have been in touch by now. He'll be wondering what happened to Lopsy, right?'

A hand appeared at the glass where the hair had been. Bart could just make out her thumb and forefinger.

'I hope so,' Skye said. 'God, I really, really hope so.'

Chapter Seventeen

Three clients stood at the door to the flat. One was a regular, although he'd never been sent to Elenuta. He had a thing for another of the women, and made sure he was always there before the late-night rush. The second Elenuta had never seen before. He was large, and his eyes were slightly turned out from one another. The effect was disconcerting. As the women arranged themselves in the corridor, little more than tins on a supermarket shelf, the third man stepped out from behind the other two. Elenuta recognised him immediately, even with his top on and the scar on his stomach hidden.

'Scalp, my man,' Finlay shouted from the doorway to Elenuta's bedroom. 'How're you doin'? I've been meaning to call.' He exited, fist extended, fingers to the floor, and stood waiting for the man he'd called Scalp to respond in kind. His knuckles remained unbumped.

'Were you meaning to?' Scalp asked. 'That's fine then, only I was worried you were avoiding me.'

'Avoiding you? You'd have to be my ex-missus for me to bother avoiding you.' Finlay tried to raise a laugh.

When none of the men at the door obliged, Elenuta took

a half step back. The other women looked on, some craning their necks forward to get a better view of the action. Scalp stayed where he was outside the flat. The other men who'd arrived with him remained at his side. The timing was no coincidence, Elenuta decided.

Scalp grinned. Finlay beamed back.

'I want my money back from the race,' Scalp said.

'I see.' Finlay rubbed his chin. He might as well have declared that a time out for thinking was needed. 'Let's talk about this in the kitchen, shall we? No need for my girls to be wasting time when they should be on the job. You two lads can go and get yourselves comfortable.'

'They're okay,' Scalp said. 'Pussy can always wait.'

'Right, well, my place my rules so, like I said, we'll go in the kitchen and the bitches can mind their own. Let's get a dram and find a way to sort this out.' Finlay moved along the corridor towards the kitchen, stopping when he realised Scalp wasn't following.

'The girls can stay where they are,' Scalp said. 'Like you said, your place, your rules, so we'll discuss this out here, neutral territory if you like.'

Elenuta kept her head low, watching Scalp from beneath her hair and her lashes. She knew better than to give him cause to notice her after what she'd seen of the race. He was wiry, his hair receding and thin on top. There were bags under his eyes that told a tale of insomnia, and his chin was weak. His eyes, though, were darts, and Elenuta wished he would just leave. Finlay was a bastard, but at least he was a predictable bastard.

'Sure, mate, sure,' Finlay said. 'But as far as the money for the race goes, you played fair and square. You knew what the price was . . .'

'The girl I caught did herself in. By rights she was mine to kill.'

'A girl died at your hand. That was the agreement,' Finlay said, his overly jolly voice a perversity relative to the subject matter. 'You had a knife, pal, let's not forget that it was you who broke the rules.'

The women around Elenuta took in a shocked breath all at once, like an outgoing wave over pebbles. They knew nothing of the race, certainly not the details, even if they'd heard rumours.

'Did I sign something?' Scalp asked quietly, matching Finlay's false grin with a quiet smile of his own. 'I must have missed that.'

'Come on, you've been to the race before. You knew the rules. You use your own hands, or anything you pick up there. You can slam their head into the wall, or shove their neck between two cupboard doors, but no weapons. If some twat decided to bring a gun, how would that be fair?'

'Two thousand, and I want it today,' Scalp announced, moving the conversation on as if he hadn't heard a word Finlay had said.

'Would you go fuck yerself? You didn't pay that much in the first place,' Finlay said, the talk of so much cash dissolving his facade instantly. 'There'll be no return of your money, Scalp, and I think you're forgetting who you're talking to.'

'Interest is due, Finlay. Enough time has passed, and you made enough on the door to return ten times that to me. I looked like a cunt in front of all those people. I'm owed something for my reputation.'

'That's a different thing, now,' Finlay said, rolling up his sleeves as if readying himself for a playground fight. His own men were at either end of the corridor, out of Scalp's line of sight, but Scalp had to have known they were there. Elenuta took a half step towards her bedroom. 'She saw it,' Finlay said, pointing in her direction. 'She saw the video. What do you think?' He reached out a hand, took Elenuta by the wrist and pulled her into the space between Scalp and himself. 'Do you think Mr

147

Scalp there was made to look like a twat because of something I did, or do you think he managed that all by himself?'

Elenuta looked from the men hovering just outside the flat door, to Finlay and his men who were now approaching slowly and quietly.

'I not understand,' she muttered with emergency diplomacy. The lie was hidden effectively beneath her genuine sense of panic. Standing between two rabid pit bulls had that effect.

'The thing is, Finlay, there's an awful lot of your punters that owe me. Money, favours, secrets, you name it. Your cash-flow's going to take a hit if you can't maintain your reputation here-abouts. If I spread the word, for instance, that no one was to go to your next race, sure you'd get a few idiots turning up, but generally speaking you'd struggle to break even. Then there would be the knock-on effect with your flats and your women. And there are alternatives, you know. Other pimps offering more exotic flavours than these, if you know what I mean. Or I could tip the wink in your direction. Put your competi-tors out of business. But only if you did the decent thing and refunded me for my disappointing experience.'

Finlay hesitated. He looked up the corridor to his second in command who shrugged his shoulders.

'All right then,' Finlay groaned. 'But I want your word that you'll send people our way. My girls give as good a servicing as any they'll get in Edinburgh. I test them all personally.' The woman nearest him shrank back into the wall as he reached for her. 'And I keep them good and scared so we don't get any shit from them. They do whatever anyone wants.'

'Really? I heard one of them escaped recently. Something about a dead body stinking up the road.'

'Aye, well, that bitch has been taught a lesson she won't forget. Stay there, I'll get you your money.'

Finlay scowled as he walked past Elenuta to his tiny office

in the boxroom at the end. He motioned to his men as he unlocked it and they stood, hands in their pockets, the unsubtle bulk of guns deliberately visible.

It took Finlay a while to emerge clutching a thick handful of twenties and fifties. He looked pained, but the tension of the previous minutes had passed. Elenuta gave the other women a half smile. *It'll be all right now*, her expression said.

'Shift yourself,' Scalp told her. 'Let me shake your boss's hand. A deal's a deal. Starting now, I'm going to be telling absolutely everyone that this is the only place to come for whoring.'

Finlay held out the cash in his left hand, and extended his right to seal the deal. Scalp took the cash, stuffed it in his jacket pocket and took Finlay by the hand, pulling him sharply forward. The man to his right squatted, grabbing Finlay's ankles and lifting them. Stepping aside, Scalp shoved Finlay towards the railings. His body went up and over, headfirst. There was a cracking noise, as if a giant nut had been forced open, and at the same time a dull thump. One of the women screamed, and another slapped a more experienced hand over her mouth. Finlay's men ran forward, stopping just short of taking action. It was pretty clear that whatever they did was going to be too late.

Scalp stepped into the corridor through the open doorway.

'Right, gentlemen, we're open for business as usual. You two,' he looked at Finlay's men. 'You can keep your jobs if you can also keep your mouths shut. You might even get a pay rise. Down you go and fetch your former employer. Gloves on, wrap him in clean plastic sheeting – there's some in the boot of my car – and we'll get rid of him tonight. Open up his office, too. Now we know he keeps his stash here, we'll be able to figure out a little bonus for you all.'

Elenuta kept her eyes on the carpet.

'And ladies, I have a gift for each of you. We'll be visiting

Finlay's other flats after this to distribute these more widely but you get to model them first, so be appreciative.' He motioned to one of his men who opened up a backpack he'd had at his feet, pulling out several plastic neck collars each with a small plastic box attached. 'These little beauties will help you remember your boundaries. We'll be running a length of wire around the apartment. Try to leave when the current's on and you'll get a nasty electric shock, probably a burn, and we'll know exactly what you're up to as it's been modified by a pal of mine to set off an alarm.'

'Like for dogs,' one of the women said.

Scalp grinned.

'Exactly, only I have a dog and there's no way I'd put one of these fucking things on him, but then he's irreplaceable to me.' He walked up to the woman and shoved a hand between her legs. 'You lot are just walking, money-making pussies, and as I understand it there's a fresh supply coming in every month through the docks. Finlay had a great set-up here, but no idea of how to scale it up. So consider this a hostile fucking take-over. There'll be more of you in each flat soon, so expect to make room. Client hours will be twenty-four hours a day. Sleep when you can, and keep yourselves clean. I don't want any complaints.'

Elenuta stared at the railings that seemed to have swallowed Finlay. It had been inconceivable an hour ago to think that she might ever miss him, but now . . . The woman next to her handed a collar along the line. She ran her fingers over its rubbery length and wondered just how bad the pain would be if she crossed the wire.

'How much electric?' she asked. She hadn't meant to. Her strategy had been to stay quiet and keep off Scalp's radar. Her mouth had opened without her permission.

'Do you want to be the first to find out?' Scalp asked. She

shook her head. 'Sensible as well as pretty. We like that. Sensible means you can be trained. Let me put it like this. There are different settings. The lowest will hurt a bit like a bee sting. The top setting will put you on the floor where you'll piss yourself and wonder why you can't control your limbs, as you try to figure out what that nasty burning smell is. Let's see, now. Who's expendable?'

He looked up and down the row of women before selecting the oldest among them. She had a noticeable slouch, which was understandable given the life she was living. Finlay's men called her the hag. Elenuta opened her mouth to protest before the woman next to her dug her sharply in the ribs.

'Shut up, or it'll be all of us,' the woman hissed.

Scalp fitted the collar around his chosen example's neck, then picked up another unit, fiddling with the settings. Elenuta knew better than to look away. He pressed a button. There was a split-second delay, then a yelp like an animal who'd been kicked with a steel-tipped boot. Scalp smiled and turned a dial. The next time he pressed the button, the yelp was a scream. Elenuta imagined what he'd look like after he'd been hit by a car twenty or maybe thirty times. The image made her feel marginally better.

'So, does anyone want to join their former boss on the floor down there,' he pointed a thumb over his shoulder to the ground floor of the flats, 'or shall we agree that this is the start of something very special and that you're all going to do everything I ask without complaint?'

Silent nods all round.

Elenuta looked down at her hands. With no Finlay there, her hands were free from the threat of amputation, even if the rest of her existence had just become even more perilous.

Chapter Eighteen

Ava's car greeted the hospital lamppost with a squeal that was her paintwork crying out in pain as it left the metal. She cursed, stopped, and got out to stare at the damage. It was six thirty in the morning. She'd set her alarm to make sure she was back at Natasha's bedside before her friend woke up. Hospital visiting hours were irrelevant. She would flash her badge to get in, then explain who she was and that she'd be on duty during the official visiting period. God help the person who tried to deny her entry to the ward. It had been ten o'clock by the time she'd got home last night, and by then she wasn't hungry. Aware that she ought to eat – the exact date and time of her last hot meal not readily coming to mind – she'd grabbed a piece of toast, cutting the slightly mouldy crusts from the edge, and smearing it with the last of the butter. At some point, she'd have to remember to go shopping.

No one stopped her as she walked onto the ward, and as pleased as she was about that, the lack of security was equally maddening. Everything made her angry at the moment. That was the truth. It wasn't going to get any better until she could hold her friend in her arms knowing that not one single cell of her was being invaded by a malicious bloody biological army. She paused at Natasha's door to take a breath. Tasha needed her positive and calm. Not over the top, but not morose. She opened the door.

A figure sat at the bedside. Ava breathed in sharply. Luc was staring out of the window at the rows of street lighting, holding Natasha's hand as she slept silently. Tears threatened and Ava bit her bottom lip as he turned his head to look at her.

'I wasn't expecting you this early,' he said.

'I wasn't expecting you at all,' she replied.

'Flying visit. I caught the nine p.m. flight out of Charles de Gaulle airport and got here at eleven. She woke up a couple of times in the night and the nurse gave her more pain relief, but the dressing hasn't needed changing. I'd stand up but I don't want to disturb her.' He nodded at his hand and Ava realised that Natasha's fingers were intertwined with his.

'She must have been pleased to see you,' Ava whispered, pulling up another chair and sitting the opposite side of the bed.

'Actually she gave me a bollocking for overreacting. Then she cried for a couple of minutes, so I countered with a bottle of champagne that we'll save for when she's through treatment, and she forgave me.'

'Of course she forgave you. You're the only man she's ever really loved.'

'There's no girlfriend on the scene at the moment?'

'No, she's single. I think that's just as well. Natasha needs to focus on herself, and I'm here to take care of her.'

'You two are useless at keeping your voices down. How the hell did either of you forge successful careers in policing? You'll have woken half the hospital by now.'

'Hey beautiful,' Ava said, standing up and brushing the hair from Natasha's face to kiss her forehead. 'I found some random bloke at your bedside. They'll let anyone in here these days.'

'I know. I'm thinking about going straight. He held my hand all night. I've never been with a woman who did that.' She tried to sit up, winced and gave in.

'Do you need a nurse?' Ava stood up.

'Sit down, and stop panicking,' Natasha told her. 'They cut a bit of me out. It's going to hurt. Luc, when are you coming home? Ava's driving me crazy.' She smiled.

'I'm not sure yet. In fact, I have to get back to the airport already. My flight leaves in a couple of hours. Can you two agree to play nicely until I'm back to referee again?'

'Can you tell her to be less bossy?' Natasha asked. 'Ava, drive the man to the airport, would you? I promise I'll survive the day without you. If you're good, I'll let you give me a really long lecture when you come back this evening.'

'There's no need,' Callanach said. 'A taxi will be quicker, and that way Ava can stay here until it's time for her to go to work.'

'No, Ava's taking you. That's an order and you do not want to mess with me at the moment.'

He picked up the hand he was still holding and kissed Natasha's fingers.

'If you need me, I can be here within a few hours. Any time.'

'If this were a romantic movie, every single viewer would be in tears right now,' Natasha said. 'But as it's not I feel entitled to tell you to get your perfectly shaped, unfortunately male butt out of my hospital room and get back to France.'

'I love you,' Callanach told her.

'I love you too.' She sighed and closed her eyes. 'Idiot.'

Callanach laughed, kissed her cheek, and left to wait for Ava in the corridor.

'I won't be long,' Ava told her, doing her coat up again.

'You know I wasn't calling him an idiot, don't you?'

'Are you really going to start this now?' Ava asked, sitting gently on the side of the bed. Her friend looked fragile against the backdrop of white sheets and grey walls.

'Drive him to the airport. Walk in with him. Buy him a coffee. Then talk to him, Ava. Really talk to him. He deserves that much, at least.'

'It's too complicated, Tasha. And it's not the right time, especially with you . . .'

'Don't you dare. You're my rock, Ava. You're always there for me and I know how much this is hurting you, but if you use what I'm going through as an excuse to hide behind, I'll never forgive you. You and Luc are adults, even if you're getting pretty good at disguising that fact in your private lives. He's in love with you. Maybe he fucked up big time. Maybe you've done that a couple of times, too. Just make a choice, even if that's only between being a coward and being brave.'

'Are you done?'

'I am, but I'd like a cup of tea. Could you find the nurse before you go and ask her if she'd mind?' Natasha smiled. 'Please?'

'After that lecture I've got a bloody good mind to say no.' Ava stood up. 'But as you said please.' She walked to the door. 'The thing is, I think the time for Luc and me has passed. I'm pretty sure I've screwed it — whatever it might have been — up.'

'And I'm pretty sure you're in charge of your own destiny,' Natasha said. 'If you want him, tell him. It's that simple. Were you off to organise that tea now?'

Ava conceded defeat and went to find the nurse.

Callanach took a knee to inspect the damage to Ava's car.

'The lamppost won,' he said. 'It's safe to drive though.'

'Thanks for that. Do you want a lift or not?'

'Are you sure you want to take me? Natasha will never know.

You can go and get breakfast and just come back later. I promise I won't tell.'

Callanach stood, hands in pockets, his dark brown eyes shining in the lamplight. It began to rain, droplets catching in his hair and running down his cheeks. He didn't move. Ava felt a rush of regret streak through her with all the fury of lightning.

'Is there time for us to have breakfast together?' she asked.

He smiled slowly, gently, the way she always pictured him when she was too tired to distract herself from the truth, late at night.

He walked around the car to the driver's side where she stood, his jaw clenching and releasing as he drew nearer. Ava realised she was holding her breath. He opened her door and stepped back to let her in.

'Thank you,' she said.

Half an hour later they were sitting at a table inside Edinburgh airport, clutching steaming cups of coffee.

'Thank you for coming,' Ava said quietly. 'It would have meant so much to Tasha, waking up and seeing you there.'

'Of course I came. What did you expect?'

'I didn't really think about it. You're in the middle of a case and it's not cheap to get a flight at the last minute.' She added unwanted milk to her coffee for something to do with her fingers.

'Why didn't you phone me as soon as you found out?' he asked.

She frowned briefly, then shook her head. 'I don't know. I suppose I figured there was nothing you could do, and I didn't want you feeling that you needed to make some grand gesture, like . . . well, like this.'

'It's not a gesture, and it was as much for my sake as for Natasha's if I'm honest. Are you sure you weren't more worried that you'd have to see me if I came back, because you can tell me. I know things aren't great between us after everything that happened.'

Ava took a sip of her coffee, realised she'd ruined it and pushed it away. He was right, of course. As was Natasha. Apparently everyone but her had a pretty good understanding of just how much she was deluding herself and messing everything up. She and Luc had been on the verge of starting a relationship that had been in chrysalis form for a couple of years. Then there'd been a night she didn't like to remember. She and Luc had become intimate, physically and emotionally, and at a make-or-break point she'd found an item he'd taken from her. Stolen, she corrected herself. He had removed it from her house without her knowledge or consent while she was being held hostage by a psychopath, and secreted it away as some bizarre trophy. He'd done his best to explain it but by then the damage had been done, and Ava had decided that whatever future they might have had was dead in the water. It meant she wasn't going to get hurt longer term and that was good. Better speedy disappointment than a broken heart that might take years to mend. Only now she'd slept with someone else to try and get Luc out of her head, and she hated herself for it. She'd sent Luc away when what she'd really needed to do was face her own fears. Detective chief inspector by day, hormonal teenager by night. It was time to grow up and take a risk. Natasha was right.

'Luc, I'm sorry,' she said. 'We should have had this conversation a long time ago, but I was so . . .'

'Don't,' he said, putting a warm hand over both of hers. 'You don't have to. Sending me back to France as Interpol liaison was the right thing to have done. I've faced my demons there and I've had time to get what happened between us in perspective. It wasn't easy, but I think you did the right thing for us both. I'd missed France at a much deeper level than I was admitting. We should never have let ourselves get carried away. There's the difference in rank to consider, we'd have had to lie to everyone on the squad, and sooner or later it would have caused problems. I wish things had happened almost any other way than they did, but now we can be friends like we were before. I'm hoping you can forgive me and that we can start again? I hadn't realised how much your friendship meant to me until I lost it. I'm sorry for taking you for granted.'

Ava constructed the mask of a smile on her face. Friends, he'd missed France, sooner or later it would have caused problems, difference in rank. Friendship. She felt the single sip of coffee she'd taken rise, sour, in her throat.

'That's exactly what I was going to say,' she said. The words came out high-pitched and strangled. 'It was all just a misunderstanding. I overreacted.'

'No, you didn't, but maybe it all happened for a reason.'

'Yeah, I think you're right. And Natasha will be so glad we've sorted all this out.' She uncovered a bare wrist. 'God, I'm not wearing my watch. It's probably time I got going anyway. Um, so email me an update about Malcolm Reilly as soon as, yeah?'

'I will,' he said, getting to his feet. 'We've got some leads to follow up when I touch down later this morning.'

'You haven't slept,' she said, sticking her hands into her jacket pockets and making fists.

'That's what the plane journey's for,' he said. 'No news on your other missing person?'

'Nothing yet, and three more dead bodies. I'm off to see the forensic anthropologist now. It's a joint meeting with the deputy pathologist. Never rains but it pours, right?' Callanach tilted his head to one side. 'That probably doesn't translate very well. Have a good flight. Tripp will call you soon to talk about Bart Campbell. He's running a reconstruction of the night he went missing, which includes getting all the people in the restaurant back together again.'

She fumbled reaching forward to kiss his cheek, bashing her nose into his ear.

'You okay?' he asked, holding her shoulder.

'God, yes, fine. Just in a hurry. Take it easy. So glad we're good.'

'Yes, ma'am,' Callanach said, picking up his bag. 'I'll call Natasha every day, but let me know if there's any news she's not telling me, will you?'

'Of course,' Ava said. 'Let's chat soon.'

She turned and headed for the exit. *Let's chat soon?* she repeated in her head. Nice retreat into corporate speak. She stopped at her car, dropping her forehead onto its roof. He was fine. That was good. All the tension and agonising over what had or still might happen between them was gone. Life was simple again. Callanach was over her. The raindrops on her face were the camouflage she needed to pretend she didn't care.

Chapter Nineteen

By the time she arrived at Edinburgh City Mortuary, Ava was soaked to the skin. Having a raincoat in her car was second nature, but worry for Natasha had resulted in sleeplessness that was taking a toll on her normal routines. She'd found her car keys in the fridge the previous day, and her last load of washing had sat wet in the machine for forty-eight hours before she'd remembered to take it out. Now, no raincoat. They were small things, but Ava knew her brain was elsewhere.

A slight figure sat completely still in the postmortem suite that Ava was directed to, hands in her lap, staring at a computer screen, head to one side as if she were contemplating a sunset rather than images of a skull. Ava had met her once before at a forensics conference. Dr Liena Chen was one of the most admired forensic anthropologists in Europe. The deputy pathologist hustled in behind Ava, shutting the door noisily behind them.

'Morning,' he said. 'Do you two know each other?'

Dr Chen stood up and extended a small hand that was cool in Ava's still damp fingers.

'DCI Turner,' she said softly. 'Pleased to meet you again. Shall we sit?'

They convened around a table with the computer screen central to them. The two skull sections from the pig farm sat in covered trays to one side.

'Time has been limited, so these are preliminary findings,' Dr Chen explained, handing out copies of a report that was several pages long. If that was preliminary, Ava thought, Liena Chen was thorough to the point of obsessive. Exactly what was needed. 'These skull sections are both current, meaning they're from recently living humans. This isn't an accidental unearthing of historic bodies or a cold case. They're both from females. Male skulls tend to be heavier, and while we did not have the full skull, we performed a pro-rata weight comparison. The bone is thinner than we usually find in male skulls, and there are positional and scale differences in the eyes and forehead.'

'We've been able to confirm that,' the deputy pathologist added. 'The pigs weren't able to get all the way inside the skull bones to completely clean out all the tissue. Even though it wasn't visible at first sight, there were sufficient cells left for DNA testing. Both were definitely female, as is the trachea. No matches have come up on the police database though.'

'Can we tell if the deceased are related?' Ava asked him.

'They're not,' he confirmed.

'Rough ages and cause of death?'

'The first skull belonged to a woman I would estimate as being in her mid-thirties. The second, which is the less complete skull section, is between late teenage and early twenties. The more intact of the two had no skull injury at all. The less complete skull belonging to the younger woman had one completely healed fracture, which I would say is historical, maybe from ten years earlier, but also a recent blunt force trauma which left an indent and a small fracture.' Dr Chen picked up one of the skulls from a tray and indicated an area at the rear. 'It's not a complete injury area as the pigs had started to consume this part of the skull, so I am unable to give precise parameters for the damage. It's possible that this injury was the cause of death, but far from definite.'

'And the trachea?' Ava turned to the pathologist.

'There's a substantial crushing injury,' he said. 'Almost certainly the cause of death, unless there were any other incidents occurring at the same time. Part of the trachea was almost flattened.'

'Could that have happened postmortem, maybe trampling from the pigs?' Ava asked.

'No, this was very localised, specific pressure and damage in a small area, as if two thumbs had been pressed into the front of the trachea. Classic strangulation marks, and the internal bruising wouldn't have shown if the injury had been postmortem,' he explained. 'We can't be precise about age but the trachea is adult in scale, with little wear or fatty deposits. We're assuming young female.'

'It doesn't make sense,' Ava said. 'If strangulation was the cause of death and the perpetrator was sufficiently careful about disposing of the body, it seems an awfully lucky coincidence that it was the trachea alone that survived.'

'Actually there might be an explanation,' Dr Chen said. 'If the trachea was the most damaged part of the body, the pigs might have been attracted to that area first, from the smell. In the rush and the fight, it makes sense that it got pushed under the fence in the melee alongside the partially consumed clavicle. We got no DNA from that but indications are that it, too, was from a recently deceased female.'

'Did all these women die at the same time?' Ava asked.

'Impossible to say precisely,' the pathologist said. Dr Chen nodded her agreement. 'The few soft tissue cells left inside the skulls weren't sufficient for us to be clear about that. The trachea, though, showed no signs of long-term degradation, so we believe that was a relatively recent death, by which I mean the death had taken place no more than a week prior to the body part being found.'

'So I have three dead women, different ages, not related, with potentially different causes of death, and none of them has an identifiable DNA match. You'd think if three women had gone off the grid at the same time, we'd have enough families complaining to the police that this would make sense.'

'I would assume death at the same time, body disposal at the same time,' Dr Chen said. 'The skulls were similarly dirty and at sufficiently close stages of being consumed. The pigs did their work well but they'd have needed another twenty-four hours to have worked through the last parts of the skulls.'

'Do we have any teeth yet?' Ava asked.

'Some, but not all,' the pathologist said. 'A couple of them have fillings, others have specific damage and wear. As soon as you have any idea of the victims' identities, if they have up-to-date dental records, we'll have a shot at confirming who they are.'

'So I just need to figure out what links them,' Ava said.

'Pain,' Dr Chen said, staring into the empty eye sockets of the most complete skull. 'The woman who had two skull injuries – that's unusual. Very few people experience two skull fractures in their lifetime. Those who do are either unlucky in the extreme or they're living in circumstances where the statistical possibility of this type of skull fracture happening is markedly raised.'

'Abusive relationships, drugs or prostitution then,' Ava said.

'Exactly,' the pathologist said. 'These women were regarded as disposable. The strangulation victim is the best example. I read an article recently that equated strangulation with water-boarding in terms of how torturous it is. It can be slow, drawn-out, stopped and started again, and it's intimate. The murderer wanted to feel powerful, to be up close and personal with their victim. People who strangle want to look into their victim's eyes while they do it. It's rarely defensive.'

'Which raises the question,' Ava mused. 'Are we looking for a single killer, or for several?'

Chapter Twenty

Callanach checked his stab-proof vest and made sure his gun had its safety engaged. He was less concerned about shooting himself accidentally than he was about the prospect of someone grabbing the gun from its holster. Saint-Denis wasn't the no-go zone in Paris that the international press had made it out to be, but the police weren't welcome there. Layers of mistrust had built up on both sides. Saint-Denis had been labelled as troubled courtesy of its high immigrant population, but that ignored the many peaceable hard-working people who lived there, and punished the many for harbouring the very few. Over time, an animosity had grown from the reputation, rendering the streets occasionally unsafe for no other reason than a lack of mutual respect and understanding.

Two undercover police officers, one male, one female, stood in a doorway waiting for Jean-Paul and Callanach to appear from their unmarked police van. Both had been in close contact with Paris' subcultures for years. Neither stepped forward out of the shadows to greet them. The woman had a scarf covering most of her face, and the man had his hood up. Callanach and Jean-Paul were dressed in tatty jeans and bulky jackets, their own hoods shielding their faces from recognition.

'She's Lebanese, Joseph's Nigerian,' Jean-Paul whispered. 'They'll get us where we need to go and translate, but any trouble and we're on our own waiting for backup. They're both too valuable to the intelligence services to be compromised.'

'Understood,' Callanach confirmed, as a door opened behind them and they wandered into a dark alleyway. A false roof had been constructed of tarpaulins, plates of corrugated iron and wooden planks strung on ropes from the windows above. Here and there buckets collected the invading rain water. It was light enough to make out where you were walking, but dim enough for privacy, and no helicopter or drone could see within. The overlooking windows offered no view. Callanach understood the desire for privacy. Paris' migrant communities had been marginalised courtesy of the terrorist few, and were largely misunderstood and harshly judged. As a result, relations with the authorities were poor and no one side was entirely to blame.

Doorways into the buildings at either side remained open, and from within the scents of incense and marijuana, coffee, mulled liquor, and every spice conceivable wafted out. Shouts came from distant rooms. Those sitting in the makeshift corridor whispered their conversations, growing silent and watchful as the team passed, heads down. Rounding a corner, they moved inside a building and into a large hallway. The heat produced by the multitude of bodies was stifling.

They stuck close together, the undercover police flanking them front and back. The largest group surrounded a raucous cock-fight in one corner. Vendors called out, offering meat from sources best left unexplored, and trays of tiny packets containing different-coloured tablets adorned several tables, all well protected by men unconcerned about showing their guns.

The Lebanese officer tugged Callanach's sleeve, pulling him

to one side and out through another doorway then up some decrepit steps that had no right still to be standing, Jean-Paul and Joseph following closely. Curious eyes watched them leave. Callanach forced himself not to turn back. Any sign of concern would only be met with even greater interest. At the top of the stairs they climbed in through an open window. A crimson-lit corridor ran in each direction. They took the left into an eerie quiet compared to the market hall below. A girl sobbed in one room as they passed. A thumping behind the next door conjured images of a man hitting the internal wall. The next door opened abruptly. A man stared out at them, bared his teeth and slammed the door again.

'Here?' Jean-Paul asked, as they paused outside another door.

'Through this door, then another,' the Lebanese officer said in French. 'I'll wait here. Joseph will go with you. Keep your hands on your guns and don't trust her.'

She turned her back as they went inside, sliding her right hand into her jacket pocket. Callanach saw the undertow of fear beneath the studied calm on her face. Inside the second room three men were laid out on the floor, a syringe hanging from one banded arm. Jean-Paul and Callanach covered their noses and mouths and stepped quietly to a smaller door with peeling grey-green paint. Beyond that, they were met with a series of sheets hung like veils for three or four metres from ceiling to floor, the glow of golden light reaching through to guide them onwards. Joseph put a finger over his lips. They kept their footsteps soft. As they lifted the final sheet, a square, low-ceilinged room opened up and a woman spun around, a lime dripping, freshly cut in her right hand, a serrated knife glinting in her left.

'What do you want?' Madame Lebel demanded, pointing the knife in Joseph's direction. Her French was fluent, the accent obscured by her native Somalian tongue.

'Information,' Joseph replied, peeling a wad of sweaty euros out from where they'd been tucked inside his shirt.

'Dirty money,' the woman hissed. 'You come here with two white men, no appointment, pushing your filth at me. I know what you are.'

She jabbed the knife into a wooden cutting board, throwing the lime onto the floor at Joseph's feet. He edged backwards.

'Take the money,' Joseph said quietly. 'Listen to their questions. If you help us, we'll leave you alone.'

The woman reached out her hand, slid her fingers into a fridge door and pulled it open. Callanach released the safety trigger from his gun. From the upper shelf of the fridge door, she pulled a chunk of pink meat, wrapped in thin wire. Holding it in front of her face, she untwisted a metal screw from the meat, running her tongue along the metal before spitting it towards Jean-Paul.

'You want me to tell you the things I know?' she laughed. 'If I told you everything I've seen you would fall down dead right there.'

Callanach frowned at the theatrics. They were costing them time, and this room had only one way in and one way out. No windows, no escape route. He'd been briefed on the woman's history in the car. There was nothing to be gained by cajoling.

'You perform operations on young girls at their parents' request,' he said. 'You were prosecuted once before, but the child's mother told the court it was another woman who'd performed the circumcision. She protected you because she was scared of you.'

The woman grinned, showing sharp teeth. Callanach realised they'd been filed. The effect was chilling. It was hard to imagine a better way to ensure the silence of her clients. Her mouth was a brilliantly constructed nightmare. The rings on her fingers weren't fake, though. Stuck in a stinking inner-city hell, she was earning serious money.

'Are you scared of me?' she asked him.

'No,' Callanach said. 'The ox tongue in your hand is just protein. The screw you took out of it is just hardware. There are no spells. You convince people that there are, but you don't believe any of it.'

'I'm a healer. I don't perform operations. It's all lies.' She ran a hand over her shaved hair, showing long nails painted bright white. The file had said she was forty-nine but she looked younger. Most people in Saint-Denis looked older than their years. She was thriving.

'Either way, you're selling a service,' Callanach said. 'So take our money. It's as good as anyone else's.'

Joseph passed her half the bundle of notes. She walked to him, counting each note out slowly, taking her time. Callanach kept half an eye on her as he flicked his gaze across their surroundings. A thin mattress on the floor was home to stains he couldn't bear to think about. A knife set laid out in a leather case sparkled in the candlelight. Bottles, jars, sprigs of leaves and feathers adorned endless shelves. If it weren't for the stench of old bodily fluids that hung in the air, it could have been a film set. Of course, for all intents and purposes, that was what it was. Just an illusion.

'Someone is selling human organs in Paris,' he said. 'We want to know who, why, and how we can find them.'

'There's certainly a market for it,' she said, rolling the money into a ball and secreting it smoothly into her sleeve. 'But human organs are hard to get hold of unless you live in a war zone.'

'Who would want them?' Jean-Paul asked.

'A chef?' She licked her lips.

'Stop it,' Callanach told her. 'You're peddling myths and hoodoo here. What use are human organs put to if they're not transplanted?'

'You're thinking witchcraft,' she grinned. 'What makes you think I know anything about that?'

'Are they used in curses?' Callanach asked. 'Or for sacrifices?'

'Why is your imagination so dark? You came here assuming that everything I do is evil and for profit. I help people. Perhaps whoever is selling these organs is trying to help people, too.'

'This is helping people?' Jean-Paul asked, his eyes fixed on the bloody mattress. 'Does anyone who comes in here survive?'

'Don't judge me. You think a fourteen-year-old girl from a strict Muslim family who finds herself pregnant can get an abortion without her parents signing the forms? Do you know what her father would do if he found out? I save lives.'

'Female genital mutilation doesn't save lives,' Joseph said.

'My knives are clean and I cut away as little as possible. My stitches are small. Ask the women whose grandmothers were given the task with kitchen knives if they'd rather their parents had come to me. Hypothetically speaking.'

'Better it didn't happen at all,' Jean-Paul said.

'It's not my job to change minds,' she said. 'Perhaps if you did your jobs better . . .'

'Have you heard of anyone offering organs for sale recently?' Callanach asked.

'Rumours,' she said. 'But I don't help the police. In case you hadn't noticed, you tried to have me locked up.'

'We have information about your daughter,' Jean-Paul said.

Callanach stared at him. That nugget hadn't been shared in the car. There was a long pause.

'My daughter is fine. She lives in the next block. You people will say anything.'

'Not that one,' Jean-Paul continued. 'You have another daughter, Elise, who disappeared. Only she turned up in Syria married to an ISIS commander. You've been trying to make contact with her for the last year. Did you really think intelligence services wouldn't pick it up?'

Madame Lebel dropped down onto an ancient couch.

'Tell me,' she said.

'Information first.' Callanach folded his arms. 'What do the rumours say?'

'That using the organs, you can be healed of literally anything. They offer a consultation and treatment. It's expensive, and clever. All a scam, of course.'

'Do you have a name?' Jean-Paul asked.

'Where's my daughter?'

'Still in Syria. She's alive but has had to move around a lot with ISIS territory losses. She's on her second husband. Her first was killed in a drone strike.'

Madame Lebel wrapped her arms around herself and rocked backward and forwards.

'I told her this would happen.'

'What do you know about the person behind this?' Callanach asked.

'Nothing factual. Someone said it's a woman, but it always is when it's medical and there's an element of mystery involved. Walk onto any city street and say the word "doctor" to a crowd and most will still immediately assume you're talking about a man. Say "black magic" and everyone thinks witches and broomsticks. Some of the very sick people who come to me for help have heard about these amazing cures. They don't want to believe it's all lies. It should be stopped. It damages all our reputations.'

Callanach bit back his desire to tell her what he thought of the services she offered and the lives they ruined. No amount of cultural differences could justify the mutilation of girls too young to defend themselves or make their own choices.

'How do people get in touch with her?' he asked.

'You don't. You make your condition – your needs – known to the right people and she contacts you. Will my daughter be allowed to return to France? Will she be arrested?'

'I don't know,' Jean-Paul told her. 'If it appears that she went willingly, if she conspired with a terrorist group, then it's possible she'll be refused re-entry into the country, or prosecuted if she does return. Technically she can't be left stateless, but she would have to agree to go into a deradicalisation programme at the very least.'

'Has she been hurt? Did they treat her well? I've heard nothing. Others have told me she's not allowed to communicate with anyone outside.' There were tears now. Callanach steeled himself against them. Madame Lebel was profiting from others' barbaric beliefs. She had no moral compass. It was easy to see how her daughter was repeating those mistakes.

'Our information is that she's had a child. You're a grandmother,' Jean-Paul said quietly. 'I have a photograph, but you need to put us in contact with the right people.'

'If anyone thinks I helped the police, my throat will be slit while I sleep.'

'So be careful,' Callanach said.

'Fuck you,' she offered in response.

'We have to get out of here,' Joseph said.

Jean-Paul took a photo from his pocket, keeping its blank face to Madame Lebel. She fixed her eyes on it.

'There's a clinic on Villa Curial. It's a support centre for people suffering from life-threatening illnesses. They offer counselling, non-medical therapies, assistance with getting benefits or dealing with employers, that sort of thing. Whoever is offering these so-called treatments has contacts inside that clinic and others. They figure out who might be a good client and make an offer. That's all I know. Now give me the photograph and the rest of the money.'

Raised voices from the room they'd walked through stopped them in their tracks.

'Here,' Jean-Paul said, handing the photo over. Callanach caught a glimpse of a young woman photographed from some distance above. It was blurred but her face was showing, and there was a baby in her lap where she sat in a tiny back yard, barbed wire marking out the boundary of the property. It was impossible to say if the wire was to keep the woman in or to keep others out. Most likely both, he decided. Madame Lebel gave a small cry and sat cradling the photo. 'Keep quiet about who we are and what we asked you, and I'll arrange to get you further updates about your daughter. Agreed?'

'Yes,' Madame Lebel said. 'Thank you. Yes.'

The door crashed open. The Lebanese police officer had her weapon drawn and pointed at the three previously sleeping men, now very much awake, knives drawn. Joseph reacted first, not hesitating to draw his own gun, stepping forward and barking orders in a language Callanach didn't understand. The effect was immediate. The men dropped back a few paces, allowing Jean-Paul and Callanach the space to get out of the veiled corridor.

'Go,' Joseph ordered.

They filed out into the main corridor, following Joseph.

'Not the way we came,' he said. 'It's not safe now. Someone will have phoned down to say we were here.'

'What happened?' Jean-Paul asked.

'White men seen going into Madame Lebel's rooms,' Joseph said as he rounded a corner, checking first that no one was waiting for them. 'The range of services she offers tends to be for minorities around here. The assumption is that you're police. Down this staircase, quickly,' he motioned them forwards.

'Shall I call for backup?' Jean-Paul asked.

'Only if you want to kick off a major incident. As soon as

they hear sirens, each door will be locked and there'll be a weapon in every hand. Let's get to a lower floor and try a window.'

Footsteps behind them were approaching fast. They opened the nearest door and slammed it behind them. There was no key. Joseph held it shut, bracing his feet against the bottom as he leaned back, holding the doorknob tight. Peeling back the paper over the windows that had been improvised as curtains in what seemed to be an abandoned storeroom, they looked down to the ground. They were fifteen feet above ground level overlooking a rear passageway that led out into the street.

The door rattled. Joseph gripped the doorknob more firmly as Jean-Paul tried to open the window. In spite of its rotting frame, it wouldn't budge. Callanach kicked a pile of boxes aside, finding nothing but mildew and a dead rat.

'Hurry,' Joseph said. There were shouts beyond the door now, more people approaching.

Callanach took out his gun, re-engaged the safety, and aimed the butt of it centrally in the window, covering his face. The third blow smashed the pane. He ran to the door, grabbing the handle from Joseph, Jean-Paul standing back to provide cover.

'You two jump first,' Callanach told the undercover officers. 'And just disappear. You don't want to get caught with us. Make sure control knows our position and is ready to pick us up.'

They didn't argue, clearing the remaining glass with the cardboard and jumping immediately. Jean-Paul waited until they were both down and out of sight, sitting on the window ledge with his feet hanging out.

'I'll cover you,' he said. 'When you're ready, run for the window and just jump. I'll be right behind you.'

The door was beginning to splinter from the kicks beyond. The fact that no one had tried to shoot through the wood yet was a good sign but, even if Callanach and Jean-Paul were the only ones with firearms, there were enough bodies out in the corridor to pose a serious threat. Callanach took a deep breath and positioned himself to run.

It was only four strides from the door to the window but by then the door was wide open and men were rushing in. There was a gunshot as Callanach grabbed the ledge to vault out, then he hit cool air and sunlight, his stomach objecting to the fall. He hit the ground hard, one ankle giving way. He let himself relax, falling, rolling, getting straight back up and seeing Jean-Paul mid-air. There were angry faces in the window above. Callanach drew his gun and fired at the wall above the window, aiming to miss any live targets but dissuading them from following.

'Come on,' he yelled at Jean-Paul. He was still on the ground, rubbing at his eyes. 'Shit, did you land badly?'

'Burning!' Jean-Paul screamed.

Callanach squatted beside him, putting one arm around his shoulders, keeping his gun aimed up at the window.

'Got to move,' he said. 'Let me help you.'

Jean-Paul got to his feet, one arm across his upper face, the other clutching Callanach's shoulder. They staggered away along the passage. As they reached the archway that welcomed them into the street, the men began to jump from the window. A black van screeched to a halt in front of them, a side door opened, and men in black clothes dragged Callanach and Jean-Paul inside.

'It's all right,' Joseph told them from the back of the van. 'You're safe.'

'Jean-Paul, let me see your face,' Callanach said.

His friend pulled his arm away. Everything from his lips to the peak of his forehead was red and beginning to blister. Small pockets of yellow liquid were already forming across the tops of his cheeks. His eyes were raw, filmy and closing as the irritant worked into his body.

'Hospital,' Callanach ordered the driver.

They screeched around a corner, meeting a horde of bodies exiting the building.

'Turn right,' Joseph said, drawing his gun again as fists began to thump the rear of the vehicle.

Callanach sat on the van floor, his friend's head resting on his thighs, his breathing laboured, rasping. As they left the angry crowd behind, joined ahead and behind by police cars that eased their passage through Paris' gridlock, he wished it hadn't taken him two years to return to France and to bridge the void between the two of them.

Chapter Twenty-One

The restaurant wasn't one of Edinburgh's best known, but it was well-loved by its regular clientele. Today it was closed to the public as the Major Investigation Team worked with a camera crew, and uniformed officers booked in those people they knew had been dining or working there the night Bart Campbell had disappeared.

It was a full house. Two people working the bar, the owner/manager was on site, five waiters including Bart, seven bodies in the kitchen, and every table full. There was only one CCTV camera, and it had captured nothing of value as there was a second door through which anyone could have come and gone without detection. A lack of internal cameras meant that there was no record of what had happened inside. Only three people had proved uncontactable in terms of bookings. All were last-minute walk-ins.

The cameras rolled. A young actor had been engaged to play Bart. He could be seen working his usual tables, moving from bar to kitchen. Witnesses were released once they'd played their parts and confirmed their earlier statements. Finally they filmed the section where Bart sat at the bar for a few minutes, all his tables cleared, the last few diners remaining, being served by the two waiters still working. He had a drink in front of him that he drained, before putting on his jacket and heading for the front door. His exit had been caught on camera, and that section was to be replaced by the original footage. Then the actor took over again as Bart headed away from the restaurant towards the lamppost where he always locked up his bike. One of the media team's liaison officers then got to his feet, explaining the procedure for contacting the helpline with useful information.

Filming was wrapping when Ava turned up. Tripp was deep in conversation with the editor from the production company they'd used, setting a timeline for getting the footage out. The restaurant manager was treading a fine line between looking deeply concerned for his employee's well-being and deeply concerned about getting his restaurant reopened for trade. A woman on the corner of the street was looking into the restaurant, hands lifeless at her sides, face blank, swaying slightly. Ava walked to where she stood.

'I'm DCI Ava Turner. Are you all right?' The woman looked at her, the skin beneath her eyes so dark she might have taken punches, but Ava recognised grief like a brand, all shallow breathing, scrunched muscles and twitchy far-away stares. 'Sorry, we haven't met. Are you Bart's mother?' The woman gave a single, sharp nod. 'Come with me.'

They walked to a table outside the restaurant and sat. Ava took the arm of a passing police officer. 'Could you ask the manager for a pot of tea, please? I'll pay.'

Mrs Campbell sat to attention, unable to take her eyes off the scene unfolding within and the young man standing in for her son who was in the process of changing back into his own jacket. He bore an uncanny resemblance to Bart, Ava saw. It must have been almost ghostly for his mother. Reconstructions were hard on victims' families. Forever having last known moments reduced to a film strip, to be viewed over and over again. More often than not such events were recorded at a stage too late to change the course of events. Ava hoped that wouldn't prove true for Bart. She waited for the tea to arrive before attempting any further conversation, pouring a cup and adding a spoonful of sugar when Mrs Campbell didn't respond to the question of whether she wanted it or not. She managed to pick up the cup and take a shaky sip.

'What's Bart like?' Ava asked.

'Easy to love,' Mrs Campbell replied. Ava felt a lump form in her throat. 'How long will you keep looking for him?'

'As long as it takes,' Ava said. 'We're just getting started. Thank you for all the photos you gave us. It really helps. Publicity is very important.'

'I don't feel anything,' Mrs Campbell said. 'I've heard people say they knew when their child was dead, or that they felt they were still alive. I have no sense of him at all. Am I doing something wrong?'

'No,' Ava said. 'Everyone feels things differently, and some-times people imagine a sensation or a link that makes processing their experience easier. It's obvious that you and Bart are extremely close, so I can see why you would feel there should be a tangible sense of what's happening to him.'

'There's a dead boy, isn't there?' she asked.

Ava hesitated. The link between Malcolm Reilly and Bart Campbell was still speculative, and she'd made the decision not to have officers pass the details of Malcolm's death on to Bart's family and friends. Now she was going to be asked questions that Mrs Campbell really wouldn't want her to answer.

'There is,' Ava said. 'I believe you were asked if Bart knew him, and you said no.'

'That's right. But then I looked it up on the internet. I found

179

an article but it was in French. The translation from the search engine was . . .'

Ava could imagine. The true facts were awful enough without filtering them through a search engine.

'There's no evidence that Bart is with the same people who were responsible for Malcolm,' Ava said. 'We need to investigate all possibilities. I know it's hard not to overthink, but speculation is a dark cave.'

'How did Malcolm disappear?' she asked.

Ava didn't want to answer, but better that Mrs Campbell got the facts from her than spending hours on the internet, wandering into God only knew what forums and true crime chat rooms.

'He was at his gym. It looks as if he met up with a woman briefly, followed her out, then he wasn't seen again. His body was found in Paris. One of our officers is over there working with Interpol and the French police.'

DS Tripp patted Ava on the shoulder.

'Ma'am, you're needed inside urgently,' he said. 'Mrs Campbell, are you warm enough? I can make space for you inside.'

'No, thank you,' she said. 'I don't think I can.'

Tripp nodded respectfully, motioning for another officer to join them, whispering in his ear. The policeman sat down at the table as Ava stood up, immediately picking up the teapot to refill Mrs Campbell's cup. A flash of gratitude hit Ava for her squad. They were fierce and relentless when needed, caring and gentle in the alternative. A rare breed.

At a table indoors, a man and woman were looking wide-eyed at one another.

'Mr and Mrs Williams,' Tripp whispered. 'They're regulars. They know Bart from the times he's served them.'

Ava sat down at the table with them and introduced herself. The Williamses were in their late sixties, maybe early seventies, and sat holding hands. Ava smiled in spite of the circumstances.

'I wonder if you could tell DCI Turner what you told me just now?' Tripp said.

'You say it,' Mrs Williams told her husband.

'All right then. We were in a bit later than usual as we hadn't been able to find our cat. We don't like her being out too long in the evening. She has a tendency to get into fights,' he said.

'She does,' Mrs Williams agreed.

'So it took a while to find her, then we arrived here at about half past eight, and then it was busy so we didn't get served for ages. That's not a criticism,' he turned his head and looked in the direction of the manager. 'Anyway, we didn't get our main course until about nine thirty. I had lasagne and my wife had the cannelloni.'

Ava didn't rush the story. Whatever spell had been cast in the Williamses' recollections by virtue of the reconstruction was worth maintaining.

'We'd had pudding and were taking our time over coffee when I moved my chair back so my wife could get to the bathroom. We'd been rather squashed into our table as it was so busy. Again, not a criticism.'

'He's such a gentleman,' his wife added.

'Anyway, the back of my chair hit something. There was no table directly behind me so I hadn't been careful and looked the way I normally would. I saw a woman standing at the bar, next to young Bart. It was her leg I'd bashed. I apologised immediately but she just tossed her hair. Didn't acknowledge the apology or me.'

'We gave each other a look, as you do,' Mrs Williams said.

'I might not have remembered. She was there one minute and gone the next, but my wife commented on the size of the ring she was wearing.' He nodded at his wife who continued the tale.

'Very ostentatious,' she said in a half whisper, as if the woman were still there and might be offended. 'A sapphire, if it was real. It looked like one of those efforts you sometimes see sold on those television jewellery sales programmes, you know dear?'

'I do,' Ava said. 'May I ask which finger she was wearing it on?'

'Her ring finger, like you would an engagement ring. My mother would have called it flashy, by which she'd have meant trashy.' Mrs Williams gave a wink.

'Can you recall anything else about her?' Ava asked.

'Brown hair. She had a long coat on so I couldn't be more specific about clothes. She'd have been in her mid-twenties. Attractive in an obvious sort of way,' Mrs Williams said.

'Could you spend some time working with one of our artists, see if you can come up with a likeness of her?' Ava asked.

'Anything for Bart,' Mr Williams announced. 'He's a lovely boy. I only hope this helps. I'd never have thought about it without doing this. Your police officer there coached us to think through each course and remember everyone around us. It wasn't until I shifted my chair back again to leave that the movement prompted the memory. He's a good one, he is.'

Ava smiled at Tripp.

'He is indeed,' she said. 'Thanks so much for your time and assistance. Will you excuse me? DS Tripp will take over again from here.'

She shook their hands and rejoined Bart's mother at the outside table.

'Mrs Campbell . . .'

'Maggie, please.'

'Maggie,' Ava smiled. 'I know you've been asked this before, but are you absolutely sure Bart wasn't seeing anyone? A woman who might have been a little older than him, for example, or someone who'd shown an interest in him at the restaurant?'

'No one,' she said. 'He's a very open boy. We don't have

secrets. I know all his friends, who's seeing who. If he's interested in a girl, he tells me. I'm not judgemental. He'd have had no reason to have kept quiet about it.'

'So there's nothing he wouldn't have told you?'

'No,' she said. 'I wouldn't have cared. Bart knows he can tell me anything. I just wanted him to find someone who made him happy.'

'I see,' Ava said. 'Thank you.'

'The only thing I put my foot down about, ever, was him messing around with someone who was already taken,' she continued. 'Bart's father felt the same. Old-fashioned values and proud of it.'

Ava looked inside at the Williamses who were writing out new statements with Tripp.

'So if there had been someone in his life who was, say, engaged or married, Bart would have known you wouldn't approve?' Ava asked quietly.

'I sincerely hope he'd never do anything so wrong. He was well aware of my feelings on the subject,' she said. 'He certainly wouldn't have dared bring her under my roof. My boy knows better than that.'

Chapter Twenty-Two

Callanach stood in the second hospital in as many days, waiting for news on another friend. He ran over the sequence of events in his head for the hundredth time, wondering what he could have done differently, wishing they'd secured a better route out of the building before getting themselves trapped. They were lucky it had only been a fifteen-foot drop. Any further than that and they'd all have impact injuries. Callanach's ankle ached like hell, Joseph had sprained his wrist in the fall and his cover was blown, his partner had already been reassigned to a different city, and still none of that compared to what Jean-Paul was going through. Interpol had called in a chemical weapons expert and all attending doctors were white-suited and fully masked.

'Detective Inspector Callanach?' a woman asked him. He nodded. 'Your friend would like to see you. Please don't touch him and keep your suit done up at all times. We have some preliminary findings but, until they're confirmed, it's not worth taking any risks.'

Ten minutes later he was at Jean-Paul's bedside, trying not to look alarmed at the bulging yellow blisters covering his friend's face and hands. His eyes were covered with patches, and a drip fed into his arm. The blinds were drawn, the only light a pale blue bulb at the far end of the room.

'Jean-Paul, it's me,' he said. 'I'd kiss you, only you look gross. I thought you should know.'

'Fuck you,' Jean-Paul sniggered then winced. 'Don't make me fucking laugh, this hurts like a bitch.'

'Have they told you what caused the damage?'

'Well, it wasn't polonium, so the Russians are off the hook, and I'm not contagious. Turns out it was a bit less low-tech. The doctors think they brushed giant hogweed across my face. When I put my hands up to rub it away, my hands got the pollen as well.'

'It's just a plant?'

'Want to swap places with me and see if you think it's "just" an anything?' Jean-Paul held his hands up for Callanach to see. 'Looks like whoever did this was cultivating it deliberately. Needs a fair degree of sunlight for the plant to reach toxicity, and they knew what they were doing. Clever. It's natural, legal to grow, cheap, and it takes your enemy down in no time.'

'Shit,' Callanach muttered. 'What about your eyesight and the scarring?'

'There are very few cases of long-term blindness. The doctors are pretty certain I'll recover. The blisters need careful treatment and some scarring is inevitable. Bloody lucky it wasn't your face in the firing line, right? By now, half of Europe would have been lined up to mourn the tragic loss of your beauty.'

'I could shoot you, and put you out of your misery if it would help,' Callanach laughed. 'How's the pain?'

'I have a morphine option that I'm currently avoiding although I suspect I'll be making use of it if I want to get any sleep tonight.' He shifted onto his side, gritting his teeth. 'I won't be back on this investigation, Luc. I have to avoid natural light for a while. I'm sorry. You'll either be assigned a new partner from

185

Interpol or you can work directly with French police. You're in charge now, though. You know this case better than anyone.'

'I just got a message from MIT in Edinburgh. The other missing person, Bart Campbell, had contact with a woman just before he disappeared. Malcolm Reilly confided in his father about being interested in a married woman. It's possible both men were being primed by the same woman to gain their trust, and who asked them to keep the relationship quiet because she was, or was pretending to be, married.'

'That would explain the Scottish end of the operation, but what are you going to do about the clinic Madame Lebel mentioned here? You'll need to establish a presence as soon as possible. Your backstory has to be credible, with paperwork available from a doctor in case they check it out. Even then, you're not guaranteed contact. It'll be almost impossible to put a trace on every person who works at or with the clinic to find the communication route.'

'I'll just have to build up a strong profile and hope for the best. We can't notify any of the clinic staff. There could be more than one person involved and if they figure out that we're watching, they'll just shut the operation down and move on to a different city. I wish this hadn't happened, Jean-Paul. It was good to be working with you again,' Callanach said.

'Are you going to cry? Only if you are, it'll be worth taking the patches off my eyes to see it. I never thought the great Luc Callanach would get sentimental. Now get out of here. You have work to do. If Bart Campbell's been taken by the same people who killed Malcolm Reilly, he's got limited time.'

'I'm going,' Callanach said. 'Are we okay?'

'You mean today or before?' Jean-Paul reached for his medication button and pressed for a dose of painkillers.

'All of it,' Callanach said.

'Catch Malcolm Reilly's killers and don't end up dead in the process. Then we'll have this conversation,' Jean-Paul muttered. Callanach opened the door. 'And bring me in a bottle of Pauillac de Latour. Bastards won't even let me have a glass of red.'

Callanach left with a smile on his face. One of his friends was going to make a full recovery. He only wished he could be so certain about Natasha's future. At least he and Ava had reached a sort of impasse, even if wasn't the conclusion he'd hoped for. Right now she needed to focus on Natasha, and that meant him backing off. At least the geographical distance between them made it easier to bear.

It took four hours for Interpol to set up a fake medical file with a registered doctor's surgery in the city, then another two hours for Callanach to study his supposed medical condition sufficiently to be conversant with all the symptoms, medications, side effects and prognosis before he felt confident enough to walk through the doors of the clinic on Villa Curial. He'd been given drops to yellow the whites of his eyes, and was wearing baggy clothes to disguise his muscle tone. The clinic was larger and busier than he'd expected. The internal decor was shades of white and pale green, with wide plastic chairs that combined relative comfort with ease of cleaning. Information posters adorned noticeboards, and there was a hush about the place that had echoes of every medical waiting room he'd ever been in. It wasn't up to private hospital standards, but it was indistinguishable from most standard doctors' surgeries. He waited in a queue to be seen, running over the details in his mind, recalling the new mobile number he'd been given. Eventually he was given a wad of forms to complete and told to hand them in to the woman at the end of the counter. Twenty minutes later and he walked slowly up to start the process of booking some therapies. The woman took her time reading his forms before giving him a sympathetic look.

'Come through to our private consultation room, Monsieur Chevotet,' she said. 'It's not easy to talk out here.'

He followed her into a room with three small sofas positioned in a triangle, a central coffee table holding a candle and coasters, and several lamps but no overhead lighting. He moved carefully, conscious of the information he'd just imparted. Ideally he'd have liked more hours for research, but time was the only resource Interpol couldn't provide. He had bank cards in his new name with actual money available and an address that could be verified with public records backing it up. Everything he needed, except a firm lead on Malcolm Reilly's killer.

'Please, call me Luc,' he said as he sat down. He'd left his first name unchanged to make the pseudonym easier to use, and to avoid immediate blunders if he bumped into anyone he knew.

'My name is Lucille Blaise. I see you have advanced liver failure, Monsieur Chevotet. I'm so sorry. The prognosis?' She sat, pen poised over her file, her nails decorated with tiny sparkling stones that caught the lamplight and reflected against the dim ceiling.

'Not good,' he said simply.

'We do ask for verification of identity for our files, and also that our professionals be able to contact your primary care doctor. Are you happy with that?'

'Of course,' he said, sliding the driver's licence that had been in his wallet for just sixty minutes across the table to her. 'I already ticked the box about contacting my doctor.'

'Wonderful. Our work here is varied.' There was a soft knock on the door and a man entered wearing slippers. Callanach couldn't help but stare at his silent feet as he glided across the room. 'Ah, this is one of our counsellors. He had a free session so I asked him to join us. I hope you don't mind. Luc Chevotet, meet Bruno Plouffe.'

Callanach kept his seat but extended his hand. Bruno Plouffe, complete with silver goatee beard and wire-rimmed spectacles, took Callanach's hand in both of his.

'Allow me to explain a little about our organisation,' Plouffe said, sitting down. 'There are individual counselling sessions that range from the factual – often doctors don't have the time to explain what all their jargon means, talk about side effects of medication, to discuss how a treatment will physically feel – to the psychological. Some patients don't want to talk about nearing the end of their lives or about the limitations a chronic illness will put on them, but others do. Some patients are single, others want counselling with their spouse or children to help the family come to terms with what's happening – the options are endless. Then there's practical help and social groups. Meeting other people in the same position can be extremely beneficial. Treatments such as reflexology, aromatherapy, massage, hair-dressers who use only products that won't inflame sensitivities during harsh medical treatments – we look at the whole you. It costs money, I'm afraid. I wish we were government funded but that hasn't happened yet. Fundraising only gets us so far.'

'I understand. That's not a problem, and I'm single with no children, so it's just me.'

'Then I hope you'll come to regard us as part of your support network. Have your doctors offered you any hope longer term?' Bruno asked.

'It's proving hard to find a donor match, but that's still an option. Certain symptoms are worse than others. I'm not too jaundiced yet but I'm uncomfortable and my diet is severely restricted. There's nausea, vomiting, and the pain is getting worse.'

'We have a wonderful pain clinic,' Lucille interjected. 'I'll put in a referral.' She made a note.

'Are you still able to work?' Bruno asked.

'I'm a freelance coder. Boring stuff for financial websites

mainly, but at least I work from home and my hours are flexible. I've had to cut my clients down to the bare minimum but luckily my parents are financially stable and helping out.'

Lucille held out a variety of glossy brochures.

'Take these, have a look through. It'll give you a great idea of what we might be able to offer you, together with other clients' experiences of the clinic and our dedicated partners.'

'Thanks,' Callanach said. 'I was wondering, and I know this sounds . . . desperate, I guess . . . but I was thinking about alternative therapies. The doctors aren't offering much and I just want to feel as if I've really explored every option. Like maybe something's been missed, you know?'

'A lot of people feel like that,' Bruno said, extending a gentle hand to rest on top of Callanach's. 'I hope it's not trite to say this, but it's almost a part of the process. We'll go through your diagnosis and of course we can discuss every treatment option that's open to you.'

'But you're getting good hospital care,' Lucille added quickly. 'The consultant you've listed on your form is known to us, and he's excellent.'

Callanach left it there. He didn't want to push too hard and arouse suspicion.

'You're right,' he said, running a hand through his hair and shaking his head. 'I'm so sorry. I must sound awful with so many people trying to help me. Half the time I don't know what I'm saying or thinking these days.'

'Luc, let's fix a psychotherapy session. You're in a bad place. The first one is free so we can figure out if it's right for you. I offer hypnotherapy too, if that's something you'd consider. My patients find it helps them deal with panic attacks. I have a space tomorrow at noon. Would that work?' Bruno asked.

'Hypnotherapy sounds interesting. Thank you, noon tomorrow is perfect,' Callanach said. 'I'm so pleased I found you.'

'So are we,' Lucille replied. 'Out of interest – we always like to know – how did you hear about us?'

'A friend over at Saint-Denis. Her daughter needed some help recently. I won't say her name. She wouldn't want me talking about her.'

'Quite, and we appreciate that sort of discretion. Sometimes we're able to offer a lot more help to people who have open minds and who are able to internalise their doubts. Sometimes when people share the concept of what we do, their loved ones talk them out of it, as if only they are able to help. It's not a criticism, a family's grief is very real, but it imposes limits on what it's possible to achieve.' Lucille stood up. 'We'll have to let you go for today, I'm afraid. This room will be needed in a minute.'

'Of course,' Callanach said. 'I'll see you tomorrow.'

He gave them both a nod as he left. Out in the foyer, he walked around, peering into the rooms with glass doors. Several corridors led off in different directions. There was a wing for physical and beauty therapies, a clinical treatment centre and other multipurpose rooms that were obviously intended for larger groups, with chairs stacked against walls. Coffee and water machines, boxes of tissues and piles of magazines offered distractions in the waiting area. Rack after rack of brochures and information leaflets filled the space against the front windows. Staff came and went calling first names only in soft voices, and escorting clients to their destinations. It was like any other clinic. Callanach wondered what Bart Campbell's chance of survival was if resorting to putting himself out there and hoping someone would find him was their best investigative path. Not great, was the honest answer. He sighed, shoved his hands deep in his pockets, and flexed his shoulders. Then there was Natasha. Here he was pretending to have a life-threatening illness when Natasha was in Scotland facing the real demon of breast cancer. He sucked in the guilt-laced irony.

'You okay?' a subtly dressed security guard asked him. 'Can I get you some water?'

'No, no, I'm fine,' Callanach reassured him.

'I can call you a cab or walk you somewhere if you need help. It's no problem, a lot of people come out feeling a bit wobbly.'

The guard was in his twenties, bordering on overweight and the design of the uniform wasn't a great look, but his face was kind. Callanach gave him a warm smile.

'It's passed. I just feel a bit off-colour every now and then. But thanks, I appreciate the concern.'

'No problem. I'm Alex. I'm here most days if you're coming back.'

Callanach introduced himself – his fake self – and made a note of Alex's surname from his lapel badge. Alex Quint. A security guard would have access everywhere, and know everyone. It made much more sense than trying to infiltrate the various departments of the clinic on an ad hoc basis.

'I'll be back tomorrow,' Callanach told him. 'Will you be on duty then? It'd be good to see a face I recognise. I seem to spend all my time in hospital waiting rooms these days.' Alex raised his eyebrows but didn't push it. 'Liver failure,' Callanach volunteered.

'Shit,' Alex muttered.

It was the most honest and best-stated reaction Callanach had heard since walking into the clinic. Sometimes all psychologically focused and politically correct response training did was water down humanity's connection to one another.

'Yeah, shit,' Callanach replied.

'Sure, I'll be here tomorrow,' Alex said. 'Take it easy, man.'

Callanach gave a mock salute and exited onto the street. By the time he'd rounded the nearest corner, he was on the phone to Interpol's headquarters, asking for a full intelligence and records check on Alex Quint. He needed some inside assistance, even if the person helping him had no idea who he really was.

Chapter Twenty-Three

DI Pax Graham looked like a giant compared to the body laid out on the postmortem suite table, and it wasn't just because of his height and frame, imposing as that was. Ava dragged herself into a disposable fluid–resistant suit and joined her detective inspector and the deputy pathologist. They all stared down at the body. Ava sighed.

'Where's his head?' she asked.

'No sign of it as yet,' Graham responded.

'Was he alive when his head was cut off, or was that done later?'

The corpse was a mess, and that was a pretty high bar considering where they were and how many bodies they'd seen between them. Ava rubbed her forehead. The body was lying on its back, a sheet revealing only the section between the man's waist and his severed neck.

'I haven't had long with the body yet but the spine is broken in several places and there are large impact bruises on the backs of the thighs, buttocks, back and the rear of the arms. Also broken ribs, three of which punctured the left lung. I'd say a fall, followed by massive internal bleeding. The decapitation looks to me to have been aimed at avoiding identification. There's very little blood on either the plastic sheeting he was found in, or on the body, suggesting there was minimal blood loss as the head was removed.'

'And the marks on the neck?'

The skin around the wound was destroyed. Strings of it lay limply against the table, and jagged slash marks went inches down what remained of the neck.

'It's a sawing wound. The long wisps of loose skin indicate the use of a manual saw, rather than an electric one, hence the scratches where the saw has gone off course down the lower neck. The problem with a manual saw is that the more soft tissue gets caught in the blade, the more it gets tangled and clumps of flesh form.' He pointed at a large lump of mangled tissue, not that his point particularly needed illustrating. The picture was already clearly drawn.

'How did you conclude that it's an attempt to prevent identification?' Graham asked.

The pathologist pulled the sheet back to reveal the ends of the arms. They stopped at the wrists.

'Great,' Ava muttered. 'How long to clear DNA processing and see if we can get a match on the police database?'

'With the amount of work you've brought us recently, you'll need to allow five days. We're short-staffed and backed up. I'm due in court tomorrow, and I have people off sick, with other reports overdue.'

'Could I see the whole body?' Ava asked. 'Just to build up a better picture.'

The pathologist peeled the sheet fully down. The lower body was intact. A variety of scars and tattoos decorated his skin. Ava stepped forward, taking a closer look at the ink work.

'Poor quality,' she said. 'They look amateur to me. Could we turn him over?'

The pathologist manoeuvred the body for Ava to view the remaining skin. She sighed, unzipped her suit, put her gloved hand into her pocket and pulled out her mobile, stepping away from the body, mindful of contamination. She speed-dialled a number, putting the call on speaker phone.

'Tell me I'm getting double time for answering a call at three a.m. when I'm not on duty,' Lively grouched.

'You can have this conversation from the comfort of your bed or you can get your arse to the mortuary,' Ava replied. 'Which would you prefer?'

'Go ahead,' Lively replied. An abrupt click suggested that he'd woken up sufficiently to switch on a light.

'A few years ago, we arrested several men for an attempted robbery of a bookmaker's, remember? The prosecution didn't stick because the defence argued serious failings with disclosing our information source, and we didn't want to reveal that there was an informant.'

'Yup. Right balls-up it was.'

'One of the men we arrested was a standing joke around the station for months afterwards. He'd just had a baby, and had got the kid's name tattooed on his back, only he'd spelled it wrong. Tiler with an "i" instead of a "y", the trade not the name. His wife had thrown a fit about it and given him a black eye. Ring any bells?'

Lively laughed.

'I'd forgotten that particular muppet,' he said. 'Damn, that didn't get old for a very long time. Finlay Wilson, what a tosser.'

'Finlay Wilson, thank you, just couldn't dredge the name out of my brain. You heard much about him lately?' Ava asked.

'Hasn't been arrested that I'm aware of, kept his head down, but he'd have been running some scam or other. Vicious little bastard by reputation, served plenty of time on and off when he was younger but we never got him for anything major. He was connected though. Everyone knows him, plenty of people scared of him too. You need me to tap some sources and bring him in for a chat?'

'Won't be necessary,' Ava said, peering at the 'Tiler' tattoo on the right-hand shoulder blade of the corpse. 'He's with me right now.'

'At the mortuary?' Lively sounded fully awake. 'You mean he's finally got his comeuppance?'

'And then some. You can get searching for his head and hands if you like. They're still currently at liberty.'

'Fuck me!' There was the sound of smashing glass and mumbled additional cursing.

'You all right?' Ava asked.

'Spilled some water but it was worth it to hear that. Where was the body found?'

Ava nodded at Pax Graham to fill in the remainder of the tale as he'd attended the scene two hours earlier.

'The body fell out of the back of a moving van at midnight, in a quiet residential area. One of the doors had obviously not been secured and the body either rolled or slid, we think. It was wrapped in plastic sheeting. Cause of death was a fall.'

'Did anyone get the licence plate?' Lively asked.

'Nope, the car behind was too busy avoiding the headless corpse that fell into the road in front of them,' Graham explained. 'The driver was elderly and is being treated for shock so we don't have much to go on at the moment. He didn't have a mobile and had to knock on doors until someone answered and called us.'

'Who could someone like Finlay have pissed off sufficiently to end up like this?' Ava asked.

'You'll have to give me the day to get out there and talk to some people. The field of candidates is pretty limited unless he tried to extend his area of operations outside of Edinburgh, but

Finlay knew better than to set up on another player's turf. Maybe there's someone new we haven't heard about yet.'

'Whoever it is can't get the help, if they forgot to lock the van doors,' Ava said.

'And the work is clumsy. It should have been obvious we'd make a DNA identification if he has multiple arrests on his record,' the pathologist joined in.

'Aye, well, chances are whoever cut off the wee git's head wants word to get out. Couple of days' delay just to make sure all the evidence is squared away, but after that there's value in making sure no one else makes whatever mistakes Finlay made. Sends a message. God, I'm never going to get back to sleep now. I might as well starting making some calls. If I leave it until word gets out, it'll be like getting blood out of a stone.'

'You're still not getting double time, you know that, right?' Ava said.

'Finlay bloody Wilson's dead. I'd work for free today if I had to. It's like a Christmas bonus.' He rang off.

'I need forensic results as soon as your computer can run them,' Ava told the pathologist. 'If it costs extra, MIT will foot the bill. I refuse to believe it's coincidence that Finlay Wilson's body's turned up the same week three other corpses are turned into pig food, when we've got the Gene Oldman case still open. Get me something I can work with.'

'Are you going to release a statement for the press?' Graham asked.

'I think that can wait a while. I'm in no rush for the decapitation jokes to start up again. Do you know how much street vendors made selling funny T-shirts the last time we found a body without a head?'

'A killing?' the deputy pathologist offered quietly as he washed his hands in a corner sink.

Ava glared at him, considered an answer, and decided not to bother. Mortuary humour at 3.30 a.m. she could do without.

Ava sat in Pax Graham's car in the mortuary car park. There was a conversation she needed to have. It was bad timing considering the bodies that were piling up, and that she needed to dash back to Natasha's to check on her friend, newly returned from the hospital, but it was her mess and she needed to clean it up.

'Any movement on the Gene Oldman murder?' she stalled.

'We've got blood drips outside on the path. We're assuming the woman was still bleeding when she left the property. It trails off pretty quickly though. The DNA is good quality. Doesn't help progress the investigation. Still no information from anyone locally. No one liked the victim but no one had an obvious reason for killing him. What's more interesting is what the woman was doing in his house. The fact that every single neighbour says they heard nothing and saw nothing means that they almost certainly did.'

'Did the bullet that killed him come back as a match for a weapon used in any other offence?'

'No. How's the Malcolm Reilly investigation going in France?'

'Slowly,' Ava said. 'My gut's telling me that Bart Campbell has met the same fate, but there's not one piece of hard evidence to back that up yet. They both had meetings with a woman who might have been married or pretending to be, then they each disappeared. We can't get a clear picture of her other than thin and pretty with long brown hair. CCTV has a possible candidate leaving Malcolm Reilly's gym but she was careful to avert her face, if it's the right person. She wasn't a member but could have signed in as a day guest using false ID and paying cash. We keep hitting walls.'

'Have we hit a wall too?' he asked, too fast for Ava to prepare for the bluntness of the question at that hour.

'Yes,' she responded. It was brutal, but easier that way. She'd taken advantage of him. The least he was owed was honesty.

'For now, or for good?'

'The latter,' she said. 'I'd say sorry only that doesn't really do it justice. You'd be within your rights to make an official complaint. I wouldn't fight it.'

'As I recall I pestered you to go out with me, bought you drinks all evening, invited myself back to your place and kissed you first. I think it's fair to say that any complaint I make that my superior officer seduced me might be met with a fair amount of disbelief.'

'I think I'd feel better if you could just be a bit of a shit for a few minutes,' she said.

'You think I'm going to let you off that lightly?'

She shook her head, staring out at the sleet. It was freezing. Finlay Wilson had chosen a grim night to die.

'Will it affect how you feel about working in MIT? I don't want to lose you, but you should know that you'll get nothing but the best recommendation from me if you decide you've had enough.'

'I applied to MIT to work with the best officers in Police Scotland, primarily you. Not because you're sexy or funny or to get you into bed. Is it so hard to believe that I want to carry on working with one of the most respected chief inspectors on the force? If it is, you need to have a think about your self-perception.'

'So you're going to torture me by being nice, and make me feel like even more of a jerk. Is that the strategy?'

'That . . . and I'll be taking my shirt off at every given opportunity. No harm in reminding you what you've rejected.'

She opened his car door and slid out, leaning down to make herself heard against the howling winds.

'It's not about you, or your rank, or the complications of work. There's someone I'm not over, and I lied to myself about it. I used you. I feel crap about it.'

'That's a lot of honesty,' he said. 'Don't be too hard on yourself. I realised what you were going through and I still went to bed with you. I just hoped I might be enough to make you forget him.'

'You knew?'

'Yeah,' he said, turning the engine over. 'You called me Luc twice that evening, and you didn't even realise you'd done it. I'll see you at the station later. Drive carefully. The roads are treacherous.'

Ava stood in the car park a while, wondering why her face was burning when it was being pelted with icy rain.

Chapter Twenty-Four

Alex the security guard greeted Callanach warmly at the door, and immediately offered to get him a coffee. Callanach accepted, wandering over to the machine with him and making small talk.

Alex Quint, twenty-six years of age, had a clean driving licence and no criminal convictions. His parents came from Marseille, and he'd moved to Paris two years earlier, registering his address for voting purposes at that time. His mother was a chef and his father, now retired, had worked for a wine wholesaler. His only sibling, a sister, was studying modern languages. The classic French family. It had taken all of thirty minutes for Interpol to turn up the information from a combination of official records and social media. Alex Quint had worked other security jobs before this one, always for decent amounts of time, for some well-respected companies. He was never going to be a CEO or set the world on fire, but he did seem to be that rare millennial – someone who had no selfies whatsoever on their online profile. Callanach liked him all the more for it.

'So who's your appointment with today?' Alex asked.

'Bruno Plouffe,' Callanach said. 'I met him yesterday. He seemed nice.'

'We have to call him Dr Bruno, as if he was a TV doctor, you know? The patients seem to like him though.'

'No complaints?' Callanach grinned. 'Only I'd rather have a heads-up.'

'Depends what you're in for. I'm guessing the hypnotherapy patients can't remember if it was actually helpful or not,' he laughed. An administrator appeared from a doorway and called Callanach's name. 'Hey, take it easy. See you afterwards.'

'Sure, and thanks for the coffee.' Callanach gave him a wave and followed as directed into a corridor, then into another room. There was no sign of Bruno Plouffe so Callanach made himself comfortable in a huge chair that made him feel as if he was drowning in cushion. The room was being scented from a lit bowl that was changing colour and releasing a soft mist into the air. Dimmed lights made the room homely rather than clinical, and there was a soundtrack playing so low he had to actively listen to hear it properly. Waves crashed on some imaginary beach, and birds cried out to their mates. Every now and then a gust of wind sailed across the room, and branches rustled in a forest that was presumably carpeted with expanses of bluebells. Callanach reminded himself of just how ill he was supposed to be.

Bruno Plouffe appeared five minutes later just as Callanach was beginning to feel sleepy.

'Welcome,' Bruno said. 'I'm so glad you decided to give this a try. I think we can offer you some real emotional respite.' He took an armchair at Callanach's side, making himself comfortable. 'We don't record conversations or make notes. My focus will be on you the whole time. This is a confidential environment, so you can say or ask anything you like. Our only request is that you're honest with us. It's difficult to help when our clients try to put on a front, or to keep us at arm's length.'

'That's fine,' Callanach said. The ambient soundtrack had turned into a ticking clock, and it seemed to be slowing down. More like a heartbeat. Or perhaps it had been that all along. It was hard to stay focused.

'I thought we'd try some hypnotherapy as a starter,' Bruno continued. 'And please don't worry about this. It's nothing like they make you believe on the television. You won't end up doing chicken impressions in the supermarket when the clock strikes twelve! In fact, you won't lose consciousness at all and you'll remain in control of the situation throughout. Nothing we do here is aimed at uncovering new information or accessing parts of your memory that might naturally be inaccessible. Our purpose is to allow you to take better control of your mind, to manage those moments where you feel stressed and panicked, and to find a happy place you can return to whenever you need it. It's more like brain training than creating new pathways.' Bruno leaned forward slightly, keeping his voice low and even as he spoke. He touched a dial on a remote control at his side and the lights dimmed further.

'Feel free to close your eyes and we'll begin. You shouldn't have to concentrate on keeping them closed. Everything should feel natural and relaxed. I'm going to count down slowly from ten, and all you have to do is relax.'

'All right,' Callanach said. His own voice sounded distant to him now, and he realised the heartbeat he could hear was his own, regular and slow, dependable. Safe. He felt completely safe.

My name is Luc Chevotet, he reminded himself, suddenly alarmed at how much he might give away during hypnosis. He should have researched it better, he realised. His breathing was slowing and deepening in response to Bruno's commands, even though he could no longer really hear them.

There was a series of questions he was supposed to answer with a single word, as quickly as possible. All about emotions.

How he felt in certain situations. How he felt when he was alone, with family, at the hospital, as he went to sleep, when he woke up. He fought to try to give the answers he thought he should in the circumstances and given his cover story, but he'd already reacted before he could find the most appropriate response. Then Bruno was asking him about other times in his life when he'd felt scared, and times he'd been truly happy. He heard himself say Ava's name, hoped he hadn't given the context, then there was a floating white space and he knew he was supposed to be meditating. A picture grew around him, element by element, as if he were painting it himself, only he was in the middle of it too – a pretend god, building his own three-dimensional world.

There was a winding road, and hills rising up around him, an expanse of water, greater than a river, surrounding a building. Not just any building – it was a castle, with a bridge to the land. The sun was setting, leaving a blood red sea beneath blackening silhouettes. He was sitting on a wall, his feet dangling over seaweed-strewn boulders, watching birds feasting on flying insects and hearing nothing. Then hands covered his eyes, fingers warm despite the chill of the air, brushing his eyelashes, the touch so soft it was silk on his skin. Laughter. He turned around and the scene reset to white and began to build itself again. Over and over, until finally the laughter became a man's voice, and he was being told to come back into the room, back into the present.

He didn't want to. The place he'd found, the moment he'd constructed, was idyllic. He was happy there. Truly happy. Content. He wanted to hide there among the rocks, never to be pulled back. He resented the man who was calling him, tried to tell him he wanted to be left alone. Then there was a chair beneath him. The sound of a clock ticking. More light in his eyes. Bruno Plouffe touched his hand fleetingly. Callanach opened his eyes. He took a few moments to ground himself.

'It's normal to feel a little disorientated,' Bruno explained. 'Don't rush. You were very engaged. Some people are naturally more receptive to being hypnotised. Such a positive quality. It suggests an openness of spirit.'

Callanach looked at the clock. He'd entered the room forty minutes earlier and the time had simply evaporated.

'So we've established a safe place for you, somewhere you can always access for a sense of calm and well-being. Do you remember it?'

'I do,' Callanach said, trying to sit up, fighting the vast comfort of the chair. He knew exactly where he'd been in his mind. Eilean Donan Castle had been one of his first trips away from Edinburgh with Ava. They'd taken fishing rods and stayed in a hotel at Invershiel. It had rained on and off all weekend. They'd eaten fish and chips doused in a lethal amount of vinegar and salt, and drunk Glenmorangie from Ava's hip flask. They'd sat and waited for the sun to set at Eilean Donan, the other tourists disappearing around them as the day had worn itself out. And Ava had sneaked up behind him, covering his eyes with her fingers, as if it could have been anyone else but her, laughing at her own silliness. That was his happy place. He'd had no idea just how deeply ingrained the image was in his memory until he'd been instructed to go looking for it.

'Is there anything you want to tell me?' Bruno Plouffe asked. 'I mean, anything I don't already know about your situation?'

'Sorry, I don't understand,' Callanach replied. He hoped he didn't understand. Plouffe was giving him a quizzical look that might all too easily translate into revelations that Callanach wasn't ill at all, and that his entire persona was, in fact, a fiction.

'Forgive me, I just got the impression, from some of the answers you gave me, that the stresses in your life rather predate the point in time of your diagnosis. There were moments when you were showing a remarkable resilience to your current situation, a much greater positivity than you talked about yesterday. It's as if your inner thoughts are at odds with the external you. Does that make any sense?'

'Not really,' Callanach lied. 'I haven't been getting much sleep and my emotions have been very up and down. It's probably just a reflection of that. So how does hypnotherapy work? Is there something I need to do to trigger a particular response or is it automatic?'

'No, it's not about programming at that level. It's much more about putting you in touch with a version of you that's beyond your illness. What we find is that when people become chronically ill, or when they're given a diagnosis of a terminal illness, they often get swallowed up. They become completely defined by it. Their former interests and achievements almost cease to exist. It's important to locate times and places beyond a diagnosis or a prognosis that more accurately define and reflect the whole individual. All I've done today is help you bring a particular memory to the forefront of your mind, encapsulated it in the present, and established it as a coping mechanism. It won't so much spring into your mind unwanted as it will occur to you as something that will help when necessary. It's still your image to build and decide to use.'

'I certainly feel more relaxed already,' Callanach smiled. 'So where do we go from here?'

'I think some counselling sessions might be helpful. Your needs and emotions change as your physical treatment progresses, so it's useful to have a place to come and unload. We recommend one session per week, and you can always add additional time when you need it. Also, do consider attending our social events, get to know some of our regular clients. There's a wine tasting tomorrow evening if you're free, with soft options for people undergoing treatment that conflicts with alcohol. Also, many of our clients benefit from using the massage or aromatherapy services. Just coming to unwind is an equally valid use of the centre.'

'Tomorrow night sounds good,' Callanach said. 'I'll book in. And thanks for this. It's good to have made a start on coming to terms with what's happening to my body.'

'Indeed. I should warn you that a small number of patients experience strange dreams the first night after a hypnotherapy session. It's nothing to be concerned about. Sometimes it's just the deep relaxation opening up doors that have been closed a while. Any concerns, feel free to phone in.'

Callanach excused himself and walked out into the foyer with the odd sensation that he wasn't fully clothed, or that he had forgotten to do something important. His mobile buzzed in his pocket and he reached inside to divert the call to voice-mail. He wasn't ready to talk to anyone just yet.

'Hey, you okay?' Alex asked. 'You look a little out of it.'

'Yeah, feels like I just had a long sleep, that's all. Have you ever tried that?'

'No, I'm way too cynical. Not sure it would work on me. I don't fancy having an audience. I'd be sure to dribble or snore or something.' He gave a short smile, then caught himself, reddening. 'I mean, not that I think you did, oh, man, I'm sorry. I shouldn't have said that. You were there for a reason, and all those people were in there trying to help you. I wasn't making light of it.'

'All what people?' Callanach asked.

'Obviously Dr Bruno, but Lucille Blaise who you met yesterday, and one of the physical therapists – I forget his name. They went in fifteen minutes or so after you, and came out a few minutes ago. Did you . . .' he trailed off, looking towards the administration area window and dropping his voice a few volume levels '. . . did you not realise?'

'You sure it was the room I was in?' Callanach asked.

'Sure, I was right opposite. The staffroom is across the corridor. I was filing my timesheet for this month. Look, I didn't mean to say anything, and I shouldn't have talked about Dr Bruno's sessions at all. The important thing is that it might help you.'

'I need some water,' Callanach said. 'I'm feeling a bit shaky.'

'Sit down,' Alex said quickly, 'I'll bring you a cup.' He fussed with the water fountain for a minute, before returning with a half-full paper cup.

'Thanks,' Callanach said, taking a sip. 'Does that sort of thing happen often? People who work here wandering into each other's sessions?' He kept his eyes on the cup. No big deal. Just making conversation.

'I really can't, you know? They wouldn't like it if I talked about the centre. There's a confidentiality thing we sign . . .'

'That's about the patients, right? It's good to know everyone takes that seriously. I was asking about the staff though. I read some reviews online from a couple of patients who were concerned their details had been passed on, and how they were being offered treatments that weren't suitable for them. I just want to know that this is the right place for me. It's important, especially if I'm running out of time . . .' He let the rest of the sentence hang.

'Don't say that.' Alex took the seat next to Callanach's. 'Most of the staff here are excellent. Not that I've had treatment as such, I just know by the way they talk about the patients and their work, how much they care.'

'Most of the staff?'

Alex didn't answer the question.

'You've got good doctors at the hospital, right? Other professionals to advise you?'

'Why, Alex? Is something bothering you?'

'No, what do I know? I watch the door, call cabs for people and show everyone where to get coffee or water. That's my whole job and I like working here.' He began fiddling with his name badge. Callanach knew Alex was a closed door for the day.

'Well, I'm glad you work here. A smiling face is a rarity in places like this. I've been invited to some wine tasting evening tomorrow. You going to be on the door? I don't really want to come if I won't know anyone at all.'

'Certainly,' Alex said, standing up again, his grin back in place. 'I can even introduce you to a few other people. You should definitely come.'

'I will,' Callanach said. 'My phone's buzzing. I'd better take it.' He gave Alex a goodbye nod and walked out onto the street, taking his phone out. Voicemail message delivery kicked on.

'Hello, this is a message for Detective Inspector Callanach. I hope I have the correct number. Your details were passed to me by a boy currently under arrest. His little sister is here too. My name is Annette Thomas from Child Services. Could you give me a call back urgently, please? The children are Azzat and Huznia. They've declined to give us their surnames at present.'

She left a number at the end of the message that Callanach wrote on the back of his hand. For a few seconds, he'd had no idea who the woman was talking about. It seemed like an age ago now that he and Jean-Paul had searched the location where Malcolm Reilly's body had been left. He'd given the two Afghan children his card. The brother had to be pretty desperate if the only adult contact they had in Paris was him. He thought of the girl crying and hiding behind the bins, hungry. Seconds later, he had Child Services on the phone. Two minutes after that he was in a cab, on his way to talk local police out of charging Azzat with a burglary that could mean prison time, and losing contact with his sister for long enough to hurt them both.

Chapter Twenty-Five

'Anyway, it turns out . . .' Lively announced to the audience gathered around him in the incident room, 'that Finlay Wilson had been spending a substantial amount of time in Wester Hailes. Suffice it to say, no one I spoke to was the least bit concerned to hear the wee bastard had passed. Someone actually thanked me for letting them know, and that was a first.'

'Any information on Wilson's most recent racket then?' DI Graham asked.

'Pimping, apparently. He's been involved before, mostly small-time. Not quite standing on street corners negotiating his workers' fees, but nothing very sophisticated.'

'Maybe if we can find some of the women he was running, they'll be able to shed light on who he'd made an enemy of recently,' Ava suggested.

'Perhaps it was one of the prostitutes that did it,' DC Swift offered.

'Sex workers,' Ava corrected him.

'You think one of his toms went to the trouble of cutting off his head and hands, gift-wrapping him, lifting him into a van then driving around the city with him rolling around in the back rather than just emptying his pockets, fleeing the scene and going to the nearest pub to get good and pissed in celebration?' Lively asked, arms crossed, shaking his head. 'Do the letters DC in front of your name stand for Doesn't Concentrate?'

'All right sergeant, that's enough,' Ava butted in. 'We need to speak with any known associates of Wilson's. If he was running girls on the street, regular patrols should know about it. If not, he's got a base somewhere. Phone records?'

'Not a chance,' Lively said. 'He was an evil little git, but he wasn't stupid. There won't be a phone contract in his name. More likely he was using burners.'

'Track down Wilson's family, find out where he was living, any vehicles registered to him. Perhaps you could make a start on that, Constable Swift,' Ava offered as a lifeline before he became forever known as 'Doesn't Concentrate', although she realised it was probably too late already.

'What's maybe more interesting is the fact that one of my sources has confirmed that Finlay Wilson and Gene Oldman knew each other. Makes sense, if Wilson was hanging around Wester Hailes a lot, but Oldman isn't exactly a likely candidate for an associate of Wilson's. By reputation he was something of a hermit, and certainly not a tough guy.' Lively reached out for the last ageing doughnut that had somehow been left uneaten in a box from the local supermarket. Ava heard the crunch as he bit into it and winced.

'What about the young woman whose footprint was found in Oldman's house, and the blood outside?' she mused. 'Perhaps Finlay was keeping his workers off the streets and offering a home delivery service? Less chance of being stopped by the police, he could control the price, send one of his men with each woman to collect the money, so he was never going to be ripped off or short-changed.'

'Still doesn't give us a suspect. Oldman couldn't have killed Finlay, the deaths are in the wrong order,' Graham said.

'Maybe it was a rival pimp. It's possible that Finlay started running his business on someone else's patch,' Lively said, mouth still full of stale dough.

'Work that as a theory. I want a list of anyone known or suspected of organising prostitution in the city. Speak with the deputy pathologist and scene examination team, would you, DI Graham? Let them know we want to double-check for any overlap between Finlay Wilson and Gene Oldman. Wilson's fingerprints or DNA in Oldman's house, make sure the footprint on Oldman's floor wasn't Finlay's, as unlikely as it seems. At present we're assuming the footprint belonged to a female, but Wilson was only five foot four tall. And find his head and hands. That's a story someone'll be itching to tell after a few pints.'

She stood up and walked to the wall that held endless photos of Malcolm Reilly, together with maps of his last known movements, and the out-of-focus likeness of the woman he was believed to have met at the gym.

'Right, DI Callanach is working on a lead in the Reilly murder that's led him to a clinic in Paris. It looks as if someone was offering to use healthy organs as some form of cure, presumably to people with chronic illnesses who could get their hands on the right amount of cash. If that's right, it means that the operation has been carefully set up, streamlined and financed. After going to that much trouble, it seems unlikely that they'll stop at selling just one set of organs . . .'

'What are they doing with them, ma'am, if not transplants?' someone asked.

'We don't have the answer to that yet. There's a suggestion of a more alchemistic element to it. Myrrh was burned and found as a residue in Malcolm's hair and the wounds suggest a level of anatomical knowledge but little surgical skill.'

'Is it witchcraft?' Swift asked.

'It's a con,' Ava replied firmly. 'There's no such thing as witchcraft. There are, however, plenty of extremely vulnerable people out there who'll do literally anything to survive, and for cranks and charlatans they're easy prey. Alternative therapies with no sound medical basis are being offered for tens of thousands of pounds. Globally, this is a multimillion-dollar industry. Take a quick look at crowdfunding and you'll see endless supposed breakthrough remedies being promoted.'

Ava had looked, and spent much more time on the variety of websites offering seemingly miracle cures than she'd intended. Natasha was still in the early stages of treatment with the best medical team supporting her, and even so it was difficult not to get caught up in the brilliantly marketed, utterly convincing scams that promised natural therapies that worked with the body's own immune system to fight the disease. The options were mind-bending, and all came complete with financial advice for those who might need to 'liberate' some cash from their home to pay for the chance to survive that they'd been persuaded their current doctors were somehow conspiring to keep from them.

She moved across to Bart Campbell's section of the board.

'The woman who spoke with Bart in the restaurant as he finished his shift matches the general description of the woman Malcolm Reilly was seeing, but I doubt if that's what she looks like now. Her hair might be shorter, or a different colour, she might have coloured lenses in, or be using different clothing and padding to alter her body shape. What does seem unlikely is that Bart met this woman for the first time that evening and agreed to hook up with her. That doesn't fit with what we know about him, so we need to investigate further back on his timeline. It might give us more detail about where they met, possibly alternative CCTV footage. Maybe one of his college friends spoke to her at some point, or perhaps he dropped her name into a conversation. Bart's mother says she has a very open relationship with her son, especially since the death of his father,' she pointed at a printout of a faded colour photo on the board that showed a man in uniform holding a baby boy, 'so it seems entirely possible that Bart was strongly urged to keep the relationship a secret, which is the main link between our two cases at the moment.'

'Except for that photo,' Swift piped up.

Every head turned.

'Sorry, which photo?' Ava asked him.

'The one with his dad there. It's been all over Facebook, that one. I knew I'd seen it somewhere before when it got pinned to the board in here, but I hadn't put two and two together until now.'

There was a long silence while they collectively waited for Swift to explain himself. He didn't.

'Are you saying that someone has shared this photo on Facebook to promote the search for Bart?' Ava asked gently. 'His mother, perhaps?'

'No, it wasn't that. Hold on, it'll come to me.'

Lively jolted in his chair and Ava put a firm hand on his shoulder to keep him in place.

'That's it, it wasn't Facebook at all. It was Twitter. You know, like those things when some kiddie loses their teddy bear at a train station, and someone picks it up and takes a photo of it? They tag it, like, please share, this lost bear was found this morning at Waverley Station. Let's see if we can't help find its way home.'

'What the fuck're you—' Lively began.

'Hold on,' Ava murmured in his direction. 'Constable, are you saying that someone else found this photo and has no idea of the connection to Bart Campbell?'

'That's right,' Swift grinned.

Ava realised there was only so long she was going to be able to prevent Lively from bursting into an act of physical violence that would require an internal investigation to be held, not to mention probable criminal charges.

'So what did the message with the photo actually say?' she asked.

'No idea,' Swift replied, eyes wide. 'I couldn't understand a word of it. I never learned French.'

Every chair scraped at once. Every computer screen was prompted into life. Social media filled the room, all bright colours and GIFs.

'Find it right now,' Ava ordered, 'and make sure we get a completely accurate translation of the message. Source the original media post, then get Interpol on the phone. I'll call DI Callanach.'

'Got it,' DI Graham shouted across the din. Ava scooted between chairs and bodies to see the screen. There it was, a photograph of a photograph, curled at the edges, tatty from years of being carried in a pocket, taken out frequently and admired. Next to it was a second photo, this time of the back, with the handwritten but legible message, 'Bart, I may not always be by your side, but I will always come back to you. Love Dad xxx.'

'That's definitely the original,' Ava said. 'The copy on our board is from a scan Mrs Campbell took of the photo in case it ever got lost. Apparently Bart had it in his pocket at all times as a way of keeping his father with him. She'd told us about the message on the back, but it hadn't been released to the media. Mrs Campbell was adamant about keeping it private.'

Below the two images, someone had already made the effort to translate the original message. It had been found on the ground in a car park outside the town of Arras, close to where the A1 road ran south to Paris.

'Map,' Ava said. The screen changed to an overall view of Paris, then zoomed in closer and closer, until the road system around Arras could be seen. 'Here,' she said, pointing at one particular junction. 'He had that photo on him. His mother said he transferred it morning and night to whatever trousers he was wearing. They'd have checked for his phone and wallet, but this would have been easy to miss, or they just might not have been bothered about it. He left us breadcrumbs.'

'So how did he get there with no passport?' Graham asked.

Ava put one finger on the map and followed the road system north. She stopped at Calais.

'So they could have driven down through England with him hidden in the boot, then taken either the Channel Tunnel or a car ferry to France. Risky though. Several opportunities for him to be found, either banging the trunk at petrol stations or passing through customs,' Graham concluded.

'Unless they sedated him,' Ava said. 'It might have been a truck rather than a car, so better soundproofed and easy enough to get him out of the country. The real risk would have been a random vehicle search on arrival in France.'

'Private boat?' Graham suggested. 'Would have made it easier to have pulled up in a cove somewhere without customs.'

'Expensive and more risky. If they'd been spotted by a customs vessel, they'd have had little chance of hiding him once they'd been boarded,' Ava said. 'Notify Interpol that we need the person who posted this interviewed immediately. Establish a timeline, and details of that specific location's weather. Let's see what the state of the photo was when it was found. Maybe we can figure out how long it had been there.'

'It's been doing the rounds on Twitter a few days now,' Swift added. 'If that helps.'

'Sack him,' Lively whispered in Ava's ear. 'Please, for me.'

'Hey, he just got the only lead in a case that no one else has made any substantial progress in for days. If you're not careful, I'll end up promoting him,' she said, dialling Callanach's mobile.

'You wouldn't dare.'

Ava looked across to where the detective constable was grinning from ear to ear.

'Yeah, maybe not,' she said as Callanach's voicemail message kicked in. 'Luc, we've identified a photo of Bart Campbell with his father that he always carried with him. It looks like he tried a Hansel and Gretel tactic. I'm emailing you a precise map, and we're contacting Interpol HQ to get officers to the person who found it. It means the theory is confirmed. Bart is on French soil. It seems likely he went through Calais, but there's no support for that as yet. If someone has taken Reilly and now Campbell, they might have others, or be planning more abductions. Phone me as soon as you get this to update me from your end. I suspect Bart's running low on time.'

Chapter Twenty-Six

There was a table and a universe between them. Azzat had greeted Callanach with an angry glare. His little sister, Huznia, was in a nearby room wrapped in a huge furry blanket and playing with a box of second-hand toys. Child Services were doing what they could, but without Azzat's cooperation, that wasn't very much.

'Are you going to talk to me?' Callanach asked the teenager.

'I only gave your name because I knew you were a cop. It stopped them from charging me,' the boy announced.

'That might have worked for an hour or two, but it won't stop the police completely. Your sister's fine, by the way. She's been given food and a hot drink. They want a doctor to take a look at her but that's just standard practice when a child comes in who's been living on the streets.'

'We weren't on the streets,' Azzat hissed. 'I take care of her. We were inside a building.'

'With furniture, and electricity? Somewhere safe that no one else had access to?' No answer. 'Listen, it's clear you love Huznia and that she loves you, but you have to realise the position you're in. If you're charged, you can be tried at fifteen, and if you're found guilty one option is that you'll be kept in a young offenders' institution. In those circumstances, Huznia would be placed with foster carers or in a home, and no one will be able to guarantee if or when you'll be housed together again.' More silence, but Azzat's lower lip was less steady than before. 'Tell me about this burglary. Why were you there?'

'It wasn't a house, it was a warehouse where lorries pick up boxes of food to take to shops. I figured I'd just get some supplies to keep us going. We'd run out of money and it doesn't hurt if it's a big supermarket. They throw so much away. It's safer to just go through the bins at the end of the night when the food shops close, only Huznia got sick last time we did that. I wanted to make sure what I fed her was safe. They're making a fuss over nothing.'

'You broke a window and got in by climbing on top of a parked vehicle?' Callanach asked. He'd been given a brief summary of the details when he'd arrived.

Azzat shrugged. 'So?'

'So someone's going to have to pay for the damage. Most of these big companies have a zero tolerance policy on prosecuting. They have to keep their workforce safe. You left a large patch of broken glass on the warehouse floor. Someone could have got hurt.'

'Doesn't it matter that we're going to starve to death if we don't eat?'

'Of course it does. I'm just explaining to you why this isn't being dealt with by a simple warning. You're old enough to know better. Have you tried any of the homeless shelters? They often have hot food, at least soup.'

'That's fine for me, but as soon as they see Huznia, they start making phone calls, then people turn up and try to take her away from me. I promised I'd never let that happen.'

'Okay. I'm here and I'm listening. What is it you want me to do?' Callanach asked.

'Stop them from charging me. Get them to let us go. You said you'd help. Are you a liar too?'

'Actually I asked you for information, and I gave you money to get food. My phone number was there in case you suddenly remembered anything that might help me.'

A social worker entered, carrying a fast-food cartoon. The smell of hot salt made Callanach hungry. Azzat grabbed it as if he were starving. Callanach saw that his arms were stick thin as he reached for a packet of ketchup to smother on the fries, and his hair was matted. Callanach waited until the boy had consumed everything in front of him.

'If you could help me, give me some information about how that body came to be at the building site, I could use that to persuade the prosecutor to drop the burglary case against you.'

'I should have known you were going to use the situation to get something for yourself. That's the only reason you came.' Azzat licked the last of his meal from his fingers.

Callanach took his time responding.

'This is serious, Azzat,' he said. 'I'm not here to argue or negotiate, not because I don't want to help you. I intend to do everything I can for you and your sister. But turning information over to me isn't optional. A young man is dead. He was brutally murdered, and he was only a few years older than you. If you know anything at all, you have to tell me.'

'Do you know how many dead bodies I've seen? I was twelve when we left Afghanistan. By then, they were already gathering any boy over the age of ten to fight for one side or the other. They took my father, then my mother sent us here with some men she paid all their savings to, just to keep me alive and to stop Huznia from being promised for marriage by some male relative once my father died. Huznia can't remember it, but I do. Men who refused to join whichever army came to their village first had their eyes burned with pokers, or they were pushed off buildings. We don't even know if our mother is alive or dead. There's no way of contacting her.'

'That might be something else I can help with. Interpol has a worldwide intelligence network. We'll need details. Name, date of birth, the town she was last seen in, any places she has relatives. And the people you think might have her,' he finished quietly.

Azzat was right. Callanach had no idea what the boy had seen, or just how tough his short life had been so far. Now here they were, living in a foreign country, without security, without even the basics to keep them safe and well.

'Give me a moment,' Callanach said. Leaving the room, he sought out the arresting officer. It took fifteen minutes to ensure that no charges would be brought, and an offer to personally make good the damage to the warehouse window to guarantee that the owners wouldn't make a complaint.

He went back to Azzat, then took him through to his sister. They sat on the floor together, Azzat admiring the way she'd set all the toys out in a row and kissing the back of her head tenderly when she told him the names she'd given the stuffed animals she'd found. Callanach was impressed. In spite of all they'd been through, Azzat had combined being a brother with being a stand-in parent, making ends meet and improvising to keep them both fed. If he'd had to steal along the way, then who could blame him?

'Now, I'm going to liaise with Child Services to make sure you're placed together. I understand after all you've been through that it's vital you're not separated. Huznia would suffer if she was taken from you.'

Azzat gave him a look that was largely suspicion with a dawning element of hope.

'You have to be careful to comply, in the future, with France's laws. I don't live here all the time, and next time you get in trouble, I might not be able to help out. So no more stealing, okay?'

The boy gave a single, brief nod.

'Huznia needs you with her, not locked in a cell. You did a good job, Azzat. You got her all the way from Afghanistan and you kept her safe. But she needs proper food, access to doctors, and a warm bed to sleep in. It's time for you to let others help. Immigration services will make sure you're allowed to stay here for as long as it's not safe for you to go home.'

Callanach bent down, picked up a small puppy toy, and waved it at Huznia.

'You'll be all right now,' he told her. 'You can trust these people to help. Make sure your big brother reads you bedtime stories, okay?'

The little girl gave a smile that would have broken the hardest of hearts. Callanach felt a pain in his chest at the thought of all she'd experienced. If there was any natural justice, her mother would be found and they would be reunited as soon as possible. Callanach exchanged a few quiet words with the social worker who was making notes in a corner of the room, asking to be notified when the children were placed, and contacted if there was any difficulty in ensuring they were kept together. As he put his hand on the door knob to leave, he felt a hand on his shoulder.

'That's it?' Azzat asked. 'No strings? You want nothing in return?'

'I want to know what you saw at the building site. I need to find that boy's murderers and keep other people safe from them. But you were right, I should never have seized the moment to get something from you. If you're going to help me, it has to be voluntary, not least because anything you tell me has to be real and true, not just so that I do you a favour in return.'

Azzat stared at his trainers quietly for a few seconds.

'There was a van,' he said. 'White, old, its bumper was coming off.'

'At the building site?' Callanach asked.

'Yes.'

'What were you doing there, so late at night? Shouldn't you have been looking after Huznia?'

Azzat frowned.

'I was getting money to buy her breakfast. One of my friends was looking out for her that night. Our gang was given a few euros a week to watch the building site, and to call the boss if we noticed anything. He didn't want to pay for proper security while no work was getting done, but they had a lot of machines and building supplies there. He knew it was our turf, so he offered us the money if we didn't screw him over and break in ourselves. Different people in our group took turns hanging there at night. Three of us were watching when the van turned up. It was dirty, old dirt, like it hadn't been washed for a year, and there were no words or pictures on it, but there was this one area that was bright white, in the shape of a large leaf.'

Callanach looked at the social worker, poised with pen and paper.

'May I?' he asked. She held both out to him.

He handed the drawing materials over to Azzat who turned the paper landscape and drew a rough outline of a generic van. Along it, filling about one-third of the van's side area, he drew a large leaf, tipped as if it was falling in a breeze, not yet landed, stalk dipping towards the bottom of the van.

'This is the best I can draw it,' he said, passing the paper to Callanach. There was no mistaking the shape. 'It's like they'd just taken a big sticker off the van, so that area hadn't had a chance to get dirty yet.'

'That's really helpful, Azzat,' Callanach said. 'Thank you. What about the people from the van. Can you describe them?'

'It was dark and they were dressed in black. They were both men, quite tall, but they had big coats on and hats, so I didn't see their faces clearly. They were white, though. I could see from the backs of their necks.'

'Could you hear them talking?'

'We were too far away to hear anything and there was music from the floor below us. We were in the high-rise building, in the corridor that runs along the outside. They just pulled the van up, took something – the body, but I didn't know that then – into the building site, then came out and left. Quickly though. They didn't hang around.'

'You didn't see the licence plate?'

'No.'

'So did you ever call the boss to report what you'd seen?'

Azzat shrugged. 'No, I mean, we were there to stop thefts or vandalism, you know? Those men dropped something off, they didn't steal anything. We made sure they didn't have anything with them when they came out so we figured they hadn't done anything wrong, and . . .' he stopped talking.

'And what?'

'One of them had a gun over his shoulder. A big one, semi-automatic I guess. I was getting ten euros for the night and I had Huznia to think about. I wasn't going to get involved with the sort of men who carry weapons like that. The others felt the same. Nothing was stolen, no harm done, better to keep quiet. If I'd known . . .'

'You couldn't possibly have known, and you were right to think of Huznia first. It wasn't your responsibility, Azzat,' Callanach said.

'We didn't know you were police when we first started throwing bricks at you and the other man. We thought you were there to steal,' Azzat offered quietly. 'I would never have done that.'

'I believe you. You know, Interpol needs agents like you. Men who understand how the world works, who want to make it a better place, who're responsible enough to keep a little girl safe even when it feels impossible.'

Azzat pulled back his slumped shoulders, and drew himself up taller. The smile on his face was priceless.

'Really?'

'Really,' Callanach replied. 'You've already learned a second language fluently. You're fit and strong, and you're never going to have a criminal record, right?' The boy grinned wider. 'So get yourself to school and work hard. Whatever has happened in your life so far doesn't have to define your future.'

The boy was against his chest in a moment. The hug so brief Callanach hadn't the opportunity to return it. Huznia beamed a smile at the two of them. Callanach figured he couldn't beat that for an outcome, said his goodbyes, and left.

Chapter Twenty-Seven

The intended dinner was a burned mess in the frying pan. Ava glared at it as if the food had left itself unattended, then dumped it in the bin.

'I'm getting dinner delivered,' she shouted into Natasha's hallway. 'Is Chinese okay?'

'Sure,' Natasha shouted back. 'Nothing too spicy for me. My stomach's not up to it. What's that smell?'

'Sorry, can't talk, I'm on the phone,' Ava replied, pulling her mobile from her bag.

Natasha appeared in the doorway.

'Home cooking. You should go on one of those food shows.'

'*MasterChef*?' Ava asked, punching a number into the dial pad and swearing at the screen.

'No, I meant one of those programmes about nightmare kitchens where they do a sort of forensic investigation and discover that if you'd eaten there you'd have died from some awful bacteria,' Natasha laughed. 'Here, use my phone, there's an app that lets you order online without calling.' She passed it over.

'You're supposed to be sitting down and taking it easy,' Ava said as she scrolled through food images and a price list.

'I'm supposed to be married with kids, watching soap operas and deciding where to go on holiday this year. Unfortunately I'm gay, easily bored in relationships, prefer horror movies, and I have cancer so my holiday this year is most likely to be spent in a chemotherapy unit. Want to get into an argument with me?'

'Just grateful you're so good at taking advice,' Ava noted. 'I've ordered. It'll be twenty minutes. Will you at least sit down and let me make you a delicious green tea?'

'In lieu of a vodka and tonic.' She took a seat and Ava put the kettle on. 'Have you heard from Luc?'

'We've had some progress in the case he's working on. He's busy and his partner was hurt on duty, so there's a lot of pressure on him at the moment. We're mainly communicating through voicemail or email.'

'But you spoke to him at the airport, right? It's just that you haven't mentioned him since.'

'It's all fine so there's nothing to tell you. Whatever mis-understanding we had has been put aside. He's worried about you, obviously, and has demanded regular updates.'

Natasha yawned, throwing her head back and making a whining noise in the back of her throat.

'God, you're exhausted, you should have said. Look, why don't you go and lie on the couch? I've put a blanket there already. If you fall asleep, I'll wake you up when . . .'

'Oh no, sorry, I'm not tired at all, I'm just incredibly bored of listening to your bullshit. But go ahead, I interrupted, which was rude.'

Ava put her hands on her hips.

'Do you suppose it's more serious to assault a cancer patient? I mean, would a judge give me a longer sentence for, say, giving you a black eye now rather than before you were diagnosed?'

'At least then I might be interested in you again. It's almost worth the swelling,' Natasha laughed.

'Fuck you,' Ava said, 'and after I cooked you dinner.'

'You cremated dinner. It was a cruel and unusual act performed on innocent protein and carbohydrates.'

Ava slumped in the chair opposite Natasha and ran her nails along a scratch in the wood.

'We're good friends,' Ava said. 'He's come to terms with that. It was all terribly grown-up and clinical. So there you go. He's over me, which is exactly what I deserved. Probably best, as what you don't know is that I got drunk to an extent that I can only call reprehensible and slept with another of my detective inspectors. Just saying it out loud makes me feel queasy.'

Natasha stared at her, mouth open for full dramatic effect.

'Go on, say something. Let it all out. I'm going to settle in for at least thirty minutes of piss-taking.' She folded her arms. Natasha let the silence hang for another thirty seconds.

'I'm not bored any more,' she said eventually.

Ava leaned forward and banged her head on the table.

'I'm a disgrace,' she groaned.

'If it helps, I prefer you disgraceful to dull . . .'

'Tasha!'

'Okay, okay, I know you feel like crap, it's written all over your face, and it's not an attractive look.'

Ava scowled at her.

'Was the detective inspector a man or a woman? Only if you finally came to your senses and switched over for a bit of female action, I think that would be perfectly sensible.'

Ava picked up a tea towel and lobbed it across the table, unable to stop herself from laughing.

'Whatever you did, it's not the end of the world,' Natasha said more gently. 'You weren't seeing anyone. You certainly weren't seeing Luc. You should probably try to limit your work conquests to, say, not all the officers who rank immediately below you in your squad,' she paused, and Ava allowed her to giggle at her own joke for a while. 'But I'm not sure what you think you've done wrong.'

'You mean apart from making things bloody awkward at work? Or using a really nice guy who the majority of women would be delighted to wake up with? Or maybe behaving like I'm a student instead of a supposedly responsible member of society who's mature, thoughtful and trustworthy? Hmmm, let me see . . .'

'Do you ever allow for the fact that you're human and therefore occasionally imperfect?'

'I shouldn't even be thinking about this stuff. I have . . . shit, I've actually lost count of the number of dead bodies in the mortuary at the moment, it's that bad. Another missing man – barely even a man – and quite possibly more on the way. When I think about Luc, or Pax, I feel like I'm being selfish. Like my life should stop, or that my personal experiences should mean less to me. And it does pale in comparison to the lives that have been lost or that are hanging in the balance, but just sometimes I'd like to be able to feel sorry for myself, or make plans and think about what I really want. When I try to do any of that, I just feel guilty.'

Natasha reached across the table, laying both her hands on top of Ava's and squeezing.

'I know that,' she said. 'You're the most on-duty person I've ever met. It's like you get dissolved by your work. But you need to remember that being human makes you a better police officer. Having a personal life. Understanding the mechanics of relationships. Being able to comprehend loss, fury, envy, exhaustion, grief – making mistakes, for God's sake. If you didn't do those things and feel those things, how could you possibly have the psychological roadmap you need to guide you in your job? So give your guilt the night off. I'm ordering you. Talk to me about how you're feeling and what you're going through without comparing the pettiness of your woes to everyone else's. You matter, Ava. Not just to me, or to your family, but to the whole community. To Edinburgh, if you want to think about it like that. You need the space to decide what'll make you happy. That doesn't change because of what's waiting on your desk tomorrow morning.'

Ava coughed and dashed at her eyes with the back of her sleeve.

'You know it's worse when you're nice to me?'

'I know, I love that!' Natasha smiled. 'So start with this, just for me, because I'm not sure when the hell I'm going to have sex next. How was it?'

'Honestly, I can't remember. Not that I'd share even if I could, but there was beer, then cocktails, then there was whisky and a bit more whisky. Some whisky chasers.'

'You're sure you actually had sex?'

'We woke up in bed together naked, and he seems to remember it vividly, so the possibility that we got into bed together and feel asleep without doing anything is not a life raft I'm going to persuade myself to cling to at this point. He's not the problem. In fact, he's been more than decent about it. He said . . .' Ava huffed and frowned at the table. 'He said I called him Luc twice during the evening, and I hadn't even realised I'd done it. Then he said he shouldn't have gone to bed with me knowing how I felt about another man.'

'Knowing you're in love with another man,' Natasha corrected her.

'Am I? I don't know any more. I think I've spent so many years avoiding relationships that my tendency towards self-destructing when anyone gets close to me isn't a defence mechanism any more, it's just me. I'm not a pessimist, so why can't I see a future for myself where I'm in a happy stable relationship? I had my chance with Luc and I blew it. Or we both blew it, if I'm being fair to myself. I'm out of energy, Natasha. I have no idea what I want.'

'As a philosopher, I can tell you that most human beings move forward only by realising what they *don't* want, rather than by experiencing a sudden revelation about what they are actually looking for. Think about it like this. When you took Luc to the airport and started that conversation with him, what did you really want him to say? What's the fantasy, ideal, dream version of his response? That's what you want. Whether or not it's what you need right now is a different thing. Now, are you going to make that tea or are you expecting me to do that myself, because I thought you'd come round to be helpful?'

'Bugger, sorry.' Ava stood up and began pouring boiling water over tea leaves. 'Isn't what I want the same thing as what I need?'

'Not necessarily. Quite often in life, not at all. Humans have terrible judgement. Examples: what I want is wine, what my body needs is water. What I want is a Creme Egg, what I need is broccoli. What I want is to sleep in until eleven a.m., what I need is to get up and fill in my tax return. The two things are quite often at odds with one another.'

Ava put the teapot and a mug on the table, then started getting out plates and cutlery.

'But those are practical examples. You're talking about physical or legal requirements. My problem is about how I feel and what I see in my future.'

'Is it? At the risk of you not being terribly careful with that knife you're carrying, I see it like this. What you wanted was for Luc to declare his love for you, to take responsibility for everything that went wrong between you, let you off the hook, and to move things forward in a way that meant you didn't have to address your own emotional shortcomings. What you need . . . lower the cutlery . . . is to understand why you constantly destroy your chances of personal fulfilment by choosing the wrong men. Why can you operate like a clinical, sharp-shooting goddess at work, but not express a single intimate emotion to a man in your personal life? What you needed to do with Luc was to have the guts to express how you feel about him at the risk of him still rejecting you. Because if you don't think he's worth the risk of getting hurt, then how can you possibly deserve him?'

The doorbell played a few jingly notes.

'Wow, I've never been literally saved by a bell before. Who knew?'

Ava dumped the cutlery on the table and made for the door. By the time she returned Natasha had poured her a large glass of red wine and was lighting a candle.

'You think I'm a coward?' Ava asked.

'I think you can't do your job, spend eighteen-hour days seeing the very worst humanity has to offer, toughen up so you don't get broken by everything you deal with, and not have that impact on your ability to be open and responsive to your personal life and emotional needs. Are you going to withhold food from me because you're annoyed? Because if you do, I should tell you I'm finding someone else to play nursemaid in the future.'

Ava put the cartons down on the table and began opening them and dumping messy mounds of noodles on plates.

'I didn't tell Luc how I felt about him because I didn't want to put him under any pressure. That wouldn't have been fair.'

'Bollocks,' Natasha said, tucking into her food.

'Could you maybe go a little easier on me? I'm in the middle of—'

'You're in the middle of what you're always in the middle

of, and it's never going to stop as long as you're still doing your job. I, on the other hand, am in the middle of trying not to fucking die. You have my opinion. Nothing more. Accept it, reject, whatever you want. Right now, if you don't shut up and eat, I'm kicking you out.'

'Shit,' Ava said quietly.

'Yeah, sorry. I was warned I'd have bursts of anger. Could you get the soy sauce out of the cupboard above the sink?'

Ava fetched it.

'I love you,' she said, handing it over.

'I love you too,' Natasha said, cramming food into her mouth. 'God, either I can't stomach the thought of food, or it's like I'm pregnant with sextuplets.'

Ava's mobile rang as she was swallowing her first mouthful of wine.

'Ma'am, it's Lively, need you in the incident room right now. Hope it's not a bad time.'

'I'm coming.' Ava hung up. She shovelled several forks of food into her mouth before standing up and dragging on her coat. 'Don't say it.'

'What?' Natasha grinned.

'Don't.'

'Just eating my dinner. Nothing to see here.'

'I know my work–life balance is screwed.' Ava grabbed her car keys and walked to the back door.

'You haven't got any shoes on!'

'Oh for crying out loud . . .' Ava stormed back into the hallway. 'I'll see you later.' She opened the door again.

'Thanks for dinner!'

The door slammed.

Chapter Twenty-Eight

The deputy pathologist was huddled in a corner of the incident room with DS Lively and DI Graham when Ava arrived. The room was remarkably full given the time of night, presumably because it was so unlike Lively to call an off-duty meeting that everyone was curious as to what couldn't wait until the next day.

'We've established a connection between the Gene Oldman killing and Finlay Wilson's death,' Lively began. 'I'm going to ask the deputy pathologist to bring you all up to speed first.'

The presentation screen lit up with photos showing the floor of Gene Oldman's kitchen and the pathway outside his house. Several areas were marked with Photoshopped arrows.

'You'll be familiar with the partial footprint inside Oldman's house,' he began. 'There were also blood droplets found outside the property on the pathway shown. We obtained DNA from this blood but have not found a match for it on the national database.'

The screen went dark momentarily, lighting up again with a photo of what remained of Finlay Wilson's body. There were a few groans from the audience. It was too late at night to be looking at a headless corpse, Ava thought.

'This body was brought in with hands and head severed postmortem – still not recovered – cause of death was internal bleeding after a fall which in turn caused his heart to stop beating. We performed urgent complete swabs for DNA, as well as fingerprinting the whole surface of the skin and checking for unusual fibres that might tell us where the body had been stored. We rushed the results through,' he gave Ava a brief glance that she hoped wasn't accusatory, 'and we did find another person's DNA.'

He hit another button on his laptop and the image changed again to a close-up of Wilson's penis. That time there were retching noises, a round of expletives and some improv comedy.

'Could they not have cut that head off as well?' someone yelled.

'Did he cut off his own head in disappointment?'

'That's all you get,' Ava said. 'Back to business. Please, do carry on.'

'We found clusters of cells here,' he pointed on the screen at the base of the penis in the pubic hair, 'and more, under the foreskin. The placement of the cells indicated that they had been deposited during sexual intercourse. It must have been reasonably soon prior to death as there is a fair amount of bodily fluid still on the corpse, including the deceased's own semen dried onto his stomach. All of this would have been reduced with friction against clothing, or washing, even urination, had much time passed. It's not possible to draw up a more accurate timeline than that, before anyone asks. We checked the cell type. These were vaginal or cervical cells, with a full DNA structure. Again, the police database did not come back with a hit.'

That drew a few disappointed sighs. The deputy pathologist raised a hand.

235

'Bear with me. After that we ran a DNA check against all the other bodies recently processed who were deemed to have been victims of crime, given the sudden and unusual influx of bodies into the mortuary. I can tell you that the DNA from the blood found at Gene Oldman's is an exact match for the cervical cells' DNA on Finlay Wilson's body.'

'So she was present immediately before, or during, Oldman's death, and again soon before, and possibly at Wilson's death,' Lively said. 'Which means she's either the killer or our best witness.'

'Are we looking for one of Finlay's sex workers then?' Graham asked.

'That's the most likely scenario,' Lively said, 'and it would explain her being at Oldman's house if Wilson had his women doing home visits. I made some calls when this evidence came through. Since word has begun to spread that Wilson's dead, the residents of Wester Hailes are marginally less tight-lipped than they were when Oldman was killed. Word is Wilson was running girls out of a number of flats across the city. No one's quite sure of the scale of it. One hundred quid got us the address of the block of flats Finlay was known to use closest to where Oldman lived. Interestingly they're all rented flats, not one single resident is claiming benefits, which is unusual for that area, and I can't contact any of the flat owners. Cash paid, no questions asked. As no one who's renting out the flats is suspected of involvement in a crime we can't bring them in under arrest.'

'Can we not just break down doors and do a sweep, see what we pick up?' DC Swift asked.

'Aye, we could, but then no one will talk, word will get out, the killer will hear about it and the broader investigation will be ruined,' Lively replied softly but firmly. Ava was put in mind of a man training a very young puppy not to pee on the carpet. 'Do you see?'

'Oh, I get it,' Swift said.

'Well done,' Lively said quickly.

'I want to get someone in there undercover first to figure out what's going on. We need more information. The addresses of all the flats, names of Wilson's associates and enemies, see if anyone knows anything about Oldman. It's no good solving these murders if we don't have the physical evidence to put the perpetrators away for life,' Ava said.

'So we need someone who has a deep understanding of how this community works, the cases themselves, and the instincts to uncover the story without jeopardising the investigation,' Graham said.

'And who's believable in the context of using sex workers,' Ava added.

There was a silence so long it was easy to imagine a dustball being blown across the incident room floor. Almost without noticing the tide of movement, all eyes were on Lively.

'You posy of pricks,' he said. 'That's ageist. I can complain to HR about this.'

'It's not ageist if it's because you're a grumpy old git, Sarge,' DC Monroe called out.

The room erupted into applause.

'Sorry, Sergeant, but you know this case, the local area, and all the key players better than anyone else on the squad.' Ava tried to quell her smile. 'Has anyone been inside the block of flats in question yet?'

'All we know about it is that it's four floors, two flats front and back in each block. Front main entrance but a fire escape at the back. Some of the windows seemed to be permanently blacked out.'

'Is the top floor high enough for loss of life if a man was pushed over the handrail?' Ava directed at the pathologist.

'Four floors is high enough to cause the injuries Wilson

237

sustained. It's survivable in some cases, but it would depend how you landed. However far Wilson fell, he landed on his back and his spinal injuries were severe. I'd say the geography of this property makes it a possible scene of the crime.'

'Then start on the top floor as that's more likely where Finlay was pushed from. Get into a room alone with one of the girls – careful how you go about it, we can't risk an obvious wire. Choose someone mature. We don't want the complications of you ending up in a room with anyone underage who starts stripping off. Pay them extra, tell them you're lonely and that you just want to talk. Finlay's dead so we need to know who's in charge now. Offer them witness protection, a guarantee of no prosecution, but if they have information they'll need to give evidence in court or the information might be useless.'

'Yes ma'am,' Lively scowled. 'Anything else?'

'Do I need to tell you to keep your clothes on?'

Lively folded his arms and stared at her.

'Right, it's eight forty-five now, so let's work towards getting you in there at eleven this evening. Lively, you'll need a name of someone local who recommended you. If a stranger turns up out of the blue, they'll be suspicious straight away.'

'Why don't I say I heard about it from Gene Oldman before he died? We found betting slips in Oldman's belongings. I can put together a backstory about using the same bookie.'

'Great,' Ava said. 'Contact the tech team about getting us ears inside with no prospect of your cover being blown. And we'll need backup as close as we can but not inside the block. If this is a professional operation they'll have a man posted on security all night. What do you want to do about a weapon?'

'Knife in my boot. If they do a body search, that'll be perfectly normal for Wester Hailes. It'd probably look more suspicious if I wasn't carrying a blade, to be honest.'

'Agreed,' Ava said. 'Let's get moving. I want the building plans obtained from the council, a full layout, better information about the occupants of each flat, and eyes on both building entrances all day today to get a feel for who's coming and going. Photos of every single person seen entering and leaving, with control room working up identifications in real time and building up profiles. Sergeant Lively, a word in the corridor?' He followed her out. 'I'll have to approve the operation with the detective superintendent. Did you want to talk to her first?'

It was an uncomfortable conversation to have. Until it had come to a recent halt, Lively and Detective Superintendent Overbeck had been having an extra-marital affair that had lasted several months. Ava had an unspoken agreement with Lively not to refer to it.

He shrugged his shoulders.

'Doesn't matter either way,' he said. 'I doubt she'll even register my name, to be honest.'

'Oh, fine, I'll deal with the super then,' Ava said. 'Are you . . . okay?'

'I'm not sobbing on my sofa watching *Bridget Jones* movies, if that's what you're worrying about,' he smirked.

Ava figured she'd probed enough.

'All right. You're to brief me in person with all the security and tech arrangements. I'll be heading up the operation in the vicinity. You sure this isn't too risky? I can find someone else. There's no pressure.'

'And pass up my chance to be a hero? I figure this'll get me a few months' free beers, and I've told all my old stories to death. I'll be fine, ma'am.'

'You'd better be, you stubborn bastard,' she said.

Chapter Twenty-Nine

Fifty press-ups twice a day was his target. That and staying on his feet, walking the perimeter of his room. If the opportunity came to escape, Bart had decided he wasn't going to get caught just because incarceration had left him unfit. He was at number thirty-seven of his first set of the day when the noise in the corridor marked an unusual amount of activity. It was neither meal nor shower time. He stood up and peered out into the corridor, holding his breath.

The party detoured off into Skye's room. Two men and two women, all wearing surgical gowns. The first woman carried a kidney tray, its contents obscured by a sheet of paper across the top. One of the men was pulling a drip stand. Another woman was pushing a machine with a large monitor with a variety of leads snaking from it. The final entrant into the room carried a video camera in one hand and a bulky tripod under his other arm. Each of them was gloved, mouths and noses covered by a mask. Just as Skye had described had happened with Malcolm.

'Hey,' Bart called out. Skye's door shut firmly. 'Hey!' he shouted, louder this time. 'Skye, fight them. Just fight.' He slammed a fist against the door. The sound echoed uselessly back at him. 'Use me instead,' he yelled. 'Don't touch her, you bastards. Don't you fucking touch her!'

No one reacted. No one came. They could hear him, he was sure of that, but Skye didn't make a sound. She didn't race to the window to take one last look at him. No guard bothered to admonish him. Because they were miles from anywhere, alone. Skye was all he had. The thought of being there without her was the death warrant of hope. He stood sentry at the glass in his door, watching as every now and again a gowned figure passed the window in Skye's room, turning, motioning, doing God knew what. He wished he could switch his imagination off. In the end, it took remarkably little time. An hour, he estimated, no more.

Out they trailed, one after the other, pushing and pulling their equipment, walking casually, as if everything they'd done was perfectly normal. As if the woman in the room was a bona fide patient, not a kidnapping victim. There was no sense from their demeanour that they were ashamed of what they were doing, or that they feared discovery. Bart pressed his face against the glass. There was no sound at all from Skye's room, only the ghost of her in his mind, standing at her door, pressing her fingers against the glass while he did the same. Holding hands in spite of the space between them. He gave up on the remaining press-ups and curled on his bed.

'Bart.' Skye was whispering to him in his dreams. He turned his head into the pillow. 'Bart! Are you there? Please?'

Not in his head. The voice was coming from Skye's room. She was talking more slowly than usual; and her voice was thick, low. He jumped from his bed, and skidded to his window. She was there. The section of her face that he could see was even paler than normal, the ends of her fingertips glowing white dots against the pane.

241

'Thank God you're alive. I thought . . . I just . . .'

'They didn't hurt me,' she said. 'It was weird but it wasn't bad. I just don't know.' She paused. He heard the sob in her voice. 'I just don't know how much longer I've got now.'

'Tell me everything.'

'They set this camera up, and told me to lie on the bed. I heard you telling me to fight and I wanted to, really, but there was no point, Bart. They said if I just lay still I'd be okay. They promised me. I didn't want it to hurt, whatever they were doing.'

'That's okay. I was wrong. You did the right thing. I was an idiot. I panicked. Don't listen to me. It wasn't fair to tell you to fight. I'm so sorry.'

She was crying. He cursed himself.

'All that matters is that you're okay now. Do you know what they wanted?'

'They put this drip in my arm. I saw a bag with "saline" written on it, but they added another drug. I kind of fell asleep. I couldn't move or speak, but I could hear them. They set the camera up in the corner of the room, I remember seeing that. I think they took my clothes off but by then everything was just fuzzy and my head felt blank. They dressed me again before they left.'

'Anything else? Did you understand what they were saying to each other?'

'The woman – the one who did most of the talking – spoke in French. And I have these weird lines on me . . .' she broke off.

Bart gave her a moment.

'What sort of lines?'

'Pen markings, in a purplish felt tip. Over my stomach, my back although I can't see it all. Round each of my breasts. Some on my face. Can you see from there?'

He tried.

'It's not clear,' he said. 'Do the marks make any sense?'

'It's kind of like an anatomy drawing. There's a circle where my stomach would be, my liver, definitely my ovaries. Maybe they're just teaching with us? Perhaps that's all this is. Do you think that could be it? Maybe they let Malcolm go after all.' Her voice got brighter, bolder. 'They haven't hurt us yet. It could be some military thing, practising for an epidemic. You know, top secret, they'll explain it all to us when it's over . . .'

Bart said nothing. The hope in her voice was killing him. He knew it wouldn't end that way. So did she.

'Shit,' she whispered.

'That's all right. We have no way of knowing what's going to happen.'

'They did the same to Malcolm. Two days later he was gone. I have a mark.'

Her voice was muffled. Bart pressed his ear to the glass.

'Say again,' he said.

'I said they didn't hurt me. It didn't hurt at the time, but it's starting to now. I have a pin prick in my thigh. Quite deep. It's not bleeding or anything, but it's bruised.'

Bart frowned.

'Think back,' he said. 'What's the last thing you remember?'

'It's not like there's a sequence,' her voice was tense. 'It's all just a muddle. Voices, images. I wanted to sleep. Just to let it all go. My body felt so heavy. One of my eyes opened on its own, then there was a light, like they were trying to look all the way into my brain.'

'Probably just checking your level—'

'That was it,' she blurted. 'That's when my leg hurt. I felt it, but I didn't. I know that doesn't make any sense. I knew something was happening to me, but it wasn't painful then, just a sense of intrusion. They stuck a pin in me.'

'Do you think you flinched?' Bart asked.

'I'm certain I didn't. Does it matter?'

It did, Bart thought. It mattered a lot. Whoever was destined to view the video needed to see Skye as unresponsive, perhaps even comatose. It was a sales video of some sort, and she was the goods.

'None of it matters,' he said. 'People are looking for us. By now, your family will have figured out that you didn't just decide to leave. They'll be searching for you. My mum will have raised hell. Sooner or later they'll figure out something that'll bring them to us. There's still time. Hey, what cocktail am I buying you at The Newsroom? How many can you remember from the menu?'

'I don't know,' she said. 'I can't think.'

'Yes, you can,' he said. 'We've just arrived. It's busy but we get the last table. It's a Friday night, or maybe a Saturday, but we both managed to get the night off work. The city's mad with stag parties. It's raining but not too hard. I've got an umbrella so you won't get too wet when we leave.'

'My brother would like you.' He could hear that she was trying to be brave but her voice shook as she said it.

'Well, next time we'll invite your brother out too,' he laughed. 'But tonight is just for us.'

'Martini,' she said. 'Nothing too sweet. With a green olive. In a tumbler. I don't like those wide V-shaped glasses.'

'I knew that,' he said. 'They're too pretentious for you. Let's set the date. First weekend back in Edinburgh. I'll pick you up at eight o'clock.'

'I'd like that,' she said. 'Hold my hand?'

Bart pressed his fingers against the glass, grateful to stop talking for a while. His brain was too overwrought for him to speak coherently any longer. Over the course of his conversation with Skye, he'd made a single, irreversible decision. The day she was taken, he would extract the loose metal screw that was sticking out of the plug socket in his wall, and open up a vein in his wrist. He'd already done a dry run and made a scratch in the right place. Without Skye to stay strong for, to imagine freedom with, his continued existence was just too painful to contemplate.

Chapter Thirty

The party was more upbeat than Callanach had been expecting. The human spirit was naturally optimistic, he thought, but more resilient in public than in private. He wondered if the laughter would stop as soon as each attendee climbed into their car or cab, or if the ebullience would last longer. Perhaps until they were in their own homes and safe to mourn their fates without feeling self-conscious. The thought made him want to call Natasha immediately.

'Luc,' Alex said. 'Can I get you a drink? There are sodas or fruit juices. Must be tough to be around wine. I'm not sure arranging an evening based on an alcohol theme was the best idea here.'

'It's Paris,' Callanach smiled. 'How many of us are really prepared to give up wine, even when we know what the consequences might be?'

'True enough,' Alex said. 'So what'll it be?'

'Just a sparkling water. I guess that means I haven't given up hope yet, in spite of the prognosis. Desperation may be making me deluded.'

'Is there really no other treatment?'

'Treatment but no cure. I'm too far down the transplant lists to make that a viable option. Unless you've heard of something I don't know about.'

'I wish,' Alex murmured. 'Dr Bruno tells everyone during our training sessions that no patient is ever beyond hope, that miracles happen, and that we should encourage all the patients to ask about options, no matter how hopeless it seems. He says there's no such thing as end game.'

'Really? Sounds like that might give false hope.'

Alex shifted from one foot to another.

'Not that Dr Bruno would do that deliberately, I'm sure,' Callanach added smoothly. 'He seems like a genuinely caring man.'

'I'll get you that water,' Alex said.

Callanach watched him go. He was going to have to work the room, make his plight known to as many people as possible, then wait and see if his efforts bore fruit. He couldn't approach Dr Bruno and ask why Lucille Blaise had gone into his hypno-therapy session without making it obvious that someone had spoken out of turn, yet the hypnotherapy wasn't supposed to leave him with a gap in his memory. Lucille herself was missing from the gathering, although there was nothing amiss about that. Staff members would have other commitments in the evenings. He made a mental note to schedule an appointment with her. It wouldn't be difficult to orchestrate a reason to do so. The clinic offered enough therapies that he could find endless questions about them all.

'Hi,' a woman said, offering her hand and giving him a demure smile. Forty, he guessed, a French national, well spoken, with long auburn hair and an attention-grabbing figure.

He shook it and smiled back, wondering if she was a patient or attending in a more professional capacity. She certainly didn't look ill.

'I'm Marie Delphine,' she said.

'Luc Chevotet,' he replied.

'I didn't want to leave you standing alone.' She slid her arm through his. 'Come and meet some people with me.'

Callanach turned to look for Alex but there was no sign of him at the drinks table or anywhere else in the room. He allowed himself to be led towards a small group of people in one corner. Apparently the networking was going to take care of itself.

Two hours later and he was no further forward. He'd exchanged details with two other patients suffering liver complaints, his conscience twinging at the extent of his lies. Bruno Plouffe had spoken to him briefly, welcoming him before moving on to other people eagerly awaiting his attention. Alex had brought his water after a while, apologising for the delay, checking Callanach was all right. Other staff had made the effort to introduce themselves; some of whom had obviously read his file while others hadn't. There was a system, one had explained. All staff were notified that a new patient was on the books, and his file could be accessed on their database for everyone to familiarise themselves in their own time.

Marie was the clinic's marketing and public relations consultant, which explained her approach. She'd seemed to know almost everyone in the room, staff and patients alike. It was some sort of grant that paid for her time, although Callanach guessed the clinic wasn't her only client, given the designer clothes and jewellery she'd been wearing. Using a bathroom break as an excuse, he sent a quick message to Interpol listing all the names he could remember, and asking for background checks.

Back out in the main foyer, in the absence of any familiar faces, he focused on a noticeboard instead. A poster with a single green leaf logo at the bottom caught his eye. Callanach pulled the pins from the corners and took a closer look. The leaf design was the same as Azzat had claimed was on the van that had delivered Malcolm Reilly's body to the building site, but this was in a vertical position, as if growing directly up from the earth.

'Are you a vegan? Laudable, but I'm afraid I'd struggle with it. I like steak tartare and lobster thermidor too much to make the sacrifice.'

Callanach looked over his shoulder to see that Marie had found him again.

'I was looking at the logo, actually,' he said. 'I thought I recognised it, but it must be a different brand. I'm not a vegan, though I've had to give up red meat since I was diagnosed, as well as a number of other things I used to love.'

'Of course,' Marie said. 'How insensitive of me. I'm in awe of the people who use this centre. You all cover the pain of what you're going through so well. Sometimes, I'm embarrassed to say, I forget what you're dealing with.'

'I'll take that as a compliment,' Callanach smiled. 'And you should forget. Who wants to walk around contemplating their mortality all the time? I know I don't.'

Marie smiled back.

'You're empty-handed,' she said. 'Can I get you anything? I know you're not drinking alcohol, but maybe orange juice or water?'

'Maybe just some help, given your expertise in marketing. Is there somewhere I can find a particular logo? I have a vague image of it in my head, but I can't quite remember the company it belongs to.'

'What product was it advertising? That would be the best place to start. Pharmaceutical, food or beauty – just a category would get you started.'

'I'm afraid I'm not sure. Sorry, that's not much help is it?' Callanach said.

'Not to worry. Do you have an image of it somewhere you could scan? There are some great image-recognition apps around on the internet.'

'Sadly, I don't. It's a leaf like this one, but on its side. I'm not quite sure about the colour of it. Pretty wide brief, right?'

'It's one of those universal symbols. Food is the most obvious product type, like the poster you're holding, but nature symbols can be helpful in lots of different marketing situations. Promoting medicines you want the public to think of as pure but which are really just a cocktail of chemicals. Makeup and beauty products that would make you rethink your need to be beautiful if you knew what was in them. It's the oldest trick in the book. Got a rotten product you need consumers to think of as natural? Use a sunflower or a leaf, a water droplet or a ladybird as a logo. Buyer sees the logo – the words that will spring into their mind are things like *unprocessed*, *organic*, *safe*, *pure*, *wholesome*, *unrefined* . . . I could go on. I have whole files of buzz words relating to images that show what consumers respond to. So don't be fooled by the leaf, is what I'm saying. The product the brand is selling is as likely to be an opioid as it is your vegan burger there,' she pointed at the image on the poster.

'Thank you,' he said.

'I'm not sure what for. I certainly haven't limited the field for you.'

'Food for thought, anyway. Possibly just not vegan.'

Marie laughed.

'The evening seems to be winding down,' he said, looking at the dwindling numbers left in the room. 'I should probably make a move too.'

'Of course.' She extended a delicate hand for him to shake

once again. As he took it, he found a business card left in his palm. 'In case you want more help with your logo research,' Marie said. 'Or anything else. It was nice meeting you, Luc Chevotet.'

'Likewise,' he said, slipping her card in his pocket. She gave him a last smile and slipped off towards the small group still chatting in one corner.

Callanach disappeared out of the door, unable to find Alex to say goodbye. He walked a while before taking a cab, thinking about what Marie had said. Logos weren't always what they seemed. He'd been thinking too literally about what sort of company might have owned the van that had dropped off Malcolm Reilly's corpse. He needed to cast the net much wider. An hour later he was back at his hotel, staring blankly at his computer screen, the enthusiasm he'd felt when he'd first sat down to begin researching a distant memory. Marie had been right about the scope of the leaf image. Leaf logos cropped up in every industry imaginable. Even limiting the search to companies based in or around Paris, the possibilities were vast. It was another dead end.

Chapter Thirty-One

Elenuta sighed. It was 11.15 and her night's work had barely begun. Who knew how many more men would parade through the door? She stared at the wall. The last man had ripped her clothes in some sort of show of bravado. He must have been trying to impress himself, because he couldn't possibly have thought she was going to be impressed by it. Now there was both screwing and sewing on the agenda before she could sleep. She brushed her hair. Some of the other women were letting theirs get matted. Elenuta understood the temptation. Make yourself unattractive, hope you got chosen by fewer men. What those women didn't understand was the jeopardy they were in. Less attractive meant you were more disposable, and that took you right up to the threshold of being selected for the race. A living hell or a brutal, early death. What a choice.

Things had been bad under Finlay – she hated how literal that was – but it was even worse with Scalp in charge. One of the girls had a burn on her neck after forgetting the electrical circuit and sticking her head through the front door to shout downstairs. It was only then that Scalp's goons had realised what a great punishment it made, particularly in moments of boredom. One of the women answers you back or refuses you a quick blow job? Throw her out of the door. Pull her back in. Throw her out again. Next time she'll comply quicker. Just when they'd all thought life couldn't get any worse.

The walkie-talkie buzzed. Two men were on their way up. Scalp kept a man on the external door these days. Finlay had never bothered, which was the only reason she'd been able to escape. No chance of that now. Elenuta did her best to pull her clothes together and make herself presentable again, before opening her door and parading herself in the hallway as instructed. She was exhausted. It occurred to her that if she put her head in and out of the front door enough times, she might actually die. For the first time, that seemed like an acceptable choice.

'Jacket off, shirt open,' one of the guards told the men at the door.

'Come on, you know me, I'm here all the time,' one of them groaned. Elenuta recognised him as a regular.

'New management, new rules,' the guard said. 'Do it or go the fuck home.'

The other man complied, slipping his arms from his jacket and opening the buttons of his shirt to show his chest and stomach.

'Empty your pockets,' the guard told him. He took his mobile and a set of car keys from one, and a wallet from the other. The guard gave it a half-hearted check. 'First time?'

'Aye,' the man said. 'Gene Oldman gave me the heads-up. I don't mind paying in advance but I'm not leaving my wallet out here for some little bastard to scam me.'

'Gene Oldman's not recommending anyone any more.'

'Way I heard it, the miserable sod blew his own brains out and now the polis are looking to pin it on someone local to make themselves look good. Bunch of wankers. Surprised they haven't knocked on my door yet,' the new man said with a broad grin.

The guard laughed. 'Leave your phone, take your wallet with you, but watch the bitches. They'll try anything. Payment's due now. How many girls?'

'Just one.'

'Any preferences? They'll all do whatever you want, mind. Any problems, just give a shout.'

'Can I get a better look at them?' he asked, moving further into the corridor.

'I want that one,' the second man in pointed at the woman to Elenuta's right. 'I'm here all the time. I should get first choice.'

'Forty.' The guard held out a hand. Once the bundle of notes was passed over, the other man looked up and down the row of women.

'I'll need someone who speaks the language,' the man said. 'I've got some instructions and I don't want to have to draw fucking diagrams.'

'Her or her.' The guard pointed first to Elenuta then to one of the younger girls.

The new man looked at them both long and hard.

'That one,' he said, indicating Elenuta. 'I've got a teenage daughter. I don't need another one rolling their frigging eyes at me and sulking.'

'Leave her in a fit state to work the rest of the night. Otherwise, you're good to go. Thirty on a first visit. Consider it an incentive to come back.'

'She'd better be fucking amazing,' the man grumbled, handing over the cash.

'If she's not, she'll be explaining why to the boss. What did you say your name was?'

'Jack Thomson. Jackie to my friends, but let's wait and see how your ho does before we get too pally.'

'I'm Paddy,' the man extended his hand and they shook. 'Off you go then. Half an hour. Anything over that, you get charged extra.'

Elenuta watched as the man plodded towards her along the corridor. Caucasian, hairline receding as his stomach expanded, he looked out of shape and sad. She supposed she should be grateful she'd make her quota of jobs for the night. Popularity kept her safe from the prospect of being forced into the race, but she so wanted to lie down and rest. Just for a while.

'Come in,' she said, standing back and letting him through her door.

He walked in and went to the window, as she closed the door behind them.

'Does that lock?' he asked.

'No, but not worry. They only come if you shout. Is private. I undress or you do it?'

'What's your name?' the man asked.

'Rosie,' she lied. None of them were supposed to use their real names. 'On bed?'

'No, but you can sit down if you like. Keep your clothes on. What's your real name?' She stared at him. 'You're not Scottish. Your English is good but not fluent. It seems unlikely that you're called Rosie. Where are you from?'

Elenuta perched on the edge of the bed, studying the stranger. Most likely it was Scalp testing her out. It was exactly the bastard's style. Get her to break the rules as an excuse to punish, making it easier to ensure the other women's compliance.

'Glasgow,' she said. 'I have to do work. What you want?'

'I'm not really in the mood, but don't worry, I'll make sure they know you did everything I asked.'

'No,' she stood up. 'I work hard. I do what told. Whatever you say.' She looked towards the door. One of Scalp's men would be the other side, listening, ready to report back.

The man followed the direction of her glance, walking across the room, then sitting down on the floor, his back to the door. There was no way anyone was going to walk in.

'On the bed,' he ordered loudly. 'Right now.' Elenuta sat down again. 'And get naked.'

She began doing as she was told, but he covered the space between himself and the bed on his hands and knees in a couple of seconds, holding her hands still and shaking his head.

'Don't,' he whispered. 'It's all right. I'm not here to hurt you. You can trust me.' He returned to his original position keeping the door firmly shut. 'What's that around your neck?'

Elenuta rubbed her eyes.

'Electric,' she said.

'There's a boundary?' She nodded. There was no point lying about the dog collar. The large battery unit attached to it made the purpose obvious enough. 'So you're not allowed out of here?' She shrugged. She didn't really see the point of the conversation. 'You're not living here voluntarily?'

'You pay to ask questions?'

'That a problem?' he asked.

'I get trouble,' she said. 'Not okay to talk.'

'I guessed that,' he said. 'So who's the boss here?'

Word was getting around about that so she supposed she was allowed to answer.

'Scalp,' she said quietly.

'Scalp? That's a new one on me. Does Scalp have a surname that you know of?'

She shook her head.

'Did Scalp put that thing around your neck?' She nodded. 'Motherfucker,' he muttered. 'Come here.' She hesitated. 'Right now. Come and sit on the floor with me.'

Elenuta sighed. This she understood. Men giving her orders. It was easier than answering questions. She braced herself for whatever was coming. He kicked his boots off, reaching inside one of them and taking out a penknife, flicking the blade open with his thumbnail.

'Not hurt me,' she flinched, throwing herself backwards.

'God, I'm an idiot, I should have explained. I won't hurt you. Not at all. Let me sort that thing out. I won't take it off you. They'll never know. You can just say it doesn't work. Better still, if you go across the boundary, just act like you had a shock.'

She frowned at him.

'What?'

'I'm going to disable the battery unit so you can't get an electric shock,' he whispered slowly.

Elenuta looked him up and down. He had no intention of having sex with her, that much was clear. His clothes were clean. His nails neatly trimmed. His voice was kind. Either she shouted for help, which would likely get her nothing but fists for dinner, or she could trust, which was something of a joke. She'd thought she was beyond such overt stupidity. On the other hand, a knife to the neck would at least be fast.

She leaned forward again, presenting the right side of her neck where the battery box was, closing her eyes.

'Relax,' he said. 'I'll be careful.' He inserted the tip of the blade into the battery box and took out the screw. 'Turn a bit more left.' She opened her eyes, getting a better look at his face as he worked. 'Hold your hair back for me.' She did. She could hear scraping, his arm made a tiny sawing action in front of her face, then his elbow banged into her nose. He stopped what he was doing and leaned back. 'Sorry about that,' he smiled. 'You okay?'

She couldn't resist a laugh. Half embarrassed, half intrigued at how worried he looked. If a bump to the nose was the worst of her problems, life would be wonderful.

'Is okay,' she said.

'All right, I've nearly got it. I just don't want to do any damage to the outside or they'll notice. This way you can claim you know nothing about it.'

'They punish me anyway,' she said, as he picked up the tiny screw and closed the battery unit back up again.

'I bet they bloody will,' he said. 'There. I don't suggest you put it to the test, but I reckon that'll keep you a bit safer.' He folded the knife blade away and reached for his boot, pausing before he secreted it. 'Do you have anywhere safe you could keep this without getting caught?'

She stared, assessing its length, then went to a set of drawers and took out a pair of tatty jeans. He held the penknife out to her. Her hands shook as she grasped it. She'd have liked the time to have sat and stared at it, but no such luxury existed. She wiggled her finger into the hem of her jeans and tucked the blade into it, manoeuvring until it was the opposite side of the hem from the small hole.

'Why give me knife?' she asked, as she put the jeans back in the drawer.

'Just in case. I'm guessing you need to protect yourself. If things ever get really bad, better to have something. And so you understand that I'm here to help you. You believe me now?'

She thought about it. It could all have been a set-up from the minute he'd walked into the flat. New customer making sure the guards followed procedure, asking questions she wasn't supposed to answer. Naming Gene Oldman as his source of information. Elenuta had cautioned herself not to react to that. Not that it affected her. She was glad the man was dead after he'd helped Finlay find her. It would have to be a pretty elaborate hoax though – disabling her electric collar, giving her the knife. Scalp was devious and manipulative, but he was also arrogant. He wouldn't have wasted so much time and energy on her. Easier to have just beaten her to a pulp to see if she was properly broken in for him.

'I believe,' she nodded. 'My name is Elenuta. They kidnap me, bring me here from Romania.'

He reached out his hand, waiting until she put her own much smaller one in his, then shook it gently and released her again.

'Lively,' he said. 'Detective Sergeant Lively, Elenuta. I'm a policeman. Do you understand?'

The air left the room. She stifled a laugh at the absurdity of it, felt the dizzying effect of adrenaline as the truth hit her. He was police. She could see it now. In his demeanour, his confidence. The way he spoke to her. And yet she was still shut in a room, still a prisoner, and he was arming her for her own good.

'Why you not arrest men?' she asked.

'You mean the men out there right now?'

She nodded.

'I want leave, now. They hurt us. Rape us. You help us leave.'

'I'm going to,' he said. 'I just need some help from you first. Would you sit down, Elenuta? Tell me what I need to know and we'll talk about getting you out of here.'

Now there were tears in her eyes. Every single day she thought she was beyond crying, something new happened to prove to her that she was still human. Usually it was an act of brutality or cruelty. Now this. The tantalising closeness of freedom, of safety, even a glimpse of something that smelled curiously like fresh cut grass and that tasted like justice. And yet it was still about making a bargain, still just out of her reach. Of course it was. Escape was a mirage in the desert. She sat down next to him, her back against the door alongside his, as she stared at the blacked-out window that she could break if she liked, and jump to her death once she'd really had enough. She sighed.

'What you want know?' she asked him.

'Finlay Wilson,' Lively said, his voice much quieter now, one ear to the door. 'Have you heard that name before?'

'He was boss here, before Scalp,' she said. 'Very bad.'

'Well, he's dead. We're trying to find out who killed him. Do you know anything about that?'

She closed her eyes. Every word she said got her further into a situation that would undoubtedly end her. Only it was too late now to go back, and she found that she didn't really want to.

'Scalp kill him. Take over.'

'You know that for certain?' Lively asked.

'I saw. Throw off . . .' she pointed towards the hallway, 'what word?'

'Railing?' Lively asked.

'Yes. Over railing. They argue. Scalp angry about money. I saw.'

'You actually witnessed it?'

Elenuta nodded.

'Did you . . . sorry to ask this . . . did you see anyone do anything else with the body after that?'

'No. They shut door. Scalp's men clear up, I think.'

'That was easier than I thought,' Lively said. 'Were there any other witnesses, anyone who could say the same thing in court?'

'Many women here. We all see. To scare us, understand?'

'I do, and I'm sorry to ask about this. We know from Finlay's body that he had sex with someone just before he died. You don't happen to remember which of the women here he'd been with?'

The rush of nausea Elenuta felt was overwhelming. She could smell Finlay's body odour, feel the roughness of his fingers on her skin. Every drop of sweat from his body had reeked of hatred.

'Okay,' Lively said gently. 'That's okay, lean forward, take deep breaths.'

'Is nothing,' she said.

'Funny shade of green for nothing.' He went to the bed and picked up a pillow, bringing it back for her to lean against. 'So it was you?'

'Yes. How you know?'

'Apart from your reaction?' He smiled. 'You're the prettiest woman in this place. Not just here. You'd be the prettiest woman in lots of places. I'm sorry. This may be the worst timing ever for paying someone a compliment.'

'Better than a slap,' she smiled back.

'I knew Finlay a bit, from way back and by reputation more recently. If he had to choose a woman from here, it was obvious it would've been you. In which case I have to ask you something else. Another man died recently. Gene Oldman, couple of minutes' walk from here. He was shot . . .'

'In the head,' she finished. 'I escaped, ran, knocked door for help but Finlay came.'

'Who shot him?'

'Finlay's man. Gene made him angry.'

'How did you cut your foot?' Lively asked.

'Glass from door. Can I leave with you today?'

'There are other police officers outside. They know about this place and what goes on here. If you're willing to give evidence, to help us find the man who shot Gene Oldman, we can shut these flats down straight away. We'll find this Scalp. If need be we'll make sure you get protection before and after the trial . . .'

'How soon you find Scalp?' she asked.

'I doubt he'll manage to avoid us for more than a week. We'll be able to figure out who his contacts are, where all the other women are being kept . . .'

'You not know?'

'Not yet. It was only because Finlay died that some of Gene Oldman's contacts told me about this place. Sooner or later we'll build up the bigger picture and then we'll—'

'But next race is tomorrow night . . . must stop it.' She was raising her voice. Lively put a gentle finger over her lips, pressing his ear to the door and waiting before he responded.

'What race, Elenuta? I don't understand.'

'Race girls and men. Finlay start it. Scalp do same.'

'Like a running race, or something else?'

'No, no! In big room . . . big building. Women run, men go after. If they catch, they kill. Must stop it.' She gripped his arm. 'More women die.'

'More? When . . . hold on . . . how many women have died already? Were you there?'

She shook her head and released her aching fingers from his forearm.

'I not there. Finlay show me on computer. Three women die. One live. She race again.'

'Do you know what happened to the bodies of those three women?'

'No,' she whispered.

'I think I might,' he said. 'This was recently? In the last couple of weeks?'

'Yes. Scalp was there. Other men watch.'

'How many men do you think?'

'Maybe one hundred. Not sure, but many. All bad.'

'All bad,' he agreed. 'Were all the women in that race taken from the flats in this building?'

'No, from different places. I never seen those women before. You must find others before race.'

'Yeah,' he said. 'We must.' Lively folded his arms and stared at his feet.

Elenuta watched him struggling for words and realised what the issue was.

'Arrest men today, Scalp will hear and maybe you not find all women,' she said calmly. 'Yes?'

'We have to get you out of here. What you're going through . . .'

'Scalp will be at race. All bad men and guards. They tell where all women are. Many women, I think.'

A fist hammered the door. Elenuta shrieked, jumping towards the safety of Lively's arms.

'Nearly finished,' he shouted.

'Time's up, pal,' Paddy, the guard, replied.

'Then I'll fucking pay for a bit more, now would you sod off while I do what I'm here for.' Lively had his hand on the doorknob, his weight pressed against it for good measure. Elenuta held her breath.

'All right, but it'll be another twenty for the extra minutes. You good for that?'

'And then some,' Lively growled.

Footsteps up the corridor indicated that the deal was done. Elenuta collapsed against his shoulder.

'I can't leave you here. You're being raped, all of you. Beaten, tortured.'

'One more day. You find race, this stops for everyone.'

'I can't do that,' Lively said. 'It's too dangerous. If we could just get Finlay's computer we'd have the evidence, maybe we'd get the other addresses he was keeping the girls at, we'd find out which men he'd invited to this race . . .'

'Scalp . . .' she tried to find the word and couldn't, making a violent motion with her foot instead, 'like this, on laptop.'

'Stamped on it?' She nodded. 'Completely destroyed it?'

'And take away,' she said. 'All papers, everything. Police watch here, tomorrow guards go to race. Only one guard stays here.

263

You catch all bad men. No women hurt. You save us.' She took his forearm in her hands, clutching hard.

Lively shook his head.

'There's no guarantee of that. If we don't find them or something goes wrong . . .'

'Must try,' she said simply.

The hammering at the door began again. They both stood up.

'I'll get you out of here, one way or another. Will you be okay tonight? I need to go and brief my boss,' he whispered.

'I will,' she said.

Lively took an awkward half step towards her, then backed away. Elenuta covered the distance herself, reaching up to hug him, wishing he didn't have to go. He felt so solid and real. She just wanted to cling to him.

'I have to go. They'll get suspicious. Quickly, loosen your clothing,' he whispered. She undid her shirt and the top button of her shorts, messing her hair up for good measure. 'I'm coming back, Elenuta. You're not alone any more.'

The door opened.

'She giving you shit?' Paddy asked.

'Just telling her what I'm expecting next time I see her,' Lively said. 'You got my phone there?'

'Here you go.' He handed it over. 'She all right, then?'

'Aye, one's the same as another once they're on their backs, right? To be honest with you, it gets a bit boring after a while. Do you not offer anything more exciting here?'

'You can have multiple girls as long as you pay. The boss doesn't care, and he turns a blind eye to what you do to them as long as they're fit to work the rest of the night.'

'If I want to give a woman a slap, I'll do that at home where I don't have to pay for it.' Lively got a bit closer to Paddy, dropping his voice and giving him a wink. 'Gene

Oldman told me Finlay used to run something a bit more exotic. He said he could never afford to go, but cash isn't a problem for me.'

'Gene was a twat with a mouth that got him killed,' Paddy said.

'Not going to disagree with you about his mouth, but his ears worked fine, and he heard stuff. Listen,' he stuck his hand in his wallet, 'I get it. These things only work if the people involved know how to keep their mouths shut. I appreciate your discretion as a matter of fact. But I can pay – not just whatever it costs to get in – but as a thank you to anyone good enough to help me.' He shoved a roll of twenties into Paddy's hand. 'If you could help me out there'd be double that in it for you. No one else needs to know.'

Paddy looked up and down the corridor before answering.

'It's not that easy. There's a list. Your name's got to be on it in advance. You have to be a client already.'

'Well, I'm here, and I think what I've been doing for the last hour qualifies me pretty bloody impressively as a client. Ask your whore if you don't believe me.'

'I believe you well enough pal, but it's tomorrow night. I'm not sure I've got time to sort it, and the list might be full.'

'Ah, room for a small one, though, right?'

'You're no' a small one, you fat bastard!' Paddy laughed.

Lively responded with a smile and gentle fist to the upper arm.

'You cheeky fucker! And there was me thinking we could be mates!'

'Listen,' Paddy whispered. 'I'll try to get you on the list, but I won't know until tomorrow. Scalp's organising the whole thing himself. The address and time go out in a text with only an hour to go, so no one gives it away. I can't guarantee anything.'

'Understood,' Lively said.

'And you can't tell anyone you gave me money. That'd drop me properly in the shit.'

'I look after anyone who looks after me. Old school.'

'Right,' Paddy said. 'Give me your mobile number.'

He handed Lively a pen and he scribbled the number onto an extra twenty-pound note, making sure Paddy saw there was plenty left where that came from.

'Watch your mobile, and be prepared to move quickly. Once the doors are locked, they don't open them for anyone.'

'You're a pal,' Lively said. 'Tomorrow, then.'

'I'll see what I can do.'

Elenuta watched Lively go through the tiniest crack between her door and its frame. He couldn't have looked less like a comic book superhero, yet the effect he'd had on her was no less than if Superman had flown in through her window – once he'd broken through the boarding, of course. She realised she was hungry. She hadn't felt properly starving like that in such a long time. The desire to eat, to make herself strong and healthy, had slowly dripped from her.

Scalp hadn't yet chosen the women who would race tomorrow. The rest of the women didn't even have it on their radar, but then they hadn't seen Finlay's video, and she hadn't had the heart to warn them. Why increase their fear when they were already living in terror? Release from captivity was only twenty-four hours away. All they had to do was survive until then. Close their eyes and imagine a better life while seeing to the clients. Eat a bit, sleep for a while, then it would all be over. The police would rescue them. She looked at her watch and began counting down not just the hours, but the minutes.

Chapter Thirty-Two

'That's all the information I have. Time was limited and the guard was in the corridor,' Lively explained.

'Where's Elenuta from?' Ava asked.

'Romania. I don't know about the other women there.'

'Any word on Scalp's true identity?' Ava asked the crowd gathered in the incident room.

'Nothing, ma'am,' Graham replied. 'Plenty of people have heard of him, but no one knows his full name. I suspect he's come in recently from out of the area, so I've issued an alert requesting information across Police Scotland, and also notified New Scotland Yard to spread the word and see if the other UK forces have any intelligence.'

'Great. So do we have any idea where this race might be held? No rumours about that circulating?'

'If anyone knows anything about it they're not saying, and we can't ask too many questions in case the fact that we're asking gets back to Scalp and he changes the venue or moves it back by a couple of days. We don't want him disappearing on us,' Lively said.

Ava looked at her watch. It was 3 a.m. Since Lively had

emerged from the flats four hours earlier MIT had done nothing but get in touch with their usual sources and check databases, all to no effect.

'I say we just go in and get those women safe,' Tripp said. 'Even twenty-four hours more of what they're living through might mean multiple additional rapes, not to mention violence and the threat of death. What if someone gets killed in there while we're making plans?'

Ava sympathised. That had been her initial view, too. They'd solved two murders, even if no one was in cuffs yet, although it was fair to say few were grieving over the loss of either Gene Oldman or Finlay Wilson. The three young women whose remains had been found at the pig farm deserved justice too. Their identities weren't yet known, but somewhere in the world they had family and friends waiting desperately to know what had happened to them. The best chance MIT had of arresting and convicting their killers, and of identifying the dead women, would be at the race. Ava stood up.

'All right,' she said. 'We can debate this all night. There's never going to be an answer that keeps everyone safe, but we'll do our best. I agree with DS Tripp that we have a serious responsibility to keep those women we already know about safe. There might be an awful lot of them in the flats at Wester Hailes. And I get it. If any of those women gets seriously hurt or, God forbid, killed, before we start making arrests, it'll be on us. Me, in fact. While that's a risk I don't want to take, I can't see a way of avoiding it. The second we go in there, the whole network will close up. Every phone, every computer, every vehicle, every witness will disappear. Worst-case scenario is that Scalp – whoever he is – hears about the first raid and decides to get rid of the other women who are too much of a liability. We might save some lives only to cause others to die.'

There was a general murmur of consent around the room.

'We've got a skeleton crew running surveillance at Wester Hailes now. DI Graham, increase that, please. If any female comes out of those flats – on foot, unconscious, or in a body bag – I want undercover units tailing immediately. Everyone in plainclothes and concealed. Avoid contact with the locals. Not a single marked car. No sirens or lights, whatever happens. Use your discretion, but obviously where there's an immediate threat to life we'll have to intervene. Other than that, we watch and wait. Get perimeters established at all major junctions in the area. We're not expecting much movement until tomorrow evening. That's when it seems logical that they'll transport the chosen women to the race venue.'

'What if none of the women from the Wester Hailes flats is in the race? How will we know where it is then?' Tripp asked.

'Some of Scalp's heavies from the flats will be going. Elenuta said they only leave one guard inside the flat on race night,' Lively said.

'Sergeant Lively, we'll need you on the inside of the race from as early as possible,' Ava instructed.

'I don't know if I'm even going to get on the list, ma'am,' Lively said. 'We might just have to follow Scalp's men, wait until everyone's inside and raid the place.'

'Not good enough. If we don't have eyes inside, hearing and seeing what's going on, we don't have any evidence. Scalp could just say the women were taking part in a race and that there was no intent to harm them at the end,' Ava said.

'But there's the last race. We can prosecute them for that . . .' Tripp said.

'That was down to Finlay Wilson, and he's dead. Elenuta says the recording on Wilson's laptop was destroyed by Scalp. Elenuta only saw it on video and without a single witness there in person and the victims' bodies largely destroyed, we won't get any murder convictions. You have to be inside, Sergeant. This whole case rests on you.'

'No fuckin' pressure then,' Lively muttered.

'We'll follow Scalp's men. Make sure you're in the area – even if you don't get the text you'll have to pretend you did and blag your way in,' Ava told him.

'It's not that easy, security on this friggin' race is tighter than Sandringham on Christmas Day.'

'Make it work!' Ava snapped. 'If you don't, either more women will die, or everyone inside walks free.'

'We'll still have them on human trafficking and every assault charge you can imagine,' DC Swift offered.

Ava glared at him. Lively took over from her.

'Aye, that's great for us, Doesn't Compute Swift, but it won't be good enough for the parents of the girls who were killed for sport the last time. The chief's right. Failure's not a fucking option.'

'Thanks, Sergeant,' Ava said quietly. 'Right, let's get this plan clear. We need to hold on until everyone is inside before we raid. A build-up of police vehicles will alert them, so we have to be cautious until we've got every single one of them trapped like the rats they are. We'll be in contact with Lively inside. He'll send us a message when everything's about to start and that's when we go. I'll need multiple paramedics on standby, but notify the receiving hospitals confidentially. Same goes for the fire service. Armed units are going in up front – we can be sure there'll be men in there with guns. This has to be a flawless operation. The second they realise what's happening, the first response will be to use any women inside as shields. Unbroken perimeter. No one gets away. Plenty of uniformed officers ready in the station to process everyone who gets arrested, and the number should be high. Briefings of the relevant units and teams all day. I'm calling in backup from the other Police Scotland areas. Lively – you'll have a concealed weapon, a mobile, and a hidden communications device.'

'If they find a weapon on me, I'll be kicked straight back out and that's the best-case scenario. It could blow the whole thing if they suspect me, then we're back to square one.'

'All right, no weapon, but you have to be able to communicate with us. See what tech can do to make sure you get through without anything being picked up. DI Graham, finding where the other women are across the city will be the priority. Brief uniformed teams on readiness to undertake further operations as soon as we start getting information from those arrested. I'll do deals with anyone who gives us useful information the second they have the opportunity, so DS Tripp, make contact with the Procurator Fiscal this morning and have someone on standby at their office too. They need to know what we're doing anyway. They're about to get an awful lot of paperwork on their desks and we'll need some legal backup when we start breaking down doors.'

'In terms of getting information from the women inside, we might need translators, ma'am,' Lively said. 'Elenuta's English is workable but not fluent enough that she can give complex descriptions. I'm guessing it'll be the same for some of the others.'

'Good point,' Ava said. 'Also, we'll need somewhere safe to house any women we remove who don't require hospitalisation. They'll have to be seen by a doctor in any event, clothes, food, beds for the night. It'll have to be somewhere secure, away both from the press and from anyone looking to help out Scalp. Contact social services, Tripp. See what they can do.'

'Where will you be, ma'am?'

'At the race, running point. I intend to go in with the armed units from the outset.'

'Ma'am . . .' Graham said.

'Too busy for any more discussion,' she said. 'You've all got a week's work to fit into twelve hours. I'll buy all the coffee and biscuits. At lunchtime I'll make sure you get as much fast food as you can eat. There are people depending on us, so no slip-ups. Thanks everyone.'

She made her way out into the corridor. About halfway along she realised no one was following her. No Tripp with endless, but always vital, additional queries. No Lively having to have the last word. No DI Graham asking if she was okay. It was too big a deal for that, she realised. She checked her watch and began making a mental to-do list. It was going to be the longest day imaginable.

Chapter Thirty-Three

By 10 a.m. Callanach had slipped into two hours' sleep after a night of research, and awoken to the sound of the email alert pinging on his mobile. He stretched and grabbed the phone. There was an update from social services saying that Azzat and Huznia had successfully transferred to a family and were settling in. After that was an email from Jean-Paul. Daily phone calls to the hospital meant that Callanach knew his friend's eyesight was recovering slowly, but that it still wasn't up to staring at a screen and writing emails. He'd obviously drafted in assistance from Interpol to help him get through the admin building up in his absence.

Luc, you have, apparently, decided against taking on a new partner while I'm temporarily out of action. That doesn't seem like a good choice given the recent difficulties we found ourselves in. I can arrange either a replacement from Interpol for you, or pair you with an experienced officer from the local French police. Also, an update once in a while wouldn't be a bad thing. What the hell's going on? Jean-Paul.

Callanach grinned. Jean-Paul could never maintain formality from the start of an email to its end. He could see him as clearly as if he were in the hospital room, trying his best to maintain an air of professionalism while stuck in bed, desperate to be up and involved.

Callanach began typing.

Jean-Paul, Many thanks for your email. I gave detailed consideration to requesting the assistance of a partner from either Interpol or the local police force but decided, due to expediency, that it would be more efficient to proceed with the investigation alone. I am aware that others continue to pursue strands of the investigation and will liaise with them as needed. Given that a second Scottish citizen is also now known to be on French soil, I believe it is crucial for me to take a lead in this case. I'm doing fine, by the way. No, I'm not taking any risks. No major shifts in the investigation. Now let me get on with the job, take the doctors' advice, and get some rest. If anything comes up, you'll be the first to know. Luc.

He clicked send and opened the email he'd been saving until last.

Luc, I'll be out of contact most of today. We have leads in two murder cases, which may also resolve three others. There will be a large-scale operation tonight in an attempt to detain multiple suspects at a single scene. If you need me urgently, please contact the incident room and they will do their best to pass a message along. As soon as this is completed I will be in touch for a full update on the Malcolm Reilly and Bart Campbell cases which I know is overdue.

And I'm sorry to email this rather than phone. Yesterday, the doctors confirmed that they still weren't content with the extent of the surgery. Natasha is due to have a mastectomy in the next few days. We're just waiting for them to confirm the appointment. She doesn't want a lot of fuss. In spite of how brave she's been, this is hitting her hard. Don't race back. I'll let you know as soon as I have more info. Ava.

Callanach threw his mobile down on the bed.

'Fuck,' he muttered, closing his eyes before drawing in a deep breath.

His mobile offered another alert tone. He didn't want to look. Enough news for one day. What he needed to do was write to Natasha, but anything he came up with sounded trite in his own head, and that was before seeing it reduced to a font. Something was better than nothing though. She needed to know he was thinking of her.

He picked up his phone again, opening his email.

The latest message sat in bold type, seemingly innocuous, its subject line proclaiming nothing other than the bland, 'Your Condition'. He didn't recognise the sender's name.

He took a screen grab, then opened the message. It was written in French and addressed to Monsieur Chevotet. He'd given a false email address to the clinic and had all messages diverted into his usual email. He took another screen grab of the complete email before beginning to read.

Monsieur Chevotet, We are contacting you privately and confidentially to offer you a consultation regarding a possible treatment for your condition. Access to our treatments is extremely limited, due to cost and practical considerations. You have been referred to us as an end of life case, and in those circumstances we are prepared to include you in our potential patients list. You will need to consent to engaging with us in absolute confidence. Big pharmaceutical corporations and governments conspire together to keep alternative treatments from the public, receiving billions of euros each year in covert payments for licensing only those drugs and treatments that serve them. We have consistently refused to engage in this corrupt process, and thus a licence has been refused. If you cannot guarantee discretion then we will have no choice but to remove your name from our list, as you will jeopardise the opportunity for many others to receive potentially life-saving treatment at a time when their medical advisors have told them their situation is hopeless. Your invitation to receive further, more detailed information will expire within one hour. You can confirm your interest by replying to this email, upon which you will be given details for an in-person meeting, with an access code and password. You alone will be allowed to attend that meeting. You must bring photographic ID and be prepared to be checked for recording devices.

It was signed from Group 2029. No name.

He messaged Interpol immediately, asking for a trace on the email, not that there would be a simple IP address that would lead them to the author. Whoever was organising international abductions of organ donors wasn't going to fail to protect themselves at the most basic communications level.

He waited half an hour, made sure Interpol was watching and recording the email exchange, then replied.

Dear Group 2029. I am interested in hearing more. My doctor has said there's no treatment available except a transplant, but my chances of getting a suitable liver in time are millions to one. I have a lot of questions. Do you have a website? What are your success rates? Would this be in France or do I need to travel? Is there a phone number I could call, as I'm anxious not to lose any more time. Yours, Luc Chevotet.

They weren't going to answer any of his questions in an email, but a failure to ask them would raise an immediate red flag. Offer this sort of potential life-saving treatment to anyone who needed it and they would inevitably come back asking for more information. It took only eight minutes for the response.

Monsieur Chevotet, Please attend at 167 Rue des Bateliers, Clichy, apartment 206, this afternoon at 4 p.m. precisely. Attend alone. Identification and a body check will be required. You will have a 30-minute consultation session. Our representative will have information for you. He is not from Group 2029, but he will be able to pass any questions you have along to us after the consultation. There is no fee payable at this stage. If you attend with other people, you will not be allowed access. If it becomes clear that you have notified other people about our services, your consultation will be terminated to protect our other patients. You will not need a medical. We offer treatments that differ from normal medical procedures. If you do not attend this meeting, no further appointment will be offered and no further communications will be entered into. We look forward to meeting you and helping to reshape your future. Apartment access code 87961, password Cathedral. Group 2029.

Callanach checked the details for the apartment. It was a new build and rooms were being offered for short-term business purposes as well as for longer-term residential lettings. Payment would inevitably have been made in cash or using an online payment facility that couldn't be traced back. Interpol would be attempting to identify the lessee already, but Callanach wouldn't be holding his breath. If it were a hotel room, they might have some success persuading the management to allow them to place surveillance in a room, but the lease would have begun in the private building already, and at that stage they'd require a court order to force the building owner to comply. It could be done quickly, but not quickly enough if there was a lease in place and rights potentially being infringed.

He emailed an update to Jean-Paul, copying in both Ava and Interpol HQ. French police would detain whoever met him in person at the end of the meeting, and an order to examine their communications would be obtained within an hour of identifying them. What they actually needed, though, was evidence of where Bart Campbell was being held. That's if he was still alive.

Chapter Thirty-Four

It had been a relatively easy afternoon. Scalp had instructed that the flat doors be closed to clients given the number of guards he had at the warehouse setting up. The new boss had been unusually jovial all day, parading around barking instructions, reminding them time and time again that his first race was going to make everything that had gone before look like amateur night at the dog track. The comparison of the women to dogs wasn't wasted on Elenuta. Like so many greyhounds, the women were being kept for business purposes only, worked until they broke, then put down as soon as they weren't earning their keep any more.

Scalp had adopted an air of superiority that, almost impossibly, made him even more dislikeable. One phone call after another had come through to his mobile. Guards had come and gone, lockable cash boxes had been unwrapped from pristine cardboard, new SIM cards had been inserted into phones to be destroyed immediately after the race was over, and Scalp himself had changed outfit three times, never quite satisfied that he was looking his absolute best for his crowning moment when he took the microphone.

Elenuta had got through the previous night quietly after Lively had gone, desperate to tell the other women that their time left in captivity was on a countdown, but convinced she'd jinx it if she did. She'd slept wearing the jeans that contained Lively's knife, reaching down repeatedly to run her fingers along its outline in the hem, and fallen asleep clutching it, even though it meant having her leg bent up at an unnatural angle. She'd woken up stiff, her hip sore, and happier than she'd felt since the day she'd been forced into the back of a truck and driven across Europe. All she had to do now was wait it out. Just a few hours and the police would be there. Safety was waiting just outside the door. It was four in the afternoon when Scalp turned up with two new goons in tow. Elenuta kept to the back of the row of women when they were called out into the corridor, head down but listening carefully. Any additional information she could give the police when they turned up would help.

She stole a quick glance at Scalp. He was paler than she remembered, a sheen of sweat across his forehead lighting him up beneath the bare bulb hanging from the ceiling.

'Right, I've got a special job on tonight,' he said. 'I'll be needing a couple of volunteers for it.'

Elenuta's stomach shrivelled. She'd known this was a possibility but hoped the women who'd be racing had already been selected from the other flats. Not that it made it any better for those women, just that she wouldn't have to live with the knowledge that she'd kept information from her flatmates that could have helped them avoid this situation.

'So who hasn't been pulling their weight?' he asked their regular guard. 'Only this would be an opportunity for them to get back in my good books.'

None of the women spoke. They might not have known what was going on, but they'd all long since stopped trusting anything they were told.

'Her,' the guard pointed at one of the oldest women in the group, Suzan, who rarely got chosen unless all the other girls were busy, 'or her.' He poked Anika in the shoulder. At just sixteen, Anika might have been a favourite with the regulars if she took better care of herself, but lately Elenuta had noticed the girl pulling out patches of her hair and eyelashes. She'd lost so much weight that every rib showed as clearly as on an X-ray, and her eyes appeared overlarge. The effect was ghoulish and off-putting.

'All right,' Scalp said. 'You can both come. If you're good, you'll get a prize.'

Suzan looked shocked and terrified, while Anika began to smile. Elenuta wanted to slap some reality into her.

'What prize?' Anika asked, stepping forward towards Scalp.

Elenuta saw heroin's delusion in her eyes, and realised she'd been using far more than the other women to cope with the day-to-day existence. Anika wouldn't stand a chance in the race. She was just as likely to sit on the floor and wait for death as she was to run and fight. If the police didn't intervene in time, whatever their plan was, Anika was almost certainly going to be the first to die. The only place she could possibly survive was in the flat with the other women to protect her.

All Elenuta had wanted was to keep quiet, stay put, and wait. The day's hours had slipped away, and now the end was in sight. She believed that Sergeant Lively, or someone under his command, would come to the flat. Any guards that remained would be arrested. Scalp would be far away, at whatever venue he'd chosen for the race, and the police would be there too, ready to stop that bloodbath before any more women lost their lives. That was why she'd waited all day – so the police had a chance to figure out everything about the race. Only nothing in life was certain. She'd learned that lesson the hard way when

281

she was abducted. It was possible that the police would be a split-second too late. Scalp might change the format for the race and start it early or, God forbid, decide to sacrifice some poor woman at the very start to prove – mainly to himself – how incredibly powerful he was. Or it might all be fine. It would have to be, she told herself. She wasn't going to die today. But she couldn't let someone as young and vulnerable as Anika die either.

'Fuck,' she muttered to herself. 'Not my problem.' But her conscience objected immediately. Reluctant hero or not, Elenuta knew it wasn't even a choice. The police would save them all, she persuaded herself, because they had to. It was that, or execution.

She'd thought this would be the last time she'd have to look at Scalp's face, unless it was from a witness box in a courtroom with police and prison officers there to protect her. She welcomed the chance to look into his eyes under those circumstances. But she couldn't send a child to her death. Much as she hated to, she stepped forward.

'I want chance,' Elenuta said. 'I want win prize.' She raised her eyebrows and stared at Scalp.

'You can get back to work,' Scalp said. 'I've got what I wanted.'

'I run away again. I did before.'

'That was you, was it? Lucky for you you've a half-decent fucking face. You're a money-earner.'

'If no prize, I kill next client. Police will come look.'

'Are you fucking threatening me?' Scalp stepped towards her, pushing the still-grinning Anika out of the way. She stumbled into the wall as Scalp grabbed a handful of Elenuta's hair and twisted her neck upwards.

'I want prize,' she repeated.

'That's because you don't know what the prize is.' He snarled in her face and she resisted the temptation to headbutt him. Scalp wasn't above strangling a woman to death out of sheer anger, even if it made no commercial sense.

'I have first go. Anika is only sixteen. She try next time.'

'She's young. The crowd will like it. Plus she's useless here. I've made my decision. Get back in your room.' He released her, letting her fall into her doorway. Elenuta got upright again and walked after him.

'I see film of race. I know what is. I escape and tell police.' She held his gaze, watching his frown turn into something closer to hatred.

'You'll die,' he said. 'Is that what you want?' Elenuta held her tongue. 'Because if that's it, I can help you with that right here, right now. Shall I?'

He bent down to look her straight in the eyes. His breath stank of stale cigarette smoke, and just below his nose were tell-tale grains of white powder. She counted down from ten, rigid, waiting for his decision.

'All right, you fucking bitch, you want to race, you can. I don't ever want to see your face again, so I might as well make some money out of you. The kid can take the next turn. And now we're fucking late, that's just great. Get these two in the car,' he told the man next to him. 'The rest of you get cleaned up. It bloody stinks in here.' He kicked a bin as he walked past, head held high, king of his castle.

One of the men took Elenuta by the arm, pulling her towards the door.

'Wait! Collar,' she remembered.

Scalp took a knife from his pocket and cut through it.

'You won't be needing it again anyway,' he told Elenuta, as he did the same with Suzan's collar.

'Maybe I win,' Elenuta said quietly.

'If you win, sweetheart, I'm going to celebrate by wringing

your fucking neck myself. How's that for an evening to look forward to?'

Scalp shoved her and Suzan across the threshold. Elenuta took a last look at the row of women staring in horror as she left. The police were nowhere to be seen as they exited the building. Either the operation had gone terribly wrong or they were doing their job exceptionally well. She was betting on the latter with her life.

Chapter Thirty-Five

Rue des Bateliers was out of Paris' centre, an innocuous enough road with the Grand Parc des Docks de Saint-Ouen on one side and semi-high-rise flats in different stages of construction along the other. It hardly seemed the place you'd go to buy a new organ from a kidnap victim, but then, Callanach wondered, where was? Officers were stationed outside the building to provide backup, but none were inside. It was too much of a risk. The apartment had been rented for the previous two weeks, and it was safe to assume Group 2029 had security arrangements in place which included monitoring people entering and exiting. A sudden influx of people would immediately arouse suspicion.

He repeated the routine, yellowing his eyes and preparing himself for likely questions. Group 2029 had paid the rent in cash, together with a deposit that limited the amount of questions asked by the landlord. There were no company records available for them, and no intelligence about them. It seemed likely that the name changed on each email. Callanach punched the entry code into the panel outside the apartment door and entered.

The man standing inside the door was all brawn. Six foot four with tattoos peeking out of the top of his shirt and below his cuffs, he could have been a doorman at any club in the city.

'Your name, please?' he asked, in an accent a long way from Paris chic.

'Luc Chevotet,' Callanach replied, making sure his hand had a just-noticeable tremor to it as he held out his fake driver's licence.

'The password?'

'Is this all really necessary? I'm just here to get more information.'

'The password has to be given before you can go through,' the doorman said blankly.

'Okay, sure. Cathedral. I wasn't sure what to expect. Will there be a presentation, or—'

'I have to check you.' He was polite but obviously not prepared to answer any questions.

Callanach put his arms up slowly, giving a faint groan as he did so, conscious of possible hidden cameras and who might be watching. The security officer ran an airport-style electrical monitor over his body, pointing at the pockets which elicited a beep.

'Leave your mobile in this box.'

'Um, I don't really like to leave it anywhere I can't see it, for privacy reasons. Do you think you could make an exception?' Callanach asked, knowing the answer, but the pretence was necessary.

'You'll get it back afterwards,' was all the response he got.

He left his mobile in the security officer's keeping and was shown through to another room. Taking the chair on the side of the desk that didn't have a file, Callanach stared out of the window and waited. The whole place was bland, anonymous. It was clever. Use an apartment for a couple of weeks, then

286

move on. Presumably not just up a floor or across a street, but to a different area of the city altogether.

An internal door opened and a man walked in, serene smile fixed in place, suited and tied, hair neat, hand ready for shaking. Callanach made a show of effort in standing up, gripping the offered hand only weakly, breathing hard.

'Monsieur Chevotet,' the man began. 'I'm here representing Group 2029. We're so pleased you decided to find out more. Please sit down. Take all the time you need. Would you like a bottle of water?'

'Thank you,' Callanach said.

The man made his way to a mini-fridge. Cheap, temporary, portable. Callanach opened the offered water and took a long drink as he studied the man in front of him. He hadn't noticed him at the clinic, but then he'd have been easy to miss. Early to mid-thirties, clean cut. Nothing remarkable. Unathletic, erring on the too-skinny side of thin. Eyes that didn't want to settle anywhere.

'So let's begin,' the man said, taking his seat behind the desk and opening the file. 'First of all I have to cover the issue of confidentiality.' He picked up a pen and ran its nib along the text as he read. 'The treatment we offer is not one you will find in any traditional hospital or practice. It has been developed—'

'Sorry,' Callanach interrupted. 'I didn't catch your name. Are you a doctor?'

'Um, no, I'm a . . .' the man's eyes flicked to the top of the page he was reading from, 'a client liaison executive.'

'And your name is?'

'We don't give out our names at this stage. As I was explaining, the confidentiality issue—'

'I understand, it's just that I was hoping for a more personal approach. I've had so many different doctors, it can be difficult to trust when there's no connection,' Callanach explained.

The man coughed into his hand.

'I wonder if I could just read this. There's a section at the end for questions. I think when you hear all the information you'll feel much better about it.'

'Sure. I get it. Go ahead.'

'Thank you. Right . . . our need for confidentiality relates to threats received from large pharmaceutical companies who have rejected our calls to understand the value, validity and nature of our treatments. The corruption of these big corporations, and the extent of their reach into the political sphere, including the police force, means that it is unsafe for us to reveal too much about our company, our practitioners and researchers. Their refusal to recognise our treatments means that we have not been able to roll them out wide scale but we continue our work, to help the few, because a single life saved is worth our time. Big pharmaceuticals receive billions each year in grants, in drug sales, and even more in fundraising. They refuse to open up the marketplace to newer, more innovative treatments because of the financial risk to them.'

'How exactly does the treatment—' The man held up a hand to stop him. 'Sorry.'

'Because of the extreme danger to our staff and our practice through breach of confidentiality and sharing of information, we ask you to pay the fees for treatment up front. The fee structure is in thirds. Two-thirds of it remains with our company, and the final third is a returnable deposit, repayable to you once your treatment is complete, and when we are certain that you have not breached the confidentiality contract. It will be repaid to you no more than seventy-two hours after treatment.

'You've been assessed as suitable for our treatment, given the lack of probability of traditional successful ongoing treatment or transplant, taking into account your age, and previous record of good health. The cost of treatment and payment facility will be notified to you by email at the end of this meeting. We recognise that our charges are high, but that's because we have to recompense the family who will contribute to your future well-being.'

Callanach watched him reading. His expression was almost blank. Whatever role he had in the company, he was either in the dark about the details or he had the best poker face imaginable.

'The treatment itself consists of specific and targeted living cell transfer. Stem cells have been used in treatments for many years now, but that is dependent on having access to the right cells. Our innovative new treatment identifies living donors without the risks involved in transplants and organ rejection, without the need for donor-to-recipient matching, and with a full consensual and compensatory practice that fulfils our legal and moral obligations to all involved.'

'Living donors?' Callanach asked.

'I'm just getting to that bit. Our donors are all in vegetative states, but prior to reaching that state, they all signed and agreed to take part in this programme. We have identified a donor who would meet your needs in terms of the age and health of their organs. None of our donors have organ damage that relates to the organ whose cells you require. We are able to provide you with medical assessments, photographs, and evidence of the donor's desire to help others live on after their death.'

'But why would they—'

'We have limited scope to discuss an individual donor's decision-making processes, as you'll understand. This is a personal decision they reach with their families. Some have received spinal injuries, for example, and are seeking end of life treatment, but wish to help others before they die. Some might have the onset of a genetic disease which you will not be affected by.'

'Where do these donors come from? Are they all French or—'

This time the man didn't bother with the hand. He just continued speaking.

'Healthy cells can be introduced orally into your body. Eating raw is a cornerstone of all good cancer advice. This is because the raw consumption of all cells . . .'

Callanach's stomach hit a zero gravity moment. He frowned, blinked, realising the man had paused and was waiting for him to compose himself.

'I'll wait,' he said. 'This is revolutionary science. It's important you understand how it works.' But his eyes were still on the page. Even this pause, this reassurance, was scripted.

'I'm fine,' Callanach said. 'You can keep reading.'

'The raw consumption of cells is the purest, cleanest way to reinvigorate the body. Contrary to popular belief, not all cells are completely broken down in the digestive process. With treatment and coating from our newly developed and proven formula, those cells can be absorbed into the body with their individual organ benefits intact, with medical properties that the body can recognise and incorporate into the body's own failing organ to begin the regenerative process.

'Our success rate with the treatment is more than fifty per cent, which in chronic or late-stage cases marks a dramatic breakthrough in life-saving procedures. Again, we stress that everything we do is consensual. If you decide to proceed with the treatment, your donor's family will be provided with your generic details – no name – so that they can treasure the knowledge of the life their loved one has helped save. Here are testimonies,' he handed over a sheaf of papers, 'from people we have already successfully treated. At this stage, I am able to offer you some details of your potential donor. Would you like that?'

'Yes, please.'

The man handed over more pages of A4 that Callanach scanned for logos. Not a leaf in sight. It was starting to look as if whatever Azzat had seen on the van had no relevance at all to Group 2029's organisation. On the first page were several photos of an adult female, Caucasian, face slightly blurred.

'We've blurred her facial features to protect her anonymity. Some donors consent to all their details being known and others opt for a level of privacy. Her medical records are on the following pages, again, with redactions.'

Callanach glanced through the photos. Some were obviously taken before the so-called donor was bedridden, standing up, showing a healthy body, good muscle tone. In the next she was in a hospital bed, hooked up to a variety of machines and monitors.

'Those last photos are a little distressing, I'm afraid, but the point is that we're very careful to prove that the patient has reached a point of unresponsiveness.'

The photos were a wide shot of a doctor — face obscured by a mask — putting something into the patient's thigh. The close-up showed that it was a needle, a substantial distance into the flesh. Certainly far enough that a normally responsive individual would be unable to remain still.

'That's very reassuring,' Callanach managed. He turned the page. A variety of convincing details were listed, from childhood immunisations to an adult diagnosis of cervical cancer.

'You'll see that this cervical cancer has been assessed as non-threatening to you, but the donor's age, race and other fitness make her cells the perfect gift for your future well-being. We cannot allow you to take these documents away, but you would see the donor immediately prior to her life support being switched off, so you'll be able to confirm that she matches the details given here.'

'Immediately before she passes?'

'Donors are kept in peace and comfort, ensuring end of life takes place in controlled circumstances at the optimum moment for transfer of cells and to add our life-prolonging formula before it's administered to you in our laboratory environment. You can now ask questions and I will provide answers as far as possible.'

'Okay, well that's obviously a lot of information. Um, is this legal? Sorry if that sounds rude, but, you know, it's something I haven't heard of before . . .'

The man scanned the page.

'All treatments are legally compliant in the same way any organ donation where consent is freely given is lawful. Donors are being kept alive by machines only. No life is terminated without the family's express consent, and terminations only take place once life would not be sustainable without artificial medical and mechanical assistance. One-third of the money you pay goes to the family or assignee of the donor, to help them in their grief. You will receive a copy of the legal donor agreement, contract and consent form at the donation ceremony.'

'Donation ceremony?'

'The donation ceremony takes place on short notice due to the nature of the donor's illness. Cells need to be transferred quickly, but no life may be shortened artificially to ensure that we at no stage breach medical oaths. You will be sent a message giving you an address, then taken via company transport to our facility. The ceremony involves a purification ritual which is important to the donor and their families, a blessing, and a period of gratitude and reflection, before organs are transferred. The donor's family or friends may also be present but in a separate room so as to respect their grief at such a delicate time. Sometimes they request a meeting with the donor, which we urge you to accept.'

'That's really amazing,' Callanach said. 'I think I'd like that. And as to the science . . .'

'Our formula is designed to maximise cellular transfer benefits, to minimise intra-patient infection and to bolster the strength of cells as they meet your own body's organ. Our formula is combined with antibiotics and a steroidal treatment to ensure efficiency.'

·'And by consume, you mean what, exactly?'

The man took a breath, and continued reading.

'The cells and medical formula are provided to you orally. You will see the organ prior to its preparation to prove its fitness. The organ will then be taken to our laboratory for preparation and returned to you for consumption with medical oversight.'

'I eat it?'

'Oral consumption,' the man repeated.

Callanach fought the desire to grab him by the throat.

'What if it goes wrong? Where do I go? Do I get my money back?'

'All medical treatment for chronic or late-stage illness is unpredictable. Our success rate is better than any other treatment offer you may receive. Our treatments have been tested in line with current regulations over a number of years. The treatment itself may carry side effects of nausea, and you will be given an injection to help prevent this. Other side effects may include stomach cramps, diarrhoea and headaches. A full list will be provided to you. You will need to sign a liability waiver as is standard in all hospitals. You'll be given a twenty-four-hour emergency phone number for the first seven days after treatment, and a doctor's appointment will be sent to you roughly two weeks after treatment for a check-up.'

'Why can't I just drive myself to the facility?'

'Corporate spies are a constant threat to our life-saving work. Information sharing, even inadvertently, can threaten our ability to work with you and for you. All arrangements are made to ensure both your safety and our ongoing mission to fight otherwise incurable diseases.' He scanned the page. 'Our session has now come to an end. You will be emailed further instructions within the hour.'

'How soon can I have the treatment?' Callanach persisted.

'Oh, yes, I can answer that one. Treatment can be assumed to be within the next forty-eight hours subject to payment being made.'

'Forty-eight hours? That's . . . wow.'

The man stood up and held out his hand to shake Callanach's. It was cold and slightly damp.

'Thank you so much,' Callanach said. 'I feel like I've been given a chance. I hope I didn't keep you too long.'

'That's all right, I've finished for today,' the man replied, giving the first genuine smile since Callanach had entered. He looked relieved it was over.

That was good. It made what they needed to do now so much easier.

'Will I see you again?' Callanach asked.

'No, I'm only involved at the front end, so to speak. I hope it goes well for you, and I'm, you know, really sorry for what's wrong with you.' He sounded vague and embarrassed.

Callanach gave a nod to the doorman as he reclaimed his mobile and left. He made sure he was clear of any prying ears or eyes, taking the stairs and exiting onto the street. Giorgia Moretti-Russo, queen of her cell in Europe's most notorious prison, had been right about the organ transplant. It hadn't been what they were expecting. Preying on the vulnerable, the terminally ill, taking advantage of people staring down the barrel of a premature death – all of that had become increasingly obvious. But unwitting cannibalism of a murder victim, paid for at vast expense? That was something he'd never imagined he might encounter. He took a deep breath and got on his phone.

'I'm out,' he told the police unit leader outside the doors. 'Two men will follow. One's a security guard, looks more like a bouncer, Caucasian, early forties, shaved head, six four, wearing a suit but with visible tattoos on his neck and hands, extremely heavy-set. Follow but do not detain. We want him acting normally. Keep eyes on him twenty-four hours a day until we make other arrests, but get access to his communications and bank account to see if there's relevant traceable activity.

'The other male, also Caucasian, is thirty to thirty-five years old, short brown hair, slim, no noticeable tattoos, five eight, brown eyes, clean-shaven and wearing a tan suit with a dark blue tie. I want him picked up as soon as you've established that he's definitely not being watched or followed by anyone else. Keep the pick-up away from this building in case other flats are occupied by the same company. Take his communications devices and let me know what you find. Immediate interview, and tell him it's in his interests to cooperate. Try to persuade him not to lawyer up. And log his phone call to his lawyer. I don't want information passed through the legal team.' Callanach hung up.

He went to dial Ava's number before remembering she was on an operation, and called the incident room instead.

'This is Callanach. Notify DCI Turner as soon as she's available that there is a third victim in the Malcolm Reilly case. Currently kidnapped but believed still alive. Female, Caucasian, late teens to early twenties, between five six and five ten, blonde hair, eye colour unclear. Slim build. I'm working on the assumption that she might also be Scottish. Please check missing persons files or crime reports asap and come back to me. We need to establish an identity.'

He rang off. A door slammed around the corner and footsteps headed for the stairs. This was their best chance at finding Bart Campbell and hopefully also saving the life of the young woman who was in the process of having her liver sold to him. Quite possibly their only chance.

Chapter Thirty-Six

The warehouse looked innocuous enough. It had taken a mammoth feat of organisation to locate it. Visitors had come and gone from the flats in Wester Hailes all day, and on each occasion a different, unmarked, suitably banged-up-looking police vehicle had to tail the leads. MIT had used up almost every undercover vehicle at their disposal, including motorbikes, vans and an old minibus, too wary of the network of Scalp's men communicating to drive the same one twice. Three journeys ended up at random houses, twice the destination was a shopping centre, one was a trip to fill up with petrol and return to Wester Hailes – difficult not to get spotted following a car to a petrol station and back again – but finally some of Scalp's muscle men had set off out of Edinburgh mid-afternoon, and led them to the right place just as Ava was starting to give up hope. Since then, they'd been tentatively moving officers into the area. A few were having a meal at a local pub and watching the road outside. Others were just driving around the area. Most were stuck, freezing, in the fields and woodland surrounding the warehouse.

Ava disliked the distance the warehouse was from any other

buildings, and the fact that all the external lights had been deliberately disengaged. Someone had been more than just diligent in researching the perfect location. It was within easy reach of the city's outer limits, but without the need to drive directly through the area's small villages and arouse suspicion. Set in a former industrial area that had fallen into disuse when a motor parts manufacturer had decided that South East Asia was a cheaper bet, the building was currently unoccupied. The fact that the car park tarmac was strewn with chunks of rock pushed up by insistent weeds indicated that no one had been in occupation for a very long time. Given that research had been time-limited to just that afternoon, MIT had no idea of the internal layout of the building – not that the original blue-prints would necessarily have borne any resemblance to its current layout. The rural location also ensured that it was practically impossible for Police Scotland to get many vehicles into the area without making their presence known. Later on in the evening, when the car park was starting to fill up, that would be an option, but for now they'd only chanced a pass with a couple of vehicles sufficiently muddied up to appear farmer-owned. Ava herself was in army-camouflage fatigues and lying on her belly in icy dirt under the hedge of a neighbouring field, watching the main entrance through binoculars.

The problem with the nature of the building was that it would have been easy for the fire exits to have been jammed shut and probably also barricaded from the inside. She had teams in place to try those exits, but she wasn't holding out much hope. The main entrance was a set of metal double doors – no window glass – and there were already two men outside those with bulky enough jackets that they could be concealing anything underneath. It was no amateur operation, and she was about to send in DS Lively, alone, without a weapon. Ava offered up a silent prayer to the gods of chaos, asking them politely to take the evening off, and crawled back out of her hiding hole, running under cover to the unmarked car parked at the end of a nearby field where Lively and Tripp were hunkered down.

'Tell me you've had a message,' Ava demanded.

'Fuck all,' Lively said, staring at his mobile.

'It's working, right? You've got a signal?' she peered over his shoulder.

'Been checking it every five minutes,' Tripp told her. 'All the messages from my phone have come straight in.'

'Damn it. Is the coffee still hot?'

Lively poured her a cup from a flask and she wrapped her hands around it, opening up a laptop and staring at the screen that showed her where her units were positioned in the vicinity.

'Are you absolutely sure Paddy didn't tell you what time to expect the message?'

'Ma'am, he said he was going to try to sort it but that he couldn't promise anything, depends on the list and on Scalp. It doesn't matter how many times you ask me the same question, the answer won't change.'

'We've got to get you in there one way or another and it's getting pretty bloody late. Tripp, do we have eyes on Scalp?'

'Yes ma'am, and a reasonable photo of his face, but no identification as yet. He's about five minutes away. DC Monroe is in the car behind him and updating us in real time. Looks as if there's a bit of a convoy. At least three vehicles left Wester Hailes at the same time – two cars and a van, exiting from different roads – but they've followed the same route since then, headed in this direction.'

'They won't keep the doors open for a minute longer than is necessary once everyone's here. Lively, how did the communications testing go?'

'Wasn't bad. Uncomfortable, but you'll be able to hear my voice, and I'm not sure why the best option was to make the earpiece look like a hearing aid. I'll take my mobile in too, but I'm guessing it'll be taken off me, like it was at the flat yesterday.'

'And all units are clear on the signal for police entry?' Ava asked Tripp.

'Yes ma'am, Sergeant Lively will say "epic". We figured it was unique enough that we'd definitely hear it, but that it would make sense in the context of what they're expecting other men's reactions to be. Is that all right?'

'Is it all right that women are going to be racing for their lives while an audience waits to watch them get killed, and the expected reaction is "epic"? No, Tripp, it's really fucking not.'

'That's not exactly what I meant . . .'

'I know it wasn't,' she sighed. 'I'm sorry. It'll work fine, Tripp. It has to. Any word on the women yet?'

'Surveillance didn't get a good look, but the assumption is that the women are en route in the van rather than the cars, to keep them hidden from view.'

'Right, I'm going back out then. How far away are our armed units?'

'Spread out at various extended perimeters. Paramedics are in the nearest village, and we have fire crew on standby. Do you think we have enough backup, ma'am? Only there are going to be a lot of people inside that building. There'll be gunfire. Scalp's men won't give in without a fight.'

'Touch some wood, Sergeant Tripp. I'm not delivering any of my team to a hospital today. And Lively, do whatever it takes to get your arse in that building. We need eyes inside to lock these bastards up forever. Just don't get yourself killed.'

Ava hopped back out of the vehicle and returned to her earlier position, khaki hood up over her hair, settling in as comfortably as she could, knowing it would likely be an hour until she could move a muscle. The first car drove into the parking area just as she was established in her ditch, and newly covered with leaves. Four men disembarked, none of them the sort she'd want to share a dark alley with late at night. They laughed and joked, entirely at ease. No indication that they'd realised the police operation was on their horizon. That was a start. They greeted the men guarding the doors with shoulder punches and expletives, delivered with a side order of stupid grins. Ava grimaced. She didn't want them to be a team. She had specifically hoped they wouldn't be friends. Friends looked out for one another and fought back. They didn't run at the first sign of trouble, or turn on each other at the blink of an indictment. The bouncer turned and knocked the door hard in a rhythm Ava couldn't make out from a distance. The use of a code was basic but efficient. It was opened from the inside. No key entry from the exterior, then. They'd been too careful for that. The four newcomers disappeared inside and the door swung heavily and loudly shut behind them, proclaiming its impenetrability.

The next car that pulled in was a Range Rover. A thug climbed out of the driving seat. Much as Ava tried not to judge by appearance, on this occasion she decided to let her prejudices rule her political correctness. He was huge, shaven-headed with a beard making up for the upper hair loss, gut spilling over the top of his black jeans, armless T-shirt in spite of the cold and encroaching evening, tattoos down his arm an actual list of previous convictions. Her binoculars told her he was claiming everything from robbery to bestiality. She'd seen her fair share of tattoos, but no one yet had had the audacity to set out his prior convictions in permanent ink. Then the passenger door opened, and out crawled a completely different shade of evil.

Ava studied the man, checked her reaction to him, and looked again. There was nothing overtly visual that made her react so strongly to him. He was just a man. But that face, the sheer force of the hatred and the utter coldness of his expression, made her bed of early spring mud seem like a hot tub in comparison.

Scalp. She didn't need to know his real-world identity. He was made up of so many other men she'd met in her years as a police officer. He believed other people – women, in particular – were dispensable. He believed he was destined for something bigger and better. He was dangerous because he liked cruelty. She checked the weapon in its holster, pressing with painful reassurance into her ribcage. She and Scalp wouldn't get on, and she had to make sure that her every action was born of necessity and procedure, not simply to rid the world of a man who seemed to walk in his own special patch of shadow.

The van that pulled in right next to the doors diverted her attention. Scalp slapped one of the doormen on the back and said something that made the guard laugh way more than anyone naturally would. A desire to impress combined with a nasty case of being terrified would do that. The van's rear doors were pulled open and two women climbed out, another male bringing up the rear. Ava saw no more than thirty seconds of the women, but that was enough. The first was older, walking with a stoop. She allowed herself to be helped into the building. The woman who followed behind pulled her arm away from the man who tried to guide her. Her head was up, eyes watchful and alert. Dark-haired, brown eyes, beautiful, with a jaw set that marked her resistance, Ava knew this was the Elenuta that Lively had described in so much detail in his initial report.

Her view was obscured when a second van pulled in. Two more women disembarked, one carried over a man's shoulder, the other dragged. Ava fed descriptions through her earpiece back to Tripp as the unloading of the vans continued. Lights were brought in, laptops, other miscellaneous computer equipment, and drones. If she'd stumbled across the activity by chance, Ava could easily have mistaken it for a reality TV set rather than the location of the world's nastiest spectator sport. The set-up was completed twenty minutes later. The girls were there, the kit was in situ, and there was a multitude of muscle both inside and out. Ava shoved her gloved hands into her armpits to warm them up, and waited. It was 6.30 p.m. and other cars were starting to arrive.

'Has Lively heard from Paddy yet?' Ava whispered to Tripp through her headset. She heard Lively cursing in the background and knew the answer. 'Never mind,' she said. 'They're obviously gearing up to get started and the car park's filling up fast. Fifteen minutes from now, we try to get Lively in there whether his name's on the list or not. He'll have to blag it. Make sure he's ready.'

By 6.45 p.m. Lively had a pocket full of used twenties, a hearing aid that he hoped like hell he'd never need in real life given the headache it was causing him, and the unshakeable feeling that something was really, really wrong. He'd been brought a car that he'd driven the three short lanes to the warehouse car park, guided by instructions from Tripp that were echoing feedback, to be met with a queue of vehicles that didn't understand the concept of orderly parking. Still no text message, which meant he had to explain how the hell he'd found the venue before he could even start worrying about how he was going to get inside.

What he really hadn't been prepared for was the scale of what he was about to walk into. Warehouse – sure – it was going to be a big place. Out of town, made sense. But there were easily more than a hundred cars parked. Assuming they weren't all single occupancy, that meant an operation that was more an out-and-out battle than a raid. In his earlier years he'd worked on the inside of football's seedier side. Organised fights after the game. Gang-style crime within supporters' clubs, extending to drug dealing and retaliatory violence. He'd marvelled at the scale of that, but this was something else. And on top of all that, he was winging it. Taking his time, tagging onto the end of a group of three other men, he walked towards the warehouse door, listening carefully to the men ahead of him.

'Names?' the security guard demanded.

'Sam Whishaw.'

'Jerry Blake.'

'Barney Wheeler,' the last one mumbled. 'We're on the list.'

The guard ran his pen down a clipboard, ticking the names off.

'Money?' he held out his hand.

Whishaw handed over a bundle, Blake counted his out in tens, and Wheeler went last, crumpled five-pound note after sticky note, most of it in a ball the guard had to flatten out, paying the last few pounds in coins. The guard gave him a look of disgust, but waved the three in.

Lively took one final look at his mobile. Still nothing. If there were armed units hiding in the tree line at the end of the car park, he couldn't see them. Wing and a prayer time.

'Name.'

'Jackie Thomson.'

The guard checked the list once, twice, then gave Lively a look that most men would take as a cue to run.

'Ah, fuck me. Is it not on there? That's typical, that is. Is Paddy around? He can sort this out.'

'He's a bit busy right now, pal,' the guard said. 'Your name's not on the list which means you've got no fucking business being here.'

'Keep your hair on! It's a fuck-up for me, too. Paddy was going to get my name on the list – he'll get it sorted. Could you no' just give him a shout so I can have a chat with him?'

The guard stared at him, slipping a hand into his pocket, his fingers bulging around a shape of some sort. Lively didn't want to think too hard about what sort of weapon he was holding.

'I'll call Paddy, then you've got sixty seconds to get this straightened out. Don't you friggin' move a step.' He hammered the door in a rapid sequence, and it opened from the inside. 'Get Paddy out here now. There's some bloke thinks his name should be on the list. If Paddy doesn't vouch for him, I'm going to have to tell the boss.'

An impatient groan from beyond the door, then footsteps walking away. Lively waited a couple of minutes before the door opened again, and Paddy's face appeared. Thunderous didn't do it justice.

'What the fuck?' he demanded before Lively could greet him.

'Aye, aye, I know.' Lively put his hands in the air. 'Let me just explain.'

Paddy took him by the arm and pulled him thirty metres away behind the first row of parked cars.

'You want to explain to me how I'm seeing your fucking face when I didn't text you the details?'

'Just a misunderstanding,' Lively smiled. 'Honest to God, give me a minute.'

There was a gun in Paddy's hand that Lively hadn't seen coming.

'I don't like this. You're fuckin' up to something.' Paddy was keeping his voice low, and Lively realised he could make that work. Paddy was just as scared of anyone finding out that he might have fucked up as he was angry at Lively for turning up without an invitation.

'Listen, I followed Barney Wheeler here. Fat fuck was in our local pub a couple of hours ago. I was in there waiting to get

304

the text from you. I recognised him coming out of the flats last night, same time as me. Must have been visiting the whores on a different floor, I guess. I knew he was a client so when I saw him in the pub, I listened in on his conversation. He was showing off about how he was going to fuck you all over with some funny money. Said he'd got hold of a load of counterfeit fivers. Good artwork, he reckoned, but the texture's a bit crap so he was planning to mess them all up before he handed them over. Go ask your man over there if you don't believe me. Anyway, I was so sure I'd get the message from you about tonight that I decided to follow him and make sure I was in the vicinity. I know I shouldn't have done, but . . .'

'Stay there and don't you say a bloody word till I get back,' Paddy said.

He walked back to the doorman, had a few words, then they began inspecting the mass of screwed-up five-pound notes Barney Wheeler had handed over. Paddy returned.

'You still shouldn't have come. Scalp said no late additions to the list.'

'I get it. Bad decision on my part. I'll go. At least you can give that wee wanker Wheeler what he deserves.'

'Aye, the boss won't like it if he's been given dodgy notes.'

'All right. Well, maybe that'll make up for me fucking up. You're a busy man. I'll be off.'

Paddy sighed.

'You got the cash on you?' he asked quietly.

'Yeah, what's due on the door and what I said I'd give as a thank you. Man of my word.'

'Ah, fuck. Come on. I never liked that little cunt Wheeler. Now you're here, you might as well come in. Boss won't like it if anyone leaves the area before it's all over, anyway. Not a frigging word to anyone else though.'

Lively slid his hand in his right pocket and drew out the

cash, holding Paddy's share of it low enough that no one else was going to see the transaction. Paddy snatched it away, shoving it into his pocket, and motioning for Lively to get moving.

'I owe you one,' Lively said quietly.

'Just keep your head down in there. Tonight's supposed to run like clockwork, so no more surprises, right?'

'Quiet as a mouse.' Lively clapped him on the back. 'You won't even know I'm there.'

'I'd better not.' They walked to the door together. 'Put his name on the bottom of the list. My fault. I'd sent him the message but forgotten to do the paperwork.' Paddy disappeared through the door as the guard held his hand out for the entry fee, then let Lively through.

Inside, he was faced with a deserted area, a staircase to his right and a closed door to his left, with no one else in sight. He tried the door first. Locked. He took a few moments to get his breath.

'Well, that was a grand-scale fuckfest,' he said quietly to Tripp, Ava and anyone else from Police Scotland who was listening to his every word. 'Assume every guard has a handgun as a minimum. Security is impressive. They know what they're doing. I'm going up.'

He was a few steps up the staircase when some other men were allowed entry, alcohol fumes preceding them. Apparently making up a pre-race trip to the pub wasn't a stretch of the imagination. Lively wished vaguely that he'd been able to do the same. The feeling of wrongness he'd experienced earlier doubled, then tripled. Laughter and shouting bellowed down the stairs as a door opened then slammed shut again. Someone had thought about soundproofing the staircase from the main building. He didn't like that at all. That wasn't just organisation. It was actual competence. Not something he regularly encountered with Edinburgh's criminals.

At the top of the stairs, he was met by another bouncer type hauling a red-faced, yelling Barney Wheeler out of the viewing gallery, ignoring his protests of innocence. Lively waited for them to pass before presenting himself to the only bouncer left on the upper level. Sliding his hand in his pocket, he prepared to hand over the mobile.

'No filming, no audio recording,' he was told. The bouncer body checked him for weapons. 'Your phone'll be examined at the end and if we find anything on it, the whole phone gets smashed as does your face, and you'll be banned.' The bouncer sounded bored. Presumably the speech had been perfected some time ago, and the thrill of delivering it had passed.

'Understood,' Lively said.

The door was opened for him.

'I get to keep my phone,' he murmured for Ava's benefit as he entered, hand covering his mouth. 'That's interesting. They must be pretty bloody sure of themselves.'

He walked into a glass-fronted balcony with tiers of seating overlooking the ground floor of the warehouse, not that it was recognisable as such. From above he could see the whole design of the maze, its construction rough but not haphazard. There were dead ends, bridges, tiny gaps that maybe someone could squeeze through but maybe not. Barbed wire was strung casually over the top of barriers that would otherwise have made tempting escape routes. There appeared to be doors every now and again, although from where he sat he could see they led to either dead ends or into walls of spikes. Run in there in a hurry and the result would be a bloodbath. Taking a seat in the third row, he tapped his hearing aid, waiting for the screech of feedback that would follow. They'd agreed silence as far as possible from the police end, but with the capacity to talk to him in the event of an emergency. Right now there was only the faintest electrical hum.

Men were still filing in behind him and filling the gaps left in the seating. Lively counted ten rows, with at least twelve men in each. As many resources as DCI Turner had thrown at it and Lively was starting to wonder if it would be enough. The armed units couldn't simply machine gun down the stampede of men who were going to spill out of the place when it became clear what was happening. They would take to the fields, abandoning their cars as soon as they realised the entrance to the car park was sealed off. It would be bloody carnage.

'Wow, there must be a hundred and fifty of us in here. I hadn't realised it was such a big deal. Scalp sure as fuck knows how to lay on a party,' he said, aiming it at the man next to him as if mid-conversation. The fact that he was talking to a turned head didn't matter. It was Tripp who needed the information.

The door to the viewing balcony slammed shut again, this time followed by the sound of locks engaging. So they were locked in. Made sense. They wouldn't want anyone coming or going during the event, or any of the girls running up to the balcony. Made it easier for MIT – keep most of the rats in one cage. It was the first time all evening he'd thought things might just work out. Then he saw Elenuta's face looking up at the window. Thin, pale and fragile as she was hauled out in front of the crowd. Suddenly there was a man holding a microphone in a pool of holiday-camp-talent-show lighting.

'Gentlemen, welcome,' Scalp said. 'I'd say ladies too but there aren't any of those here!' The audience began to whoop, and Lively got to his feet to blend in with the animals around him. 'Welcome to the race, under new and improved management.' Scalp extended the hand not holding a microphone, enjoying the spotlight.

Lively kept his eyes on Elenuta's face. She should have been back at the flat. She'd done her part, giving him all the information MIT needed.

'It's starting,' he said, no longer afraid that anyone would notice him randomly talking to himself. The last thing on anyone's mind in that crowd was what he was doing. 'Tripp, I reckon three minutes. Close off the car park and get everyone in entry positions.'

'Four women racing tonight. Last time's winner — don't say we don't play fair.' He pushed the first woman forward. She stumbled, got up, edged away. 'Then there's this old bird — don't write her off yet though. She may have a few tricks up her sleeve. Benefit of experience, and all that.'

Lively recognised the woman from the hallway of the flat the previous evening. She was crying already and shaking, petrified. He looked up at the screens flickering on above the audience, showing close-ups of the women. He'd been wrong earlier. It wasn't even just competence. It was real professionalism. Someone with a good grasp of technology had been involved in the set-up.

'Make that one minute,' Lively said. 'No delays. They're about to start.'

'Contestant number three, who took a razor blade to a client's balls two days ago!' Scalp announced, shoving another woman into the light. She spat at him. The audience booed, and yelled.

'And finally, this little beauty, but we know what other men don't, isn't that right, lads? We know that the only good cocky cunt is a dead cocky cunt.'

The crowd went wild. Lively couldn't hear anything at all. There was no hope of him hearing anything useful Tripp had to tell him. Elenuta stepped forward of her own volition before Scalp could push her. Then Lively saw the men destined to chase her and the others to their deaths enter from the side door, and couldn't wait any longer.

'Epic,' he shouted. 'This is epic. It's absolutely epic.' No one paid him any attention. All eyes were focused below. 'Epic!' he bellowed again.

'And these are the three lucky bastards who get to live out a lifelong fantasy tonight!' Scalp continued.

Lively put his hands over his ears and tried to drown out the noise around him, waiting for an acknowledgement from Tripp.

Down below, three men positioned themselves in the light, hands raised, fists punching, roaring their own sick self-approval.

Lively heard nothing.

'It's absolutely fucking epic!' he shouted at the top of his voice. 'Epic. Epic!' He pushed his way to the front through the cheering men, looking down to the door that could only lead out into the hallway and the double-door exit. No sign of any disturbance at all.

He drew out his phone. No bars. He checked his internet connection instead. His data was on, but no search engine was responding to his request for access.

'Won't work in here,' the man next to him yelled.

'What?'

'I said it won't work in here. Nothing does. They've got some sort of fucking communications shutdown in here. No signals at all coming in or out. Not that you should try. I saw a bloke try to stream the footage once. They took a crowbar to his skull.'

Lively looked back down to Scalp.

'. . . giving them a sixty-second head start. Not that these bitches deserve it, but we don't want all the good stuff over too soon, do we?'

Another roar from the crowd.

'Epic,' Lively shouted again. Nothing. He tried dialling a number, then opened his email. Everything was dead. 'Fuck,' he said. 'Fucking fuck.'

He had to get the doors open one way or another. Sooner or later, they'd figure it out and raid the place anyway, but if that was a minute too late, then some if not all of the women would be dead. Lively staggered to the door, knocking on the glass, trying to attract the bouncers' attention. Below, he could hear Scalp giving a countdown. They were out of time.

A bouncer turned round. Lively pointed at his chest, fell against the door, his mouth lolling open, and clutched his upper left arm dramatically. The bouncer grabbed his fellow doorman and they got closer to take a look. Lively crashed to the floor as they unlocked the gallery door.

Chapter Thirty-Seven

The women ran. Elenuta yelled after them, shouting their names, calling them to her. She'd had too little time to explain properly what they needed to do, and language was a barrier. Grabbing the older woman from her flat, Suzan, by the arm, she pulled her down an alley, chasing after the previous race's winner who was already well ahead. The countdown was booming in her head but she was waiting for another sound. For the doors to be blown in, for feet to pound through the warehouse, announcing the fact that the police had arrived, and that no one should move. Only she'd been waiting for that a while now, and it hadn't come. There was no DS Lively to rescue her. Not a sign of a police car in the car park. It was exactly like the video Finlay had shown her. The options were fight or die. She was glad Anika was safe back in the flat. She only wished she was, too. It wasn't supposed to have come to this. If she'd known just how terrified she would be, she'd never have put herself in the line of fire. Where the hell were the police?

From the corner of her eye, she caught slices of glistening light, raced back, stooped down and picked up the biggest shards of glass she could find on the floor, then took hold of Suzan's hand again and raced deeper into the maze. Around a corner, she ran head first into the woman who'd spat on Scalp.

'It's all right,' Elenuta said. 'Stay together.' She reached down to take hold of the woman's hand, pushing a piece of lethally sharp glass into it. 'We fight.' She pointed at herself, then at both of them. 'Together, fight.'

The woman took a look at the spike in her hand, nodded slowly, then again faster.

'Fight,' she said.

'Four, three, two, one,' Elenuta heard Scalp shout. 'It's time to hunt for cunt!'

'Come,' she shouted at the other two women. 'Follow.'

They ran into a dead end, turned back the other way and found a bridge over a barrier. From the top, Elenuta could see the drones hovering over the maze, and in the distance two of the three men making their way steadily closer. Three women wouldn't be enough. Suzan wasn't going to keep it together. It had to be all four of them or they didn't stand a chance.

She turned round to check the other direction. There was an alley which led into three other lanes, but which had only one entrance. Plenty of options for backing up if they needed to, but they couldn't be taken by surprise from behind, or surrounded. Kicking one leg over the side of the bridge, she got her balance, threw the remaining glass down ahead of her and jumped.

'Come,' she said. 'Quick.'

The younger woman didn't wait to be told again, but Suzan stayed up on the bridge, shaking her head. It wasn't far, but it was far enough.

'Jump or die,' Elenuta said. 'Jump, we help you.'

Suzan climbed clumsily, falling at the top, coming down hard on one ankle and knocking Elenuta off her feet in the process. There was a scream from a different area of the warehouse.

'Here!' Elenuta shouted. 'Come here, to us!'

She was giving away their position and she knew it, but she wasn't leaving another woman to die. Their only strength was in standing shoulder to shoulder. Footsteps pounded and there was a crash, another scream, this time pain rather than fear. Then the previous winner's face appeared around a corner, bloody and torn, a length of barbed wire streaming from her shoulder.

'Faster!' Elenuta shouted, her hand outstretched.

She sprinted. Together they retreated to where the passageway offered them a chance of making a stand. They shared out the glass as Elenuta crouched to the hem of her jeans and retrieved the knife. If that was all Lively had to offer her now, then she had to make the best use of it.

The bouncers had argued over Lively for a good minute, before grabbing him under the arms and pulling him out into the corridor then locking the viewing gallery door up again. He lay, maintaining the charade, clutching his chest on the floor.

'What the fuck are we going to do?' the first bouncer asked.

'There's nothing we can do. It's fucking started. We've got orders. No one in or out until it's over.'

'So we're supposed to let him fucking die?'

'Are you going to be a pussy over a fucking corpse now? Have you forgotten what we'll be cleaning up later?'

'No one knows about the whores. They go missing and no one's gonna come looking. This bloke looks like he might have a job or a family, or something. He dies and if anyone knows where he is tonight, the police'll get involved, then Scalp'll fucking kill us.'

The second bouncer didn't have an answer to that. Lively took the opportunity.

'Pills,' he rasped. 'In my car. Get me . . .' gasping for

breath '. . . into the car park . . .' letting his head flop back down to the floor.

'You're shitting me,' bouncer two groaned. 'Why the fuck did this have to happen now?'

'Just look at him. He was a fucking heart attack waiting to happen.'

In the main warehouse Lively could hear a woman's screams.

'Make a decision,' bouncer two said.

'Well, we can't just leave him here. Help me get him down the stairs.'

They got either side of him and lifted him to his feet. Lively made it just believable enough that they struggled with his weight, but not so difficult that they gave up. Between them, they got him to the top of the staircase. A wave of yelling from the audience marked a new level of excitement.

'Hurry,' Lively said.

'What the fuck is going on? Why can't we hear anything?' Ava demanded through her earpiece to Tripp.

'I don't know. I don't think he can hear me either,' Tripp said. 'We're getting nothing.'

'It's been too long,' Ava hissed. 'There's only one guard left outside. We heard them bolt the doors from within. No other cars have turned up since.'

'What do you want to do?' Tripp asked.

'We're going in,' she said. 'Non-lethal force on the guard outside the door, but it's got to be fast. Disable him. He doesn't get to send a message inside.'

'Got it. All units, prepare to move,' Tripp ordered.

Ava put her binoculars back to her eyes. Four men dressed in black made their way silently, two from each side of the warehouse, rushing the guard. He put one hand towards his trouser pocket and the other into his jacket. Phone and gun,

Ava thought. He wasn't fast enough. They took him down, gagging and disarming him before he could do more than issue a single shout.

'Shit,' Ava said. 'If anyone heard that they'll be straight out. Armed units, I want guns on the door. If they come out firing, respond in kind. No hesitation. Now get that door down.'

Wishing her legs were more responsive after lying in the cold dirt, she ran for the door. An army of officers appeared from other bushes and trees. Vehicles screeched into the car park, accompanied by the rhythmic crunch of boots on gravel.

Then the door ram arrived, three officers positioned on either side.

'Go,' Ava told them.

They swung their arms back and let loose. The only response was a dull thud. The door showed no sign of giving way.

'Again,' Ava said.

The second blow had no more effect.

'Report,' she ordered.

'Reinforced steel, additional barriers on the inside, double-thickness metal. This door was built to withstand the force we're applying. I guess they saw this coming.'

'Just do whatever you have to do to get us in there,' Ava commanded.

'All we can do is try the fire exits, although I suspect it'll be the same story.'

'Do it,' Ava said. Tripp appeared at her side.

'They've got to come out sooner or later, ma'am,' he said.

'That doesn't help the women in there right now. Get me the bouncer. If all I've got left is announcing our presence, then that's what we'll have to do. We'll negotiate with them. They won't carry on with the race knowing we're out here.'

'They'll use the women as shields, ma'am,' Tripp said

'But they'll need them alive. If they kill those women, they've got no way of making it out and into vehicles. Get it set up, Tripp. Notify all units of the change in plan.'

The metal doors squealed as the internal bolts were disengaged. Twenty officers jumped away. The right-hand door opened, and Lively fell face down into the car park.

'Now which fucking car's yours, pal? I'm going to get your bloody pills then you're on your—'

The bouncer finally got his eyes to focus in the gloom. Ava leapt forward as Lively rolled over and punched the bouncer in the back of the knee. He fell, tree-like onto Lively. Ava grabbed his arms and folded them behind his back as Lively used his own head as a weapon.

'Door!' Ava screamed. 'Don't let it—'

A shot rang out. The bullet hit the nearest car, taking out the windscreen. Ava gave up on securing the first guard's hands, leaving Lively to wrestle with him, and ran for the area behind the open door as an officer returned fire. There was momentary silence, then the second guard staggered out of the doorway, hands on his stomach. Ava reached for the door handle. It slipped through her fingers and she threw herself after it, catching the last centimetre before it slammed shut again.

'Lively, you okay?' she yelled.

'I'm fine. I'll deal with this bastard. Get inside. It's already started. Save the women.'

Ava ran in, gun drawn.

Elenuta stepped to one side, allowing the previous winner to fit into the gap. As soon as she was in place, one of the men appeared. There was a hollow thud that stopped them all for a second, an odd moment where everyone in the warehouse responded the same way, human and curious. Even Scalp ceased his incessant commentating. Then the first male walked into their line of vision, showing tobacco-browned teeth as he grinned.

'One step back,' Elenuta told them.

Keeping their line formation, they moved a foot further away.

'That's it, you'd better be scared,' he told them. Two drones hovered, one before them, one behind, capturing the view of both their faces and his. He drew closer still. 'I'm having one of you. You can either decide who it's going to be, or you can run and see which of you I catch first. Honestly, I don't fucking care either way.'

'One more step,' Elenuta said.

He kept walking. Twenty feet. Fifteen feet. There was a second thud in some distant place, almost thunder, but without the defining whipcrack. This time no one stopped to ponder it.

At ten feet he began to sprint. As one, the women jumped. Elenuta had known they would, however firm they were resolved to remain. It was vital, the burst of adrenaline that might keep them alive. Suzan cried out, ran back behind them. That was okay too. As she opened a gap in their line, Elenuta stepped aside, giving the man the space to break through them.

As one, they brought their weapons up to his neck, stabbing, slashing, making the best of what limited space they had to manoeuvre. He brought his fists into play, but the wounds they'd inflicted were too much for him. As the first slash of blood sprayed the wall, he began to crumble. Elenuta finished the job, pushing him to the floor and clutching a handful of his hair with her left hand, sticking the depth of Lively's blade into his jugular, and shoving his twitching body to the floor face down.

She directed a level gaze at a second man who'd moved into their line of sight, waiting, watching, further down the corridor.

'Your turn,' she told him.

Suzan stepped over the corpse to retake her place in the line.

'Sorry,' she whispered to the other three women. Elenuta smiled at her, and put a gentle hand on her arm.

'This isn't what I paid for,' the watching man shouted. 'They're not supposed to do this. That's not in the fucking rules!'

Elenuta couldn't help herself. She watched the man-child rant, all pointy fingers and pouty lips, as if he hadn't paid money to be allowed to hunt and kill one of them. As if he were the wronged party. As if death was only ever on one person's terms. She stepped forward out of the line and raised her knife. It wasn't Lively's any more. Not now. Not with another man's blood dripping from it.

She ran, springing away down the lane. It took him a few seconds, but he reacted, spinning, screaming with high-pitched panic and racing away. Elenuta stopped rather than taking the corner and following him any further. She was enraged, but she wasn't stupid. To stand any chance of surviving, she needed the group and the group needed her.

'You fucking bitches,' Scalp's voice came from the speakers. 'You stay right where you are.'

Scalp was coming for them, and he was furious. There was no doubt whatsoever in Elenuta's mind that he was heavily armed. Shards of glass and a small knife wouldn't be any match for guns.

The sound of weapons firing reached them before Scalp did. A door opened – smashing violently – then there was shouting, yelling, feet hitting concrete.

'Run,' Elenuta shouted to the other women. 'Hide. Stay down.'

That was the end of their line. Two of them went into the pathways behind their standpoint, splitting in different directions to the rear. Elenuta and the spitting girl went forward, both heading for the bridge. Instinct was telling Elenuta to keep her head down and stay out of sight, but she wanted to know what was coming. She paused below the bridge, looking at the walls, figuring out how to climb up. By the time she was taking her first handhold, Scalp appeared around the corner, his gun stuck deep in spitting girl's mouth, walking with a swagger in his stride as if he were doing nothing more than strolling down a high street.

'Get on your knees,' he ordered Elenuta.

'No,' Elenuta replied. If she was going to die, she was going to die on her feet.

'Get on your knees or I'll cover you in her brains.'

That was when Elenuta heard the shouts more clearly.

'Police. Remain where you are. Put down your weapons!'

More gunfire. More screaming.

'Too late,' Elenuta told him. 'Fuck you.'

Chapter Thirty-Eight

Ava didn't get more than three metres into the building before the stampede hit her. They came down the stairs three at a time, pushing and shoving each other. Then one lost his footing, and it became a human slide. Throwing herself backwards, Ava tried to yell some order into the throng but panic had set in. They jumped over each other, hit their way through, elbows and knees jabbing. Other police officers attempted to enter but by then the first of the escaping men were at the front door and shoving outwards.

Ava pointed the gun at the heart of the group, but firing wasn't an option. They had to be restrained outside in the open. A man went down in the doorway and others merely trod on him. Ava pushed forward, reaching an arm down, trying to grab his hand, yelling at the others to stop, but it was herd mentality. They'd been caught in the shitstorm of their lives and not one of them was going to stop running. Desperate eyes swivelled up at her, a silent plea, then Ava took a punch to the face and staggered backwards.

'Stop!' she shouted, pointing her gun at the ceiling, ready to fire, but the construction of the mezzanine floor above her had involved metal plates on the ceiling. The shot would bounce, as likely hitting her as any of the men. Gunfire stuttered across the main warehouse through the doors behind her, and was repeated outside.

'Police, stay where you are!' she yelled.

But bodies continued to pile through the doors. More than they'd been expecting. Not enough boots on the ground outside, Ava thought. There was an ear-splitting crack as an enormous man barged into the back of the exiting crowd and used the neck of the man on the floor as a stepping stone. Finally they began to tail off and Ava stuck her head out of the exit door to request that medics retrieve the bodies tangled on the stairs and in the doorway. The scene in the car park took her breath before she could make any such demand.

Men were running across adjacent fields with officers in pursuit, others were locked in their cars with armed police aiming weapons through windscreens, ambulances were unable to enter the car park, three fights were going on with so many bodies involved – some police, some escapees – that no one was getting a clean shot. The shouting alone was deafening.

She grabbed a uniformed officer who was handcuffing a suspect.

'Get him in a van, then I need paramedics in the entrance hall. Several bodies, some critical.'

'Got it,' the officer told her, hauling his detainee along as more shots rang out from inside the warehouse.

Ava turned and sprinted for the entrance again, Lively and DC Swift following her as she went in. The internal ground-floor doors had been bashed open and Ava ran forward into the maze, following the sound of women's voices. A man stepped into her path, gun raised, the muzzle close into her face.

'Die, you bitch,' he hissed, as he raised his second hand to keep the gun steady against the coming recoil.

Someone wrenched at her clothes from behind, spinning her off to one side, and down onto her knees. She hit a tripod, and a camera crashed to the floor over the top of her. A gun went off close enough for her ears to ring, and a body staggered backwards, tumbling, turning, without so much as a cry. Blood spattered Ava's face and she wheeled around to see Swift clutching his shoulder, just at the edge of where his protective vest would have stopped the shot, his hands and the floor beneath him a liquid red mess. The shooter ran for the exit as she scrambled to Swift's side.

'Lively!' she yelled. 'Get here now.'

He was there in a second, on his knees, putting pressure on Swift's wound.

'It's bad,' she said. 'He was too close to the gun. There's a lot of damage.'

'Can't get paramedics in here while there's still live fire,' Lively told her.

'Then get him out. Carry him, drag him, just get him in an ambulance.' There was a scream from the far end of the maze, a woman, desperate and furious all in one. 'He saved my life,' Ava said, standing and picking up her gun from where she'd dropped it. 'Save his for me.'

Other officers were running in and scattering in all directions. Bursts of gunfire necessitated running low, head down. Up above her Ava could see a bank of screens showing bodies flying around the maze. On one she could see two women together, a man between them. Another screen showed an overview of the maze. Figuring out the route – lefts, rights, bridges – Ava went as fast as she could combine with reasonable caution. Deeper inside the maze, footsteps behind her neared, stopped as she stopped, then moved again, at times sounding as if they were in adjacent alleyways, sometimes fading altogether as shots rang out.

Finally at the far end of the warehouse, Ava heard a low groan ahead of her and rounded the corner to see the rear view of a man, his left arm wrapped around a woman's waist, half pushing, half dragging her forwards. His right arm was up high, elbow crooked. She didn't need the front view to understand that the man was Scalp, and that he was holding a gun.

Slowing her pace, Ava crept forward. He was talking to someone else, someone hidden from her view.

'Fuck you,' a woman enunciated clearly and precisely.

'Oh really, fuck me? You asked to be here tonight. Isn't this exactly what you wanted?'

'Let her go,' the woman said.

'Yeah, let her go,' Ava repeated behind him.

Scalp turned away from the woman he'd been talking to, dragging the woman in his grasp with him, aiming the gun at his hostage's temple as he looked Ava up and down.

'Am I supposed to find you threatening, sweetheart?' he laughed.

'You're supposed to do what I say. The building's surrounded. There are armed police everywhere. You're not getting out of here, so let her go, right now, or I won't hesitate to use lethal force.' Ava levelled her gun and took a step towards him.

'You shoot Scalp, I shoot you, bitch.' The new voice came from behind and to her left.

Ava glanced sideways at the man pointing a gun at her face. He must have rounded the corner behind her silently. She cursed her own sloppiness, failing to cover her back, but in the thin corridor the choices were face forwards or backwards. No other options.

'The area is full of police officers. You can shoot me,' she said, 'but you're just adding a murder charge to everything else you're about to be charged with. No way this ends well for you.'

'Paddy, just get her out of my fuckin' way. I'm coming through and I'm bringing this one with me as a shield. You grab that police bitch, we'll tell them to get us a car and that if they follow us they both die. Don't you worry, mate, we'll be fine.'

Scalp began walking towards Ava, dragging the woman at his side.

'Step this way, gun down,' Paddy told Ava.

'I don't think so,' she said. 'You're not going to shoot a police officer. Does Scalp here know it was you who let us inside tonight?'

'I did no such—'

'Jackie Thomson?' Ava said. 'That would be Detective Sergeant Undercover to you.'

'You did fuckin' what?' Scalp screeched. 'This was you? Holy mother of shit, what the . . .'

The girl Scalp had been holding in his right arm lashed out, nails flying in the direction of his face. He whipped the gun round at her head as another figure flew at him from behind, using the moment to her advantage.

Ava focused, ignored the gun pointed at her face, and took the shot. Her bullet flew as a second blasted across the corridor, ricocheting on the makeshift metal barriers at either side. The sound in the constructed alleyway was deafening. Ava threw herself to the floor, rolling as she fired at Paddy. Scalp, the woman he'd been holding, and the other woman he'd been talking to, dropped to the floor as if a sinkhole had opened up beneath them. A pool of blood was spreading beneath the tangle of bodies before Ava could get there.

'Don't move,' she shouted. 'I need paramedics over here!'

One of the women raised her head from the floor, eyes wide, mouth slack.

'It's all right,' Ava said. 'Just stay still. Help is coming.'

She scrambled over to where Scalp lay, pushing his body over with one hand as she kept her gun aimed at his head with the other. It was in fact only half a head, she realised, as his corpse rolled. Her bullet had hit its mark.

Getting up, Ava reached for the woman Scalp had been holding hostage. Her head flopped uselessly, the back of her neck ripped apart.

'Bullet hit there,' the other woman said, pointing up at a cabinet that had been used to construct a barrier. There was a clear dent in the metal, with sideways brush-stokes showing the bullet's path after impact. Scalp had managed to kill the spitting girl not by skill, but by sheer bloody accident.

'Are you Elenuta?' Ava asked her.

'Yes.'

'Okay Elenuta, you don't need to be scared any more. Are you hurt?'

'Not bad,' she replied.

'Can you walk?' Ava asked.

Elenuta nodded, and Ava reached out to pull her up, slipping an arm around her waist as they limped back toward the exit. She cast a look down at Paddy. Her bullet had hit his chest, straight into the heart, by the look of it. He hadn't got a shot off. Maybe what she'd said about adding a murder charge had resonated, or maybe he just wasn't cut out for killing. Either way, she hadn't been prepared to leave a potential shooter aiming a gun at her. She should have felt more disturbed by it, Ava thought, as she helped Elenuta hobble out through the maze. Two bullets from her gun, two men dead. Killing was remarkably easy when you felt it was completely justified.

There was no gunfire now. Calmer voices were in control. Ava counted a total of seven additional bodies as she exited. It wasn't exactly a clean operation, but it wasn't quite the massacre it could have been.

Officers appeared from other corners of the warehouse, two of them supporting the other women. Three were helping injured colleagues get outside to the waiting paramedics.

Tripp met Ava at the door.

'Swift?' she asked.

'On his way to the hospital now. They're doing everything they can to save him.'

'Tell me no officers have been killed,' she said.

'No. Other than Swift, there's one nasty knife wound, another got caught in barbed wire, a third took a bullet in the leg but it passed through the muscle. He'll be okay. Cuts and bruises, maybe some broken bones from the fights.'

'Thank you,' Ava said.

Then Lively was at her side, putting his own arm around Elenuta's waist, guiding her towards an ambulance. The woman rested her head on Lively's shoulder, and gripped him tight.

'How bad is it in there?' Tripp asked Ava.

'One dead woman. We need to get her identified as fast as possible and locate her family. She fought Scalp. I suspect that if she hadn't, she might still be alive. It was a ricocheted bullet.'

'I'll make the identification a priority. Are you okay?'

'I killed two men. Scalp, and the guy Lively was dealing with, Paddy. We need to make sure everything's properly documented for an internal investigation. How many under arrest?'

'Too many to count out here, and we're already getting addresses for the other flats where the women are being held. DI Graham is leading those raids now. The women from the Wester Hailes flats are already on their way to hospitals and safe houses.'

'Thank God,' Ava said. 'Some good came of it.'

'A lot of good, I'd say.'

Ava gave Tripp a brief, hard hug and went to find DS Lively.

She found him sitting in the back of an ambulance, tucking a foil blanket around Elenuta's shoulders.

'How are you doing?' Ava asked her.

'Okay,' Elenuta replied. 'Better now. Girl who died. You can find her family?'

'We will,' Lively reassured her. 'What about your family? Who can we call for you?'

'My mother is in Romania. I give you her number.'

'How did you end up here?' Ava asked as a paramedic pushed between them with a gauze pad and began work.

'I was told could get work in next town. Got onto truck, they did not stop. Put us inside a van. We went many days, more women get on.'

'They drove you all the way across Europe. How did you cross the Channel?' Lively asked.

'In France they stop. Big lorry with . . .' she put her hands in the air and drew the outline of a huge rectangle.

'On the lorry?' Lively checked.

Elenuta nodded.

'To go on ship . . . on sea,' she added.

'A container ship?' Ava said.

'Yes, that. They stop van, open door. Wood box inside. One man get out. Put us in, with water, food, bucket. Onto road then ship. Then arrive here.'

'How many women?' Lively asked.

'Eight on ship,' Elenuta said.

'You said a man got out of the box,' Ava said. 'Can you tell me anything more about him? Was he with the men who kidnapped you?'

'No. Young man, not okay. He looked weak. Ill.'

'His age?'

'Maybe twenty. Dark hair. Pale skin. Scottish. Did not know accent then. Now I know.'

Ava grabbed her mobile from her pocket and scanned through her documents.

'Was this him?' she asked, holding a photo up for Elenuta to see.

'Yes. I think,' Elenuta replied. 'Who is he?'

'His name was Malcolm Reilly,' Ava said. 'And I need to know anything, absolutely anything you can tell me, that might help me find where he was taken in France after he was pulled out of the container.'

Elenuta put a gentle hand on the paramedic's arm, pausing his work as she considered it.

'Finlay in charge, but one other man there from Scotland.'

'Would you recognise him again?' Ava asked.

'He is here. Tonight. One of guards.'

Lively stared at Ava.

'Let's hope he's still alive then,' he muttered. 'Tripp! Over here. Get every guard lined up here now, before anyone gets taken to the station for processing.'

'But they've all been charged now. They've got to be given access to lawyers. If we break with procedure—'

Lively walked up, put one firm hand on Tripp's shoulder and looked hard into his eyes.

'Son, you're a good policeman and I like working with you, but if you don't understand by now that there's a time and place to say fuck proper procedure, then I'm not sure you and I can continue working together.'

Tripp didn't miss a beat.

'Got you,' he said.

Five minutes later a line of men stood grumbling before them, two being held up by a combination of paramedics and uniformed officers. Elenuta didn't need to climb out of the back of the ambulance.

'Third from right,' she said. 'Spiky hair. Nose ring.'

'Get rid of the rest of them,' Ava ordered. 'You. Back of that police van, right now. Lively, Tripp, you can join us. Everyone else stays clear.'

No one argued as they climbed into the van and she slammed the doors shut. Spiky hair was pushed down firmly onto a seat, hands double-cuffed behind his back, Lively's guiding hand on the back of his neck. Ava seated herself so she could look him directly in the eyes.

'One chance,' she said, slowly and loudly. 'You get one fucking chance. If you don't tell me everything – absolutely every bloody detail – not only will I refuse to explain to the judge that you assisted the investigation. I will appear at court and make it very clear that you put additional lives in jeopardy and that you withheld details that led to the torture and potential deaths of other innocent victims. And that you attempted to assault me inside this van.'

'But . . . I . . .'

'I only just stopped you in time. If I hadn't grabbed your arm, you'd have broken the boss's nose, easy,' Lively said. 'Attempting to assault a police officer on top of everything else. Boy, are you in the crap.'

'And I think I heard you say you were going to kill the DCI here,' Tripp added. 'Making a threat to kill carries one hell of a sentence.'

'Wankers,' Spiky muttered.

'Good,' Ava said, frowning at Tripp. He was more like Lively than she'd realised. 'Now, somewhere in France you and a few others opened up a cargo container with a box inside. You took out a young Scottish man and put several women inside to ship them to Edinburgh. I want to know about the boy. Where did he go? Who took him? Who organised it? Who got paid? What was he needed for?'

Spiky was sweating. That was a good enough start for Ava. He knew something.

'I don't know much,' he mumbled. 'I just did what Finlay told me to do. There was a woman who delivered the boy to us. He was out of it, like he was pissed but not. He was still walking, just about. I don't know her name, but a couple of the other blokes do. I'll tell you who they are.'

'The woman had long hair. She was pretty and thin?' Ava asked.

'Aye, that's her. We put him in the container at the docks. Then we travelled to France for when the ship was due to arrive, to do the handover.'

'Where?' Lively said.

'Some car park, like a gravel area, at the side of a big road on the way to Paris.'

Ava nodded. That much he'd got right.

'And from there?' she asked.

'He was put into the boot of a car. They were taking him towards Paris. I don't have an address.'

'You must know more than that,' Ava said.

'I fuckin' don't,' he moaned.

'Lively, hit me in the face,' Ava said. She stood up. Even Lively looked a bit uncomfortable. 'On your feet, Sergeant.'

'She's got a screw loose, that one,' Spiky said in Tripp's direction as Lively got ready to throw the punch. 'You wouldn't.'

'He'll obey my orders,' Ava said. 'And if I tell him to punch me, he's going to punch me. And you're going to get charged with it.'

'Don't you punch her,' Spiky yelled.

'Get on with it,' Ava told Lively. 'Right now.'

'Shit, give me a minute, would you? I can't think,' Spiky blabbered.

'Better hurry up,' Ava said.

'Finlay said something about a closed-down factory. The lad was wanted for some sort of medical thing, like he had a special blood type or something.'

'He was transported in a container ship against his will and you fell for the special-blood-type story?' Lively asked.

'Hey, I didn't ask questions. You asked Finlay questions and you got your fucking head blown off. Did you not see what happened to Gene Oldman?'

'This was all Finlay's deal?' Ava asked.

'Aye, he had a contact in France who agreed to split the shipping cost with him. Finlay was a bastard but he always knew how to save money.'

'Who else did you move out of Scotland and hand over in France?' Tripp asked quietly.

There was a moment of silence, before Spiky visibly wilted.

'Another lad, and a girl. I felt bad for her. She was pretty, you know? A proper Edinburgh girl.'

'Not this European trash you've been pimping out against their will, then?' Lively snarled. 'I suppose you think there's a difference. Anyone who doesn't speak your language deserves to be treated like shit.'

'Describe her,' Ava intervened.

'Tall, thin, good-looking. Bit messed up by the time we got her off at the other end.'

'Did you hear her name?'

'We weren't supposed to ask names. It was against the rules.'

'Weren't supposed to, or didn't?' Ava asked. 'There's a difference.'

'She told me her name while I was getting her out. Asked me to contact her parents. Skye. I didn't catch her surname.'

'Right. You're going to be charged with an ungodly amount of offences now, and taken to the police station where a lawyer will be provided to you if you don't have one. But before you go, let me just assure you that if you stop assisting us at this stage, I will make it my mission in life to get you the longest sentence permitted by law, then I'll spread a rumour around whatever prison you end up in that you're a rat. I want every single fact, every address, every name, every fucking detail you can remember. Got it?'

Spiky whimpered his assent.

'Get him processed straight away,' Ava told Tripp. 'And Lively, keep your hands off him, I know what you're thinking.'

'Where are you going?' Lively asked.

'Home to pick up my passport, then straight to the airport. Get in touch with Callanach and update him. I'm booking myself on the next flight to Paris. And figure out who Skye is. I'll call you from Charles de Gaulle airport.'

'You're still going to write a letter to the judge saying I helped you, right?' Spiky whined.

'Fuck you,' Ava said as she opened the van door. 'You kidnapped people, trafficked them, and stood guard while women were murdered in front of an audience. I could write a million letters and you'd still never see daylight again without bars obscuring the view.'

'Bitch,' he squeaked.

'I'm still armed.' Ava paused, slipping one hand inside her jacket. 'I could accidentally shoot you if you like. I'm quite happy to deal with the fallout.'

'She's insane,' Spiky appealed to Tripp.

'Just the way we like her,' he replied, grabbing Spiky beneath the arms as Ava strode away.

Chapter Thirty-Nine

All the direct flights had already left for the day, leaving Ava no choice but to detour via Brussels then down to Paris. By the time she made it out of the airport, she still had no hotel booked and all the currency exchange booths were closed. Armed with a credit card and a backpack, she walked out into the night. Her mobile rang as she waited in line for a taxi.

'Lively, ma'am. It's about Detective Constable Swift.'

'Go on,' Ava said quietly.

'He's out of surgery. Shoulder's a mess, and he needed a substantial blood transfusion. He's in intensive care, but the doctors are confident he'll be okay. Thought you'd want to know.'

Ava smiled and fought tears. Exhaustion, lack of food, a near-death experience and international travel were a bad combination.

'Thanks, Sergeant,' she said. 'When he wakes up, tell him I said thank you.'

'Aye, well he's a brave bloody idiot, I'll give him that. I guess this means you can't really transfer him to traffic now.'

'I guess not,' Ava said. 'I'd better go.'

'You be careful there, ma'am. That's probably enough excitement for one day.'

Ava rang off as a taxi pulled up.

'I just need a decent hotel. Not expensive, but nothing below three stars,' Ava told the driver through the window. He was replying in French, shrugging like it was going out of fashion, and managing to look her up and down so obviously that she was more astounded by it than enraged.

'I don't think so,' Callanach said from behind her, reaching out to take her backpack and pulling her away from the edge of the pavement in a single move. The cab driver offered up one final shrug and drove away.

'Are you insane? It's three in the morning. You were about to get in an unlicensed cab without a definite location, holding just one tiny bag, looking like a runaway. Do you read newspapers? You know what can happen to women in those circumstances? Never consider a career in the police.'

'I need coffee,' Ava told him. 'And a shower. I think I still have blood on me.'

'Glad this isn't a blind date,' he smiled. 'Come on, my car's over here. Lively got in touch. I gather last night was rough.'

'It was,' Ava said. 'One woman died, and I wish we could have avoided that. Everyone else had it coming. There was an awful lot of bloodshed, though. Did Lively give you a proper update?'

'He said they've rescued a total of eighty women across the city and new information is still coming in during interviews. One hundred and forty men arrested. Every police station in the city is packed. What you achieved was amazing, Ava.' He started the car. 'You must be exhausted.'

'Not really. Furious and horrified. Exhausted can wait a few more days. Have you heard about the young woman we believe is being held captive?'

'Actually, I've seen photos of her. We're going to my hotel. Did you at least bring a change of clothes?'

'Just a pair of jeans.'

'Literally . . . just one pair of jeans?'

'I had trouble finding my passport so I emptied all my drawers onto the floor, then I ran out of time. I figured I'd buy something on the way but all the airport stores were shut last night and again this morning,' Ava said. 'Hold on, did you say you've seen photos of the woman we think is with Bart Campbell? How come? Did Lively locate a missing persons file?'

'He did. The woman was reported missing by her brother a month ago, but the photos I saw were more recent than that. I left you a message with someone in the incident room but you'd already moved on the warehouse. I've made contact with the organisation involved in the kidnappings of Reilly, Campbell and Skye Kelso. They're exploiting end of life patients with the promise of a miracle cure, apparently replacing the dead or infected cells in their bodies with good cells from another human.'

'So it is transplants?'

'It's cannibalism,' Callanach said, pulling into a parking slot in front of a twenty-four-hour cafe. 'Still want that coffee?'

Ava stared out of the windscreen.

'You okay?' he asked.

'Define okay.'

'Able to breathe and swallow,' he said.

'Then I'm okay.' She opened her car door and swung her legs out. By the time they had burning hot cardboard cups in their hands, she'd found her voice again. 'I'm ready now,' she said. 'Tell me everything.'

They drove back to Callanach's hotel as he ran through the sequence of events.

'What's happening right now?' Ava asked as they took the lift to the ninth floor.

'Interpol is arranging the bank transfer to Group 2029 this morning. As soon as they receive the funds, I'll be sent another email with the next steps.'

He unlocked his hotel room door and showed her in.

'What about the man you met who gave you the details? Can we not get any better information from him to close it down faster?'

'He's under arrest and being held in custody, but he was just a pawn with no inside involvement. An out-of-work actor, in fact, delivering a brief. Group 2029 are well organised. Each individual they use, right up until the final operation, is completely separate from the organisation. The man I met was given information sheets, told the bare minimum, paid cash, never given any real names or real company information. We picked him up as he left the building and I interviewed him for an hour, during which time all he did was cry. At one point he actually asked if we could phone his mother, which for a man in his thirties . . .'

'Great,' Ava said. 'What about the money trail?'

'It's an online account routed through various international banks outside of Europe, two of which require us to get court orders by attending in person within their jurisdiction before they will release the information we need. We'll get there eventually, but not in time to prevent another death.'

'So we just wait?' Ava kicked off her shoes and sank onto the sofa.

'No,' he said, reaching down to take her hand and pull her back on her feet. 'You're going to shower, then you're going to sleep. We're going to make sure we're both ready for tomorrow.'

'I can't,' Ava mumbled. 'I totally forgot. One of the guys at Skye Kelso's handover said she was being taken to some disused factory. I need to get researching.'

'Interpol is already working with French police. We have an outline of a logo from the van that dropped off Malcolm Reilly's body. We're already narrowing down the possibilities.'

'That doesn't mean I can't help. Another set of eyes on it . . .'

'Ava, it's nearly four a.m.'

'And I'll only lie awake wondering what it is I don't know. Come on. Give me the potted version then I'll shower.'

'Fine. The logo is only an outline, it's a leaf on its side, stem out to the right, as if it's falling through the air. Interpol and French police have been working on it since we got the information but the possibilities are endless. I spoke to a woman in marketing about it. Honestly, it could be anything from arms sales to kids' toys.'

'She actually said that?'

'Not in those words, but she said don't be fooled by the concept. Marketing is all about creating masks. The more a company has to cover up, the more they want to create an image that suggests the opposite, so the logo won't help us. Malcolm Reilly's body gave no clues. There were traces of lanolin left at the scene when his body was deposited, but that has several potential sources. It's really all or nothing. If they suspect me, and don't invite me for the operation or whatever they're calling it, all our leads might be lost.'

'Great. What could possibly go wrong?' Ava yawned.

'How long have you been awake now?' Callanach asked. Ava folded her arms. 'That's what I thought. Now listen, get in the shower. I'm not talking to you again until you smell less like a butcher's shop.'

'Don't be gross.'

'What's that ridiculous phrase I could never understand, the one you love so much? Kettle and pot?'

'It's pot and . . . never mind. Thank you for letting me stay here.'

'As opposed to leaving you on the street?'

'Luc, last time we shared a bedroom . . .' she let the sentence finish itself. Nothing between them had been the same since.

'We're both a little older and a little wiser. This is a professional scenario. I'm sure we'll cope.'

She nodded, draping her coat on the arm of a chair and picking up her backpack to take into the bathroom with her.

'I'm going to insist on sleeping on the couch, though. Looks comfy enough,' she said.

'If that's what you want.' Callanach pulled two spare pillows from the bed and set them on the couch instead.

'It is,' she said, walking to the bathroom door and opening it an inch. 'We'll be in time to save them, right? Only I let a young woman die earlier tonight and I don't want that to happen two nights in a row.'

Callanach took a blanket from the wardrobe and laid it out along the couch.

'Fighting to save someone, even if it goes wrong, isn't the same as letting someone die, Ava.'

'I know that,' she said. 'But still.'

'I'll organise a wake-up call and breakfast for eight, then we'll head into the Paris Police headquarters for a joint agency briefing.'

'Perfect,' she said. 'Thanks.'

By the time Ava emerged from the shower to find a T-shirt left on the sofa for her, Callanach was already in bed, eyes closed, and silent. She settled herself on the sofa and pretended to sleep.

Chapter Forty

Ava sat in an unmarked van with a French drone operator whose grasp of English was limited to song lyrics, which was fair enough given that her French was entirely menu-based. They'd shaken hands, smiled at one another and settled down to a conversation consisting of gestures. It was 5 p.m.

The day had been spent engaged in a frustrating holding pattern. Briefing, text messages, reactions, preparation. Repeat. The incident room at police HQ in Paris wasn't physically dissimilar to the one the Major Investigation Team used in Edinburgh, except there was an unfamiliar hush to the place. No one shouted loudly across the room, or took the piss out of each other. She'd felt a sudden longing for Sergeant Lively's tendency to walk through the crowd, stuffing himself with a sugary offering and using homemade expletives unrepeatable in the outside world. A number of sharply dressed speakers, using English first then French in deference to her, had addressed the gathered force fast and with minimal interruptions. Ava had made a mental note to find out what training they'd undergone.

By 9.30 a.m. a payment of thirty-five thousand euros, approximately thirty thousand in British pounds, had been made. A text acknowledging the payment had pinged back within minutes. At 11 a.m. Callanach had been sent another message with directions for his personal preparations later in the afternoon, including bathing, not eating after midday to prepare his stomach to receive the purportedly 'life-giving cells', and wearing clothes that were easy to take off as he would be given a new set to wear for the journey, excluding the possibility of sewing in a GPS unit. He was to have no electronic equipment with him whatsoever. A representative from Group 2029 would be left in the car park with his keys. Ava had felt then quickly resented a vague respect for the set-up. Directions for Callanach to attend at the pick-up site hadn't been sent until 4 p.m., by which time it had become clear that following him wasn't going to be possible by traditional means.

Callanach had left the flat he'd given as his address alone and in good time. There was no guarantee that his journey wasn't being watched. He was currently driving out of the city to the north-east of Paris. The rendezvous point was just outside Coubron, a small and relatively quiet town.

By the time Ava had awoken that morning, Callanach was already up, showered, and setting breakfast on the writing desk in the hotel room. He'd loaned her a fresh shirt for the day, then given her the room as she changed. They'd hardly spoken during the journey into police HQ, both of them wrapped up in their own thoughts. It occurred to Ava that she hadn't told him to be careful. She couldn't even remember saying thank you for the fact that he'd picked her up from the airport, housed and fed her. Not that there'd been any bad atmosphere, not even an element of awkwardness. Just polite professionalism, to an almost vacuous extent. She hadn't wished him luck.

'Is it ready?' she asked the drone operator, pointing at the tiny four-rotor drone, and miming it going up and down. The operator nodded.

It had been her idea, thanks to Finlay Wilson and the drones he'd used in the warehouse to relay footage of each woman's personal nightmare back to the audience. Less obvious than a vehicle, safer than having police officers hiding in the ditches of all the possible routes out of town, the drone could track the van Callanach was in by simply hovering at a sufficient height and taking shortcuts over fields and buildings. It wasn't easy, and it certainly wasn't recommended to lose visual contact with a drone when you were operating it, but without GPS on Callanach it was the most surefire means of checking where he was taken.

Before she'd left police headquarters, her limitations had been made very clear to her. She had no legal status in France. There was no way she was being given a weapon. Her French wasn't good enough for her to follow orders quickly, so she hadn't been included in the entry team that was to follow Callanach in. Ava was relegated to the sit-and-wait brigade. She was stuck in a vehicle, watching a van speed away with her detective inspector, with her friend, in circumstances and a jurisdiction entirely beyond her control. The fact that she was there at all, as someone had kindly translated for her, was a matter of international policing courtesy. Ava was not to overstep.

It had been a cold experience, walking into the middle of a new team who couldn't really see why she hadn't simply phoned instead of turning up in the middle of the night. It had been her first experience of feeling like an outsider while surrounded by other police officers. Not dissimilar to Callanach's first day with Police Scotland, she supposed. He'd been stand-offish and aloof. Hard to like. Her first day within a foreign police squad had given her more insight as to why. Someday, she thought, she and Callanach ought to talk about it. The only substantial conversation they'd had the night before was about using logos to create a better impression of companies with less than pure purposes or products. She wished she'd arrived in Paris earlier and been able to . . . the thought stopped there.

She grabbed the drone operator's laptop.

'Can I use?' she said, pointing at it frantically.

'*Oui*,' he nodded.

Opening a search engine, she rubbed her eyes, trying to gel the fractured pieces of thought flying around in her head. The logo. Covering up a real purpose. And what was found at the building site? What was it Callanach had said?

'Damn it,' she muttered, typing the name of the nearby town into the box on the screen.

'Coubron. Company. Leaf logo.' Ava hit the enter button. The options came back numerous but vague, with nothing that looked helpful.

'Lanolin. It was lanolin,' she muttered. 'Lanolin from sheep. Farming. Too obvious. Cosmetics. Clothing. Factories.' She stared at the screen. The drone operator had stopped what he was doing and was staring at her as if he might call for backup at any moment. 'Animal products. Companies trying to cover up their real purpose.'

'Coubron', she typed again. 'Animals. Products.' She hit enter.

The two seconds she had to wait for results felt like two hours. The top search result bore the legend. 'Coubron animal testing facility closes.' Ava clicked the link to bring up the full article from an online magazine.

The Beaulieu Corporation has moved its centre of operations to an undisclosed location in Belgium following repeated protests that resulted in serious injuries to employees and millions of pounds of damage to property and increased security needs. The facility outside Coubron, near Paris, will be available for rental. Beaulieu handled a number of prominent international accounts,

from government biological defence testing to cosmetics and
medical products, but it was a whistleblower revealing details of
animal testing that led to the mass protests that resulted in the
closure. Beaulieu issued a statement in which they made clear
that they complied with all EU regulations as far as the
welfare of animals was concerned, and that animal rights groups
had acted in an illegal manner, posing a risk of harm, even
threat of loss of life, to their employees and contractors. Some
2,000 employees were asked to move with the Beaulieu
Corporation to Belgium or face redundancy. The corporation
reported a loss of almost 28% of its market value during the
protests and subsequent move.

'That's it,' Ava said. 'I know where they're going.' The drone operator shrugged at her. 'We have to go. Now! We might be able to stop what's about to happen.'

He babbled at her in French, pointing at his drone, then outside to the other units, then at his watch.

'Oh, sod this.' Ava climbed from the van and sprinted for the nearest unmarked police car, climbing into the front seat. The female officer in the driver seat stared at her.

'Speak English?' Ava asked.

'Of course. Are you all right?' the officer replied.

'Thank fuck. Listen, I know where they're going. I've found the logo and I know where the company is based. If we go now we can get there before Callanach, and maybe stop anyone from getting hurt. I'll need wire cutters.'

The officer shook her head at that one, so Ava checked the translation on her phone and held up the words in French.

'Ah yes, in the boot of the car. But you cannot be sure. We are supposed to wait and follow the drone, no?'

'You want to wait until people are dead? Because that's the most likely outcome,' Ava growled.

The officer sighed. 'But I am supposed to close the road after the van has left.'

'That's it? That's your only job? Move, right now.'

'I should tell the operation coordinator . . .'

'Wonderful, do that as we drive.' The officer looked unconvinced. 'What's your name?' Ava asked.

'Jojo Berger.'

'Good, now Jojo, I'm going to take full responsibility and we'll call this in, but either you move straight away or I'm going to kick you out of this car and steal it from you.'

Berger laughed.

'The British are so dramatic.' She turned over the engine, hitting a dial on the dashboard that operated the radio and speaking in rapid French as she pulled out of the parking place and sped away. A retort of bullet-like speech came back. Berger switched it off.

'Did we get the go-ahead?' Ava asked.

'Depends how you want to translate it,' Berger said.

'Are they at least sending other vehicles there with us?'

'No, they say it's too late and too dangerous to deviate from the plan. The more vehicles, the greater the chance that we'll alert whatever security Group 2029 has in place. Also, they think you're probably wrong and a bit crazy at this stage. They told me to just keep you out of the way.' She grinned. 'Now give me directions because I have no idea where we're going.'

The roads were empty. No other police unit tried to stop them – presumably, Ava thought, for fear of being seen. They went from a main road to side roads to what was little more than a track, as Ava navigated to avoid the main entrance and skirted the compound via what must have been an emergency vehicles access road.

'God, it's massive,' Ava said, sliding down in her seat. A female driver alone if spotted on CCTV in an unmarked car could be taken for someone lost. No threat. Given what Ava suspected they were doing inside the buildings, seeing a lone woman bumping up the track wasn't going to be a priority. 'Those are all heavy industrial buildings,' she said as they passed a complex of warehouses, garages and chimneyed factories. 'We're looking for a building that shows signs of inhabitation. Do you have binoculars?'

'In the glove compartment,' Berger said. 'How do you know this is the place?'

'The company had a logo, a leaf, that a witness saw. It matches the company who used to own this place.'

'Really? A leaf? This and a million other companies.' Berger shook her head.

'But the set-up's perfect. The original company left, so the place was available to rent. It's got great security, no reason for anyone to attempt to enter without invitation, a double-perimeter fence, and, best of all, endless laboratories, meeting rooms, offices, all of which also means they'll have kitchens, bathrooms, and full medical facilities. The fact that they would have been originally intended for veterinary purposes makes no difference at all. It's ideal.'

Berger stared at her.

'Okay, not so crazy,' she said.

'How about that?' Ava pointed.

Berger pulled the car up smoothly under a stretch of trees, and squinted at a low-level building a short distance from a larger, newer complex, joined to it by a covered corridor.

'Why that one?'

'Because the windows are boarded up, and they haven't boarded any other buildings on the site,' Ava explained.

'Could be just to stop vandalism. Not many of the other buildings have ground-floor windows.'

'I'd agree,' Ava said, 'but take a look.' She handed Berger

the binoculars. 'The boarding is secured over the outside. A determined vandal or burglar could take it down.'

'But if anyone is on the inside, there's nothing they can do about it.' Berger smiled at Ava. 'All right. What is it you need?'

'You'll keep me safest by staying here and watching through the binoculars to make sure I don't get in trouble. If you come in with me, there won't be anyone to report a problem.'

'It's a risk,' Berger said.

'I know, but you're just a minute away if I need you, and backup can be here in minutes. The risk is minimal.' Ava wasn't sure she believed that herself, but it sounded reassuring enough. 'I'm cutting through both sections of fence. If you see anyone coming, hit the car horn. I'll use the wire cutters to take a window board down and get inside the building. Give me your phone.' Berger handed it over and Ava punched her number in, then sent a text. 'I'll send a message once I'm in and safe. 999 if I'm in danger. If I'm not back out or you don't hear from me in ten minutes then call for backup anyway.'

'Okay,' Berger said. 'Are all Scottish police officers like you?'

'I'm one of the tame ones,' Ava smiled at her. 'You should visit. I think you'd fit in.'

Exiting the vehicle, she kept low, moving away from the car so as not to draw attention to it if she was seen. Then she went for the fence. It was thick, rigid wire. Every time she snapped the cutters through a section it pinged wildly as the tension was released. Her hands were aching within sixty seconds, and her breath was noisy in her ears. She scanned the compound for security. Once she'd cut through three sides, she sat back and pushed a makeshift doorway into the fence, crawling through on her stomach then pulling the wire shut behind her. Between the two fences she had no cover at all, but the second fence was made of slightly less high-grade wire. She clipped away at it, falling backwards as a section of wire flew towards her face, cutting into her cheek. Warm blood flowed down into the corner of her mouth. She spat it out as she continued to cut, more conscious of her eyes, and just how close a call the accident had been.

A dog barked somewhere in the distance, and Ava flattened herself on the ground, hoping Berger had her back and was watching carefully. No movement. She started cutting again, creating an entry point and shoving the wire aside before creeping through, then replacing the wire section as best she could once more to avoid detection. Her mobile buzzed in her pocket. She grabbed it to read the message.

Callanach is in a van and headed in this direction. Expect activity soon.

Ava hit the thumbs-up icon in the messages app, put the phone away, took a deep breath and began to sprint the distance between the inner fence and the boarded building. It was longer than it had looked from the car. As she drew nearer, it was clear that a series of cameras were cleverly mounted in the shade of the roof, almost impossible to see from outside the fence. There was no way to avoid them completely, and no way to know if they were active or manned, but the risk was unavoidable. It was time to take a chance or retreat. She put her head down, and continued.

By the time she reached the wall, she was out of breath and shaking. Sprinting while carrying heavy-duty wire cutters wasn't like being on the treadmill at the gym, and she didn't do that often enough for it to count. Great time for resolutions, she thought, as she stood up and tested the boarding on the nearest window. Sturdy hooks had been fitted into the fabric of the brickwork at each corner of the window and they weren't going to budge, but she could just about shove the point of the wire cutter blades into the gap. Hammering on the handles, she shoved the cutters into the space between the wall and the boarding, jiggling them until she had them in position around the metal clip that fixed the boards to the hooks. Ava squeezed, rested, applied more pressure, and eventually the first clip gave way. The boards didn't budge. She moved the wire cutters and repeated the manoeuvre on the second clip. That took less time, with more flexibility since the first corner had given way. It was only with the third clip gone that she was able to pull the boarding away and see inside.

It was disappointing. There really wasn't anything there. A disused office with an abandoned plastic chair to one side and a dirty-looking green jacket slung over the back of it. Ava checked the perimeter again. Still no activity, and she couldn't hear any vehicles approaching, although the site was at least a mile long so that wasn't entirely surprising. If there were guards inside the building though, they were inevitably going to be disturbed when she broke the glass. Raising the alarm prematurely might blow the whole police operation, and if Skye and Bart were already at risk their lives might be put in even more jeopardy if she acted without backup in place. She took another look inside as she weighed the options, trying to peer beyond the small pane of glass in the office door to the corridor beyond, but she was kidding herself. There was nothing to see, and no basis for risking carefully made plans.

Lowering herself to the floor, back to the wall, she prepared for the run back to the fence and the waiting car. She set off then skidded to a halt, freezing cartoon-like mid-run, catching her breath. The jacket. Throwing herself back towards the building, she hit the ground once more and took out her mobile. It took a while before she could access the right file, but she found what she was looking for. A still shot of Malcolm Reilly leaving the gym the night he disappeared. Green jacket over a T-shirt and jeans. Standing once more, she pressed her face against the glass. No collar, zip front, a pocket on either side. It was possible that the jacket had belonged to someone else. Anything was possible. But Ava had long since stopped believing in coincidences. She checked the landscape one last time for security patrols, satisfied herself that the area was clear, then stood to one side of the window to avoid the worst of the shrapnel and smashed the glass with the wire cutters. If anyone walked past now, the damage would be obvious, but it was too late for caution. It took three blows to get through the double glazing then Ava leapt into action, sliding the cutters along the sill to get rid of the remaining shards, and pulling herself up and inside, moving straight to the glass pane in the door and peering out, expecting raised voices at any moment.

There was a resounding silence. The hairs on Ava's arms stood up. She wasn't superstitious. The limits of the supernatural for her was someone cleaning the Major Investigation Team kitchen without being ordered to, yet she turned around in the small office space fully expecting Malcolm Reilly, or what little remained of him, to be standing behind her, eyeless, lost in the pain of his death, and looking for someone to blame.

She turned the door handle slowly, as quietly as she could, gritting her teeth. Nothing. Absolutely no sound. The building was tomb-like in its stillness. She checked the room to her right. Completely empty. Then she reversed direction in the corridor, moving fast and quietly along. The next room she checked showed signs of recent inhabitation but no occupier. There was a dinner tray on the floor, barely touched. A put-up bed that had been slept in, but the sheets were long-since cold. And a metal dish with a hypodermic syringe and some cotton wool bearing bloody patches.

She took her mobile out and messaged Jojo Berger.

Someone was kept in here. Needle and blood traces. I'm ok. She hit send.

Exiting that room, she moved across the corridor. There was another door further up, locked, and as silent as the others. Her stomach cramped, and a rush of nausea hit her. Too much adrenaline, she decided, breathing deeper. She'd spooked herself, that was all.

At the glass pane in the door, she peered through. The bed was unmade but empty, and there was little else to see except the edge of a shoe on its side. She could just make out the toe of what looked like a man's trainer. Shifting to the other side of the door to get a better view, she looked again.

'Bart,' she whispered. The shoe was still attached to a foot and a leg. His head had to be right up against the door. The odour hit her before she could decide what to do. Sweet and slightly nutty, ripe and coppery, it was unmistakable when you'd smelled it enough times. She brought up the wire cutters again, this time using them on the door handle, smashing them down hard enough to jar both her shoulders, but she kept going. The prospect of an alarm being raised had become irrelevant. She was there to save lives, and if she was going to save Bart's this would be her only opportunity. Standing back she kicked the door hard, five times, six, seven, before raining more blows at the lock with the wire cutters. The door began to move in the frame, the handle flying loose and the metal complaining. Ava kicked again and it flew forward, only to bounce back at her.

'Shit,' she said, grabbing it and stepping forward more carefully, hoping the door hadn't bounced off Bart's head.

His eyes were open. That was the first thing she noticed. On his back, one arm an island in a sea of blood. He was gone, and Ava was as sure as she could be that he'd inflicted the damage on himself.

'Not yet,' Ava said. 'No, you don't.'

She threw herself to her knees, one palm over the other on his chest, starting to pump, only pausing to pull out her mobile

351

again and dial Berger's phone. After thirty chest compressions and two breaths, she began talking into the speaker phone.

'I need paramedics,' she shouted. 'Now, Jojo. I've found Bart Campbell, no pulse, not breathing, severe blood loss. And there's . . .' she looked down at his wrist '. . . something metal sticking out of his wrist. I'm performing CPR. Get someone in here now. Fuck the consequences.'

'Got it,' Berger said, ending the call.

Ava continued with the compressions.

'Come on,' she said. 'Come on, Bart. Don't give up now.' More breaths into his mouth and she ripped off her shirt, wrapping it around his wrist and pulling it tight, before elevating it on his stomach as she started pumping his heart again.

'Your mum needs you, Bart. I need to take you home. You're not dying like this. I won't let you. Don't you bloody dare.'

Callanach had followed his satnav through Coubron and out the other side of town, pulling into a makeshift car park in a field where a gate had been left open. Several other vehicles were already parked there, each with a single person sitting expectantly in the driver's seat. He'd counted nine cars. That meant nine patients each paying thirty-five thousand euros. In total, the revenue from Skye's body was going to be in the region of two hundred and seventy thousand pounds. None of it would be repaid as promised, obviously. Not when the recipients became even more ill, just as it dawned on them that they'd taken part in what was an incredibly serious offence. He'd parked and waited for the transport to arrive. It was cruel to allow the others with him in the car park to go any further, but there was no choice. Interrupt proceedings then and they might never find Skye and Bart. He'd had a few seconds to realise he hadn't even said goodbye to Ava at police HQ before two windowless minivans had pulled in.

Six people climbed out, wearing caps and sunglasses. They

looked professional but well disguised. One by one, they invited the driver of each car to climb into a van and change. Another staff member took the original clothes and shoes back to the relevant car, using the keys to lock up. Callanach went second to last. There was no conversation other than the basics. Inside the van, they were each asked to take their allocated seat and not talk. He made eye contact with a woman he'd been introduced to at the clinic's social evening, and another man he thought he recognised from the waiting room, but no one broke the rules and broached a conversation. If the circumstances weren't oppressive enough to ensure silence, a guard remained with them in the back of the van to ensure compliance. There was no view through the front window, and as they left the field, the sense of fear was palpable.

Callanach understood the reality of what they were driving towards, but the saddest, most desperate part of it was that he could sense that his companions did too. To admit that, though, meant coming to terms with the most awful of truths. That this was the end. That acceptance of mortality was the inevitable path. There was no conspiracy between drug companies, doctors and governments to keep alternative treatments from public knowledge. The reality was an unfair, random, pointless death before a full life had been lived. It was there on every single face, hidden behind the blankness and control. The knowledge that they were pretending to believe rather than genuinely believing.

Without a watch he was only guessing, but Callanach estimated they travelled for around twenty minutes before slowing then stopping, slowing then stopping. There were voices, the sound of metal protesting against metal – double electric gates, he decided – then concrete became gravel beneath the tyres and the minivan bumped along for a few more minutes. Wherever they were, it was a substantial distance between the outer perimeter and their final destination. For the police drones

353

to remain unseen, they would have to keep a long way back from the perimeter. Too far, and it was possible the drones would lose sight of the van completely, particularly if there was tree cover or a heavily built-up area.

The van stopped. The driver and guards climbed out, then the glare of electric lights intruded as the rear doors opened. Callanach made himself wait to take position at the back of the queue, maximising his opportunity to look around. At some point the van had entered a large indoor unloading bay. The massive garage doors rumbled the final metre back to the ground as they were met by yet more guards, this time suited, the juxtaposition of five-star treatment with guns.

'Ladies and gentlemen,' a man announced. The flat accent gave away the fact that French was his second language, although Callanach couldn't guess his nationality. Not Scottish, in any event. 'If you'd follow me, we are about to begin. You will each be made comfortable in a viewing gallery together. It is extremely important that you respect one another's privacy and confidentiality, and therefore do not attempt to speak with one another. When you leave here you will wish to maintain your anonymity, and sharing information will jeopardise that. There will be a brief explanation of security procedures and then we'll begin.'

Large interior doors opened, and everything beyond that was bright white, washable plastic, glass or tile. One by one, they went through a medical-grade clean room, washing their hands and faces, then applying antiseptic lotion to any exposed parts of their skin. After that, they entered an office space. On the windows of the abandoned conference rooms Callanach could make out the ghostly outlines of a large leaf, over and over again. At some point a substantial company had occupied the building, with breakout rooms, individual offices, spaces where vending machines must have sat against the walls. All very normal and corporate, but high security just the same.

'Nearly there,' the guard told them, as they proceeded towards a set of double doors, with tiered seating beyond.

Callanach almost missed the safety instructions on a plastic sticker, fixed onto a pane of glass as they walked past. He paused and bent down, pretending to do up the lace of one of the cheap trainers they'd each been given.

'One moment,' he indicated to the guard holding the doors open, overseeing everyone else getting to their seats.

Callanach flicked his eyes up cautiously as he slowly retied the knot.

'During fire alarms, proceed immediately to the designated area. Do not go beyond the designated areas. Animal research facilities can be subject to attacks and false alarms with intent to do harm. All employees must follow manager instruction, ensure doors are closed behind . . .'

That was all the time Callanach could afford, and all the time he needed. It made sense. In lots of ways, it was genius. Any normal medical facility would have the internal set-up required, but not the security. He'd been to a number of animal testing complexes over the years. They were often subjected to acts of vandalism, attempts to enter to release animals, or bomb hoaxes. With barbed-wire-reinforced fences and boundaries, it would prove time-consuming and difficult for even the police to break into. Standing up, Callanach followed everyone else into the auditorium and took a seat. He looked back up the corridor, at the doors that were swinging shut, and wondered how long it would take for backup to arrive.

In front of them was a vast glass partition, beyond which was an operating theatre. Had it been decked out in wood rather than chrome, it might have belonged to a Victorian medical school. The theatre was as yet unoccupied, but the guard held another door open and from it emerged a woman in scrubs, surgical mask covering her face.

'Good evening,' she began in French. 'In a moment we will

355

bring your donor into the theatre. Please be quiet and respectful. Her family are in another part of the building and have spent the last hour saying their final goodbyes and coming to terms with their loss even as they give you their blessing and hope very much that each of you will benefit from this extraordinary gift. Occasionally families in this situation feel able to spend time with recipients afterwards. I'm afraid today that this young woman's parents are not able to take that step. You'll understand that their grief is too raw.'

There were a number of nods from the audience. Callanach suspected an amount of relief, too. It was no small thing, if you believed what was about to happen, to be given a chance to live through someone else's death.

'For some of you with strong religious beliefs, we have agreed that a multi-denominational blessing is in order. We will purify the body, and say a prayer for the young woman whose life span has nearly reached its full conclusion. Her natural life, in fact, would have ended some time ago if it were not for life support. We pray, also, for you as you prepare yourselves physically and mentally to go into the treatment phase. If you do not have a religious or spiritual leaning, please respect those who do, and perhaps take those few moments to consider how lucky you are to have this opportunity, and to meditate on what it means to you.'

She was good, Callanach thought. Completely credible. Stopping just short of patronising in tone. Professional but compassionate. Astoundingly real. Not looking at all like someone who was about to murder a perfectly healthy woman in cold blood.

'A word of warning. I'm sure you're all aware of this by now, but I am duty bound to reiterate the need for you to keep details of what we do here secret. You all know and understand that the government has conspired with pharmaceutical conglomerates to refuse to license our innovative treatments. What you may not have thought about is the fact that therefore the treatments we offer here are considered – wrongly, we would state – criminal activity.'

There were a couple of muffled coughs at that, but no objections.

'Therefore, whatever happens after this, do not contact the authorities. Do not give details to other medical practitioners. Our own legal counsel has looked carefully at the law, and you would be charged as conspirators. Obviously that's something we wish, for your sakes, to avoid.'

Callanach waited to see if anyone would lose their nerve and attempt to leave. No one did. If you were facing an early death, of course, the threat of legal proceedings was not terribly impactful.

'Lastly this. We will bring in your donor, for you to assure yourself that what we have told you is real. After the ceremony, we will remove her to a surgical-only area, for her organs to be processed. During that period of time, you will be shown to your individual rooms while your treatment is prepared. A staff member will remain with each of you during that time period, and from now on you will not be permitted to go anywhere without a staff member accompanying you. It can be a stressful time, and we need to make sure that both your emotional and physical needs are fully met. Let us begin.'

She disappeared out of the door. Footsteps echoed beyond, and within sixty seconds additional lights were switched on in the operating theatre. Almost as one, the people watching, waiting to have their lives saved, leaned forward for a closer view. Callanach shifted in his seat. By now, the auditorium should have been full of police, guns pointed in every direction, no door left closed. Instead he was in a room with two armed guards, several innocent but desperately misguided people, and no weapon.

The doors at the back of the operating theatre swung open dramatically. An orderly pushed in a gurney upon which, beneath a green surgical sheet, lay the unmoving body of Skye Kelso. Another woman pushed in a drip, and on the other side a man in scrubs was setting up a vital signs monitor.

Finally, a third woman entered carrying a candle, which she lit as she stood at Skye's head. Skye herself was wired into a variety of machinery. The drip was feeding into her arm. She had a mask over her face. There were electrical pads covering what showed of her upper chest. In truth, she looked dead already. Callanach took stock. If he made for the door now to let officers in, either he'd be shot in an instant or everyone involved would get away. It wasn't until he heard the voice from behind the mask of the woman with the candle that he realised he was looking at Lucille Blaise, the administrator from the clinic. Her hair was hidden by a surgical hat, and not an inch of her body showed save for her eyes – devoid of makeup – but the voice was clear. She lit the candle and myrrh-scented smoke wafted around Skye's body, the odour leaking into the auditorium through the air-conditioning vents.

'We purify and commend this brave young woman. Let us acknowledge the tragedy of her passing, as we accept and give thanks for the gift it has given us. Let us continue our work in the knowledge that more lives can and will be saved this way. We should now each take a moment to be silent and grateful.'

The police weren't coming. The ceremony was over. Callanach could see other so-called staff members amassing in the corridor beyond the auditorium, ready to take them to their rooms and deliver their medically prepared meal of human organs. There was no way out in that direction. He felt under the seat for any metal spike or heavy object he could use. Nothing.

In the operating theatre, Lucille Blaise extinguished the candle, and with dignified slowness turned to those around her. Callanach slipped forward in his seat, tensed to move. The machines were removed from Skye's body, the drip detached, electrical pads peeled away, her mask taken off, although staff were careful to shield the body at that point. He guessed it would have been obvious that there was no substance to the illusion if there had been no tube in Skye's throat. The vital signs monitor flatlined, and the surgeon who had issued the criminal liability threat took Skye's pulse, flashed a light in her eyes and gave a nod to her team. Skye was out of time.

Callanach stood up, walking briskly towards the nearest guard who frowned at him, put one hand up in a 'stop right there' gesture then raised his gun. Callanach leapt the remaining distance between them, left arm pushing outwards to direct the gunfire away from the stunned spectators, right arm drawn back, ready to punch. He connected with the guard's jaw as the first bullet flew, hitting only the rear wall, but by then the second guard had woken up. He was the other side of those watching, yelling instructions to them to get down to give him a clear shot. Callanach let himself roll, pulling the guard on top of him, wrapping an arm around his neck and taking control of the weapon.

In the operating theatre, the staff were making a rapid getaway, rushing the gurney through the rear door. The people waiting for their life-saving treatments were screaming, trying to run for cover as the second guard returned fire. Callanach hauled the first guard up as a shield, aiming at the enormous glass window and letting loose with the automatic rifle. The first few bullets created splintered cobweb patterns across the partition, and then it was raining glass. Callanach pushed his face into the back of the guard's neck, shutting his eyes tight, hoping that everyone had the sense to get down and stay down.

The guard began to crumple in his arms, screaming before he hit the ground. Callanach threw himself to the ground at the base of the bottom row of seats and waited for the shooting to stop. Somewhere further up the auditorium a woman was shouting for help. He took the gun from the guard's increasingly slack grip, and vaulted the low wall between the auditorium and the operating theatre, his hand registering the pain of the glass shards that were still in place, catching a glimpse of the carnage behind him. The second guard had chosen self-preservation over loyalty to his employers and was pushing past the confused and terrified patients to get out into the corridor. The guard Callanach had used as a shield was bleeding out on the staircase and two other people were down – either because of their already weakened state, the glass or the bullets – but there wasn't time to help them now. He shoved through the double doors, looking left and right along the corridor to figure out where Skye had been taken. He chose left for no better reason than gut instinct and began to run.

The baseball bat that smashed into his ribcage was all the more forceful for the speed at which he was moving. He went straight down, winded and gasping for breath, as the boot he was staring at kicked upwards, smacking him in the soft flesh beneath his jaw. Teeth slamming together, Callanach's head whiplashed to one side, seeing Alex's sweet, round face above him.

The baseball bat was coming for his face. He got an arm in front of it first, the subsequent pain in his forearm matching the agony in his mouth. The gun was lost to him, spinning off down the corridor. Alex took a step away, giving himself additional space to swing the bat. Callanach managed to get up on his knees before the next blow, driving forward, head-butting Alex's testicles. The baseball bat clattered down onto his back, the worst of its force gone.

'You lied!' Alex screamed as he doubled up. 'You said you had liver failure, and I believed you.'

By then Callanach was up on his feet, and he drove the outer part of his bent elbow with brutal precision into the back of Alex's neck. He met the floor face first, hands still cradling his balls.

'I lied to help people. You lied to help kill people for money. Where have they taken Skye?'

Alex gurgled as he writhed on the slippery floor. Callanach couldn't wait for him to start making sense. Grabbing the baseball bat, he took off again. The corridor rounded to the right, opening into a larger open room where the surgeon and Lucille Blaise were furiously attempting to destroy two laptops as they stuffed bags and fought loose of the fake, pointless scrubs.

Callanach skidded to a halt.

'Don't come any closer,' the would-be surgeon said. She picked up a syringe and held the tip of it to Skye's throat. 'She's still alive and you can have her, but we get out of here first.'

'I need proof,' Callanach said. 'I can't see any sign that she's breathing.'

'She's fully anaesthetised. Her systems are starting to shut down. If I give her another dose of this,' she waved the hypodermic needle, 'I guarantee you she'll never wake up and that'll be your fault.'

'I want to check her pulse,' Callanach said. He stepped forward slowly, reaching one hand out to Skye's wrist. The beat he felt was weak and erratic, but she was holding on. 'Okay, how do you want to do this?'

'I'm going to keep holding this needle to her neck while my friend ties you up. You're going to stand still, hands behind your back, and agree not to move. There's enough anaesthetic in that syringe to kill the girl first and have enough left over for you, so don't make me nervous.'

'Fine.' He dropped the baseball bat on the floor and put his hands together behind his back. Lucille approached him hesitantly, stethoscope in hand, as if he were a wild animal. 'You had me fooled,' Callanach told her. 'I'd have put money on Bruno Plouffe being the contact at the clinic. You and Alex working together was clever. Alex pretending to be wary of Plouffe, so innocent and friendly there was no way I'd have suspected him of being involved in something like this.'

'Hurry up,' the surgeon demanded. 'And stop talking.'

'He's police,' Lucille muttered as she pulled the knot of the stethoscope tight. 'There'll be more on their way.'

'They won't know all the exits and entrances yet. Do his ankles with that sheet.'

Callanach drew his feet together and allowed Lucille to wrap the sheet several times around his legs, doing the best she could to bind them together.

'Done?' the surgeon asked. Lucille nodded. 'Good, now pick up that baseball bat and hit his skull as hard as you can. I don't want any chance of him following us.'

'What if I kill him?'

'It'll be worse if you don't. He knows who you are.'

'I can't kill a policeman. I was only supposed to pass over the information from the clinic, and to pretend to be a member of your team. I can't kill anyone.'

'Don't,' Callanach said quietly. 'You don't know what it'll do to you. At the moment you're involved in a conspiracy. When you get caught, if you've refused to kill, then you're in a good position to strike a deal in court—'

'Fuck you,' the surgeon said. 'I'll do it myself.' Leaning forward with the syringe, she went to jab it into Skye's neck.

Callanach let his weight carry him forward between the surgeon and Skye, the needle painlessly entering his shoulder, no more than a scratch, as he covered Skye's body with his own.

'Oh my God,' he heard Lucille cry, his consciousness already dimming as if he were listening through a wall. 'He'll die.' Something heavy clattered to the floor. Sounds of feet running.

Callanach tried to turn his head, but the only thing he could see was fairground ride movement of light and colour. Skye lay motionless beneath his chest, and he held on as long as he could before slipping to his knees, then crashing down into oblivion.

362

Chapter Forty-One

The first bursts of gunfire echoed through the complex just as the paramedics and Jojo Berger reached Ava.

'What's happening?' Ava demanded, stepping back and allowing the medics the space to do their work.

'The drone followed the vans to the gates of the complex but it's taking some time to find the right building and gain access,' Berger told her.

'Skye Kelso?'

'No news yet. Are you hurt? You're covered in blood.'

'I only wish it were mine,' Ava said. 'Look after him and get the paramedics whatever they need. Just keep him safe.'

'There's an air ambulance on its way. You go.'

Ava went. The door at the end of the corridor was unlocked. She took the covered walkway to the next building along, which was more modern – glass and chrome. Further gunfire. Shouting now. Sirens, and the sound of multiple vehicles. To her right were double doors into a large auditorium. Those were locked. To her left there was a fire escape. She took the latter, and found herself back outside, gaining pace as she raced towards the sirens, round the vast curved exterior of the enormous building.

Ava arrived at the edge of a crowd of police officers just as the first of Group 2029's guards rushed out. Then came a straggle of people in cheap white cotton garments, and others in scrubs. As they exited, Ava ran in. Guns had been discarded along the corridor. Group 2029 had known the police were on their way, then. Callanach had started something.

As she rounded a corner, a woman fled through a side door, marked as the entrance to the incinerator. Ava looked around to alert other police officers to pursue, but they were scattering in all directions. Wrenching the door open, she followed.

It was dark inside. Someone had turned off all the lights in the passageway. Only emergency lighting remained, set into the floor, casting shadows everywhere. Ava reached out for the right-hand wall, keeping herself steady.

In front of her was a glass doorway to an office, beyond which she could see the giant incinerator, a wall of metal. A huge notice declared the incinerator out of use awaiting repair. As she read the sign, a reflection rippled above the words and behind her.

Ava swung round, hands together and clasped in one large fist, ducking her head and driving for the abdomen. Her aim was good. The woman she'd struck tumbled back into the opposite wall, one arm flying out and an object spinning from her fist. It took Ava half a second to assess the surgical scrubs and realise she was dealing with one of the monsters responsible for Malcolm Reilly's death. It seemed a fair call to make doubly sure the woman was incapacitated.

Grabbing a handful of her hair, she pulled the woman's head away from the wall, then brought it back again, harder. There was a grisly but satisfying crunching noise, and the woman's forehead came away bloody. Ava told herself to breathe. She'd overstepped. As she moved away, something smashed beneath her foot. The syringe was in pieces, a few drops of liquid seeping out. That's what the woman had been holding, with God only knew what chemical destined for her veins. To call it a lucky escape was an understatement.

'Paramedics!' Ava yelled, racing for the door into the main corridor.

As the medics entered, she left, shouting for Callanach as she went. The rumble-squeak of wheels was even louder than the feet running alongside them. Ava picked up the pace to meet the stretcher head on.

'Is that Skye?' she shouted. 'Is she still alive?'

'Yes, clear the corridor,' the paramedic ordered.

A second stretcher approached. She recognised the hair before she could solidify the thought. It was Callanach, one arm flopping off the side, his head lolling as the paramedics jogged alongside.

'Luc?' she shouted. 'What the hell happened? Oh shit,' she tried to take his hand but it slid uselessly from her fingers. 'What's wrong with him?'

'Out of our way.'

'You have to tell me . . .'

'You want him to live, then get out of our way.'

She got the message, clearing the space, making sure they were far enough ahead of her before she followed, telling herself to keep breathing. Trying to persuade herself that Callanach and Bart would both survive.

As the medics left, a stream of police officers entered. Ava grabbed the nearest of them and led the way to the woman she'd left unconscious on the floor in the incinerator area. She was put on a stretcher, hands cuffed over her stomach, and lifted out. So many bodies, Ava thought. So much spilled blood. And all because people would do – and pay – almost anything to live. The irony of it was depressing.

'Did Skye survive?' were Callanach's first words, three hours later from a hospital bed. A doctor had given what amounted to an antidote to the huge dose of anaesthetic he'd been given, but then decided his body would need some time to recover from the shock of the dosage he'd received, leaving him mildly sedated.

'She did,' Ava said, sliding her hand gently from where it had been wrapped around his. 'And she's going to be fine. Certainly in a better state than you.'

'What's wrong with me?' he asked. The words came out mushed.

'Oh, right, you probably can't feel your face yet. They gave you some painkillers while you were asleep. Hold on.'

She picked up a shiny metal kidney bowl, turned it over, and held it up for him to see. 'From the baseball bat, I assume?' Ava said as Luc surveyed the damage to his face.

He nodded.

'No fracture, but your jaw's going to hurt like hell for a couple of weeks, the swelling on your skull will go down, you're being watched for concussion, you have various cuts and bruises, some nice swelling on your arm. Combine that with the anaesthetic they injected into you that was designed to end Skye's life and you've had what some people would regard as a difficult day at work.'

'Enough,' he said.

'Yeah, you're right. That is enough. You should have waited for backup. We were on our way into the building.'

'They were about to kill her. I didn't know where you were.'

'You did okay. Bart Campbell is in the intensive care unit. He cut his wrist and lost a lot of blood. Paramedics revived him, but the extent of any brain damage isn't yet known. Everyone involved from Group 2029 is in custody. There's one dead guard, one patient who got in the line of fire and who didn't make it, and plenty of other injuries but none life-threatening. The female surgeon who was carrying a syringe, you know her?' He nodded. 'She and I met up, and I guess you could say I felt that I had no choice but to use consider-able force to ensure my own safety.'

Callanach smiled then grimaced.

'Wish I'd seen that,' he said.

'Sounds more exciting than it was. What you don't know is that she turned out to be your friend Alex's mother. It was all carefully thought out. He worked in the clinic, gained the trust of suitably desperate candidates, and offered other staff members large amounts of money to be involved.'

'He had me completely fooled. Alex was a nice kid, quiet and unassuming. So clever.'

'Don't feel too bad. It looks as if they've been working medical scams for years, but there was never any firm evidence, no witness testimony. Alex always held down real jobs with good recommendations while his mother stayed under the radar. The family made sure they left a convincing trail of previous jobs and social media. Interestingly, Alex has a sister who is currently believed to be in Scotland . . .'

'The woman who met Malcolm Reilly in the gym and Bart at the restaurant?'

'That's the theory we're working on. She's just been arrested in Edinburgh. Now that the police have started digging, I suspect the operation will widen substantially.'

'This one's closed down, but there'll be others. There's always someone ready to rip off the vulnerable. Lucky we made it in time,' Callanach said.

'Only just, as far as you were concerned. You scared me. I'm a bit pissed off with you, to be honest.'

'Am I supposed to be able to remember a time when you weren't pissed off with me?'

'Touché.'

'Wow, you can speak one whole word of French.' He closed his eyes and settled back into the pillows.

'You're going to have to stay here a couple of days. Interpol are insisting. You were their liaison officer when this happened, so they're responsible for you until you're back in Scotland.'

He took a few deep breaths.

'I'm going back to Scotland?' he asked quietly.

'Yes. You are.' She wiped her cheeks quickly and turned to look out of the window before he opened his eyes again. 'I'm travelling back tomorrow. Debrief today, then I'll write up my statement. Bart and Skye can both be returned to their families tomorrow, and they're anxious to get as far away from here as possible. I'm going to escort them home. Then there's all the fallout from arresting a couple of hundred people in one operation. I think we've poached officers from every other city in Scotland to help.'

'You must be popular,' he said.

'You know me. Why do anything simply when it's possible to create a massive bloody mess?'

He gave a soft laugh.

'Truce?' she asked. 'Get better, do what you have to do here, close the file and come home. Plus, Natasha needs you.'

'Just Natasha?'

'You going to make me beg?' She folded her arms. 'All right. I need you. You're my best detective inspector. Even Lively's missing you. It's just not the same.'

'Ava, of course I'm coming back. I was always intending to. And I wasn't trying to make you beg.'

'Right. Good. I'm glad you're conscious. Sorry about your face. Can I take a quick photo to show the squad?' He glared at her. 'Spoilsport. I'll see you in Edinburgh then.' Ava walked to the door. 'Get strong, okay? I don't have enough money in my budget to have an officer out on long-term sick leave.'

Chapter Forty-Two

Luc put his suitcase down and took his passport from his pocket. Charles de Gaulle airport was strangely quiet, as if the whole place was being respectful of the hangovers Jean-Paul and he were suffering. He was winging it on two hours' sleep, glad he wouldn't have to drive when his plane set down in Edinburgh. Between the two of them, they'd consumed five bottles of wine, which given the antibiotics Jean-Paul was taking and the painkillers Callanach had been prescribed, had been not just stupid but reckless. Jean-Paul, still hypersensitive to sunlight after the skin burns, had insisted on wrapping his face up in a scarf and donning dark glasses to deliver him to his flight.

'You going to be okay?' Callanach asked.

'If I haven't thrown up by now, I'm pretty sure I won't,' Jean-Paul laughed.

'I wouldn't bank on that, but actually I meant are you okay about everything that happened. Your face . . .'

'Is nearly mended. I'd be more concerned about yours. How do you feel about going back to Scotland?'

'Good actually,' Callanach said. 'I've missed it. You should visit some time.'

'Oh no, I don't do British food,' he grinned. 'So is there any chance of you coming back to live here? Interpol wants you back. I said I'd get you drunk and persuade you, but apparently I only managed the first part of that.'

'I doubt it, and not because of what happened in the past. I want to try and make Scotland my home. It's been good, getting a sense of my father, where he came from and my roots. I'll miss France – especially the food – but Scotland is beautiful. It has history and this amazing sense of community.'

'And a woman you're in love with,' Jean-Paul finished for him.

'There's always a woman,' Callanach laughed it off.

'Not like Ava Turner, it seems. It's a shame I didn't get to meet her. There's a rumour she's pretty handy with her fists and not afraid to use them.'

'That's not just a rumour. Anyway, I don't think it's going to happen,' Callanach said. 'I messed up. It's like I broke her into too many pieces to even start putting her back together.'

'I think I actually might vomit after that.' Jean-Paul laughed, stepping forward to throw his arms around Callanach's shoulders, squeezing long and hard. 'Stop overthinking it. People screw up. Even you, golden boy. Women love you. It's pissed me off for as long as I've known you, but if you've found the one woman in the world who doesn't fall for your looks and your accent, then I'm delighted for you. Sounds to me as if she's the only one you've ever met who's worth fighting for.' He released his hold and stepped away. 'Come back soon. It's not the same without you. Sooner or later I'll have to get myself a wife and a bunch of kids if the party days are really over.'

'You're really considering passing those genes onto some unsuspecting kids?' Callanach picked up his bag. 'You know you have to find a wife willing to sleep with you first, right? And with that face . . .'

'Fuck you,' Jean-Paul laughed. 'If you hadn't been so slow jumping out of that goddamned window, I wouldn't be in this mess.'

Callanach waved and began walking away.

'Oh hell, Luc, wait! Come back!' Callanach turned round, apologising to the people already queuing behind him, and returned for another dose of Jean-Paul's sarcasm. 'I completely forgot. They found those kids' mother, the two Afghan children you helped. She's flying out here to be reunited with them.'

Callanach's heart double-timed for a few seconds. He'd resisted the temptation to visit Azzat and Huznia before leaving Paris but he'd been told they were settling well into foster care, and that Azzat had even started school. It was a rare triumph in a system that struggled to cope.

'Will she be allowed to stay or will they all have to go back to Afghanistan?' he asked.

'They'll be able to make an asylum application. She was subjected to a substantial level of violence and abuse, and she was living on the streets, begging. Interpol identified her as she was using an international charity's medical service regularly. Don't get a hero complex, but I guess it's fair to say those kids'll be pretty grateful to you.'

Callanach considered answering then gave up on it. Some things didn't require a response. He stepped forward, kissed Jean-Paul on each cheek, then disappeared through into security. Half of him longed to stay in France and the other half was counting down the minutes until his feet hit the ground in Edinburgh. He felt the pull of his dual nationalities, no longer running away from one or the other, but equally invested in both. Settling on the plane, he closed his eyes and let himself drift back in time to a day he spent at Eilean Donan Castle.

★ ★ ★

Lively shoved the bunch of flowers forward, looking off in a different direction. Elenuta took them carefully, putting her face to the orange roses and breathing deeply.

'Thank you,' she said. 'Beautiful.'

'I just figured you wouldn't have had many visitors except for immigration and doctors. Shall we sit?'

Elenuta glanced at the sad, hard chair next to her bed in the hospital room where she'd been left – in theory – to recuperate. The authorities were still processing her and the other women, and leaving them in the hospital was easier than organising a longer-term solution.

'Can we walk? I am allowed to leave room if police with me.' She smiled, looking out of her window at the grounds below. It was chilly, but not raining. Lively could sympathise with her desire to get fresh air. Hospitals made him feel ill as soon he walked in the door. It was enough to make anyone long for freedom.

'Will you be warm enough?' he asked, as she put the flowers by her bed then pulled on a patchy denim jacket, obviously donated from a charity store.

'I don't mind cold,' she said, pushing her feet into trainers and moving for the door. Lively followed her, showing his ID to the officer who stood at the end of the corridor, though he didn't check it anyway.

They took the stairs rather than the elevator, and headed for the car park. Elenuta turned her face up towards the weak sunshine and smiled.

'So how're you doing?' Lively asked. 'I mean, I know it's only been a couple of days, so it's probably a stupid question . . .'

'I'm alive,' Elenuta smiled. 'Must not be sad. Others dead.'

Lively shoved his hands hard in his jacket pockets and gave a small cough.

'I, er, think you were very brave. Maybe braver than anyone

else I've known. You could have asked me to stop it all earlier on. Maybe we should have done, too. What happened during the race when I couldn't get to you . . . Shit, I don't even know how to say sorry properly. It just doesn't do it justice.'

'You save me.' She tipped her head to one side and smiled. 'Why sorry?'

'It should have gone down differently,' he said. 'You shouldn't have had to fight the way you did. I don't know why we didn't anticipate them blocking phone signals to the outside. It makes absolute sense now. And as for locking the doors into the viewing area . . . we tried to be too clever, and . . . hell.' Lively hung his head. Being stuck for words wasn't something that happened to him very often. Perhaps ever.

'You did best, right? All the women found. So many of us. All safe now. You are hero.'

'Not at all,' he muttered. 'You are hero.'

'Perhaps both,' she laughed and Lively marvelled at the sound. 'Come, we walk,' she said, slipping her hand into the crook of his elbow, pulling him away from the hospital doors and around the side of the building.

'So, am I in trouble?' she asked quietly.

'What could you possibly be in trouble for?'

'I kill man. Stab him, in race.'

She looked up into Lively's face, eyes wide.

'No,' he said softly. 'There'll be no charges. You're not in trouble. We'll take statements from everyone there, but we already know the circumstances. It was as clear a case of self-defence as I've ever seen. The man you killed had it coming.'

'Thank you,' she whispered.

'Please, don't thank me. You should never have been there. If I'd known you were going to be chosen for the race . . .'

'I make Scalp choose me,' she said. 'It was me or sixteen year old.' She shrugged.

Lively dashed the back of one hand against his cheek and turned away for a second, coughing loudly before looking at her again.

'Have you been told what will happen to you now?' he asked.

'I go home,' she said, raising then dropping her shoulders. 'I have no passport here. Not legal. People wait for me there.'

'Of course,' he said. 'That's what I figured. Obviously Scotland is the last place you want to be after everything you've been through.'

'Scotland did not do this,' she said, shivering suddenly at a blast of wind that hit them. 'Bad people everywhere in world.'

'That there are,' Lively said. 'I wish I could show you what it's really like here. The cities, the lochs, the castles and the Highlands. It's not all bad.'

'Maybe I come back? With passport this time. But not by boat.'

'I hope you do,' Lively said. 'Could I maybe write to you?' he blurted.

'Write letters?' Her eyes opened wide. 'I would like.'

'I mean, I'm not much of a writer. Can't remember the last time I put pen to paper, to be honest, so don't expect anything grand.'

'You are kind man.'

'I'd just like to know that you're home safe, and that your family are looking after you,' Lively said, managing a direct smile. 'I wish none of it had ever happened to you. The things I see in this job . . . every time I think it can't get any worse, someone ups their bloody game.'

'So we . . . I don't know word. We make like was different, you know?'

'Pretend?' Lively asked.

'Yes!' She waved an excited hand in the air. 'In letters, we

374

not talk of it. Tell me about Scotland. I tell you about my life, my country. You want this?'

'I do,' he nodded. 'I should walk you back now. You're turning a bit blue.'

'Cold but happy,' she said. 'For first time in many months. You make me feel safe.'

Elenuta stepped forward and hugged him fiercely. The gesture took Lively by surprise. He raised a tentative hand and patted her back.

'You're all right now,' he said. 'Every bastard involved is going to rot in jail, I promise you.'

'I just try to forget,' she said. 'Too much hate inside me. I need peace.'

She was right, Lively thought, as they walked back towards the hospital entrance. He wanted to find peace, too. For the first time in more than thirty years of policing, he wondered if he was finally done.

Bart and Skye sat at a table near the back of The Newsroom, the music playing just quietly enough for them to talk. The bandage on Bart's wrist poked out a fraction below the sleeve of his shirt, but the wound was healing. A blood transfusion and an amazing medical team had saved his life. In spite of a lengthy period of unconsciousness, there had been no brain damage. He was due a scar, but it would fade with time. Faster than the memories would, anyway. Skye had a half-full pack of cigarettes set on the table in front of her, the lid open a crack and a lighter balanced on top.

'You took up smoking since we got back?' Bart asked, topping up her glass with champagne. The choice of drinks was a gesture of celebration. He'd have preferred beer or red wine, but the gold label and ridiculous bubbles were so iconically happy and alive that it had been a no-brainer.

'I'll never smoke,' Skye said in a half whisper. 'But if that's what it takes to stop anyone from ever thinking my body would make a good sales product in the future, then I'll never be without a pack again.'

'It won't happen again,' Bart told her. 'It was nothing we did. Wrong place at the wrong time, maybe, but you can't live scared.'

'I don't care if I live scared, terrified, or under my bed forever.' She raised her glass. 'The fact that I have a chance to live at all is a fucking miracle as far as I'm concerned. Tell me it's not just me. You're so calm, and after everything you went through . . .'

'It's in the past. I don't want to think about it any more.'

'But I wake up twenty times a night back in that building, waiting for them to come for me. The only thing that keeps me from screaming is knowing that you were always in that room across the corridor. I have to imagine your voice to stay sane. The only way I can get back to sleep is by replaying our conversations in my head. God, that sounds so pathetic.'

Bart reached out, slipped an arm around her shoulders, and pulled her towards him until her head was resting on his shoulder.

'This, here, is what kept me going, and it's why I couldn't cope when they took you,' he said. 'Until that moment, the thought of being here with you some day was everything. The idea that we would find a way to fight or to escape, or that someone would finally come the way they did. I pictured the tables, the menus, the lamps in the window and the passersby looking in. It was always raining in my head, just like it is now, because when it rains in Edinburgh at night, all the lights from the cars, the shops and street lights reflect on the roads and I think the city's even more beautiful like that.'

'I used to imagine Paris like that,' Skye said. 'There's a painting by an artist called Gustave Caillebotte. *Rainy Day*, I think is the title. Anyway, it's this Parisian street and everyone has an umbrella. The flagstones are wet and the sky is this stormy yellow colour but it's just so atmospheric and romantic. I used to have a poster of it in my bedroom. Now I'll never go back to France again. Not if I live to be a thousand.'

She looked up at Bart but kept her head against his shoulder.

'There are lots of other places to visit,' he said. 'California?'

'I always fancied Australia.' She smiled. He didn't need to look at her to know. He could feel the muscles of her cheek lift against his chest.

'What about Hawaii? I could learn to surf.'

She laughed. He felt as if he'd won the lottery.

'You think you could pull off one of those flowery shirts?' she asked, taking a sip of champagne and picking her head up. She stayed close, though, and he kept his arm around her shoulders.

'Sure, and I'll let my hair grow like those guys who live in a camper van next to the beach all year round. I used to skateboard a bit. How much harder could it be?'

'Hawaii it is then. I reckon I could get a bar job to pay the rent.'

'And I can get work as a waiter, buy all our food and suntan lotion. Is it a date?' He grinned.

'Is this a date?' Skye asked quietly.

'Do you think you'll ever be able to look at me and not think of the time we spent watching each other through toughened glass wondering if we'd survive? Because I don't want to be only that man to you. Sooner or later I can see how you'd need to leave that behind.'

Skye put her drink down delicately on the table and shifted her body round to face Bart front on, her hands together in her lap.

'You're right,' she said. 'I will need to move on. We both

will. But you're not the man who reminds me of being locked in a room thinking I was going to die, or the person who reminds me of the city I was abducted from. Bart, you're the man who made me laugh during the darkest moment of my life. I know you. Maybe not everything about you, and I get that ours has been a brief and entirely bizarre meeting, but you're never going to hurt me, or be cruel, or take advantage. I know you're good, brave, and resilient. If you actually want to give . . .' she gestured from herself to him and back again '. . . this a go, then I think I'd have to be a strong candidate to win luckiest girl in the world.'

Bart looked at her demure hands. Her right middle fingernail was still missing from the damage it had sustained inside the cargo container, scratching at the walls. Her face bore faint yellow bruising around one eye from rough treatment forcing her to comply with orders. Her ribs, elbows and collarbones were visible reminders, even beneath her black top, of the fact that she had been too desperate and stressed to eat in captivity. In spite of what she thought, her soul was hopeful. Bart took a moment to remember the way she looked right then. She was the most beautiful girl he'd ever seen.

He leaned forward, stopping an inch away from her face.

'Do you think it would be okay if I kissed you?' he asked.

Skye closed the distance between their lips and gave her answer.

Chapter Forty-Three

Natasha's kitchen was warm and bright as they sat around the table, drinking coffee. Ava perched cross-legged on her chair, staring into her cup. Callanach studied Natasha as she pulled her blanket closer around her shoulders in spite of the blasting heating. The after-effects of surgery and chemotherapy were wearing through her.

'Dinner'll be ready in ten minutes,' Natasha said quietly. 'Nothing fancy, I'm afraid. I just threw a quick curry together.'

'You shouldn't have cooked at all,' Ava scolded her. 'I said I'd pick something up on the way.'

'I know. I appreciated it, but I still love to cook and there are a certain amount of fresh vegetables I need in my diet that takeaways occasionally forget to include. The point is that I want to carry on as normal when I'm up to it.'

Ava turned away. Callanach wondered how long it had been since she'd been able to look her best friend in the eyes without tears forming in her own.

'I'll learn to cook,' Ava muttered. 'Properly. I'll do a course or something. We can all eat raw, or clean, or whatever the phrase is. Fruit and vegetables three times a day. I'll get deliveries set up . . .'

'Ava . . .' Natasha said.

'No, it's fine, I can make sure I'm here at set times each day. We're fully staffed in MIT again now that Luc's back. I'm due a ton of leave in lieu of overtime . . .'

'Stop, please. I know you feel like you need to fix this, but it'll be easier on all of us if you just accept that you can't. Not this time. As for the cooking lessons, please – for the sake of us all – don't even contemplate spending time in my kitchen. That really would kill me.'

Still no smile from Ava.

'Then I'll get someone in to cook. I can afford it. It's not like I've had a holiday in the last five years and I haven't touched the money my mother left me . . .'

'Actually I need more from you than that,' Natasha said. 'I asked you both here for a reason, and it would be quicker if you'd just listen. Let me finish. If at the end you need some time to think about it, or if you know it won't work, then that's fine.'

Ava frowned, opened her mouth, but Natasha shook her head.

'No, you're at my table. That means I get silence when I want it.'

'Go ahead,' Callanach said. 'I'm sure we can stay quiet for a few minutes.' He looked to Ava for a response. She studied the wall.

'All right,' Natasha said. 'Here goes. I have something to ask of you both. It's a big thing, too, but given the position I find myself in, I've decided I'm entitled to take advantage a little.' She smiled and topped up her mug from the cafetière. 'I've got plenty of chemo left to go, probably followed by radiotherapy. My doctors say I'll need rest, emotional support, help making sure the house is as clean as possible while my immune system is down, and just . . . everything, I guess. Anyway, I think the thing that scares me more than anything is being alone through all this. Nights when I can't sleep. Evenings when I'm sick of listening to my own scared voice in my head . . .'

'Tasha . . .' Ava said, crumbling, reaching for her friend's hand across the table.

Natasha folded her fingers over Ava's and gave it a tiny shake. 'No,' she said. 'You have to be quiet or I won't get through this.'

Ava swallowed a sob and used her sleeve to dash away tears.

'I can't sit in this house alone. I don't want there to be silence around me. My parents have asked me to go home. They decided after years of being ashamed to have a gay daughter that the prospect of me dying was worth compromising over, but they're not really my family any more. Family, it turns out, are the people you want around when you suddenly discover that death is a realistic possibility. In case you hadn't figured it out yet, I'm talking about you two idiots.

'Anyway, I want to stay in my own home. I need my bed, my paintings, and my own oven. And I need you to move in with me, Ava. Not to stop work. You'd be unbearable after twenty-four hours, and the point is that I need you to come home each day full of incredible stories about what you've seen and done, with all the gossip . . .'

'Yes,' Ava said. 'Of course. If you hadn't asked, I'd have broken in anyway. I'll be here for you every day. We can watch movies, I can drive you to all your appointments . . .'

'Wait until you hear the whole deal,' Natasha said. 'Because this is non-negotiable. I get everything I'm asking for or nothing at all. My doctor says selfishness is necessary at the moment, and that I'm to do whatever I need to get through this, so I'm taking that literally. I need you here, Ava. You're more than my best friend. You've been a sister, a mother when I needed one, and occasionally like an irritating child to me, and I love you with all my heart. But I won't let you be dragged down by this fucking disease. I can't see you exhausted and scared by it, and I can't impose all my worries on you, but I need to dump all the crap on someone else's shoulders sometimes because I have days when I'm convinced the sheer weight of the sadness I feel will crush me long before the cancer decides my fate.'

Callanach reached across and took hold of Natasha's free hand. She squeezed his fingers hard.

'So Luc, this is where you come in. I want you to move in, too. It's a four-bedroom house. There's plenty of space for everyone.'

'You know I will,' Callanach said. 'Whatever I can do to help.'

'This isn't for me,' Natasha said. 'If Ava is going to move in and support me, she'll wear herself down. She'll worry, she'll stop smiling, she'll be no fun, and ultimately that'll be no use to me at all. And yes, this is all about me. You're just my minions for these purposes.'

'Fuck you,' Ava sniffed, smiling finally through the tears.

'Swear as much as you like, Turner, but I know you, and you'll forget yourself in a heartbeat. I need someone to fetch you takeaway, and to pour you a glass of wine when I'm not looking. Obviously you're both banned from drinking in front of me while I'm not allowed it.'

'Can we at least drink out of the house?' Callanach laughed.

'Only if you don't come back drunk. That would be too unfair,' Natasha smiled. 'So that's what I need from you, Luc. Someone to look after Ava while she looks after me, and an extra person to keep this house alive. If you can alternate your shifts, then Ava won't worry about me when she's at work. Three of us means no awkward silences, no one overwhelmed.

Ava to help me up the stairs when I'm exhausted, and you to rub Ava's shoulders when I've leaned on her too heavily, physically or metaphorically.'

'Natasha, things between Luc and I have been strained. You know more about it than anyone else. I'm not sure this will work,' Ava said gently.

'You have to make it work,' Natasha said. 'Both of you. For me. Pretend nothing ever happened. Or work through it. Make peace, make friends, just find a way. You've both been miserable apart so I don't see what either of you has to lose by being close to one another for a while and seeing how that works out.'

'Ground rules?' Callanach asked.

'No dating anyone else while you're both living under one roof. That would be too awkward. And no sex with each other either, even if you both come to your senses. It wouldn't be fair while I'm incapacitated.'

'I don't think you need to worry about that.'

'Ava, I love you, but know when to shut up,' Natasha said, turning to look at her straight on. 'You have one life. I'm telling you it's time to start actually living it.'

Ava reddened, glanced at Callanach, then looked away again.

'That's all,' Natasha said. 'It's a big imposition but I figured if I don't ask, I won't get. Take your time and mull it over. You'll be giving up a good six months of your life, maybe longer depending on how treatment goes. I won't think any less of either of you if you decide it's too much. I love you both. You've been a late addition, Luc, but you're the only person who could possibly look after Ava the way she needs looking after. She needs someone who isn't scared to tell her off, and who knows her better than she knows herself.'

'Natasha—' Ava said.

'No, I want to finish,' Natasha said. 'Whatever you and Luc—'

'I was just going to say yes,' Ava said. 'That was all. Yes to all of it. To living here and sharing this part of your life with you. And to having Luc here and letting him take care of me. All the drinking, dating, cooking rules – honestly I got a bit bored and lost track about halfway through; I'm not sure how your students stay awake in your lectures – but yes. We'll be here, together, for as long as you need us, or want us, and probably refuse to leave at the end of it. That was all I wanted to say. Luc?'

'There isn't a Frenchman in history who's turned down the opportunity of living with two women. I'm in charge though, right?'

'No!' they shouted together.

'Well, it's not ideal then, but I'm willing to compromise. I'll need decent coffee in the house at all times and I'm not prepared to share a bathroom with Ava. There's only so much chaos I can cope with.'

'You mean you need so much time in front of the mirror that you're not prepared to share one,' Ava said.

'This is exactly what I was talking about,' Natasha grinned.

She stood up, reaching an arm out to put around Ava's shoulders as Callanach moved around the table to join them. They stood there together long enough for dinner to burn. No one cared.

Read on for an exclusive extract from Helen Field's new standalone novel.

Coming February 2021.

Chapter 1

A sleeping woman watched over by the stranger who had hidden for hours in the shadowed bay of her bedroom curtains. That's all there was to the scene. He was a spider, patient and unmoving, poised to drop and stun his prey. There was no malice to it. Only need. The white sheet covering her body rose and fell with each breath in the oblivion of slumber. Three steps forward and he could reach out and touch her, run his hands through her long, dark hair, press the half moon of his finger nail into the dimple that punctuated her right cheek as she smiled. His arms would wrap around her frame perfectly. In his mind he'd measured every part of her. Twice he'd passed by close enough to brush her body with his, once in the street, once in the school playground. The latter was a risk, but it had proved fruitful. In the beginning, he'd been concerned that the watching phase might be dull. How wrong. Familiarising himself with the lives of the ones he'd chosen had become his oxygen as the rest of his world had started to fade.

He ran appreciative fingers over the top of the dresser at his side. No dust. No sticky fingerprints from the children. Angela was all wife, mother and homemaker. Her bedroom was the epitome of family. Photographs adorned the walls. A wedding, more than a decade ago, with a bride leaning into the arms of her groom, her dress demure, hair pinned up with just a few curls left hanging. A promise for later that night, Fergus thought. It had taken months of patience to find a time when her husband would be away, then he'd struck gold. The man of the house had treated the children – a boy of seven and a girl of five – to a camping trip for a night, enjoying Edinburgh's idyllic August. The husband couldn't have realised it, but the experience would be good practice. After tonight, he would be a single parent unless he married again. Fergus couldn't imagine why anyone would try to replace Angela. She was everything.

Each morning she walked her children to school, the boy racing ahead, sometimes on a scooter, while the girl held fast to her mother's hand. He liked to watch them all together. Angela's face wore an indelible smile when she was with her offspring. He'd never seen her looking tired or cross. In all the hours, all the journeys he'd witnessed, she hadn't rolled her eyes, yawned or snapped at them. In the photos on the bedroom walls, she was not just a parent but utterly engaged in the act of parenting. He studied those pictures one last time, committing each to memory. There she was hugging her son as he clutched some sports trophy, and there she was laughing as she made cupcakes with her daughter, beaming with love. And there they were as a family on their bikes, pausing as a passerby took their photograph, defining togetherness.

Fergus had been in that bedroom before, but never when Angela was in bed. He'd taken pieces of her home with him. A silky soft shirt from the laundry basket. A lipstick from her handbag. Nail clippings from her bathroom, still showing the colour of her toe nail varnish. There was a whole shelf of her in his own bedroom, and a file. Paper, not digital. He was ill, not stupid. Computers could be hacked. The information he'd gathered was from the real world. Her date of birth and marriage certificate had been obtained from official records. He knew where she shopped, which doctor's surgery she attended, who her friends were. A timeline constructed from his labours provided an accurate structure of her week. Her kitchen bin was an endless source of intelligence. She rarely chose precooked meals or processed foods, preferring fresh fruits and vegetables. There were no magazines, but the odd newspaper was recycled. Angela liked hard soap bars rather than liquid soap dispensers. And she was on the pill. The discarded wrapper from the previous month was in his file, too. No more children planned, for now at least. She was content.

Edging closer to the bed, he breathed in her scent. She'd bathed before slipping between the sheets. He'd been in the house long before that. Easier to allow her the reassurance of checking each window and door, believing that anything that might do her harm was safely beyond the boundaries of her home. As she'd soaked in the steaming water, lavender bubbles caressing her skin, he'd made sure her curtains were drawn and taken the keys from the lock in the back door. No point taking chances. If she got spooked or surprised him and ran, he couldn't allow her to exit the property. When all was secure, he'd sat outside her bathroom door and listened to her humming. He'd imagined her running the pale green flannel up and down her arms, her legs, between her breasts and around the back of her neck. He'd waited as she'd read the book he'd noticed on her bed, resting on a freshly laundered towel and her dressing gown. When he'd heard the cascade of water that signalled her standing, he'd shifted position into the window alcove, behind her curtains, focusing on breathing silently and remaining still. There were windows open in the upstairs bedroom to allow some of the cooler night air in, and he'd planned to close those once she was sleeping soundly. If she screamed, the noise would travel out into the crescent and her neighbours would be alerted. Fergus couldn't allow that to happen.

Now she was right in front of him. So much hard work had brought him to that moment, he almost couldn't bear for it to end. Until he looked in the mirror. Hung on the end wall of the bedroom, opposite the window, it reflected Angela's pretty head on her pillow, and the man looming over her. While her hair was gleaming and vibrant, his was greying prematurely, thinning more than anyone in their late thirties should have to tolerate, dangling lank from his scalp, as if trying to slide away. His eyes were pale in the scant light that entered from a street-lamp beyond the curtains, but he could still make out their watery blue, surrounded by creases of red on white. But it was his skin that told the real story. A greener shade of white. Waxy, sallow, wanting.

Fergus Ariss was dying.

However long he had left, there was insufficient time to achieve everything. He'd dreamed of travelling. In his twenties, he'd had a world map on his wall. The idea was to scratch off a section of chalky paint every time he took a trip. A school visit to France had offered one country beyond the United Kingdom's borders, then came a friend's stag weekend in Amsterdam. He'd always wanted to go the USA. To explore Peru. The Great Wall of China was his ultimate goal. Now he had to fulfil all his dying wishes in Scotland. Even the borders were too far to cross at this stage. His body had betrayed him. There was nothing the doctors could do, in spite of their protestations that he should let them assist. He could smell the rot of his own body. No herb or spice could mask the taste of death in his mouth. There was pain and grief, then there were moments of clarity when he understood that death would be a release. Months of hospital treatment weren't the answer. Prolonging life regardless of the quality of that time was nothing

392

more than fading away. He didn't want to fade any more than he already had. He wanted to blaze a trail into the next life. But there was so little time, and so much left to do. Starting with Angela. She was to be his first. But not his last.

Creeping around the end of the bed and slipping off his shoes, he slid his body weight gently onto the mattress. A smile flitted across Angela's face as his body joined hers. He fitted behind her like a puzzle piece, and she murmured as he slid his arm over her waist, pushing his face gently into her neck and breathing the scent of her shampoo. She was so warm in his arms. So soft. Destined for him.

Then she woke. She took a breath sharp enough to push Fergus's chest from her back, and every muscle in her body seized. She jolted but he'd been ready for it. He squeezed his arm around her, dragging her backwards into him, snaking his free hand under her neck and over her mouth.

'It's all right,' he whispered. 'Angela, you have to trust me. I'm not here to hurt you.'

She tried kicking, going for his shins with her heels, but the sheet hampered the force of her movements and Fergus shifted his right leg on top of both of hers. Her breath was hot and wet in his hand, and her head was a wild creature whipping left and right. He waited it out. There were no surprises. He'd played the scenario out in his head hundreds, maybe thousands, of times. In his pocket was a handkerchief, and on it was a carefully measured dose of chloroform. There were things he wanted to do with Angela, and those things required her not to fight him. Fergus wanted her pristine.

'Let it out,' he said. 'I know you're scared and confused, but I chose you. I need to tell you that I think you're incredible. You don't know who I am, but I know you. I really do.'

Angela heaved forward, rolling her mouth hard onto his fingers and biting down. Fergus tried to keep his grip on her, but his hand betrayed him. His fingers shot out straight and his wrist flicked backwards, giving Angela the space to bend her head forwards then smack it backwards into Fergus's face, the rear of her skull a true weapon, splitting Fergus's nose from between his eyes to below the bridge. The pillow became a mess of bloody hair. He couldn't see, and his face was a mask of agony. Only his right arm and leg remained steadfast, holding her in place. Angela spat hard. A chunk of something warm and soft landed on his hand as he pinned her to the bed. The flesh was from his finger, he realised, as he shifted his body on top of hers before she could attempt an escape.

'S'allrigh', lemme help you,' he muttered. Blood droplets from his face burst juicily as they hit hers. Angela began to sob. 'I'm not cross. Don't cry. Nothing to be sad about.'

Fergus pulled the handkerchief from his pocket with his right hand, shifting his left forearm to rest solidly across her breast bone. She gushed air and spat tears.

'Please don't…'

'Hurt you? Why would I? I'm your one true love, Angela.' He pressed the handkerchief to her lips. A cotton kiss in the dark.

Angela's hips bucked beneath him, and he imagined a different bed, her holding him, wanting him on top of her. Her neck arched. She did her best to fight, but he wanted her compliance more than she wanted her freedom. Desperation had fine-tuned him into an extraordinary beast. He could smell her toothpaste and it was a field of wild mint. The diamonds in her eyes were more riches than he had ever imagined he would own.

Then the bedside lamp was arcing through the heavy air. Had it been switched on, he knew it would have left a rainbow of light in its wake. Even as he saw it coming, he recognised it was too late for avoidance. Shattering on contact with his cheek bone, the pottery base turned to gravel and took root in his flesh. Angela fought harder as he swayed, his head a wasp nest. He pressed his forehead down on top of his own hand as it covered her mouth. If he lost consciousness now, it was over. If she got out from under him, he was done. Everything he wanted, what pathetic time he had left, would be smoke.

She battered at him with one fist. Slamming his whole body weight onto her rib cage, he grabbed her wrist with his free hand. Her fingertips scratched weakly at his knuckles. The bed was wet, he realised. His knee rested in a damp, warm patch. That was fine. A success, in fact. She was relaxing. Surrendering. The whole head buzzed and burned, tidal nausea swept inward. Fergus let her hand slide from his grasp as the world pixelated then faded.

Was it possible that death was coming for him so much sooner than he'd anticipated? Fergus breathed deeply, trying to catch hold of the pain, yearning to stay in the moment with Angela, but there was a roundabout spinning mercilessly in his head and he couldn't get off.

Her body juddered beneath his.

He couldn't get off.

Angela's gasps were ragged and raw.

He couldn't get off.

The last breath he heard leave her body was an inhuman rattle. He longed to comfort her, to tell her he was sorry. There was so much he'd wanted to do with her and it had all gone so dreadfully wrong. Now he had to start over. And first, he had to find someone new.

Loved *Perfect Kill*? Then why not get back to where it all started with book one of the DI Callanach series . . .

A gripping crime thriller that will leave you breathless.

Available in all good bookshops now.

Welcome to Edinburgh.
Murder capital of Europe.

A dark and twisted serial killer thriller that fans of M. J. Arlidge and Karin Slaughter won't be able to put down.

Available in all good bookshops now.

**The worst dangers are the
ones we can't see . . .**

DI Callanach is back in the stunning third novel from
the bestselling Helen Fields.

Available in all good bookshops now.

When silence falls, who will
hear their cries?

Relentlessly dark and twisty crime that will
keep you up all night . . .

Available in all good bookshops now.

**Your darkest moment is your
most vulnerable . . .**

An unstoppable crime thriller from the #1 bestselling
Helen Fields.

Available in all good bookshops now.